UN
LUN DUN

China Miéville

 BALLANTINE BOOKS / NEW YORK

Copyright © 2007 by China Miéville
Illustrations copyright © 2007 by China Miéville

Published in the United States by Del Rey Books, an imprint of
The Random House Publishing Group, a division of Random House, Inc., New York.

DEL REY is a registered trademark and the Del Rey colophon
is a trademark of Random House, Inc.

ISBN 978-0-345-49516-7

Printed in the United States on acid-free paper

www.delreybooks.com

2 4 6 8 9 7 5 3

Book design by Susan Turner

To Oscar

Acknowledgments

With huge thanks to Talya Baker, Mark Bould, Lauren Buckland, Mic Cheetham, Deanna Hoak, Simon Kavanagh, Peter Lavery, Claudia Lightfoot, Tim Mak, Farah Mendlesohn, Jemima Miéville, David Moench, Jonathan Riddell of London's Transport Museum, Max Schaefer, Chris Schluep, Jesse Soodalter, Harriet Wilson, Paul Witcover, and everyone at Del Rey and Macmillan.

As always, I'm indebted to too many writers to list, but particularly important to this book are Joan Aiken, Clive Barker, Lewis Carroll, Michael de Larrabeiti, Tanith Lee, Walter Moers, and Beatrix Potter. Particular thanks are due Neil Gaiman, for generous encouragement and for his indispensable contributions to London phantasmagoria, especially *Neverwhere*.

Note to Reader

People speaking British English and people speaking American English mostly understand each other fine. But there are a few words we use in Britain that you might not recognize, or that we use differently from you. Should you encounter a strange or difficult word in the story, please flip to the short glossary, which is located in the back of this book.

In an unremarkable room, in a nondescript building, a man sat working on very non-nondescript theories.

The man was surrounded by bright chemicals in bottles and flasks, charts and gauges, and piles of books like battlements around him. He propped them open on each other. He cross-referred them, seeming to read several at the same time; he pondered, made notes, crossed the notes out, went hunting for facts of history, chemistry, and geography.

He was quiet but for the scuttling of his pen and his occasional murmurs of revelation. He was obviously working on something very difficult. From his mutters and the exclamation marks he scrawled, though, he was slowly making progress.

The man had traveled a very long way to do the work he was doing. He was so engrossed it took him a long time to notice that the light around him was fading, unnaturally fast.

Some sort of darkness was closing in on the windows. Some sort of silence—more than the absence of noise, the presence of a predatory quiet—was settling around him.

The man looked up at last. Slowly, he put down his pen and turned around in his chair.

"Hello?" he said. "Professor? Is that you? Is the minister here . . . ?"

There was no answer. The light from the corridor still faded. Through the smoked glass of the door, the man could see darkness taking shape. He stood, slowly. He sniffed, and his eyes widened.

Fingers of smoke were wafting under the door, entering the room. They uncoiled from the crack like feelers.

"So . . ." the man whispered. "So, it's you."

There was no answer, but beyond the door came a very faint rumble that might just have been laughter.

The man swallowed, and stepped back. But he set his face. He watched as the smoke came more thickly around the edges of the door, eddying towards him. He reached for his notes. He moved quickly, dragging a chair as quietly as he could into place below a high ventilation duct. He looked afraid but determined—or determined but afraid.

The smoke kept coming. Before he had a chance to climb, there was another rumble-laugh-noise. The man faced the door.

PART I

Zanna and Deeba

The Respectful Fox

There was no doubt about it: there was a fox behind the climbing frame. And it was watching.

"It is, isn't it?"

The playground was full of children, their gray uniforms flapping as they ran and kicked balls into makeshift goals. Amid the shouting and the games, a few girls were watching the fox.

"It definitely is. It's just watching us," a tall blond girl said. She could see the animal clearly behind a fringe of grass and thistle. "Why isn't it moving?" She walked slowly towards it.

At first the friends had thought the animal was a dog, and had started ambling towards it while they chatted. But halfway across the tarmac they had realized it was a fox.

It was a cold cloudless autumn morning and the sun was bright. None of them could quite believe what they were seeing. The fox kept standing still as they approached.

"I saw one once before," whispered Kath, shifting her bag from shoulder to shoulder. "I was with my dad by the canal. He told me there's loads in London now, but you don't normally see them."

"It should be running," said Keisha, anxiously. "I'm staying here. That's got teeth."

"All the better to eat you with," said Deeba.

"That was a wolf," said Kath.

Kath and Keisha held back: Zanna, the blond girl, slowly approached the fox, with Deeba, as usual, by her side. They got closer, expecting it to arch into one of those beautiful curves of animal panic, and duck under the fence. It kept not doing so.

The girls had never seen any animal so still. It wasn't that it wasn't moving: it was furiously *not-moving*. By the time they got close to the climbing frame they were creeping exaggeratedly, like cartoon hunters.

The fox eyed Zanna's outstretched hand politely. Deeba frowned.

"Yeah, it is watching," Deeba said. "But not *us*. It's watching *you*."

Zanna—she hated her name Susanna, and she hated "Sue" even more—had moved to the estate about a year ago, and quickly made friends with Kath and Keisha and Becks and others. Especially Deeba. On her way to Kilburn Comprehensive, on her first day, Deeba had made Zanna laugh, which not many people could do. Since then, where Zanna was, Deeba tended to be, too. There was something about Zanna that drew attention. She was decent-to-good at things like sports, schoolwork, dancing, whatever, but that wasn't it: she did well enough to do well, but never enough to stand out. She was tall and striking, but she never played that up either: if anything, she seemed to try to stay in the background. But she never quite could. If she hadn't been easy to get on with, that could have caused her trouble.

Sometimes even her mates were a little bit wary of Zanna, as if they weren't quite sure how to deal with her. Even Deeba herself had to admit that Zanna could be a bit dreamy. Sometimes she would sort of zone out, staring skywards or losing the thread of what she was saying.

Just at that moment, however, she was concentrating hard on what Deeba had just said.

Zanna put her hands on her hips, and even her sudden movement didn't make the fox jump.

"It's true," said Deeba. "It hasn't taken its eyes off you."

Zanna met the fox's gentle vulpine gaze. All the girls watching, and the animal, seemed to get lost in something.

. . . Until their attention was interrupted by the bell for the end of break. The girls looked at each other, blinking.

The fox finally moved. Still looking at Zanna, it bowed its head. It did it once, then leapt up and was gone.

Deeba watched Zanna, and muttered, "This is just getting weird."

2

Signs

For the rest of that day Zanna tried to avoid her friends. They eventually caught up with her in the lunch queue, but when she told them to leave her alone it was in such a nasty voice that they obeyed.

"Forget it," said Kath. "She's just rude."

"She's mad," said Becks, and they walked away ostentatiously. Only Deeba stayed.

She didn't try to talk to Zanna. Instead she watched her thoughtfully.

That afternoon, she waited for Zanna after school. Zanna tried to get by in the rush, but Deeba wouldn't let her. She crept up on her, then suddenly linked an arm into one of hers. Zanna tried to look angry, but it didn't last very long.

"Oh, Deebs . . . what's going on?" she said.

They made their way to the estate where they both lived, and headed for Deeba's house. Her boisterous, talkative family, while sometimes exasperating with all their noise and kerfuffle, were generally a comfortable backdrop for any discussion. As usual, people looked at the girls as they passed. They made a funny pair.

Deeba was shorter and rounder and messier than her skinny friend. Her long black hair was making its usual break for freedom from her ponytail, in contrast to Zanna's tightly slicked-back blondness. Zanna was silent while Deeba kept asking her if she was okay.

"Hello Miss Resham, hello Miss Moon," sang Deeba's father as they entered. "What have you been doing? Cup of tea for you ladies?"

"Hi sweetheart," said Deeba's mum. "How was your day? Hello Zanna, how you doing?"

"Hello Mr. and Mrs. Resham," said Zanna, smiling with her usual nervous pleasure as Deeba's parents beamed at her. "Fine, thank you."

"Leave her alone, Dad," said Deeba, dragging Zanna through to her room. "Except for the tea, please."

"So, nothing happened to you today," said her mother. "You have nothing to report. You had a totally empty day! You amaze me."

"It was *fine*," she said. "It was same as always, innit?"

Without getting up, Deeba's parents started loudly consoling her about the tragedy of how nothing ever changed for her, and that every day was the same. Deeba rolled her eyes at them and closed her door.

They sat without speaking for a while. Deeba put on lip gloss. Zanna just sat.

"What we going to do, Zanna?" said Deeba at last. "Something's going on."

"I know," said Zanna. "It's getting worse."

It was hard to say exactly when it had all started. Things had been getting strange for at least a month.

"Remember when I saw that cloud?" said Deeba. "That looked like you?"

"That was weeks ago, and it didn't look anything like anything," Zanna said. "Let's stick to real stuff. The fox today. And that woman. What was on the wall. And the letter. That sort of thing."

It had been early autumn when the odd events had started to occur. They had been in the Rose Café.

None of them had paid any attention when the door opened, until they'd realized that the woman who'd come in was standing quietly by their table. One by one they looked at her.

She'd been wearing a bus driver's uniform, the cap at a perky angle. She was grinning.

"Sorry to butt in," the woman said. "I hope you don't . . . Just very exciting to meet you." She smiled at all of them but addressed Zanna. "Just wanted to say that."

The girls stared in dumb astonishment for several seconds. Zanna had tried to stutter some reply, Kath had burst out with "What . . . ?" and Deeba had started laughing. None of this fazed the woman. She said a nonsense word.

"Shwazzy!" she said. "I heard you'd be here, but I wouldn't have believed it." With one more smile, she left, leaving the girls laughing nervously and loudly, until the waitress had asked them to calm down.

"Nutter!"

"Nutter!"

"Bloody *nutter!*"

If that had been all, it would have just been one of those stories about someone a bit loopy on London streets. But that had not been all.

Some days later Deeba had been with Zanna, walking under the old bridge over Iverson Road. She'd looked up, reading some of the cruder graffiti. There behind the pigeon net, far higher than anyone could have reached, was painted in vivid yellow: ZANNA FOR EVER!

"Cor. Someone else called Zanna," Deeba said. "Or you've got long arms. Or someone massive loves you, Zan."

"Shut up," Zanna said.

"It's true, though," Deeba said. "No one else's called Zanna, you're always saying. Now you've made your mark."

* * *

A little while after that, the day after Guy Fawkes Night, when London was full of bonfires and fireworks, Zanna had come to school upset.

At last, when she was alone with Deeba, Zanna had pulled a piece of paper and a card out of her bag.

A postman had been waiting outside her front door. He had given her a letter with no name on the envelope, just handed it straight to her as soon as she had emerged, and disappeared. She hesitated before showing it to Deeba.

"Don't tell any of the others," she had said. "Swear?"

We look forward to meeting you, Deeba read, *when the wheel turns.*

"Who's it from?" Deeba said.

"If I knew that I wouldn't be freaked out. And there's no stamp."

"Is there a mark?" Deeba said. "To say where it came from? Is that a *U*? An *L*? And that says . . . *on,* I think." They couldn't read any more.

"He said something to me," Zanna said. "The same thing that woman did. 'Shwazzy,' he said. I was like, 'What?' I tried to follow him, but he was gone."

"What does it mean?" Deeba said.

"That's not all," said Zanna. "This was in there too."

It was a little square of card, some strange design, a beautiful, intricate thing of multicolored swirling lines. It was, Deeba had realized, some mad version of a London travelcard. It said it was good for zones one to six, buses and trains, all across the city.

On the dotted line across its center was carefully printed: ZANNA MOON SHWAZZY.

That was when Deeba had told Zanna that she had to tell her parents. She herself had kept her promise, and never told anyone.

"Did you tell them?" said Deeba.

"How can I?" said Zanna. "What am I going to say about the animals?"

For the last few weeks, dogs would often stop as Zanna walked by, and stare at her. Once a little conga line of three squirrels had come down from a tree as Zanna sat in Queen's Park, and one by one had put a little nut or seed in front of her. Only cats ignored her.

"It's mad," said Zanna. "I don't know what's going on. And I *can't* tell them. They'll think I need help. Maybe I do. But I tell you one thing." Her voice was surprisingly firm. "I was thinking it when I looked at that fox. At first I was scared. I still don't want to talk about it, not to Kath and that lot. So don't say nothing, alright? But I've had enough. Something's happening? Okay. Well, I'm ready for it."

Outside it was storming. The air was growling and rumbustious. People crammed under eaves, or huddled into their coats and shuffled through the rain. Through Deeba's window, the girls watched people dance and wrestle with umbrellas.

When Zanna left, she ran out past a sheltering woman with a ridiculous little dog on a lead. As it saw her, the dog sat up in an oddly dignified way.

It bowed its head. Zanna looked at the little dog and, obviously as surprised by her own reaction as by the animal's greeting, bowed her head back.

3

The Visiting Smoke

The next day Zanna and Deeba wandered through the playground, watching their reflections in all the puddles. Bedraggled rubbish lurked by walls. The clouds still looked heavy.

"My dad hates umbrellas," said Deeba, swinging her own. "When it rains he always says the same thing. 'I do not believe the presence of moisture in the air is sufficient reason to overturn society's usual sensible taboo against wielding spiked clubs at eye level.'"

From the edge of the playground, near where the respectful fox had stood, they could see over the school's walls, into the street, where a few people passed by.

Something caught Zanna's eye. Something strange and unclear. By a playing field at the end of the street, smudges were just visible on the road.

"There's something there," said Zanna. She squinted. "I think it's moving."

"Is it?" said Deeba.

The sky seemed unnaturally flat, as if a huge gray sheet had been pegged out from horizon to horizon above them. The air was still. Very faint dark stains coiled and disappeared, and the road was unmarked again.

"Today . . ." Deeba said. "It's not a normal day."

Zanna shook her head.

Birds arced, and clutch of sparrows flew out of nowhere and circled Zanna's head in a twittering halo.

That afternoon they had French. Zanna and Deeba were not paying attention, were staring out of the windows, drawing foxes and sparrows and rain clouds, until something in Miss Williams's droning made Zanna look up.

". . . choisir . . ." she heard. ". . . je choisis, tu choisis . . ."

"What's she on about?" whispered Deeba.

"Nous allons choisir . . ." Miss Williams said. "Vous avez choisi."

"Miss? Miss?" said Zanna. "What was that last one, Miss? What does it mean?"

Miss Williams poked the board.

"This one?" she said. "Vous avez choisi. *Vous:* you plural. *Avez:* have. *Choisi:* chosen."

Choisi. Shwazzy. Chosen.

At the end of the day, Deeba and Zanna stood by the school gate and looked out at where they had seen the marks. It was still drizzling, and by the playing fields, the rain looked to be falling as if against resistance, as if it had hit a patch of odd air.

"You coming to Rose's?" Kath and the others were standing behind them.

"We . . . thought we saw something," Deeba said. "We was just going to . . ."

Her voice petered out, and she followed Zanna. Behind them, a scrum of their classmates were rushing by, heading home or meeting their parents.

"What you looking for?" said Keisha. She and Kath stood watching quizzically as Zanna stood in the middle of the road a few meters away, and looked around.

"I can't see nothing," she whispered. Zanna stood for a long time, as the others huffed impatiently. "Alright then," she said, raising her voice. Kath had her arms folded and one eyebrow raised. "Let's go."

The stream of their classmates had ended. A few cars emerged from the gates and swept past them as their teachers headed home. The little group of girls were alone in the street. With a sputtering crack, the streetlights came on as the sky darkened.

Rain was coming down hard like a typewriter on Deeba's umbrella.

". . . don't know *what* she's doing . . ." Deeba heard Becks saying to Keisha and Kath. Zanna walked a little ahead of them, her feet sending up little sprays of rainlike mist.

A lot like mist, a dark mist. Zanna slowed. She and Deeba looked down.

"What now?" said Keisha in exasperation.

At their feet, a few centimeters above the dirty wet tarmac, there was a layer of coiling smoke.

"What . . . is that?" said Kath.

Wafts were rising from the gutters. The smoke was a horrible dirty dark. It emerged in drifts and tendrils, reaching through the metal grilles of the drains like growing vines or octopus legs. Ropes of it tangled and thickened. They coiled around the wheels of vehicles and under their engines.

"What's going on?" whispered Keisha. Smoke was beginning to boil out of the sewers. A smell of chemicals and rot thickened in the air. Far off and muffled as if by a curtain, the noise of a motor was audible.

Zanna was standing with her arms out, focusing intensely into sudden fumes that circled them. For a second, it looked as if the rain that was pelting them was evaporating, like drops on hot metal, a few millimeters *above* Zanna's head. Deeba stared, but dark drifts hid her friend.

The motor was louder. A car was approaching.

The girls were shrouded in gritty smoke. They spluttered in panic and tried to call to each other. They could see almost nothing.

The noise of the motor grew, and glints of reflected streetlamp-light winked momentarily through the fumes.

"Wait a minute," Zanna shouted.

Through the fog headlights suddenly flared, heading straight for Zanna. Deeba saw her, turned in to a shadow, sidestepping neatly as the lights bore down, her hands seeming to glow.

"It's my *dad*!" Zanna shouted, and moved fast as the car raced into the smoke, and there was a rush as the fumes dissipated and—

—there was a *bang*, and something went flying, and there was silence.

The clouds undarkened and the rain stopped. The strange fumes dropped out of the air and flooded like thick dark water back into the gutters, gushing soundlessly out of sight.

For several seconds, no one moved.

A car was skewed across the road, with Zanna's dad sitting in the front seat looking confused. Someone was shouting hysterically. Someone fair was lying by a wall.

"Zanna!" Deeba shouted, but Zanna was beside her. It was Becks who had been hit, and who lay motionless.

"We have to get a doctor," said Zanna, pulling out her mobile and starting to cry, but Kath was already through to 999.

Zanna's dad staggered out of the car, coughing.

"What . . . what . . . ?" he said. "I was . . . what happened?" He saw Becks. "Oh my God!" He dropped to his knees beside her. "What did I do?" he kept saying.

"I've called an ambulance," Kath said, but he wasn't listening. Now the light was back to normal and there was no fog lapping at ankle-height, people were peering out of doors and windows. Becks moved uneasily, and made groggy moaning noises.

"What happened?" Zanna's dad kept asking them. None of them knew what to say. "I don't remember anything," he said, "I just woke up and—"

"It hurts . . ." Becks wailed.

"Did you see?" Zanna whispered to Deeba. Her voice sounded as if it were cracking. "The smoke, the car, everything? It was all thick around *me*. It was trying to get *me*."

The Watcher in the Night

That night, and the two that followed, Zanna stayed over at Deeba's house. Just then, she preferred it to her own place across the yard of the estate.

Her father was in a bit of a state. The police kept asking him to tell his story again, and telling him there was no sign of the "chemical spill" he thought might explain the smoke that had made him light-headed. While he had to deal with the questions, Mr. and Mrs. Moon gratefully accepted the Reshams' suggestion that Zanna stay with them.

The police had also asked the girls what had happened, of course, but Zanna and Deeba couldn't explain what they didn't understand.

"She's had a real shock, Mrs. Resham," Deeba heard one officer say. "She's not making a bit of sense."

"We have to make them believe us," Zanna insisted.

"What?" said Deeba. " 'Magic smoke came out of the drains.' Think that'll help?"

Becks had broken a couple of bones, but was recovering. So, at least, Zanna and Deeba understood. Becks herself wouldn't speak to them. She wouldn't see them when they came to the hospital, nor would she answer her phone.

And it wasn't just her. Kath and Keisha ignored Zanna and Deeba at school, and wouldn't answer their calls, either.

"They're blaming me for what happened," Zanna said to Deeba, in a strange voice.

"They're scared," Deeba said. The two girls were sitting up late in Deeba's room, Zanna in the foldout bed.

"And they're blaming *me*," Zanna said. "And . . . maybe they're right."

In the next room the Reshams shouted at the television.

"Idiots!" Deeba's mother was saying.

"They're all fools," her dad said. "Except that Environment woman, Rawley, she's alright. She's the only one does any good . . ."

The Reshams were still having the conversation—the same one they had many times, about which politicians they disliked most, and the much more rare species, which they liked (a shortlist of one)—much later, when they went to bed. Zanna and Deeba were still whispering.

"It must have been an accident," Deeba said. "Something with the pipes."

"They said it wasn't," Zanna said. "And anyway . . . you don't believe that. It's something else. Something to do with . . ." *With me,* was what she didn't say, but what they both knew she meant.

They had the same conversation every day. There were no conclusions they could come to, but there was nothing else they could talk about, either. They talked themselves out, and eventually fell asleep.

Much later, in the small hours of the night, Deeba woke, quite suddenly. She sat up in her bed by the window and pulled aside the curtains a little, to look out across the estate and try to work out what had disturbed her.

She watched for a long time. Occasionally a figure might hurry by, following the tiny red glimmer of a cigarette end. At this time of night, though, the concrete square, the big metal bins, the walkways were mostly empty.

On the other side of the yard she could see Zanna's flat, its windows dark. The wind turned corkscrews in the courtyard, and Deeba watched bits of rubbish turn. It was raining a little. The moon glinted in puddles. In the far corner was a pile of full black rubbish bags.

There was a tiny scratching sound.

Deeba thought it must be a cat, searching in the rubbish. There was quiet except for the fingertip drumming of rain and the whisper of wastepaper. Then she heard it again, an insistent *skritch-skritch.*

"Zanna," she whispered, shaking her friend awake. "Listen."

The two girls looked out into the darkness.

In the shadows by the bins, something was moving. A wet black shape, rooting in the plastic. It moved toward the light. It didn't look like a cat, nor a crow, nor a lost dog. It was long and spindly and flapping, all at once.

It extended a limb out of the shadows. Something glinting and black fluttered. Zanna and Deeba held their breath.

Shaking with effort, the claw-wing-thing hauled itself through shadows, spidery and bedraggled. It approached Zanna's house. It huddled in the dark by the wall, leapt suddenly up, and hung below the window.

The two girls gasped. The thing was just visible, now, in the faint lamplight.

It was an umbrella.

For a long time it hung like some odd fruit below the windowsill, while the rain increased, until the watching friends began to tell themselves that they had imagined the motion, that there had been an umbrella hooked on the ledge for hours. Then the dark little thing moved again.

It dropped and crawled with its excruciating slowness back to the darkness. It opened its canopy a little way, gripped the concrete with a metal point, and dragged itself along. It was bent, or battered, or bent and battered, or torn, and it crawled like something injured, into the shadows and out of sight.

The courtyard was empty. Deeba and Zanna looked at each other.

"Oh . . . my . . . God . . ." whispered Zanna.

"That was . . ." squeaked Deeba. "Was that an *umbrella?*"

"How's that possible . . . ?" Zanna said. "And what was it doing by your window?"

5

Down to the Cellar

The two girls crept out into the estate night.

"Quick," Zanna whispered. "It was over there."

"This is mad," hissed Deeba, but she moved as quickly as her friend, in the same half-bent run. "We don't even have a flashlight."

"Yeah but we've got to look," Zanna said. "What is going *on*?" They shivered a little in the clothes they had quickly put on, looking nervously around them into darkness and halos of lamplight. They headed for the bins, and the hollow full of rubbish where they had seen the impossible spy.

"So it was some sort of remote control thing, innit?" Deeba said as Zanna looked around in the smelly dark. "And maybe . . . I dunno, maybe it had a camera or something . . . and . . ." Deeba stopped, as what she was saying began to sound more and more unlikely.

"Come help me," Zanna said.

"What you doing?"

"Looking for something," Zanna said.

"What?"

Zanna poked about in the rubbish, holding her nose as she prodded the overspill from the bins with a stick.

"There's going to be rats and stuff," Deeba said. "Leave it."

"Look," said Zanna. "See that?" She pointed at one streak among many across the cement of the estate.

The smear, just faintly visible, stretched from the rubbish tip, towards the dark ground-floor windows of Zanna's house.

"That thing. These are its tracks."

Zanna got on her hands and knees.

"Yeah, see?" she said. "You can see scratch-marks. Where it's dug in with its . . . you know . . . metal points."

"If you say," said Deeba. "Let's *go*."

"Look. It was watching, or listening or whatever, at mine. Now we can see where it went."

"We don't even know what we're after." Deeba followed Zanna, who bent carefully over and traced her way through the dark estate. Deeba peered over her friend's shoulders, trying to make out the tracks Zanna could see.

"You blatantly look like a mad person," Deeba whispered. "If anyone sees you, what they going to think?"

"Who cares? Anyway, there's no one. If there was, I'd be out of here."

"I don't even see nothing."

"Marks," Zanna said. *"Tracks."*

She headed into the backs of the estate, between the brown concrete of those huge buildings. They were heading deep into the dead zones behind all the towers, into a maze of walls, bins, garages, and rubbish. Deeba looked around nervously.

"Come on, Zann," she said. "We dunno where we are."

"I've got a feeling . . ." Zanna said. She was distracted.

"This way . . ." she said, glancing down without slowing. In fact, she looked now as if she were following a memory, or an instinct, rather than a trail. She wound between the enormous buildings, lit here and there by inadequate yellow lights.

"I can't see it," Deeba said anxiously. "There's nothing."

"Yes, there is," said Zanna dreamily. She pointed, almost without looking. "There, see?" She sounded surprised. "It came this way." She accelerated.

"Zanna!" said Deeba in alarm, and trotted to keep up with her. "How can you even *see* that?"

The main road was just out of sight: even at this hour, they could hear traffic. Zanna turned a corner, mov-

ing almost as if she were being tugged.

"Wait!" said Deeba, and came up behind her.

In front of them, in the base of one of the monoliths, surrounded by puddles of pretty oily water, below a weakly shining lamp, the girls saw a door. It was ajar. On its threshold, even Deeba could see it was marked with a smear of oil.

"No way," Deeba said, eyeing Zanna. "You are *not* going there . . ."

Zanna stepped inside. Behind her, shouting, "Wait! Wait!" Deeba followed.

"Is anyone there?" Zanna said, not very loud. They were in a narrow corridor below ground level. The only windows were stubby ones by the ceiling, cracked and flecked with cobwebs and fly husks. The one or two bulbs let light out resentfully, as if they were misers who hoarded it.

"We are *going*," Deeba said. "There's nothing here."

Pipes and wires ran along the walls, and meters ticked.

"Hello?" Zanna said.

The corridor ended in a huge basement. It must have stretched underneath almost the whole tower block. Along its walls were old tools; there was rope in thick puddles; and sacks; and rusted bicycles; and a dried-out warmed-up fridge. Here and there were faint illuminations, and the light from streetlamps came through the filthy windows. The girls could hear the moan of traffic.

In the middle of the room was a pillar of pipes, where needles jerked up and down on gauges, and pressure was channeled by fat iron taps. In the dead center was an ancient, heavy-looking one the size of a steering wheel. It looked like it would open an airlock in a submarine.

"Let's go," whispered Deeba. "This place is scary."

But, slowly, Zanna shuffled forward. She looked like a sleepwalker.

"Zanna!" Deeba moved back towards the door. "We're *alone* in a *cellar*. And no one knows we're here. Come *on*!"

"There's more oil," Zanna said. "That thing . . . that umbrella, was here."

She touched the big spigot experimentally.

" '. . . when the wheel turns,' " she said.

"What?" said Deeba. "Come on. You coming?" She turned her back. Zanna gripped the wheel, and began to turn it.

It moved slowly at first. She had to strain. It squeaked against rust.

As it went, something happened to the light.

Deeba froze. Zanna hesitated, then turned the wheel a few more degrees.

The light began to change. It was flickering. All the sound in the room was ebbing. Deeba turned back.

"What's happening?" she whispered.

Zanna tugged, and with each motion the light and noise faltered a moment, and the wheel turned a little farther.

"No," said Deeba. "Stop. Please."

Zanna turned the valve another few inches, and the sound and light shifted. All the bulbs in the room flared, and so, impossibly, did the sound of the cars outside.

The iron wheel began to spin, slowly at first, then faster and faster. The room grew darker.

"You're turning off the electricity," Deeba said, but then she was silent, as she and Zanna looked up and realized that the lamplight shining through the windows from outside was also dimming.

As the light lessened, so did the sound.

Deeba and Zanna stared at each other in wonder.

Zanna spun the handle as if it were oiled. The noise of cars and vans and motorbikes outside grew tinny, like a recording, or as if it came from a television in the next room. The sound of the vehicles faded with the glow of the main road.

Zanna was turning off the traffic. The spigot turned off all the cars, and turned off the lamps.

It was turning off London.

PART II
Not in Kilburn

6

The Trashpack

The wheel spun; the light changed; the sound changed.

The glow from outside went from the dim of streetlights, down to darkness, then slowly back up to something luminous but odd. The last of the car engines sounded very far away, and then was gone. At last the wheel slowed and stopped.

Deeba stood, frozen, her hands to her mouth, in the strange not-dark. Zanna blinked several times, as if waking. The two looked at each other, and around at the room, all different in the bizarre light, full of impossible shadows.

"Quick! Undo it!" Deeba said at last. She grabbed the wheel and tried to turn it backwards. It was wedged stubbornly, as if it hadn't moved for years. "Help!" she said, and Zanna added her strength to Deeba's, and with a burst of effort they made the metal move.

But the wheel just spun free. It wasn't catching on anything. It whirred heavily around, but the light didn't change, and the noise of traffic didn't return.

London didn't come back on.

"Zanna," said Deeba. "What did you *do*?"

"I don't know," whispered Zanna. "I don't know."

"Let's get out of here," Deeba said. Zanna grabbed her arm and they ran back into the corridor.

The peculiar light was shining around the edges of the doorway they had come in by, as if a giant black-and-white television were playing just outside. Deeba and Zanna went for it full-tilt, and shoved it open.

They stumbled out. And stopped. And looked around. And let their mouths hang open.

It was not night anymore, and they were not in the estate. They were somewhere very else.

Just as it had when they entered, the door opened on waste ground between tall buildings, and to either side were big metal bins and spilt rubbish. But the tower blocks were not those they had left behind.

The walls just kept going up. Everywhere they looked, they were surrounded by enormous concrete monoliths that dwarfed those they remembered, and stood in more chaotic configurations. Not a single one of them was broken by a single window.

The door swung shut, and clicked. Zanna tugged it: of course it was locked. The building they'd emerged from soared into a sky glowing a peculiar glow.

"Maybe that room's, like . . . a train carriage . . ." Deeba whispered. "And we've come down the line . . . and . . . and it was later than we thought . . ."

"Maybe," whispered Zanna doubtfully, trying the door again. "So how do we get back?"

"Why did you turn it?" Deeba said.

"I don't *know*," said Zanna, stricken. "I just . . . thought like I had to."

Holding each other's arms for comfort, peering everywhere wide-eyed, Zanna and Deeba crept into the passageways between the walls.

"I'm calling Mum," Deeba said, and took out her phone. She was about to dial when she stopped, and stared at the screen. She showed it to Zanna. It was covered in symbols they'd never seen before. Where the reception bar usually was was a sort of corkscrew. Instead of the network sign was a weird pictogram.

Deeba scrolled through her address book.

"What's that mean?" said Zanna.

"Those aren't my friends' names," whispered Deeba. Her phone's contact list contained random words in alphabetical order. *Accidie, Bateleur, Cepheid, Dillybag* . . .

"Mine's the same," said Zanna, checking her own. "Enantios? Floccus? Goosegog? What is *that*?"

Deeba dialed her home number.

"Hello?" she whispered. "Hello?"

From the phone sounded a close-up buzzing like a wasp. It was so loud and sudden in that silent place that Deeba turned it off in alarm. She and Zanna stared at each other.

"Let me try," said Zanna. But dialing her number led to the same unpleasant insect noise. "No reception," she said, as if that were all that was wrong. Neither of them said anything more about the strange words or pictures on their phones.

They went deeper into the cavern between the windowless buildings.

"We have to get *out* of here," said Zanna, speeding up.

They ran past windblown old newspaper, deserted tin cans, and the rustling of black rubbish bags. In growing terror they turned left then right then left, and then Zanna came to a sudden stop, and Deeba bumped into her.

"What?" said Deeba, and Zanna hushed her.

"I thought . . ." she said. "Listen."

Deeba bit her lip. Zanna swallowed several times.

For long seconds there was silence. Then a very faint noise.

There was a rustling, what might be a light footfall.

"Someone's coming," whispered Zanna. Her voice was halfway between hope and despair—would this person help, or be more troubles?

Then she slumped, and pointed.

It was just a torn black rubbish bag, billowing nearby. It scraped gently against the ground.

Deeba sighed and watched it despondently as it fluttered a little closer. There was more rubbish behind it: with a clatter a can rolled into view, and there was the whisper of newspaper. A little collection of discarded stuff swirled at the passage entrance. The girls leaned against the wall.

"We got to think," Deeba said, and tried and failed to use her phone again.

"Deeba," Zanna whispered.

There was more rubbish than had been there a moment before. The black plastic, and the can, and the newspapers, had been joined by greasy hamburger wrappers, a grocery bag, several apple cores, and scrunched-up clear plastic. The rubbish rustled.

More rolled into view: chicken bones, empty tubes of toothpaste, a milk carton. Debris blocked off the way they had come.

Deeba and Zanna stared. The rubbish was moving towards them. It was coming against the wind.

As the girls began to creep backwards, it seemed as if the rubbish realized they were onto it. It sped up.

The cartons and cans rolled in their direction. The paper fluttered for them as madly as agitated butterflies. The plastic bags reached out their handles and scrambled towards the girls.

Deeba and Zanna screamed and ran. They heard the manic wet rustle of the predatory rubbish.

They raced through the maze of walls, desperate to get away.

Behind them there was a scrunching of paper, a percussion of cardboard, the squelch of damp things moving fast. The girls were fighting for breath.

"I . . . can't . . ." said Deeba. Zanna tried to pull her along, but Deeba could only flatten against a wall. "Oh help," she whispered. Zanna stood in front of her, between her friend and their pursuers.

The rubbish was close. It had slowed, and was creeping towards them. The stinking heap came with motions as careful and catlike as its odd shapes would allow. The stench of old dustbins was strong.

Ragged black plastic reached out with its rip-arms, trailing rubbish juice like a slug's slime. Zanna raised her arms in despairing defense, and Deeba held her breath and closed her eyes.

7

Market Day

"Oy!"

A voice came from behind them, and stones began to whistle past them. Someone grabbed Deeba and Zanna by their collars and hauled them backwards out of the alley.

It was a boy. They stared at him as he elbowed in front of them, chucking more pebbles and bits of brick and brandishing a stick at the rubbish. Which was cowering.

"Go on!" he said. He threw another well-aimed stone. The rubbish flinched, retreated. "Get out of it!" the boy shouted. "Disgusting!" The rubbish scrambled to get away.

Zanna and Deeba stared. The boy turned to them and winked.

He was about their age, very thin and wiry, dressed in odd patched-up grubby clothes. His hair was messy, his face shrewd. He was raising an eyebrow.

"What's that all about?" he said, putting his hands on his hips. "You ain't scared of a trashpack, are you? Pests like them? Need a much bigger lot'n that to do you any damage." He lobbed another stone. "If you're that yellow, why you off walking in the Backwall Maze? You wouldn't like it if they came swanning into *your* manor, would you? Mind how you go."

He nodded and half-grinned, gave them a little salute, then strode off away from the wall, brushing dirt from his already dirty clothes.

"Wait a minute!" Deeba managed to say.

"We don't know . . . where . . . we . . ." Zanna said. Their voices trailed off as they turned to watch the boy go, and saw the square he had pulled them into.

It was big, full of stalls and scores of people, movement, the bustle of a market. There were costumes and colors. But above all the girls' attention was taken by the light shining down from above.

In the narrow alleys, they had only seen slivers of sky. This was the first time since emerging from the door that they had had a clear view.

The sky was gray, not blue. Here and there were a few scurrying clouds, unfolding like milk in water. They moved in all different directions, as if they were on errands.

"Deebs," said Zanna, swallowing. "What is *that?*"

Deeba's throat dried as she looked up.

"No wonder the light's weird," whispered Zanna.

The orb above them was huge, and low in the sky—a circle at least three times the size of the sun. It shone with peculiar, cool dark-light like that of some autumn mornings, giving everything crisp edges and shadows. It was the yellow-white of a grubby tooth. Deeba and Zanna looked directly at it without hurting their eyes, for long seconds, their mouths wide open.

The sun had a hole in it.

It hung over the city, not like a disk, or a coin, or a ball, but like a donut. A perfect circle was missing from its middle. They could see the gray sky through it.

"Oh . . . my . . . God . . ." Deeba said.

"What *is* that?" said Zanna.

Deeba stepped forward, staring at the impossible sun shining like a fat ring. She looked down. The boy who had rescued her was gone.

"What's going on?" Deeba shouted. People in the market turned to look at her. "Where are we?" she whispered.

After a few seconds people went back to their business—whatever that was.

"Okay. Okay. We have to figure this out," said Deeba.

Behind them was a blank concrete wall, the edge of the maze they had come through, broken by a few alley entrances. In front, the market stretched as far as they could see.

"Why'd you turn that *stupid* wheel?"

"Like *I* knew we were going to end up here?"

"Can't ever leave anything alone."

Hesitantly, the two girls stepped into the rows of tents, buyers, and sellers. There was nowhere else to go.

They were immediately surrounded by the animated jabbering of a market morning. Deeba and Zanna kept looking up at that extraordinary hollow sun, but the scene around them was almost as bizarre.

There were people in all kinds of uniforms: mechanics' overalls smeared in oil; firefighters' protective clothes; doctors' white coats; the blue of police; and others, including people in the neat suits of waiters, with cloths over one arm. All these uniforms looked like dressing-up costumes. They were too neat, and somehow a bit too simple.

There were other shoppers in hotchpotch outfits of rags, and patchworks of skins, and what looked in some cases like taped-together bits of plastic or foil. Zanna and Deeba walked farther into the crowd.

"Zann," Deeba whispered. "Look."

Here and there were the strangest figures. People whose skins were no colors skin should ever be, or who seemed to have a limb or two too many, or peculiar extrusions or concavities in their faces.

"Yeah," said Zanna, with a sort of hollow, calm voice. "I see them."

"Is that *it*? You *see* them? What *are* they, for God's sake?"

"How should I know? But are you surprised? After everything?"

A woman went by above them, pedaling furiously as if she were on a bicycle, striding on two enormous spindly mechanical legs. Strange little figures flitted by at the edges of the market, too fast to clearly see. Deeba murmured an apology as she bumped into someone. The woman who bowed politely to her wore glasses with several layers of lenses, lowered and raised on levers, seemingly at random.

"Lovely arrangements!" the girls heard. "Get them here! Brighten up the home."

Beside them was a stall bursting in flamboyant bouquets, carefully arranged in colored paper.

"They're not flowers," Deeba said. They were tools.

Each was a bunch of hammers, screwdrivers, spanners, and levels, bright plastic and metal, carefully arranged and tied together with a bow.

"What on earth are you wearing?" someone said. Zanna turned as someone picked at her hoodie. The man was tall and thin, with a jagged halo of thick, spiky hair. His suit was white and covered with tiny black marks.

It was print. His clothes were made from pages from books, immaculately sewn together.

"No, this won't do," he said. He spoke quickly, tugging at Zanna's clothes too fast for her to stop him. "This is very drab, can't possibly keep you entertained. What you need—" He flourished his sleeve. "—is this. The hautest of couture. Be entertained while you wear. Never again need you face the misery of unreadable clothes. Now you can pick your favorite works of fiction or nonfiction for your sleeves. Perhaps a classic for the trousers. Poetry for your skirt. Historiography for socks. Scripture for knickers. Learn while you dress!"

He whipped a tape from his pocket and began to measure Zanna. He yanked at his head, and Zanna and Deeba winced and gasped. What had looked like hair was countless pins and needles jammed anyhow into his scalp, a handful of which he pulled out.

The man did not bleed or seem to suffer any discomfort from treating himself as a pincushion. He wedged some of the pins back into his head, and there was a faint *pfft* with each puncture, as if his skull were velvet. Busily, he began to pin bits of paper to Zanna, scribbling measurements on a notebook.

"But what if it rains, you say? Well then rejoice as your outfit cuddles you in its gentle slushing, and you're given the opportunity for an *entirely new book*. How wonderful! I have a vast selection." He indicated his stall, crammed with volumes from which assistants tore pages and stitched. "What genres and literatures are to your taste?"

"Please . . ." stammered Zanna.

"Leave it," said Deeba. "Leave us alone."

"No thank you . . ." Zanna said. "I . . ."

The girls turned and ran.

"Hey!" the man shouted. "Are you alright?" But they did not slow down.

They ran past chefs baking roof-tiles in their ovens and chiseling apart bricks over pans, frying the whites and yolks that emerged; past confectioners with jars full of candied leaves; past what looked like an argument at a honey stall between a bear in a suit and a cloud of bees in the shape of a man.

At last they reached a little clearing deep in the market containing a pump and a pillar. They stopped, their hearts pounding.

"What are we going to *do*?" said Deeba.

"I don't know."

They looked up that empty-hearted sun above them. Deeba dialed her home once more.

"Hello Mum?" she whispered.

There was that frenetic buzzing. From a little hole in the back of her phone burst a handful of wasps. Deeba shrieked and dropped the phone, and the wasps flew off in different directions.

Her phone was broken. She sat heavily at the pillar's base.

Zanna stared at her, and her face began to crease.

"It'll be okay," said Deeba. "Don't. It'll be alright."

"How?" said Zanna. "How will it?"

Zanna and Deeba stared at each other. From her wallet, Zanna drew out the strange travelcard she had been sent, weeks ago. She stared at it as if it might contain some clue, some advice. But it was only a card.

Pins and Needles

Deeba put her arm around her friend. Neither of them wanted to attract the attention of the strange market-goers. They sat quietly for a couple of minutes.

"Ahem . . ."

Cautiously, the two girls looked up. Standing before them was the boy—the boy who had scared off the trashpack. He eyed them with a look somewhere between sarcasm and concern.

"I was just wondering . . ." he said slowly. "Is that yours?"

He pointed near their feet, at an empty cardboard milk carton. Zanna and Deeba stared at it.

The carton moved eagerly towards them, opening and closing its folded spout. Deeba and Zanna yelped and withdrew their feet. It was one of the pieces of rubbish that had chased them earlier.

"I was going to kick it back into the maze," he said. "But I thought maybe it was a pet . . ."

"No," Deeba said guardedly. "No, it's not ours. We was . . . It was . . ."

"It must have followed us," said Zanna.

"Righto," the boy said, stuck his hands in his pockets, and whistled a tune for a second or two. He looked at them quizzically. "Well I'll . . ." He hesitated. "Can I just ask . . . Are you okay?"

He sat down beside them. "What're your names, then? I'm Hemi. Pleased to meet you and all that." He stuck out his hand. Zanna and Deeba looked at it suspiciously. Eventually they shook it and said their names. "So what's up with you two then?" he said. "What's happened?"

"We don't *know* what's happened," Zanna said.

"We dunno where we are," said Deeba. "We dunno what that is . . ." She pointed up into the sky.

"We don't know what's going on," Zanna finished.

"Well . . ." the boy Hemi said slowly. "You two don't know a lot, do you? But I might be able to help you. I can tell you where you are, for a start." His voice dropped, and the girls eagerly leaned in close to hear him.

"You're . . ." he whispered slowly, "in . . . Un Lun Dun."

The girls waited for the words to make sense, but they didn't. Hemi was grinning. "Un Lun Dun!" he repeated.

"Un," said Zanna. "Lun. Dun."

"Yeah," he said. "Un Lun Dun."

And suddenly the three sounds fell into a different shape, and Zanna said the name.

"UnLondon."

"UnLondon?" Deeba said.

Hemi nodded, and crept an inch closer.

"UnLondon," he said, and he reached for Zanna.

"Hey!" A loud voice interrupted. Zanna, Deeba, and the boy jumped up. The milk carton squeaked out air and scuttled behind Deeba. There in front of them was the pincushion man, his needles winking in the light. "Don't you *dare*!" the book-wearing fashion designer shouted. "Get out!"

Hemi leapt up, made a rude noise, and sped away, ducking at astonishing speed between the legs of passersby, into the crowd and out of sight.

"What you doing?" Zanna shouted. "He was helping us!"

"Helping?" the man said. "Do you have any idea who that was? He's one of them!"

"One of who?"

"A ghost!"

Deeba and Zanna stared at him.

"You heard me," he said. "A ghost. He's from Wraithtown, and . . . Did he make you get really close to him? I saw him trying to grab!"

"Well . . . we couldn't really hear him, so we was leaning in . . ." Deeba said.

"*Aha.* I knew it. One more minute and he'd have possessed you! That's what they want: they're desperate for bodies. They'll possess you soon as look at you. Sneaky little wisper."

"Possess me?"

"Absolutely. Or you." He nodded at Zanna. "Why do you think he was talking to you?"

"But . . . he *has* a body," said Zanna. "We shook his hand."

The man looked a little put-out.

"Well, yes, technically he has a body, that one. If you want to be really precise about it, he's a half-ghost. But don't you be fooled by his whole 'Flesh-and-bone, just like you' act. He'll steal your body just like the rest of his family.

"It's just as well I came looking for you," the man said kindly. "You worried me back there. I suppose I can just understand someone not wanting to benefit from the astonishing opportunity of this new form of apparel, which literally *clothes* you in education . . ." Seeing their faces he cut this patter off with visible effort. "Sorry. Anyway. The point is you both looked so scared. I wanted to check you were alright."

Zanna stared into the crowd.

"What *is* this place?" she said.

"What do you mean?" the pin-haired man said. "It's Rogueday! This is Rogueday Market, of course. You can't seriously tell me you haven't been here before? What's that?" Before Zanna could stop him, he had reached out and taken the travelcard from her.

"Give that back!" she shouted. The man's eyes were growing wider and wider, and he gaped at the piece of card, and back at Zanna.

"Oh my fizzy dog," he said. "No wonder you're confused. You're not from here at all. You're the *Shwazzy!*"

There was an intake of breath from the little group of market-goers around them. Zanna and Deeba looked at each other, and at the people watching.

Among the women and men in those unconvincing uniforms were odder figures still, like a woman who seemed made of metal, and someone wearing one of those old-fashioned diving suits with weighted boots and a big brass helmet, windowed with dark glass. Everyone was staring at Zanna.

"Unstible's boots," someone said reverently. "I can't believe it. The Shwazzy."

"Well," Zanna said. "I don't know much—"

"Wait!" the pin-headed man said, and looked around. "We have to be careful. We need to take you somewhere safe. Just in case." Some of the onlookers

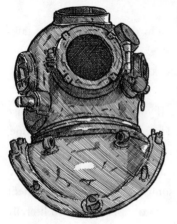

were nodding and glancing around. "I can't believe you're here! And . . . you brought a friend." He nodded politely to Deeba. "But there'll be time for all this later. Right now let's get you out of here.

"Skool," he said, "you go check the schedule. You know where we're going, and how." The diver gave a laborious nod and headed off. "I'll get the Shwazzy and her friend ready . . . if," he added with sudden nervous politeness, "that's alright with her. And everyone else . . ."

He looked at the people listening. "Not a word about this. Shtum! This is our chance!" The onlookers nodded.

"If you'll follow me, we'll get ready. It'll be my honor to take you." Zanna said nothing, but he continued: "You're willing? That's marvelous, really. We've not been introduced: you are the Shwazzy, and as I say it's an honor." He said the last phrase so quickly it was like one word: anazahsaytsan*onn*a.

"I'm Obaday Fing, the couturier. Of Obaday Fing Designs. Perhaps you've heard of me? Not the wearable books, I know, but perhaps . . . the edible cravat? No? The two-person trouser? Doesn't ring a bell? Never mind, never mind. I'm at your service."

"This is Deeba," said Zanna. "And I'm . . ."

"The Shwazzy, absolutely," the man said. "A pleasure. Now if you please, Shwazzy . . . I don't want to alarm you, but you've already had a run-in with an attempted flesh-theft, and I'll feel much happier if you stick with me."

From behind them was the clatter of the milk carton.

"Go away," Zanna told it, and pointed. The carton retreated a few centimeters. Air whistled from its spout. It sounded like whimpering.

"Shwazzy, please!" Fing said, beckoning.

"Oh alright," Deeba said to the carton. She nodded at Zanna. "I'll sort it. You can come," she said to the rubbish. "But if you gang up with your friends again, you're gone." Deeba jerked her head in invitation, and the milk carton scampered after her, rolling over the cobbles.

Behind them, the last of the little gathering dispersed. Several people watched Zanna go. They looked excited, and secretive, and very pleased.

One man was standing still. He was chubby and muscular, squeezed into painter's dungarees, complete with streaks of paint. Deeba looked back, and he met her eyes for a moment, then looked back at Zanna, very thoughtfully.

He disappeared into the crowd, moving fast.

"What?" said Zanna, pulling Deeba to come.

"Nothing," said Deeba. "I just feel like someone's watching us."

Watching you, she thought, and looked at her friend.

Location Location

"I should've realized," Obaday said, "that you're arrivals, when I saw you talking to that ghost-boy. He hangs around, stealing, looking for strangers, but so far we've managed to get rid of him before he does anything terrible. You don't want to make it into *his* phone book!"

"What?" said Zanna.

"In Wraithtown," said Obaday. "They keep a list of all the dead. On both sides of the Odd!"

"Our phones don't work," Deeba said. "They're bust."

"You have phones? What in the abcity for? It's too hard to train the insects. As far as I know there are about three working phones in UnLondon, each with a very carefully maintained hive, and all of them in Mr. Speaker's Talklands."

"No wonder you're confused. When did you get here? You must have been briefed? No? Not briefed? Hmmmm . . ." He frowned. "Maybe the Prophs are planning on explaining details later."

"What Prophs?" Deeba said.

"And here we are!" said Obaday Fing, waving at his stall.

* * *

Obaday's assistants looked up from their stitching. One or two had a few nee-dles and pins wedged into their heads, in among plaits and ponytails. At the rear of the stall sat a figure writing at a huge sheet of paper. Where its head should be was a big glass jar full of black ink, into which it dipped its pen.

"Simon Atramenti," Obaday said. The inkwell-headed person waved with stained fingers and returned to its writing. "For clients who insist on bespoke copy."

The stall looked as if it was only about six feet deep, but when Obaday swept aside a curtain at the back there was a much larger tent-room beyond.

It was silk-lined. There was a table and chairs, a cabinet and a stove, ham-mocks hanging from the ceiling. Plump pillows were everywhere.

"Just my little office, just my little office," Obaday said, sweeping off dust.

"This is amazing," said Zanna. "You'd never know this was here."

"How come there's space?" said Deeba.

"I beg your pardon?" Obaday said. "Oh, well, I stitched it myself. After all my years I'd be embarrassed if I hadn't learnt to stitch a few wrinkles in space." He looked expectant. He waited.

Eventually Zanna said: "Um . . . That's brilliant." Obaday smiled, satisfied.

"No, it's nothing," he said, waving his hands. "Really you embarrass me."

He picked things up and put them down, packing and unpacking a bag, talk-ing all the time, a stream of odd phrases and non sequiturs so incomprehensi-ble that they quickly stopped hearing it, except as a sort of amiable buzzing.

"We have to go home," Zanna said, interrupting Obaday's spiel.

Obaday frowned, not unkindly.

"Home . . . ? But you have things to do, Shwazzy."

"Please don't call me that. I'm Zanna. And we really do have to go."

"We have to get *back*," said Deeba. The little milk carton whined air at her miserable voice.

"If you say so . . . But I'm afraid I've no idea how to get you back to, to what's it called, to Lonn Donn."

Zanna and Deeba stared at each other. Seeing their faces, Obaday continued quickly. "But, but, but don't worry," he said. "The Propheseers'll know what to do. We have to get you to them. They'll help you back after . . . well, after you've done what's needed."

"Propheseers?" said Zanna. "Let's go, then."

"Of course—we're just waiting for Skool with the necessary information. Traveling across UnLondon—well, it's quite a thing to take on." He disappeared behind a screen and flung his paper-and-print clothes one by one over the top. *"Moby-Dick,"* he said. "Even with small print, I have to wear too many undershirts." He emerged, in a new suit of the same cut, but adorned with visibly larger letters. *"The Other Side of the Mountain."* He smiled, flashing his cuff. "Considerably shorter."

"Zann," said Deeba urgently. "I want to go *home.*"

"Mr. Fing, please," Zanna said. "You really have to help us get out of here."

Obaday Fing looked miserable.

"I simply don't know how," he said at last. "I don't know how you got here. I don't know where you live. There are plenty of people who don't believe in Lonn Donn at all. I'm truly sorry, Shwazzy . . . Zanna. All I can do is take you to those who can help. As fast as we can. Believe me, *I* want you to . . . get started ASAP."

"Get started?" said Zanna.

"With what?" said Deeba.

"The Propheseers'll explain," Obaday said.

"No," shouted Zanna. "Get started with *what?*"

"Well," said Obaday hurriedly, "with everything. We have to get you out of here. There are those working against you. Working for your enemy."

"My enemy?" said Zanna. "Who's my enemy?"

Before Obaday could respond, the curtain was pulled back and there stood Skool, the figure in the diving suit, tapping its wrist urgently.

"Now?" Obaday said. "Already? Right, right, we're coming, off we go." He grabbed a few more things, hauled his bag over his shoulder, and ushered everyone out.

"Who?" Zanna said.

"What? Oh, honestly, Shwazzy, it's really best you let those who know these things explain . . ."

"What enemy?" The two girls stared at Obaday, and he faltered, and was momentarily still.

"Smog," he whispered. Then he cleared his throat and walked hurriedly on.

10

Perspective

"What did you mean *smog*, Obaday?" Zanna said.

The topic obviously made him very uncomfortable. Zanna and Deeba could make very little sense of what he said. "Hold your breath," he said, and, "We shouldn't talk about it," and, "You got it once before, you can help us get it again." "The Propheseers . . ." he said, and Deeba finished for him.

"They'll explain," she said. "Right." She and Zanna exchanged exasperated glances. It was obvious they would get nothing useful from Obaday, nor from the silent Skool.

They passed people standing in front of walls, avidly reading graffiti.

"They're checking the headlines," Obaday said.

Most people looked human (if in an unusual range of colors), but a sizeable proportion did not. Deeba and Zanna saw bubble-eyes, and gills, and several different kinds of tails. The two girls stared when a bramble-bush walked past, squeezed into a suit, a tangle of blackberries, thorns, and leaves bursting out of its collar.

There were no cars, but there were plenty of other vehicles. Some were carts tugged by unlikely animals, and many were pedal-powered. Not bicycles, though: the travelers perched on jerkily walking stilts, or at the front of long carriages like tin centipedes. One goggled rider traveled by in a machine like a herd of nine wheels.

"Out of the way!" the driver yelled. "Noncycle coming through!"

They passed curbside cafés, and open-fronted rooms full of old and odd-looking equipment.

"There's loads of empty houses," said Zanna.

"A few," Obaday said. "Most aren't empty, though: they're *emptish*. Open access. For travelers, tribes, and mendicants. Temporary inhabitants. Now we're in Varmin Way. This is Turpentine Road. This is Shatterjack Lane." They were going too fast for Zanna and Deeba to do more than gain a few impressions.

The streets were mostly red brick, like London terraces, but considerably more ramshackle, spindly and convoluted. Houses leaned into each other, and stories piled up at complicated angles. Slate roofs lurched in all directions.

Here and there where a house should be was something else instead.

There was a fat, low tree, with open-fronted bedrooms, bathrooms, and kitchens perched in its branches. People were clearly visible in each chamber, brushing their teeth or kicking back their covers. Obaday took them past a house-sized fist, carved out of stone, with windows in its knuckles; and then the shell of a huge turtle, with a door in the neck hole, and a chimney poking out of its mottled top.

Zanna and Deeba stopped to stare at a building with oddly bulging walls, in a patchwork of black, white, and gray bricks of varying sizes.

"Oh gosh," said Deeba. "It's *junk*."

The entire three-floor building was mortared-together rubbish. There were fridges, a dishwasher or two, and hundreds of record players, old-fashioned cameras, telephones, and typewriters, with thick cement between them.

There were four round windows like a ship's portholes. Someone inside

threw one open: they were the fronts of washing machines, embedded in the facade.

"Shwazzy!" Obaday called. "Shwazzy . . . I mean, Zanna. You'll have time to stare at moil houses later." The girls followed him, and the milk carton followed them.

"How long will it take to get there?" Zanna said. "Is it dangerous?"

"Is it dangerous? Hmm. Well, define 'dangerous.' Is a knife 'dangerous'? Is Russian roulette 'dangerous'? Is arsenic 'dangerous'?" He did the little finger-thing to show quotation marks, tickling the air. "It depends on your perspective."

The girls looked at each other in alarm.

"Uh . . ." said Zanna.

"I don't think it does depend on perspective," said Deeba. "I think that's all definitely *dangerous*. I don't think you need none of this . . ." She did the quote motion.

"If we planned ahead, sent a few messages," Obaday went on, "maybe got a gnostechnician to check the travel reports on the undernet, stayed each night with friends in safe places in whatever borough we reached . . . then it would be perfectly safe. Well . . . reasonably safe. Safe-esque. But, yes, it would be 'dangerous' if we didn't think ahead, and we took a wrong turning into Wraithtown, or met some scratchmonkeys or a building with house-rabies, or, lord help us, if we ran into the *giraffes* . . ."

He shivered, reached up absently, and touched his fingertips on the ends of his pins and needles. "But we're not walking. We're going to get there today. This is . . . well, a 'special occasion' doesn't cover it, really, does it? We have to get you to the Propheseers *one*, as quickly as possible, and *two*, as safely as possible."

They turned into a cul-de-sac of brick homes, houses on stilts, and a windmill made of a helicopter on its side. Skool pointed. He, or she, beckoned them to a shelter with a very familiar logo.

"Now," said Obaday, "we have only to wait."

Zanna and Deeba stopped. The milk carton bumped into Deeba's foot and squeaked.

Zanna said, "We're getting a bus?"

11

Public Transport

"I know!" said Obaday. "Hard to believe. But yes. I think we need to."

Zanna and Deeba looked at each other. They didn't speak, but messages went between them in a series of looks and raised eyebrows: *What's the big deal with a bus? Don't know* . . .

"I've got the fare," Obaday said. "They never turn anyone away, but it's traditional to pay what you can."

They were joined at the stop by an elderly woman in a coastguard's uniform, and a hulking figure in a dress at whom Zanna and Deeba had to force themselves not to stare. It was a lobster, waddling on two stubby legs, clacking her pincers.

Obaday looked at his watch, leaned against the pole, and began to read his sleeve. The girls watched the sky. A sliver of the hoop-sun was visible over the roofs. Troupes of starlings, pigeons, and crows crisscrossed in front of the clouds, in rather more organized fashion than they ever seemed to manage in London.

"Look," said Zanna, pointing. There were other birds among them, half-familiar from pictures, like herons and vultures. There was at least one thing in the air that didn't look like a bird at all, something that *caw*ed enormously as it disappeared.

"So," Deeba whispered, knocking the post of the bus stop. "What do you think'll turn up?"

"Don't know," said Zanna.

"A load of camels?" said Deeba.

"A boat?"

"A carriage like in Sleeping Beauty?"

"A sledge?"

The girls' smiles froze when they heard the familiar coughing of a big engine approaching. A double-decker red bus turned the corner.

"It's just . . ." said Deeba.

"It's a bus," said Zanna.

Obaday Fing looked enraptured.

"Isn't it *magnificent*?" he said.

The bus looked severely battered. Where it should have had a number was instead a strange sign that might have been a drawing of a roll of paper or might have been a random pattern. It was an old-fashioned Routemaster of the type that had been retired from London, with a pole and an open platform at the back, and a separate little compartment at the front for the driver, a woman in an antiquated uniform and dark glasses.

"The helmswoman," said Obaday. "And with her one of UnLondon's champions. Protectors of the transit, the sacred warriors."

"Morning," said a man, jumping out of the vehicle.

Obaday whispered, "The bus conductor."

The conductor wore an old-fashioned London Transport uniform. It had been torn and fixed many times, and it was clean, but scorched and stained. Strapped to his front was a metal contraption, on which he drummed his fingers. He wore beads, and charms, and a copper truncheon on his belt.

"Mrs. Jujube," the man said, pushing back his cap and bowing to the elderly woman. "Always a pleasure. Manifest Station again? And madam?" He inclined his head at the lobster. "Let me guess . . . the estuary? You know you'll have to change buses? Please, go on in. And sir . . ." He turned to Obaday.

"This is, I must, I cannot tell you," Obaday stammered. "It is an honor, a real, I cannot, I am overcome! On behalf of all of UnLondon—"

"Well," said the uniformed man, in what sounded like polite boredom. "You're very kind. May I ask your destination?"

"I am Obaday Fing, and this is my associate Skool, and this is Deeba, and *this*—" He swept his arm at Zanna. "—is the reason for our journey. Your route takes us towards the Pons Absconditus, I think?"

Obaday rummaged in his pocket and brought out a handful of money. There were francs and marks and ancient English pound notes, and colorful currency Deeba and Zanna didn't recognize. "One young lady has her own ticket."

Zanna held out her travelcard. "*This*," said Obaday, "is—"

"The Shwazzy," the conductor whispered. He grabbed the travelcard and examined it.

"I know that look," he said to Zanna, smiling. "Astonished, bewildered, excited, frightened . . . awed. That's the taste of the first few days in UnLondon. It takes one who's swigged it to recognize it. Shwazzy, it's a great honor."

"You recognize it . . . ?" Zanna said.

"You came here, too?" Deeba said.

"Where d'you think I got this?" he said, pointing at his uniform, and the box around his midriff. "Where you two from?"

"Kilburn," said Zanna.

"Ah. I'm a Tooting boy originally. Joe Jones—pleased to meet you. I went abnaut—that's what it's called, crossing down, or up, or sideways, from there to here—and came to UnLondon, what, must be more than a decade ago."

"You did?" said Zanna. "Thank God! You can explain things."

"We dunno what's going on," said Deeba. "We need to get *back*, I want my mum and dad . . ."

"Hey, Rosa!" Jones shouted, and the driver leaned out of her window. "See who we've got on this trip?"

She peered over the top of her glasses.

"Blond . . ." said Jones. "Young lady. From out of town. As things are getting nasty in the abcity . . ."

Rosa's eyes grew wider and wider.

"That is *never* the *Shwazzy*!"

Zanna and Deeba looked at each other.

"Oh my lord!" Rosa went on. "I heard rumors from the old place that something was happening, on the drivers' grapevine . . . one of them even said she'd tracked the Shwazzy down to a café! But I thought it was just foolishness . . . But it's finally happened! It's time!"

"It is indeed!" the conductor said. "And it's down to us to get her to the Pons Absconditus."

"So, she's going to fight for us! She'll fix things!"

"Hold on," said Zanna. "I don't know anything about that . . ."

"What's the holdup?" the elderly woman shouted.

"Coming, Mrs. Jujube!" Joe Jones spoke quietly to Obaday and the girls. "We should be careful who knows about this. There are . . . those who'd like to get in the way. The Pons is a few stops away. We'll go as usual, so no one knows anything's up. Get you there in a few hours.

"Please." Jones closed Obaday's fingers around his money without taking any. "You're escorting the Shwazzy. Now remember—not a word. As far as anyone's concerned, you're just regular petitioners, come to ask the Propheseers a question. And what about that? Is that with you? Does it have a name?" He pointed at the milk carton, hesitating by the bus's platform.

"Yes," Deeba said. "It's called . . . Curdle. Come on, Curdle."

Zanna crossed her arms and raised her eyebrows.

The carton leapt happily inside after them.

"Curdle?" whispered Zanna.

"Oh shut up," said Deeba. "Just get on with being Shwazzed, will you?"

There were a few other passengers on the bottom deck, oddly dressed men and women and a few even odder other things. As they always did on buses, Zanna and Deeba headed for the staircase to the upper level. The conductor stopped them.

"Not this time," he said. "Wait a bit."

He rang the bell, and the bus moved. Obaday and Skool sat, but Zanna and Deeba stood next to Jones on the platform at the back.

"Our next stop's Manifest Station," he said. "We're heading straight there."

"Not *straight* there," Deeba said. She pointed through the front window. "I mean, there's a wall in the way." They did not seem to be slowing down.

"We're going to hit it," said Zanna. The bus gunned straight for the bricks. Deeba and Zanna winced and closed their eyes.

"Hold tight, please," Jones shouted.

There was a hissing sound, the flapping of heavy cloth, and the thrumming of ropes. Zanna and Deeba opened their eyes again, hesitantly.

A tarpaulin bulged from the bus's roof like an enormous fungus. It inflated into a huge balloon, tethered by ropes from the upper windows. The bus sped up, and the rugby-ball–shaped balloon stretched longer than the vehicle beneath it.

There was a thump behind them, as if something had hit the vehicle's rear, a scuffing like an animal ascending the metal. Deeba and Zanna turned in alarm, then gasped and rocked and held on, as with a stomach-jolting tug, the bus started to rise.

Dangling below the balloon, it passed over the wall, leaving a threadwork of streets and buildings below, ascending over UnLondon.

12

Safe Conduct

"It's beautiful," Zanna said.

The girls held on to the pole and leaned out over the roofs.

"God," said Zanna. "My dad would be *sick* if he saw me doing this."

"Eeurgh," said Deeba. "Imagine." She leaned over and made a puking noise. "It'd go *everywhere.*"

Conductor Jones stood on the platform with them, and they both knew somehow that if they were to slip, he'd be there to grab them.

The bus puttered low over the streets. Towers poked up around it. UnLondoners looked up and waved at it.

They passed squat tower blocks, arches of brick and stone, the hotchpotch slopes of roofs. There were stranger things, too: skyscraper-high chests of drawers in polished wood, spires like melting candles, houses like enormous hats and bats. Deeba pointed at gargoyles and pigeons on some of the houses, then started: some of the gargoyles were moving.

"Your eyes," said Jones. "Bigger than fried eggs. I remember seeing it the first time."

He pointed out landmarks to them.

"That's Wraithtown, where the roofs flicker. That's the market. Those windowless towers? Backwall Maze. That big fat chimney-thing? It's the entrance to the library."

"Why you here?" Zanna said.

"I couldn't do this back in London, could I?" Jones held on to the pole with one hand and leaned out over the city. "Do you see that?" He pointed at a building made from typewriters and dead televisions.

"We saw one like that before," Zanna said. "Obaday called it . . . what was it?"

"A moily house?" said Deeba.

"You'll see a lot of moil technology here," Jones said. "Em Oh Aye Ell. Mildly Obsolete In London. Throw something away and you declare it obsolete. You've seen an old computer, or a broken radio or whatever, left on the streets? It's there for a few days, and then it's just gone.

"Sometimes rubbish collectors have taken it, but often as not it ends up here, where people find other uses for it. It seeps into UnLondon. You might see residue: maybe a dried-up puddle on a wall. That's where moil dripped through. And here, it sprouts like mushrooms on the streets.

"The money your friend has? All the out-of-date and foreign coins and notes Londoners throw away. A few years ago when Europe got rid of its old money and you were all left with loads of useless old bits and bobs, so much found its way down here we had too much, and that meant terrible inflation. We had to feed loads of it to the moolaphage . . . Anyway. That's sort of how things get down here.

"You could say I was a bit like that," he said thoughtfully. "Obsolete, they said. If you find just the right manhole you can get here. The hard part wasn't coming through, it was getting the *bus* through.

"I always worked on the buses, back in London. You probably grown up paying the driver, right? Or travelcards? Didn't used to be that way. It used to be that most of the buses in London had a driver *and* conductor.

"I'd take the money and give the tickets." He patted the machine he wore. "It was quicker, because the driver didn't have to deal with everyone. And it was safer. Two of us there, all the time. But they decided they could save money if they got rid of half of us. Of course it messed things up. But them who made the decision were people who never took buses, so they didn't care.

"We knew what we did was important. Look in the dictionary. 'Conduct:

verb. To *lead, control,* or *guide.*' Some of us weren't prepared to stop being guides. We look after travelers. It's . . ." Conductor Jones looked down, suddenly shy. "Some people say it's a sacred duty."

"UnLondon . . . Well, sometimes, it can be a dangerous place. We had to be really ready to *conduct.*" He tapped the weapon on his belt, pointed into the cabinet beside him, at a bow and arrow, and coils of wire. "The drivers who came down swore to get the passengers from where they are to where they want to go. And to protect them."

"Protect them from what?" Zanna said.

"There's the occasional skymugger," Jones said. "Airsquid, though mostly they hunt high, where the deep-sky fisherfolk go. And there are other things. Conductors on other routes, if they're *real* unlucky, sometimes get attacked by giraffes."

The girls stared at each other.

"You're the second person to say that," Deeba said.

"I've seen giraffes," Zanna said.

"They're so not scary . . ." Deeba said.

"Ha!" The whole bus looked up at Jones's laugh. "They've done a good job making people believe that those hippy refugees in the zoo are normal giraffes. Next you'll tell me that they've got long necks so they can reach high leaves! Nothing to do with waving the bloody skins of their victims like flags, of course.

"There's a lot of animals very good at that sort of disinformation. There are no cats in UnLondon, for example, because they're not magic and mysterious at all, they're idiots. You'll find pigs, dogs, frogs, everything else getting through to here, though. There's a lot of traffic back and forth. They know when things are happening. They pass messages."

"Zann," said Deeba. "That makes sense. All those animals, they knew you were . . . whatever you are."

"The Shwazzy," said Zanna.

"But no cats," Jones went on. "Too busy trying to look cool. Anyway. You know what the main danger is down here. And it's a danger that's been growing. For years."

"The Smo—" Zanna said, and he put his finger quickly to his lips.

"Yes," he said. "That's why you're here."

"But what *is* it?" she said. "What does it want?"

"Can't talk about it here," Jones whispered. "Better safe than. You know what I mean. The Propheseers'll explain."

"Next stop," he yelled. "Manifest Station."

They passed an enormous building like a cathedral, within a few meters of its windows, and people peered at them out of offices. The edifice was perforated in several places with what looked like random holes, and bursting from them were railway lines. They sprang in different directions: horizontal; up like a roller coaster; corkscrewing down. A few hundred meters from the great building, they plunged into holes in the street, and down into darkness.

"Manifest Station," Jones said. A dark-windowed diesel train burst out of the building, close enough to make the bus shake. It helter-skeltered downward into the earth.

"Where's it going?" Zanna said.

"Crossing the Odd, to some of the other abcities," Jones said. "If you're brave enough to try, you might be able to catch a train from UnLondon to Parisn't, or No York, or Helsinkı, or Lost Angeles, or Sans Francisco, or Hong Gone, or Rome- less . . . It's a termi- nus."

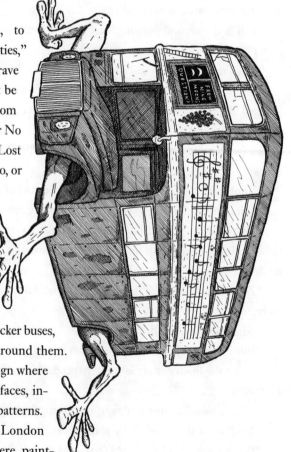

They hovered above a big yard at the side of the station containing twenty or thirty double-decker buses, with passengers milling around them. Each bus had a different sign where the numbers should be—faces, in- sects, flowers, random patterns. On their sides, where London buses carried adverts, were paintings, short stories in big print, pictures of chessboards with games in progress, musical scores.

But these were details. What made Zanna and Deeba stare and make little sounds of wonder was how the buses moved.

UnLondon's terrain was difficult. There were thin tangled streets, sudden steep hills, deep pits, patches where roads seemed to be made of something too soft for wheels, on which pedestrians bounced. To deal with the various difficulties of their routes, the UnLondon buses had adapted.

They trundled on caterpillar treads. They rolled on enormously inflated rubbery wheels. They coasted on skirts of air like hovercrafts. In the sky was another aerobus, below a round balloon. Conductors leaned out of the vehicles, bristling with weapons.

A bus approached the terminus from a thicket of tall spindly towers. It picked its way over the roofs on four enormous lizard legs that sprouted from its wheel housings. The driver spun the wheel and tugged at levers, and the bus's padded gecko feet closed gently around buttresses and splayed on slanting roofs, leaving no marks behind.

"Manifest Station Terminus," Jones belted. "Who's changing here?"

They winched Mrs. Jujube and two other passengers down in a basket. "This is the Scrollscrawl bus, and you want the Rusty Star Sigil bus," Jones told one. "And you, sir, look for the Terrible Mouse Sigil."

As the bus swung in position, Deeba looked up and made a little startled noise.

"What is it?" said Zanna.

"I thought I saw something," said Deeba, pointing up. "Like . . . a crab. Moving on the ceiling."

"Well . . ." Zanna looked around. "It's gone now. This place is full of weird things."

The basket dangled between a bus on stilts and another on what looked like giant ice skates. The three passengers got out. At the last moment a man wearing a toga ran and caught the basket; said good-bye to a companion, who hurried off; and got in.

He was big and heavy to haul. When he stepped onto the platform, there was a hissing. The milk carton was huddled behind Deeba, exhaling aggressively.

"Curdle," Zanna muttered. "Deeba, keep your manky pet under control."

The new passenger stared huffily at Curdle from behind his beard.

"See that?" Deeba whispered.

"That bloke does *not* like us."

They went much higher this time, midway between the roofs and the strangely lit sky. UnLondon sprawled to the horizon. A few animal-footed buses crawled carefully over and around houses. Light from the empty sun gleamed on a million surfaces. It was a ragged and jagged landscape. Low clouds buzzed below their wheels, obscuring neighborhoods, moving in various directions purposefully.

"That?" Jones pointed at what looked like a shirt, racing madly through the air. "When washing blows away in London, if it stays in the air long enough, it blows all the way here. Then it's free. Never has to come down."

They passed a stepped pyramid, a corkscrew-shaped minaret, a building like an enormous *U*.

"I wish my mum was here," Deeba whispered. She couldn't even look up as the thought took her. "And my dad. Even my brother Hass."

"Me too," said Zanna.

" 'Course you do," said Jones gently. The sadness and homesickness that filled the two girls was sudden, but it didn't feel like it came out of nowhere. It had been there many hours, underneath everything, and now that things were calmer, with the beautiful view below them, it sort of ambushed them.

"My mum must have the police and everything," Deeba said.

"Actually, I wouldn't worry too much about that," said Jones.

"What do you mean?" said Zanna.

"Difficult to explain. The Propheseers'll tell you." The girls shook their heads in exasperation. "Just . . . I wouldn't worry yet."

Deeba and Zanna were quiet. Sensing their mood, Curdle snuffled up to Deeba's foot. She picked up the little carton and, ignoring its sour smell, stroked it.

"Yet?" Zanna said. Conductor Jones looked evasive, and started muttering something about air currents and tacking and the directions. "You said," Zanna insisted, "don't worry *yet*?"

"Well," he said grudgingly. "Londoners can get out of the habit of thinking about some things. Things that come here. But I wouldn't worry yet."

13

Encounters on a Bus

Obaday and Skool could tell Zanna was upset. Obaday offered to read to her from his jacket. "Although," he added doubtfully, eyeing his lapels, "I confess this story isn't quite the alpine romance I was expecting . . ." When she declined his offer, he opened his bag and handed Zanna and Deeba what looked like two tiles and cement. They stared at them dubiously, but they were both starving, and the strange sandwiches had a surprising—and surprisingly enticing—aroma.

They bit experimentally. The tiles tasted like crusty bread—the cement like cream cheese.

Below them was the Smeath, the great river of UnLondon, drawing an amazingly straight line across the abcity. A few spirals, curlicues, and straight lines—tributaries and canals—poked off from it in various directions, into the streets. Bridges crossed it, some familiar in shape, some not, some static, some moving.

"Look at that!" Deeba cried out. Far off, there was a bridge like two huge crocodile heads, snout-to-snout.

Deeba started humming a tune, and Zanna snorted with laughter and joined in: it was the theme song to the program *EastEnders*, which started with an aerial shot of the Thames.

"Dum dum dum dum dum, deee dum," they sang, looking down at the water. The passengers looked at them as if they were mad.

A few birds and intelligent-seeming clouds examined the bus curiously. "Here comes a highfish," said Jones, and the girls jerked back in horror at the approaching jackknifing body, its ferocious teeth and unmistakable shark fin. It glided with a faint burring sound. Where its ocean cousins' side fins were, it grew dragonfly wings.

Jones leaned out and banged the side of the bus. "Get out of it, you dustbin!" he shouted, and the big fish darted off in alarm.

"What is *that*?" said Zanna. They were approaching a truly enormous wheel. Its base dipped into the river, and its highest point arced hundreds of meters up, almost to the bus.

"The UnLondon-I," Jones said. "It's what gave them the idea for that big wheel in London. I saw some photos. Ideas seep both ways, you know. Like clothes—Londoners copy so many UnLondon fashions, and for some reason they always seem to make them uniforms. And the I? Well, if an abnaut didn't actually come here and see it, then some dream of it floated from here into their heads. But what's the point making it a damn fool thing for spinning people round and round? The UnLondon-I has a purpose."

He pointed. What had looked at first like compartments were scoops, pushed around by the river. The UnLondon-I was a waterwheel.

"The dynamos attached to that keep a lot of things going," Jones said. Above the wheel was the ring of sunshine. The two circles echoed each other.

"Some people say," Jones said, "that the bit missing from the middle of the UnSun was what became the sun of London. That what lights your days got plucked out of what lights ours."

Zanna held out her thumb. The hole in the UnSun's center *was* about the same size as the sun from their usual life.

"Every morning it rises in a different place," Jones said.

The UnSun glowed. Strange shapes flew around it, the air-dwellers of UnLondon. There were chimneys all over the abcity, but very few were venting smoke. A dark shape approached over the miles of sky.

"Conductor Jones," Zanna said, and pointed at the incoming smudge. "What's that?"

* * *

He pulled a telescope from his pocket and stared into it for a long time.

"It's a grossbottle," he muttered. "But why's it so high? It should be down feeding on dead buildings . . ." Suddenly he yanked the telescope to its full extent. "Uh-oh," he said. "Trouble."

The shape was close enough to see clearly now. It raced towards them. It was at least the size of the bus. All the passengers were crowding the windows, alerted by the drone of its approach.

The grossbottle was a fly.

"It would never normally come for us," Jones said. "But look—see the howdah?"

On the creature's huge thorax was a platform full of figures. "It's being driven," he said. "Airwaymen. Thieves. But I don't understand. They go for solo balloons, maybe deep-sky trawlers. They know buses are defended. Why risk it?

"Time to go to work." He unhooked his bow from the cabinet. "Rosa," he shouted. "Aerobatics!"

The grossbottle fly careered towards them. The airwaymen whipped it, prodded it with barbs, and readied weapons. Obaday and Skool were staring at it, aghast.

Deeba saw motion above her again. She nudged Zanna. There were two little moving presences, but they weren't crabs. They were *hands*, poking through the ceiling, fingers scuttling, emerging from the metal—then they were gone.

Someone stood. Deeba looked down into the face of the bearded man. Alone among the passengers, he did not look afraid as the grossbottle came closer. He met Deeba's eyes. Through a gap in the toga, she saw familiar paint stains.

Before she could speak he had leapt up and grabbed . . . Zanna.

"Help!" Zanna shouted. "Deebs! Obaday! Skool! Jones!"

Deeba was helplessly pointing at the man, and up at the ceiling.

"He heard us in the market!" Deeba said. "He must've run to Manifest Station. He was waiting for us. He sent a message to them." She pointed in the direction of the oncoming fly. "And there's someone upstairs, there *is*—"

"Shut it!" The man gripped Zanna by the neck. She struggled, but he was too strong. He held her in front of him like a shield.

Curdle launched itself at him, but he kicked the little carton away. The passengers huddled terrified. The man tightened his grip on Zanna.

"Nobody move!" he said.

14

Attack of the Manky Insect

The man swung Zanna from side to side. The passengers were frozen in their seats.

"Stay back," he said. "My colleagues'll be here in a moment. I don't want any trouble. We'll take her with us and let the rest of you go. You know you can't outfly a grossbottle, and you don't want my associates joining us."

"Airwaymen mercenaries?" Jones said, stepping forward. "No, I suspect we don't."

"You stay back!" the man said, and drew a sword with his free hand. Deeba screamed.

"Who you working for?" Jones said. "What do you want with her?"

"Shut up!" the man said, and yanked Zanna.

"Leave it!" Deeba said. "You're making him angry!"

The man held Zanna by the throat. Jones faced him, his hands half-out, but he looked at the sword and held back. Obaday was huddling behind Zanna's attacker, his head down, too terrified to move. The grossbottle was coming closer.

Suddenly, there was a grunt of effort, and something dropped from the ceiling. A body. A pale boy. The boy from the market. Stark naked. He fell out of nowhere, landed with a smack right in front of Zanna and the bearded man. The man yelped and staggered away—and backed his bum directly onto Obaday Fing's pincushion head.

It was the blunt ends of the needles that jammed into his posterior, but they were still easily sharp enough. The big man leapt and shrieked, loosed his grip on Zanna, and swung his weapon.

Everyone moved. The boy gasped, reached for Zanna, missed, ducked, and dropped out of sight. Deeba shrieked. Jones grabbed Zanna. Obaday shouted, "It's that boy again, that ghost. He's in on it too!" He slipped and whacked the back of his head on a metal chairback, groaned, and lay still.

Jones swept Zanna behind him.

"Zann!" Deeba hugged her. They crouched behind the conductor. Zanna's attacker was waving his sword.

The hands that Deeba had thought were crabs were on the floor between the man's feet. And poking up from between them was the top of Hemi's head, his two eyes staring at the girls, then abruptly sinking out of sight.

"What are you going to do?" the man shouted. "My friends are nearly here." They could hear the grossbottle. "Give us the girl!"

"I'm a conductor," said Jones, and stepped closer.

"I warn you!" the man shouted, and extended the sword into Jones's path.

"I conduct passengers to safety," said Jones. "I conduct myself with dignity. And there's one other thing that all of us who take the oath learn to conduct." He reached up and, so slowly his opponent didn't respond, touched his forefinger to the point of the sword.

"Electricity," Jones said.

As his skin touched the metal, there was a loud crack. An arc of sparks raced down the metal, into the big man's hand.

He jerked, and flew back, landing on his back, dazed and shaking. His false beard was smoking.

Jones shook his finger: there was a single drop of blood where he had pricked it. He checked Obaday's head. "He'll be alright," he said to Skool.

"It was that Hemi!" Zanna said. "We saw him in the market."

"He *was* upstairs," said Deeba. "He was looking through the ceiling . . ."

"He must've jumped on just as we set off," said Jones. "Maybe he was the lookout for this charmer." He pointed at the still-shuddering attacker. "That went a bit wrong, then, didn't it?" He took handfuls of cord and ribbon from Obaday's paper pockets. "Tie him up!" Jones shouted, and several passengers obeyed.

"I dunno," said Deeba doubtfully. "Didn't look like that to me . . ."

Jones looked around. "Well, he's gone now, straight through the floor. Keep an eye out, alright?" Deeba and Zanna were looking about avidly, but Hemi was gone. "We'll deal with that later. Have to focus now. That grossbottle's coming. As quick as you can, stay down and hold on. Rosa! Evasion!"

The bus veered, pitched, and accelerated. Passengers shrieked. Jones hooked a leg around the pole and leaned out, notching an arrow into his bow.

With a growl of wings the grossbottle came close. Jones fired. His arrows thwacked into the fly's disgusting great eyes and disappeared inside. The insect buzzed angrily but did not slow. The men and women it carried aimed a collection of motley guns. Their faces were ferocious.

One of them called out, "Prepare to be boarded!"

Jones drew his copper club.

"You maggotjockeys!" he yelled. "Leave my bus alone!" He leapt out straight at them.

Zanna and Deeba cried out. Jones flew through the air, shouting: "Un Lun Dun!"

"Look!" said Zanna. Jones's belt was attached to the bus pole with bungee cord. The tether stretched and Jones grabbed hold of the howdah.

The startled raiders tried to aim at him. He kicked, then whirled his club at them, crackling with electricity. When the pirates rallied, Jones simply let go of their vessel. The elastic catapulted him back across the air into the bus. He somersaulted and landed perfectly.

Deeba said: "That was *amaz-ing . . .*"

"Tell me later," he said, and ran up the stairs, the girls following.

"What was that you shouted?" Zanna said.

"A war cry," he said. "Very ancient. The battle call of UnLondon."

The top deck was cramped with pumps and gas machines. In one corner was a pile of dirty clothes. Jones aimed an enormous harpoon out of the rear window. He swiveled as the grossbottle veered.

The bus lurched, brought them almost face-to-face with the grossbottle itself. Jones fired.

A bolt shot straight between the fly's enormous shining eyes. It jerked, its wings shuddered, and it dropped away.

"You got it!" said Zanna. The dirty body of the fly was spinning as it fell. Little dot-figures leapt from its plunging carcass, parachutes blossoming.

"And don't come back!" yelled Jones.

"Conductor Jones," Deeba said in a strangled voice. "Look."

Far below was a patch of waste ground, dotted with crumbling buildings on which enormous insects busily fed. Two more grossbottles—one vivid blue, one a shining purple—rose above their revolting siblings and flew towards the bus, figures visible in the platforms on their backs.

15

A Sort of Delivery

"This is the plan."

The bus juddered and arced. "Rosa can't avoid both those grossbottles. We have to get you out of here," Jones said to Zanna.

"What about the passengers?" Zanna said.

"Don't worry about them," he said. "I'll make sure they're looked after. But the longer those things follow us, the more of a head start you'll have."

The toga-wearing man was gagged, blindfolded, and tied up. "We'll get him to the Propheseers," Jones said. "And we'll meet you there. Okay?"

"You're going to make us go on *alone?*" Zanna said.

She and Deeba stared at each other, aghast.

"You can't!" said Deeba. "We don't know anything about where we're going!"

"We don't know where we *are* . . ."

"We just *can't* . . ."

"I know," Jones said gently. "Believe me, I wouldn't if I had any choice. We don't have much time. There are two gangs of skyjackers on the way, and we *have* to get them off your trail. They know where you're trying to get, but we can mislead them as to how you'll get there."

"Please . . ." said Zanna.

"You're the *Shwazzy*," he said, silencing her. "You can do this."

"What about me?" said Deeba. "I'm not."

"Look to your friend," Jones told her. "Together, you'll be okay."

"Obaday," Zanna said. She squeezed the unconscious man's hand. He muttered, "I wish you could come . . ."

"Can you . . . ?" said Jones to Skool, who slumped in dejection and pointed at the heavy diving boots, miming *I am too slow*.

"You can do this, Shwazzy," Jones repeated.

The bus plunged. Passengers screamed. The grossbottles homed in.

"We have one go at this," Jones said. "We'll only lose them for a few seconds. We'll drop you at the edge of Slaterunner territory, then lead them away. Slaterunner hunting grounds lead almost all the way to the Pons Absconditus.

"Tell them if they give you safe passage they'll have earned the gratitude of the UnLondon conductors. Now hold on. Rosa's going to do her stuff."

UnLondon came so fast all Zanna and Deeba could see was a rush of colors. The aerobus hurtled down. It sped below roof-level, lurching left and right along streets. Crouched on the platform, the girls glimpsed the astonished stares of UnLondoners, saw hats yanked off heads by the bus's passing. Rosa took them under a bridge so low that the top of the balloon scraped on its arch.

"Now, Rosa!" Jones shouted.

Instantly the bus zigzagged and, so suddenly that the shock sent them lurching forward, stopped.

"Now! Now!" hissed Jones, bundling Zanna and Deeba to the edge of the platform. Deeba held Curdle. The terrified little carton tried to burrow into her hands. The bus dangled a few feet above acres of roof, over a valley between ridges.

"Jump," said Jones. They hesitated a second, then thought of the flies close behind them. First Zanna, then Deeba, jumped.

They landed in the bottom of the V, and the air was knocked out of them.

The bus was hovering. "Are you okay?" Jones hissed, Skool peering over his shoulder. The girls nodded. "*That* way to the bridge. Stay high and find Chief

Badladder. Tell her I sent you. Show her the pass. Tell her I'll owe her. *Stay safe.*" He blew them a kiss, and shouted at Rosa to go.

The bus soared, something pale seemed to drop from it, and it shot away. The two grossbottles droned into view, buccaneers on their backs, and scudded in the bus's wake.

"What was that?" said Zanna. "Did you see something . . . falling? From the bus?"

"I dunno," whispered Deeba.

Wind chilled Zanna and Deeba. The noise of the flies ebbed away.

The two girls sat in the cold. Silence settled on them like damp. They shivered. They were tired and overwhelmed, and suddenly very, very alone.

16

Stuck

"Come on," said Zanna eventually. "We can't just sit and feel sorry for ourselves."

"I bet I could," Deeba said, but she stood, holding Curdle.

"We *deserve* to," Zanna said. "We just *can't.*"

The UnSun was getting lower, and the sky darker.

"We have to find somewhere to shelter," Zanna said.

"And food," said Deeba.

They clambered laboriously up the slope, hauled themselves onto the ridge, and stared.

They were in the middle of undulating roofs, a slatescape in red and gray and the color of rust. It rose and fell like mountainside, steep, shallow, deep, flat, interrupted by trenches where streets must run, unlit alleys between houses. The angles were broken by dormer windows, by squat chimneys like patches of mushrooms, by tangles of antennae, wire fingers pointing in all directions.

They stared for a long time in the direction Zanna thought she had seen something fall. They could see nothing moving over the up-and-down of the tiles.

"What do we do?" said Deeba. "How do we get anywhere?"

"I don't know," said Zanna. "Let's try this . . ." She began to shuffle along the ridge. Deeba stared.

"You're kidding," she said. Sighing, she put Curdle in her bag, and—slowly—followed her friend.

They stopped, suddenly, as an awful bleating cry sounded nearby, and was answered from a long way off.

"What was that?" whispered Deeba.

"How should I know?" Zanna whispered back.

"Well *I'm* not Shwazzed. You know everything, Shwazzy. *Shwa* me what you can do."

"Shut up," said Zanna.

"*Shwat* up yourself." Zanna couldn't help laughing at the ridiculous riposte.

They gripped a chimney stack and waited for their hearts to slow down. Far off, they could see the rise of tower blocks and the odd shell or vegetable or typewriter-and-fridge roof of UnLondon, but for a long way, it was just foreboding hillocks of slate.

The air was darkening. Deeba leaned into the chimney. Curdle nuzzled her forlornly.

"Oh *man*," Deeba said. She couldn't stop herself saying, "I want my *mum* and *dad*. How do we get down?"

"Why in the name of Unstible," a loud voice said, "would you want to get down?"

Zanna and Deeba whirled around. Curdle squeaked.

They were surrounded.

There were men and women on the ledges. They wore tough-looking furs and padded boots.

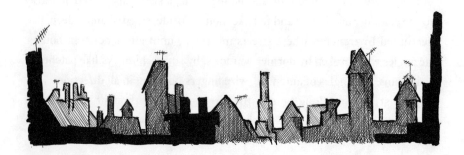

They trotted carelessly on brick ledges, somersaulted like gymnasts, and landed poised on slopes. One man had a baby strapped to him in a harness on his chest. It gurgled happily as he scampered up and down giddying slopes.

" 'Get down' indeed," the same voice said.

On a roof overlooking them was a tall, athletic, imperious-looking woman. She strode casually, reached a gap between buildings, jumped calmly over it, and landed on her toes. She took hold of an antenna and swung around it.

"You, young grubs, are in the territory of the Slaterunners. So might I ask just what exactly groundlubbers like you are doing in the Roofdom? Because we prefer guests *ask* before they come in."

Zanna and Deeba swallowed.

"We're looking for someone called Badladder," Zanna said.

"Oh *are* you?" the woman said, and the Slaterunners laughed. "And what might you want with Badladder?"

"Conductor Jones dropped us here," Zanna said.

"He had to go," said Deeba. "He wanted to stay but—"

"We were being chased by grossbottles," Zanna said. "He said Badladder'd help us. He said he'd owe her one." The Slaterunners were blinking, surprise breaking through their arrogance.

"What help is it you need?" the woman said.

"People want to stop me," Zanna said hesitantly. "I don't know why. It's because of . . . this." She held up the travelcard.

"Shwazzy!" The whisper went through the Slaterunners. "Shwazzy!" "Shwazzy!"

"You're here?" someone said. "It's happened!" And: "At last!" "Is Unstible with you?" "Did you bring the Klinneract?"

"I don't know what any of that means," Zanna said. "Jones said the Propheseers would explain."

"We have to get out of here," Deeba said.

"Will you help me?" said Zanna.

"Of *course,*" the woman said. "I can't believe you're here. At last. Now the bloody Ess Emm Oh Gee better watch itself!" She vaulted and landed in front of them. "I'm Inessa Badladder. This is Eva Roadshun; Alfred Stayhigh; Jonas Ridgetrotter; Marlene Chimneyvault . . ."

"I'm Zanna. This is Deeba. Pleased to meet you."

"The Propheseers live in Pons something," Deeba said.

"Shwazzy, it's an honor to be of help," Badladder said, ignoring Deeba.

"We have to go to the bridge," said Zanna.

"The Pons Absconditus," said Badladder. "Of course."

17

The Upside

"The secret," said Inessa Badladder, "is not to look down."

"I wasn't going to," said Zanna.

The Slaterunners led Zanna and Deeba laboriously over the roofs. They threw up rope bridges over the gaps of streets and guided the girls over, whispering, "Look straight ahead." Once there was that sudden plaintive bleating again. Zanna and Deeba froze.

"Don't worry," Inessa said. "It's just a trip."

"A what?"

Clattering elegantly down the slates came a line of goats, staring with their strange eyes.

"That's what you call a group of them," Inessa said. "A trip of mountain goats." The animals watched them go. Deeba stared back, thinking she had seen something flit pale and fast behind the goats, but only the chewing herd moved.

"I can't understand how you lot can live down there, without this freedom," Inessa said. "Walled in. I'm third-generation groundless. My mother never touched down, nor my grandmother. My *great*-grandmother once had to. It was an emergency. The roof was on fire."

* * *

"Look," said Zanna, and the two girls paused in their exhausting climb. As it set behind the bizarre silhouettes of UnLondon, the UnSun was rainbow-shaped, an arch of light.

Flocks of birds gathered, circled, and separated into species. Swirls of pigeons and starlings and jackdaws headed towards the tall, thin rectangular towers that dotted the abcity. The buildings' fronts broke with thousands of drawers, into each of which one bird flew. The little compartments slid shut. "They *are* chests of drawers!" Deeba said. "That's where the birds sleep!"

"Of course," said Inessa. "You couldn't just have them all over the place; it would be chaos."

The UnLondon moon rose, and Zanna and Deeba stared at it in astonishment. It was not a circle, nor a crescent. Instead, it was a perfectly symmetrical spindle, pointed at the top and the bottom, like the slit in a cat's-eye.

"Our way will be lit," Inessa said, "by the light of the loon."

Stars appeared in the dark. They were not still like the stars of London: they crept like luminous insects every which way. There was a sputter as streetlamps came on in the streets below and orange light shone up from the gaps between the roofs.

"What was that?" said Deeba. She pointed past the edge of a gutter, into one of those narrow unseen alleys.

There was nothing there. "I swear I'm going mad," Deeba muttered. "I keep thinking I see something."

The girls followed their guides, clambering onto an apex, and into a sudden glow. The light source came into view. It was only a few streets away, just beyond the edges of Roofdom.

"It's . . ." Deeba whispered.

". . . beautiful," Zanna said.

For a moment it looked like a fireworks display, the most amazing, huge, impressive one ever. But it wasn't moving. It was an enormous tree of firework-bursts, stuck together and motionless.

The trails of several rockets made a trunk. They jutted off at various heights in boughs of light and curved down like a willow tree. Colors filled the rocket-trail branches like leaves, in glimmering red, blue, green, silver, white, and gold. Catherine wheels and the bursts of Roman candles, the buds of sparklers hung motionless and silent like fruit.

"The November Tree," Inessa said.

* * *

"This is a good time to see it," Inessa said. "It was a bit forlorn a couple of weeks ago. Almost at the end of its life. But Guy Fawkes Night is springtime for the November Tree."

Fireworks were obsolete the instant after they ignited. Every November on Fireworks Night, the most choice effects of the most impressive displays in London would seep through into UnLondon as they became moil, and blossom into the November Tree. Over the year the tree would dim, shedding its glow and colors, until by November the fourth it was little more than a skeleton of smoke trails.

Then the cycle would begin again. The rejuvenated tree would light up the night.

Several small, crackling shapes scampered up the November Tree. Squirrels. Their claws gripped the solid glow. Their coats smoldered, but they did not seem uncomfortable.

"This is where the toughest red squirrels moved," Inessa said. "After the grays came. They're fireproof, though they keep that to themselves. Once or twice a gray makes it here and tries to follow them. Don't get very far." She mimed an explosion.

"I wish I had my phone," Deeba whispered to Zanna. "I want to take a picture."

At the shining highest branches, something swooped. Most of the birds were gone from the sky now, but above the tree was one that had not joined any of the throngs. It circled.

"There's something weird with that bird's head," said Deeba.

Its skull bulged wrongly. The November Tree's light glinted from its eyes.

"You're right," said Zanna. But it wheeled off too fast to see—into a last, sleepy flock of ducks—and disappeared.

"What was that?" said Zanna, but she was interrupted by Inessa's shout.

"Hey!" Deeba and Zanna turned and screamed.

Creeping without sound from around a chimney pot behind them, hunched over like a monkey, draped in what looked like a curtain, was Hemi. He was only inches away. He was reaching out, his fingers actually touching Zanna's pocket.

He leapt up as the Slaterunners launched themselves at him, his look of concentration becoming one of alarm. Hemi scrambled up and down the roofs to get away, Inessa's tribe quickly after him. They gained on him, but he reached the edge of a roof, gathered himself, and jumped, the cloth he wore flapping like a cape, down into the dim gap between the buildings and out of sight.

When his pursuers reached the building's edge they looked into the alley in both directions, and shook their heads.

"He's gone," one shouted.

"Who was that?" Inessa said. Deeba and Zanna were shaking.

"A ghost," Deeba managed to say.

"That *was* him off the bus," said Zanna. "He's following us."

18

Highs and Lows

"The Pons Absconditus isn't much farther," Inessa said. "Well, I mean, it's all over the place. But one fairly constant anchorage isn't much farther. We'll get you there and that little wisper won't have a chance to get near you again. Then the Propheseers will explain everything. They'll show you the book." The UnSun was gone, and Zanna and Deeba pulled themselves, exhausted, over the roofs. The Slaterunners surrounded them closely now, kept watch on all sides.

"What book?" Zanna said.

"I've never seen it," Inessa said. "Not many people have. But you hear things. It's big. It's old. It's thick, bound in devilhide and printed in kraken ink. But that's considerably less important than what's inside."

"Which is?" said Zanna.

"UnLondon. The history, the politics, the geography. The past . . . and the future. Prophecies." She looked at Zanna. "Prophecies about you."

Zanna looked thoughtful. The two girls stared back at the motionless fireworks of the November Tree behind them. "You do realize," said Zanna, "that you're stroking a milk carton."

"You're just jealous," said Deeba. She was holding Curdle in one hand, gently rubbing it with her other. " 'Cause it's the one thing here more interested in me than you."

"I am jealous," said Zanna. "That is *exactly* it."

They were tired and hungry and homesick, and Hemi's sudden appearance had frightened them.

"It'll be alright," Zanna whispered.

"I wonder how Obaday and the conductor and that lot are doing," Deeba said. "I hope they got away from the flies by now."

"Oh," said Zanna. "Yeah. I hope." Deeba looked at her suspiciously.

"You hadn't thought," said Deeba. "You're too busy thinking about what's in that book."

Zanna said nothing.

They crept on through the ivory loonlight, Deeba and Zanna miserable with exhaustion. After a long time climbing, Deeba realized that Curdle was shifting in her hands, sniffing, whiffling, and puffing with its opening.

"Zann," she whispered.

"What?"

"Listen," Deeba said. "Curdle's being funny. Something's . . ." The two girls stood still a moment, motioned the Slaterunners to stop, were silent.

Faintly, from behind them, they heard a pattering.

It came closer. Something was approaching, was only a few streets away, below them.

"It's him again!" whispered Zanna.

"But . . . it's too heavy . . ." Deeba said. "And there's more than one . . ."

"Footsteps." The two girls jumped as Inessa slid in between them and hunkered close to the roof, her ear to the slates. "Someone knows you're here. They're coming."

"He must've been a spy," said Zanna. "He's sent them after us . . ."

"There was that weird bird, too," Deeba said.

"Jonas, Alf," Inessa said to two strong-looking Slaterunners. They squatted by Zanna and Deeba, offering their backs. "Hang on," Inessa said.

"You must be joking," Deeba said.

Inessa pointed.

Several streets away, dark shapes were bobbing above the gutters. Heads in strange masks jutted into the roofworld itself.

"Oh my God!" Zanna said. "They're giants!"

"Quickly," Inessa said. "The rest of the tribe'll delay them, but we're going now. Hang on."

Zanna and Deeba felt the lurch of their carriers, the faint huffs as they cleared clay and slate, the long moments of soaring as they jumped over the gaps of streets.

"Help," Deeba wheezed, her eyes clenched.

Behind them was a sound of shattering tiles and the *phut*s of blowpipes as the Slaterunners ambushed the intruders.

"Who are they?" Zanna said as Jonas roofran.

"Know who . . . you are . . ." Jonas said between breaths. "Must be . . . with the Smog."

"Keep going," said Inessa. "They've got up here."

Zanna opened her eyes. Strange figures silhouetted against the sky, approaching steadily across the roofs.

"Deeba," she said. "They're coming after me."

"There's nothing for it," Inessa said after a moment, sounding despairing. "We're going to have to . . . descend."

"No!" said Alf and Jonas.

"We've no choice!" Inessa said. "They'll never expect it. It's the only way we'll lose them.

"Three generations," she said wistfully. "Well . . . Anything for the Shwazzy. *Follow me!*"

She ran to the edge of the roof. She leapt, somersaulted, plunged towards the street below . . .

. . . and landed almost immediately. She stood up. Her head was only a little below them.

Jonas and Alf dropped off the roof. The pavement started just inches below the eaves. The roofs slanted directly up from the ground.

"Where are the houses?" said Deeba.

"What houses?" Inessa said.

Deeba and Zanna stood in the little alley, embedded with the bulbs of streetlamps, staring astonished at the roofslopes they had just left.

"I can't believe it!" Deeba said. "Even if you fall off you'll only scrape your knee."

"You thought there were *houses* under the roofs?" Inessa said. "That would be madness! Just because we want to live free doesn't mean we shouldn't consider safety . . ."

"The people following aren't giants at all," Zanna realized.

"On which topic . . ." Jonas said.

"Yes, now's not the time," Inessa said. She gestured, and she, the Slaterunners, Zanna, and Deeba dropped to their hands and knees and rolled into the tiny space below the eaves.

They waited, then froze when they heard bootsteps overhead.

There were hunters on the roof above them. It sounded as if they were milling from one corner to another, poking into shadows. None spoke.

Deeba held her hand over Curdle's opening, so it could not whimper.

For a horrible moment one of the unseen figures was directly above them, so close the guttering shook by Zanna's head. She and Deeba stared at each other, their eyes very wide. None of the Slaterunners, nor either of the girls, dared breathe.

At very long last, the searchers moved away. Zanna let out a trembling sigh. Silently, Inessa beckoned and crawled on.

What seemed like hours later, they reached the edge of the Roofdom.

Zanna and Deeba emerged from under the eaves. Before them, the streets sloped away, and the real walls of UnLondon rose, in bricks and wood and the mixed junk called moil.

"Not far now," Inessa said. Alf and Jonas trod gingerly, and grumbled about how much they hated it down on the ground.

Behind them, the roofs sloped directly up from the pavement like slate tents. Zanna and Deeba rolled their eyes.

The Evasive Bridge

Rising from the night streets of UnLondon was the arc of the Pons Absconditus. It was a suspension bridge, with supporting up-down iron curves like two dorsal ridges. It should be spanning a river. It was not. Instead, it rose out of backstreets, from nowhere in particular, went over the roofs, and came down several streets away, in a different nowhere in particular.

There were few bulbs on in few windows. Occasionally, Deeba and Zanna saw four lights rush by through the UnLondon streets, two white lights at the front, two red at the back. The first time, they thought it was a car, but there was nothing there, only a glow like headlights. It was as if in the absence of automobiles, UnLondon had provided their pretty illuminations itself, to leave glowing trails in its night-streets.

The headlights veered past the obstacles that littered the abcity, some half-grown out of the tarmac, some lying ready to be used: old sofas; dishwashers; skips full of glass; chairs emerging from London, growing on their rusty legs like flowers with four stalks.

"Why'd they build the bridge here?" Deeba said.

"They didn't," Inessa said. "This is just somewhere people know they can find it. It's like any bridge: it's to connect somewhere to somewhere else. That's what bridges are for."

There was no one in the streets. The streetlamps shed a dim, dirty light. Below the bridge were a load of dustbins. The corrugated metal cylinders were about half Zanna's height. They all had their round lids carefully on.

"Now," said Inessa. "We need to get onto the bridge, to see the Prophe-seers."

"It comes down over there," Deeba said. "Behind those houses."

But behind those houses, there was another row between them and the end of the bridge. Frowning, Zanna and Deeba turned another corner, and came to a sudden stop.

The bridge still came down close to them—but still just behind another brick row.

"What's going on?" Zanna said. "We're not getting any closer."

Walking under the Pons was no problem. Zanna and Deeba went back and forth below it several times, and it stayed politely immobile. They tried to walk onto it, and its ends stayed stubbornly one or two streets beyond them. They came at it slowly, quickly, sneakily, in full view. It was always just out of their reach.

Zanna and Deeba and the Slaterunners stopped in the dark under the bridge, among the dustbins. Deeba stroked Curdle.

"It's like a rainbow," Zanna said. "You can't reach its end. How are we sup-posed to get on?"

Something flitted quietly through the air. They tensed, but it was just a scrunched-up piece of paper, dropping from the bridge. It settled among the dustbins.

"I wondered how they kept undesirables off," Inessa said. "I didn't realize the bridge was shy."

"Yeah," Deeba said. "Looks like they don't need any guards."

"Actually," Inessa said, "I think they have them too." She pointed.

One by one, dustbins around them were standing up.

There were seven or eight of them. A pair of skinny legs jutted from each of their round metal undersides. From their sides sprouted thin, muscly arms. Their lids teetered, then tilted. They opened just a slit. Inside was darkness, in the thick of which were eyes.

The dustbins stepped closer.

* * *

They moved with an athletic precision. The Slaterunners circled warily, ready for attack. But the bin in front raised its hand, and spread surprisingly dainty fingers, as if to say, *Wait*. It tapped the side of its lid, and cupped its hand in an ostentatious listening motion. There was that sound again. The noise of boots.

"They've found our trail!" Inessa said.

The dustbin put its finger to where its lips should be. It made quick gestures, and two of its companions ran fast and soundlessly out of the shadows.

In the light of the streetlamps they retracted their arms and legs with a faint *shlp*, leaving only grubby stains where each limb had been. They were instantly disguised—just a pair of dustbins. After a moment they sprouted limbs again. They stood in karate poses. Then they opened their own lids, reached into their own dark interiors, and drew out weapons.

One took out a sword, and the other two pairs of nunchucks, which Zanna and Deeba recognized from martial-arts films. The two dustbins ran off towards the sound of the pursuers, disappearing in shadows.

You: the dustbin leader pointed to Zanna and Deeba, then pointed straight up, to the bridge above them. Beckoned.

"It wants us to go," Deeba said.

"Not without the Slaterunners," Zanna said. "They're the ones got us here . . ."

"It's alright," Inessa said. "I've no business with the Propheseers, whereas you . . . you're expected. You go, Shwazzy. We need to get back to the Roofdom. These are the Propheseers' protectors. They'll get us out of here safely. We'll be alright, and so will you."

Zanna and Deeba gave each of the Slaterunners a hug.

"Thank you," Zanna said.

"Take care of yourself," Inessa said. "Shwazzy . . . we're counting on you. *All* of us."

The dustbin crept, Zanna and Deeba behind it, through the same streets that they had just walked. This time, however, the end of the bridge grew closer with every turn.

"How did you do that?" Zanna muttered. The dustbin motioned her to silence.

The Pons Absconditus rose in front of them. To either side were the doorless backs of houses. UnLondoners might be able to see the bridge from their rear windows, but without a guide, they'd have no success reaching it.

It rose like the back of a sea serpent. At its apex were moving figures.

The girls' dustbin escort walked them onto the bridge.

"Finally," said Zanna. "The Propheseers."

"We can go *home*," Deeba almost gasped.

"And find out the truth," said Zanna quietly.

The Welcome

There was an office on the bridge.

In the middle of the road was a collection of desks and chairs, telephones, weird-looking computers, bookshelves, and potted plants. Twenty or thirty men and women were working away. Mostly they wore shabby suits. They read reports and shuffled files. None of them noticed Zanna, Deeba, and the dustbin approach.

The girls could see to the Roofdom; they could see the waterwheel; they could see the outline of Manifest Station and across the skyline of UnLondon.

Eventually, one by one, the people on the bridge looked up. One by one, their mouths fell open. Deeba moved closer to Zanna. The two girls stood quietly, and waited.

"Um . . ." said Zanna eventually. "Hello. We were told you could help us."

"Can I . . . help you?" It was an old man who spoke. He wore a nondescript suit and an extraordinarily long beard. He spoke hesitantly, and his voice contained disapproval, surprise . . . and, though he was trying to hide it, excitement. "May I ask how you managed to get here? Who exactly *are* you?"

"My name's Zanna. This is Deeba. Are you . . ."

"I am Mortar of the Propheseers. But . . . but who *are* you?" He spoke more breathlessly, and quickly. "Where are you from?"

"I'm *Zanna,* I said. I'm from London. I think you know who I am." She spoke with sudden authority that made Deeba stare at her. "I'll show you."

All the Propheseers gasped as Zanna reached into her pocket—

—and hesitated, and fumbled, and groped in another pocket, and another, more and more frantic.

"Deeba," she whispered. "It's gone! The travelcard . . . it's gone!"

"What do you mean?"

"It's *gone.* It was in my back pocket and now it's not." The Propheseers and the dustbin were watching, puzzled.

"That . . . that ghost-boy!" said Deeba. "He must've took it! On the roofs . . . Excuse me," she said more loudly, to the old man. "It's just . . . my friend had something that sort of said who she was, and, and we've been using it to get here, and now it's been *stole,* and we . . ."

Her voice petered out at the sight of the Propheseers' faces.

"I knew it wasn't possible," one muttered.

"Remember," said another, "the enemy'll try anything." She looked at Zanna unpleasantly.

"Who are you *really?*" said a third.

"I had a *card,*" Zanna said, stricken. She searched her pockets again. "It'd show you . . ." She and Deeba began to back away.

"Wait." It was the old man who spoke. "We have to be sure. Lectern! Bring it!"

A woman came trotting towards them through the desks. In her arms, she carried a huge, mottled book.

"Is it her?" whispered the old man.

"I don't know," she said. "Hold on . . ."

"Wait a minute, wait a minute."

Zanna and Deeba started. This new voice was reedy and self-important. It rolled sounds around. It seemed to come out of nowhere. "Check page three-sixty-five," it went on. The woman flicked to the right place.

"Who is that?" said Deeba. She and Zanna looked around.

"Tall for her age, blond hair," the voice went on. "Let me have a good look . . . Decent-enough aura, brustly at the spectrids. Resonating in at least five or six dimensobilities . . . Let's check the history. Page twenty-four please."

"Deeba," whispered Zanna.

"I know."

The voice was coming from the book.

"Oh my," it said, suddenly hushed. "Well tear me up and shove me in a hutch. It's her. It is."

The woman slapped the book shut. Her mouth went slack.

"It's her," she said.

"It is," the book said. "It's the Shwazzy. We've found her."

"*You've* found her?" Deeba said. "I don't *think* so. She found you, more like. And it wasn't easy, neither."

"What . . . ?" said the old man again. "Lectern, who *is* that? Why's she here?"

"I don't know, Mortar . . ." the woman said.

"It's alright," the disembodied voice interrupted. "She's in here. Page seventy-seven, 'Shwazzy's First Appearance.' Look her up in the index: 'Shwazzy, Companions of the.' Um . . . something like that, anyway."

The woman riffled through the pages and read silently.

"It's right," she said. "Fits the description. This . . . is how it's supposed to go." She and the man were staring at Zanna, rapt.

"Everyone!" the old man shouted. "Attention, please! I have an announcement! All of you know what's been happening. All of you know of the danger we face. I'm sure many of you have despaired. That what was promised would never come. There's no shame in it: it's understandable. But despair is over.

"The Shwazzy *is here*! She's come!"

One by one, the Propheseers stood at their desks and began to applaud. The UnSun began to rise. It illuminated Zanna's face full-on, momentarily blinding her. She couldn't see the clapping Propheseers, but she could hear their shouts of welcome.

An Unlikely Place of Work

"I didn't think it could be true!" the woman Lectern said. "We got a garbled message from a conductor, couriered through several hands. Told us that you were coming!"

"Jones!" Deeba said. "Is he okay?"

"What?" said the old man, looking away from Zanna and glancing at Deeba in surprise. "Yes. I don't know. He must be. Said he was hiding south of the river. But the point is he told us you were coming. We thought that was all nonsense. But . . .

"This is extraordinary. You've met our guards." He gestured at the silent cylindrical guide. "The secret warriors: the binja. It's just as well we passed on the message. We thought the conductor was confused, but we dropped a communiqué down, just in case. But we had to be sure, in case they'd been confused, escorted in some imposter. In fact, we should tell them to stand down. Jorkins!" he shouted. "Memo to the binja. 'Shwazzy received safely. Many thanks. Yours, et cetera, et cetera.' "

A scrawny young man nodded and speedily typed. He whipped the piece of paper from his typewriter, crumpled it up, and threw it over the edge of the bridge.

"Amazing guards," Mortar said. He stroked his long beard thoughtfully. "An ancient, ancient order. The right mixture of chemicals left to marinate long enough in the right conditions in those bins, some secret training, and *voila*."

"Are they all loyal?" said Deeba. "Do any of them go off and be baddies?"

"You're a talkative young lady, aren't you?" he said. "All sorts of interesting questions."

Zanna and Deeba sat with Mortar and Lectern a little way away from the office area. The binja stood nearby, scanning the area from under its lid, constantly. Curdle played under the table.

"We were being followed," Zanna said. "What if they get past the binja?"

"Don't you worry," Lectern said. "This bridge is rarely just where you want it to be. Only once you're actually *on* it. And only Propheseers and our guests know how to get there. It's all a question of remembering what a bridge does—gets from somewhere to somewhere else."

"Now look," Zanna said. "I'm knackered and hungry. I've got no idea what's going on. *We've* got no idea what's going on."

"We just want to go *home*," Deeba said. "We didn't want to be here in the first place."

"I don't know what you lot want," Zanna said. "I don't know why some people are so pleased to see me. And I don't know why some people aren't."

"Everyone's said the Propheseers'll explain, blah blah blah," Deeba said. "And that you'll *tell us how to get back*."

"Well, here we are, and we need to know."

"We're being chased by flies and nutters," Deeba said.

"People are asking me if I've got the Klin . . . something," Zanna said. "I don't even know what they're on about. Who's chasing me? And what's the Smog? And why's it after *me*?"

"Of course, of course," Mortar said. "I can't imagine how confused you must be, Shwazzy. And we will help you home again. But there's something you can do first. We have tried to contact you, over the years. We've heard rumors of where you might be. From the clouds, and the animals, and a few savvy abnauts. And from the book."

"That's right," said the voice from the book, smugly.

"There's always a difficulty of interpretation. But from careful reading—over generations!—we've learnt many things."

"Many, many things," the voice went on.

"Hush," Lectern said, and looked apologetically at Zanna.

"We tried to ease your journey. Sent you the Pass. A pity that was stolen. It took . . . some effort to send it across the Odd, believe me."

In the distance, UnLondon's giant chests of drawers were opening up, and flocks of birds were setting out into the dawn.

"Shwazzy," Mortar said. "UnLondon is at war. We're under attack. And it's been written, for centuries, that you—*you*—will come and save us."

"Me?" said Zanna.

"Her?" said Deeba.

"I'm just, I'm . . . just a girl," said Zanna.

"You're the *Shwazzy,*" Mortar said. "You're our hope. Against the Smog.

"What is the Smog? Just exactly what it sounds like—thick, smoky fog. And why's it out to get you? Because it hates being beaten."

"Why does it think I'll beat it?" Zanna said.

"It doesn't think you will," Lectern said. "It knows you already have."

22

History Lessons

"Not you personally," Mortar explained. "But you, Londoners. Even if you didn't know it."

"Let me tell the history," the book said grandly. "Page fifty-seven." Lectern flicked through to the relevant place. The book cleared its nonexistent throat.

"Abcities have existed at least as long as the cities," it said. "Each dreams the other.

"There are ways to get between the two, and a few people do, though very few know the truth. This is where the most energetic of London's discards come, and in exchange London takes a few of our ideas—clothes, the water-wheel, the undernet.

"Mostly such swaps are beneficial, or harmless. Mostly."

Mortar and Lectern were staring intently at Zanna.

"Back in your old queen's time," the book said, "London filled up with factories, and all of them had chimneys. In houses they burnt coal. And the factories were burning everything, and letting off smoke from chemicals and poisons. And the crematoria, and the railways, and the power stations, all added their own effluvia."

"Their own what?" said Zanna.

"Muck," said Lectern.

"Add all that to the valley fog, and what you get's a smoke stew," the book went on. "So thick they called it pea soup. Yellow-brown and sitting on the city like a stinking dog. It used to get into people's lungs. It could *kill* them. That's what smog is."

"Well," said Mortar. "That's what it *was*. But something happened."

"As I was about to *explain*," said the book testily. "As I was *saying*. At first, it was just a dirty cloud. Nasty but brainless as a stump. But then something happened.

"There were so many chemicals swilling around in it that they reacted together. The gases and liquid vapor and brick dust and bone dust and acids and alkalis, fired through by lightning, heated up and cooled down, tickled by electric wires and stirred up by the wind—they reacted together and made an enormous, diffuse cloud-brain.

"The smog started to think. And that's when it became the Smog."

Lectern shivered and shook her head at the thought. "It's no surprise it wasn't . . . nice," she said. "Its thoughts are clotted from poisons, and things we've burnt to get rid of."

"It was never going to be our friend," Mortar said.

"As smoke kept going up," the book said, "the Smog got bigger and stronger and smarter. But no kinder. It wanted to grow.

"It had always strangulated some people who breathed it in. At first it didn't set out to, but then it realized that some of the dead would be cremated, and that their ashes would blow up and fatten it . . . So it became a predator."

"It knew it would be safer if Londoners thought it was just dirty fog, so it kept its new brain to itself."

"Mostly . . ." Mortar sighed and hesitated, appalled by what he had to say. "It had some allies. Believe me, there's nothing so terrible that someone won't support it. It has allies here, too."

"Yeah, we know that," said Deeba.

"One of them set airjackers on us," Zanna said.

Mortar and Lectern shook their heads in disgust.

"For ages, the fight went on," Mortar said. "But slowly, the Smog was losing. Even without knowing you were fighting, you were winning. Then it counterattacked. For five days, half a century ago, it assaulted London. It killed *four thousand people.* Its worst single attack. And still, most of you didn't even know you were at war!

"After that . . ." He breathed out and threw up his hands. "Well . . . it gets a bit vague."

"He's right," said the book. "There are hints, in me, but I'm about UnLondon, not London. There's nothing clear."

"We know a little bit, from stories," said Lectern.

"From travelers," said Mortar. "Secret histories. The Smog was beaten. There was a secret group of guardians. Weatherwitches. The Armets. It's an old word for helmet, and they were like London's *armor,* you see? And we've heard how they won. They had a magic weapon."

"The *Klinneract,*" announced Lectern.

Lectern and Mortar looked at Zanna. Eventually they looked at Deeba. They seemed a bit disappointed by their lack of recognition. "As I say," Mortar went on. "It was a *secret* group.

"So with magic and a secret war, Londoners drove the Smog away, but they didn't manage to kill it. It got away."

"By coming here," the book said.

"There was so much rubbish in it, it could slip through the crevices through which moil comes to UnLondon," Mortar said. "It was weak for a long time. It arrived . . . depleted.

"At first, even we Propheseers didn't think it was a threat. The book . . . we saw no clear references to it."

"We've talked about that," the book whispered. "You're being unfair."

"That wasn't my *point,*" Mortar muttered. "Can we discuss this later?"

"Yeah, please do," Zanna said.

Mortar cleared his throat. "It crept into chimneys. It looked for smoky fires to feed at. We ignored it. But it was preparing. It remembered the way to London. It would send a few wafts through the gaps, and they'd reach your factories and suck the smoke down. Drank from you as well as us. It took years. It was patient.

"We should've realized. But the first we knew what was happening was when . . . it started providing its own food."

"It . . . what?" Zanna said. "How?"

"It started fires. Or it got its followers to."

* * *

"There's so much rubbish in the Smog, it can concentrate it and move things. Pick things up. It's got as many chemicals in it as the best laboratory, and it can mix them, make poisons and flammables and tar and whatever. It can squeeze the coal and metal and ash it carries, and throw it around.

"It rains petrol, lights it by squeezing metal dust into shards and dropping them until they spark. We realized, at last, what we were facing. And it made sense of warnings in the book, too."

"Yes, it did," said the book. "So less of your 'It wasn't mentioned,' please."

"We've been fighting it awhile now," Mortar went on. "Since we understood. With vacuums, and extinguishers, and everything we can find. But then about a year ago, it suddenly stopped attacking."

"Isn't that good?" Deeba said.

"No, 'cause it's waiting for something," Lectern said. "It's planning something."

"And this we know because?" the book said expectantly.

"Because it's in the book?" Zanna said.

The book said "Bing!"

"Sometimes the words are riddles," Lectern said. "But there's not much controversy over 'The choker will rest, then rise, and fire, and grow, and return.' "

"Who was the man on the bus?" said Zanna.

"Someone who thinks it'll help him," Lectern said. "But there are heroes, too. For every one like him, there's someone like Unstible."

"We heard that name before," Deeba said.

"Who's Unstible?" Zanna said.

"Our greatest mind," said Mortar. "Benjamin Hue Unstible. Propheseer. Also inventor, scientist, explorer, statesman, artist, banker, furniture designer, and cook. You see, you have to remember we know very little about London's secret war with the Smog. Unstible researched and researched, all the stories he could find, about the Armets and their secret weapon, and about the Smog itself. He knew more about it than anyone else, ever. In the end, he decided that our best chance to defeat it was to know how it had been beaten before.

"He was sure the Smog would move against us. So he decided to find the Armets.

"That's why he crossed over, to search. More than two years ago. We haven't heard a word from him since." Mortar looked forlorn. "Hopefully we'll hear from him . . . any day now."

"And he was right, too," Lectern said. "The Smog *is* attacking again. And now we know what it's been waiting for."

"It's been waiting for you, Shwazzy," Mortar said.

"We knew it was approaching your time," the book said. "Word's been spreading. We heard your face had appeared in the clouds over London. That was the first sign."

Zanna looked at Deeba.

"*Told* you," Deeba muttered.

"Seven-oh-one," the book said. Lectern turned pages. " 'One shall come from that other place. She shall be called the Shwazzy. To her alone it is given to save UnLondon.' The Smog's heard the prophecy. 'She shall prevail in her first encounter, and again in her last.' *It knows you're its enemy.* And it wants you gone. That's why its forces are emerging at last. It'll attack you as soon as it can."

"Actually," said Zanna, "it already has. In London."

"But we didn't know what it was," said Deeba.

"It found you *there*?" gasped Lectern. "Oh, you poor thing."

There was a long silence.

"Look," Deeba said reasonably. "This is all . . . y'know, important and that. But you still haven't told us how to get *out* of here—"

"Wait a minute," Zanna interrupted her. "This is stupid. Why did Unstible go?" She stared at Mortar and Lectern.

"I mean . . . I'm supposed to defeat the Smog, right?" she demanded. "The prophecy says. It's . . . mad, but just say for a moment, right? So why did Unstible go looking for the Armets? What was he worried about if I'm going to take care of it? It's not his *job*."

Mortar and Lectern looked at each other uneasily.

"He . . . always had certain ideas, about what was written," Mortar said. "He said he wanted to be sure. 'It's *given* to her to save us,' he used to say. 'That doesn't mean she'll *take* it. I'll go see what I can do.' "

"So . . ." said Zanna, "he disappeared 'cause he was trying to help me?"

23

The Meaning of the Trail

"What happened to Jones and the others?" Deeba said. "The ones who sent the message to you?"

"I've given orders to the binja to let them in if they reach us," Mortar said, looking at Zanna. "Conductors can take care of themselves. And their passengers. Shwazzy, are you . . ."

"This is *crazy*," Zanna said. "I'm just a girl. How's a Shwazzy get chosen anyway? Why's it a girl? Why not a local? How d'you even know I'm it? None of it makes *sense.*"

"That's how prophecies work," Mortar said gently. "They're not about what makes sense; they're about what *will be.* That's how they work. And not only do you fit the description, but you're *here.* You crossed over . . . with your friend, even. What greater evidence could there be than the fact that you're here, now? That you found your way through the Odd, and through UnLondon, to us, the only people who could tell you what you are?"

Zanna looked at Deeba.

"You felt something, Zann," Deeba whispered. "You did. You knew you had to get us here."

"Did you turn a wheel?" Lectern said. "You did, didn't you? How *did* you get down here?"

"Well," said Deeba. "There was this smoke, and then there was this umbrella."

In a confused, overlapping way, Deeba and Zanna told the Propheseers about the attack of the terrible smoke, and the umbrella that had come to listen at Zanna's window.

"And then Zanna followed a trail," Deeba said at last.

"Not on my own," said Zanna. "We were both following it . . ."

"Whatever," said Deeba. "We ended up here."

Mortar and Lectern stared at each other.

"I wonder," said the book.

"What *is* he doing?" Lectern said.

"Who?" said Zanna.

"The man whose servant you saw," Mortar said. "Mr. Brokkenbroll. Head honcho of the Parraplooey Cassay tribe. The Unbrellissimo. The boss of the broken umbrellas."

"Lots of the moil tribes have leaders," Mortar said. "Certain substances in Un-London exist in prologue form in London, and enter a second life-cycle *here* with new purposes, even as sentient denizens of the abcity. They are *moil*, which is an acronym, the letters thereof standing for—"

"Mildly Obsolete In London," interrupted Deeba, raising her eyebrows. "We know what moil is." She leaned in to Zanna. "Old manky rubbish," she muttered.

"Ah . . . well," Mortar said. "Quite correct. And as I say, many of the tribes of moil have leaders of various calibers. Like that princess of discarded typewriters."

"What's her name?" Zanna said.

"Can't pronounce it," Lectern said. "It's all punctuation marks. Then there's Shard, the jack of cracked glass."

"Arthur Poise-Catching, the pope of empty mousetraps," Mortar said. "And the others. Some of the moil never seem to care. I don't know quite what the nabob of ring-pulls ever gained from his reign. But he seemed happy.

"Brokkenbroll's different. He really does command. And he takes our side. He's always been one of UnLondon's protectors. An umbrella's for keeping off the rain. But as soon as you break it, it doesn't have that purpose anymore, and it seeps through to here. It becomes something else."

"An *un*brella," Lectern said.

"An unbrella. And when it's that, here, Brokkenbroll commands it."

"This one didn't *seep* nowhere," Deeba said.

"It was dancing around," said Zanna.

"Yes. That's what's confusing," Mortar said. "Brokkenbroll must have been actually calling it all the way from here. That would take an awful lot of energy."

"He's not just *waiting* for them to come through," said Lectern. "He's *recruiting*. But why?"

"Is there anything about it in, er . . . ?" Mortar nodded at the book.

"Doesn't ring any bells," the book said. "Page two-twelve? Three-oh-three? No . . ."

"What's he doing?" Mortar said. "Having unbrellas keep watch on the Shwazzy after she's attacked. What's his plan?"

"I'm sorry, but why can't you just get us home?" Deeba begged. "Our families . . ."

"My mum and dad . . ." Zanna said. "They'll be *desperate*."

"They won't," Mortar said.

"What?" said Zanna.

"Of course they will!" said Deeba. "So'll mine! They love us."

"I don't doubt that," Mortar said. "That's not what I mean. Something happens, you see. There's a zone somewhere between London and UnLondon we call the Fretless Field."

"What does it do?" said Zanna.

"Is time standing still in London?" Deeba said.

"Well, no. But I promise you your parents aren't panicking. There's something called the phlegm effect . . ."

"That's disgusting." Deeba said.

"Not that sort of phlegm," said Lectern. "But you don't have to worry about them panicking. And we can help you make contact before there's any problems."

"What?" said Zanna.

"We still need to go back," said Deeba.

"Soon as we can," said Zanna.

"We'll try," Mortar said. "But we *have* to find out what's going on. If

Brokkenbroll's putting that kind of effort in, sending commands to unbrellas that far away, it sounds like he knows something we don't."

"UnLondon needs you, Shwazzy," Lectern said.

"I'm sorry, but this ain't our problem!" said Deeba. "We have to *go*."

"Go back and what?" Mortar said. "Wait for another attack?"

The girls stared at him. "Please," Mortar said. "UnLondon needs your help, it's true. But in any case, *it isn't safe for you to leave.* You're followed. All the way in London. If you left now, there'd be nothing to protect you."

"Think about it," said Lectern gently. "You think the Smog won't try again? How safe do you think you are? You're here for a reason, Shwazzy. For your own sake as well as ours. So we need to know what Brokkenbroll knows. And so do you."

Zanna and Deeba stared at each in horror.

"We'll see if we can't track Mr. Brokkenbroll down," said Lectern. "Don't you worry."

"So he can explain why his umbrella was watching my house?"

"That's the idea."

24

An Interruption in the Process

"That thing came after you," Deeba said. "Becks . . . she's alright, but she might not have been. That was meant for you."

Deeba stroked Curdle. The girls sat in the middle of the Propheseers' bridge-office as their hosts scurried around them.

"Put out a message on the walls?" the girls heard someone say. The Propheseers had been debating strategy. They rummaged in files, pulled up information on their strange computers, bickered over how to proceed. "Who do we know who might give us an in?" they heard Mortar say over the tapping of type-writers.

"I thought you might be hungry." It was Lectern, carrying a plate of strange-looking cakes. The girls eyed and sniffed them, but despite their peculiar colors, they smelt like food. Deeba and Zanna ate.

"Sorry this is taking awhile," said Lectern. "Normal service. You know. Resumed as soon as possible." She watched them until they were uncomfortable. "Sorry," she said hurriedly. "I know this must be hard for you. We're doing everything we can. This is . . . a very big time for us. I've been Mortar's second for, well, an embarrassing number of years, and no one knows the book better than me—I'm its bearer, after all—and I still can't believe it." She couldn't stop smiling. It was infectious.

The UnSun was halfway across the sky, but Zanna and Deeba's body-clocks were totally confused. They fought not to doze. Every so often a Propheseer would bring them cups of tea. "We'll be with you very shortly," she or he would say. "Sorry for the delay." Birds flew overhead, along with bigger, odder-looking things.

From the street under the bridge came a faint whistle.

"Did you hear that?" said Deeba. Curdle skipped back and forward.

"Oy," someone below shouted. The voice was very faintly audible.

"No," said Zanna, standing. "But I heard that." There was a commotion.

"Something's coming," Zanna said. A figure was stumbling slowly up the bridge, Propheseers running to help it.

"What's happened?" Zanna shouted. She ran towards them, Deeba and Curdle on her heels.

Helped up the slope of the Pons Absconditus was a binja. Its metal was cracked, and bleeding a tarry goo.

"We're under attack!" a Propheseer said. "The binja were ambushed! Thank goodness they heard something."

From the empty street where the bridge touched down, several other binja were coming. They walked backwards, weapons up, guarding the end of the bridge.

"They're watching both ends," Mortar said. "No one should be able to get past us."

"I thought no one could get on the bridge," Zanna said.

"Well no one's *supposed* to," he snapped. "But no system's perfect. That's what the binja are for. Just in case."

The binja congregated in front of their injured friend and the cowering Propheseers. They stood with weapons ready. They waited.

And waited.

"So . . . where are they?" Deeba whispered.

There were tiny whispering noises. The Propheseers and the binja looked frantically around.

"There!" said Zanna.

Meters *behind* them, in the center of the bridge by the office, grappling hooks were soaring up from below, trailing ropes. They coiled around the girders.

"A trick!" Lectern said.

"They know they can't get on from either end," said Mortar, "but now it can't shake them off . . . they've snared the middle. Quick!"

Tumbling like acrobats, the dozen binja ran to fend off the intruders. But even as they reached the little maze of desks and cupboards, dark and horrifying figures were clambering over the bridge's side.

The intruders outnumbered the binja. They wore dirty jumpsuits, rubber boots, and gloves. They aimed hoses like guns. What chilled Zanna's and Deeba's blood were their masks.

They wore bags of canvas or leather over their entire heads. Their eyes were smoked glass circles. The masks dangled rubber tubes like elephant trunks, stretching to cylinders like divers' tanks on their backs, covered with oil and dirt, and stenciled with biohazard and danger signs.

"Oh my God!" hissed Zanna. "What are they?"

Lectern had gone pale.

"Lord help us," she whispered. "Stink-junkies."

25

The Addicted Enemy

The stink-junkies were people the Smog had caught and, horribly, forced to breathe it. It synthesized powerful mind-altering drugs with its chemicals, shoved them into its captives' lungs, and took them over. If they were conscious it was in a deep dream. They would do anything the Smog made them do, while they breathed it. The stink-junkies were the Smog's addict-slaves.

The binja came at them. Perhaps because the stink-junkies were such tragic figures, victims themselves, even the ruthless binja didn't use their weapons. They attacked with chops, punches, and spinning kicks, their metal bodies twirling too fast to follow. They tried to subdue their enemies without hurting them permanently, but the Smog made the stink-junkies strong.

They were not so restrained. Their hoses sprayed oily fire. The binja dived between jets of flaming Smog.

"Quick!" said Mortar, hustling Zanna and Deeba away. Propheseers were scurrying frantically. "Lectern! We have to get the book and the Shwazzy out of here!"

"You *what?*" wailed Deeba.

A binja was caught in a blaze. It slammed down its lid to protect its eyes, and retracted its arms and legs. The flame licked harmlessly over its metal body.

"Where are we going?" Lectern shouted.

"Anywhere," Mortar said. The stink-junkies were getting closer. "Let's go!"

"*Where?*" said Zanna. Everyone looked around at the sound of her voice. "That's Smog, in their tanks?" Mortar nodded. "It keeps finding me! How'm I going to get away?"

She turned, her fists clenched; she stamped, looking halfway between petulant and impressive. She grabbed a slat from one of the broken chairs and raised it like a club.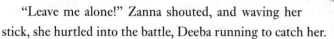

"*Just leave me alone!*" she shouted, and ran towards the fight.

"*Zann!*" shouted Deeba. "*No!*"

"*Wait!*" said Mortar, as Deeba and several Propheseers stepped forward to intercept Zanna. Mortar's voice was resonant with tense triumph. " 'She shall prevail in her first encounter . . .' "

"Leave me alone!" Zanna shouted, and waving her stick, she hurtled into the battle, Deeba running to catch her.

"It's time," Mortar said.

Zanna crooked her fingers. Wind whirled unnaturally about her.

"Feel it rising, Shwazzy," Mortar shouted. The Propheseers stared.

"What you *doing*?" shouted Deeba.

"What she was born to do," Mortar said.

The stink-junkies came close. Deeba clutched Curdle. Air streamed around Zanna.

She raised her right hand, with its club-wand-splinter, and a wave of wind swept through the fight, and made the stink-junkies stagger. The binja leapt to Zanna's side. She turned her head, caught Deeba's eye. For a moment, she seemed to glow. Deeba stared.

"Zann," Deeba whispered. "Shwazz . . ."

A stink-junkie shoved through the cordon of binja and smacked Zanna on the back of the head.

Instantly, Zanna collapsed.

"Zann!" screamed Deeba.

"What . . . ?" shouted Mortar.

Zanna lay motionless. The wind that she had seemed to conduct blew suddenly random.

The binja surrounded her, trying to shove back the attacker. It raised its arms.

"Stop it!" Deeba shouted. "It's going to kill her! What's happening?" Deeba grabbed Mortar's lapels.

"I . . . I . . . I . . ." he gabbled, staring at the unconscious Shwazzy. "Book?"

"I don't know," the book whimpered. Lectern was flicking through it rapidly, her expression appalled. "That . . . wasn't supposed to happen."

"Help her," Deeba said.

The stink-junkies outnumbered the binja. Despite the dustbins' heroism, the attackers were closing in, stamping towards Zanna, their massive boots pounding.

26

Folders and Unfolders

There was a frantic sound like wings. Dark flapping shapes suddenly raced through the air around the bridge.

"Cut the hoses!" a voice came from below. "And let me in!"

"It's Brokkenbroll!" said Lectern. "What do we do?"

"Uh . . ." Mortar said. He stared at the supine Zanna, and at the approaching stink-junkies.

"Let me *in*," Brokkenbroll called.

"I . . . I'll connect the bridge near him," Mortar said. He clenched his jaw, and concentrated.

A tall, spindly man in a dark suit came running up the Pons, his trench coat billowing around him. The Unbrellissimo. Flying around him with little squirts of air, opening and closing like squid-bat hybrids in a hundred colors, were broken umbrellas, doing his bidding.

Some were bent, some were ripped, some had no handles, but all moved fast and aggressive. They swirled around the stink-junkies. They were like fighting crows, poking at goggles with their jags, hooking breathing-tubes and flame-throwers with curved handles.

One big, tenacious unbrella
with bent spokes yanked the
pipe from Zanna's attacker's
hood. It came with a *pop* and a
jet of filthy smoke.

The stink-junkie screamed.
It scrabbled for the hose, which
flailed like a snake, gushing
Smog. The unbrellas opened
and closed vigorously. Deeba
saw several binja unfold iron
fans and wave them ferociously
at the smoke.

"Tessenjutsu," Lectern said,
crouching by Deeba. "The art of the
war-fan. It's been indispensable against the Smog."

"We have to get Zanna," Deeba said.

"Cut the hoses!" Brokkenbroll shouted again. Ducking under flames, the
binja went back into the fray. This time they knew what to do. One by one the
Smog's addict-troops went down, sucking at their torn or cut pipework. They
sucked desperately for their poisoned smoke, then were still.

The hiss of escaping Smog continued for several seconds. Layers of stomach-
turningly foul smoke hung in the air, and crawled against the air currents as the
binja and the unbrellas dissipated it.

With Mortar and Lectern behind her, Deeba ran to Zanna, wincing at the
sight of the blood and bruising on her friend's head.

"Book," she heard Mortar say. "*What* is going *on?*"

As she knelt by Zanna, she saw a clot of Smog crawl like a malevolent slug
into her nose and mouth.

"It's gone in her!" she shouted. "Help!"

"She breathed it?" said Lectern. "Book?"

"I, I've got nothing," the book said. "Page seventy-six? Page five-twenty?"
Lectern flicked hurriedly through its pages. "This *isn't what's written.*"

Mortar listened at Zanna's chest. Even unconscious, Zanna wheezed and
coughed as she breathed. "I don't think it's enough to kill her," Mortar said. "But
it's not doing her any good." Deeba could see confusion and terror in his eyes.

With a visible effort, he tried to exercise some control. "Lectern," he said, and indicated the stink-junkies.

Lectern nodded. "We'll see what we can do," she said. "Some may not be too far gone to save."

"But what about *Zanna*?" Deeba shouted.

"Propheseers." Mr. Brokkenbroll approached them, escorted by unbrellas.

"Unbrellissimo," Mortar said, shaking his hand. "We're indebted to you. Forgive the chaos. We find things going . . . not according to plan . . ."

"What's happening?" Deeba said to the book in Lectern's arms.

"I've been watching for attacks like this, Propheseer," Brokkenbroll said to Mortar. He spoke in a dry, quiet voice, only a little above a whisper. "And I heard you were looking for me. It looks like I got here just in time. Do you know what they were after?" He eyed Deeba.

"Of course. The Shwazzy."

"What?" The Unbrellissimo looked stunned. "I . . . had no idea the Shwazzy was here. There were rumors, of course, but I thought . . . they couldn't possibly be right. So, Shwazzy . . ." He stared at Deeba. She looked back miserably.

"Ah, no," Mortar said. "An easy mistake, Brokkenbroll. This isn't the Shwazzy. This young lady is Deeba Resham. She's in the book, too, I think you'll find, but not as the Shwazzy."

"What good's it being in the book?" Deeba said. "The book's wrong."

"How *dare* you!" the book said.

"Well?" she said, pointing at Zanna. There was shocked silence.

"That," said Mortar, "is the Shwazzy."

"Ah," said Brokkenbroll. "I *see*." He looked down at her. "She *is* blond," he said gently. "I thought I'd heard that. Is she . . ."

"No," said Mortar quickly. "We chased off most of the Smog. Only a very little got in."

"But enough to . . . cause difficulty?" Brokkenbroll said quietly. Mortar nodded.

"Oh my," the book said suddenly. Its voice was hollow and horrified. "She's right. It's wrong. The stuff in here. In me. It's *wrong*."

"Things aren't very clear right now . . ." Mortar said to Brokkenbroll.

"What's the point?" the book whispered. "What is the *point*?"

"Book, please," Mortar said, and swallowed. "What we'd thought we knew . . . turns out there were a few surprises. And yes, we wanted to speak to you, to understand what's been happening. Maybe you can make sense of some things . . ."

"Why you calling umbrellas down from London?" Deeba said, in tearful rage. "Why did you send one to watch my friend's house? It's because of that we came *down* here. What did you *do*?"

"Ah," said Brokkenbroll slowly. "At long last, things begin to make a bit of sense."

"So explain," Deeba said. "And then we can do something about Zanna, and . . ." She pointed at her friend, and her voice suddenly dried.

The pall of dirt-colored smoke that had gushed out of all the stink-junkies' tubes, that the unbrellas and the binja had tried to waft away, had been quietly coagulating again. It hung over the scene of the fight, a concentrated smudge, creeping closer to Zanna's body.

"A smoggler!" Mortar said. "A separate nugget. Keep it from the Shwazzy! We have to stop it joining the main mass of itself. If the Smog finds its way onto the bridge we're finished!"

It was a dense cloud, three or four meters across. It coiled and darkened like a baleful pygmy storm. From deep in its innards came a grinding, like teeth.

The cloud seemed to gather itself. Then with a rattling like a machine gun, it spat a rain of stones and coal and bullets, straight at Deeba.

A Wall of Cloth and Steel

So fast he was a blur, Brokkenbroll leapt in front of Deeba. In each of his hands was an open umbrella.

The Unbrellissimo twirled as if he were dancing. He spun the bent umbrellas in his hands, holding them like shields. Impossibly, with a *pud-pud-pud*, the smoggler's missiles bounced off the canvas.

Brokkenbroll swung the umbrellas so quickly they looked like a shimmering wall of colored cloth and thin metal fingers. He shouted an order. The other umbrellas flapped up, opened, and spun and joined in blocking the Smog's attack. Some were torn, some bent, some inverted into bowl-shapes. But each made itself a shield.

The onslaught slowed as the smoggler depleted. As its bullets ricocheted away, they dissolved in puffs of smoke, and drifted back towards the Smog. But the unbrellas didn't give it a chance to regroup. With frantic opening and closing, they made a wind.

The smoggler sent out smog tendrils, groping, trying to hold on to the bridge. But the unbrellas were remorseless against the nasty little miasma. They blew it in clots off the bridge and into the wind.

It was too small to hold firm. It grew paler, and see-through, and then was just a stain in the air, and then was gone.

Deeba and the Propheseers stood in the thick light of the setting UnSun and watched the unbrellas drop, one by one, as if exhausted, beside Zanna.

"Those were bullets," Lectern said. "And darts. Your unbrellas are *canvas*."

"So," said Mortar to the Unbrellissimo. "How in the name of bleeding bricks did you do that?"

"I wasn't sure when to tell you," Brokkenbroll said. "I hadn't yet done a final test. But events, as you see, forced my hand. At least now we know everything works. Instead of trying to explain, it would be easier if I could show you.

"You can get from the Pons Absconditus to anywhere, can't you?"

"Of course," said Mortar. "So long as it's somewhere. That's what bridges are for—getting to somewhere. Where do you want to go?"

"Please come with me," Brokkenbroll said. "And . . ." He looked thoughtful, and was silent for several seconds. "Yes. You too, young Miss Resham. I think you deserve an explanation. A little while back, I found something. Where to? Set course. We're going to Ben Hue Unstible's workshop."

"What?" said Mortar.

"I'm not leaving Zanna," Deeba said. "Look at her."

Zanna lay on a sofa, tended by Propheseers. Her eyes were closed. She was sweating, and pale, and with every breath her lungs made an ugly sound.

"I didn't know," the book whispered.

"You can't help her," Brokkenbroll said. "Not *here*. Not yet. But come with me, and I'll show you how you may be able to."

"She won't be safe," Deeba said.

"She will," said Lectern. "We can keep the bridge moving."

"The main mass of the Smog doesn't know what's happened," Brokkenbroll said. "Eventually, a few wisps of this battle may reach it, but there's time."

"I just want to go home," said Deeba, "and take Zanna with me."

"Of course," said Brokkenbroll. "That's what I'd like to facilitate. Believe me."

Mortar, Lectern and the book, Deeba and Curdle, the Unbrellissimo, and his obedient unbrellas walked down the curve of the bridge.

"Even when the Smog does find out what happened," Brokkenbroll said, "I think the course of events might put some fear into it.

"It knows that we're approaching a big fight," he said. "It's been preparing for years. Now it's started. That's why it attacked the Shwazzy," he said to Deeba gently. "It was scared of her. It wanted her out of the way before the war. It's going to attack UnLondon soon.

"But now we've given it something to think about. I'll explain everything."

They were near the end of the bridge. Mortar and Lectern focused thoughtfully on the streets ahead.

"Let's go . . ." Mortar said, and stepped off the end.

"Don't worry," Lectern said to Deeba, and tried to give her a reassuring smile. "I know you want to take care of your friend. We'll make sure everything's okay." She beckoned, and followed Mortar, Deeba only a few steps behind.

She took several steps before realizing that the buildings beside her didn't look much like they had a few seconds before. They were unfamiliar charcoal-colored edifices in the light of the early-evening loon.

There was no bridge behind her.

She walked past some of UnLondon's odd buildings. A house like a fruit with windows, one in the shape of the letter *S* and another like a *Y*, a house in a giant hollowed-out ball of string. It made the building that Brokkenbroll took them towards stand out all the more.

"I remember this place," Mortar said. "Used to get supplies round the back, by canal . . ."

It was a perfectly ordinary-looking brick factory. It was several floors high, with a tall chimney-cum-clocktower rising from its heart.

The Laboratory

The Unbrellissimo led them through the building in absolute darkness.

They stumbled through corridors and rooms and up flights of stairs, following his voice.

"What if there are traps?" Lectern said.

"Shut up," the book said urgently. "I want to hear this. I need to know what's going on."

"It's been obvious for a while that the Smog's been preparing something," Brokkenbroll said. "The Smog's always hidden, set the odd fire, rushed out and drunk it, disappeared again. Lurking in deserted buildings or under the ground. But things have been changing.

"People have been wondering for months now if the Shwazzy's due. I think that's what's got the Smog so nervous. It must think it's quest season.

"It was obvious that Unstible was worried, though. I don't think . . ." Brokkenbroll looked momentarily at the book, then away, seemingly embarrassed. "I'm not sure he ever quite believed the prophecies were true." ("Might have been sensible," the book said morosely.) "When I heard he'd gone, it made me think. Perhaps he was right. Just in case the Shwazzy didn't come . . . I thought Unstible was onto something. UnLondon needs a backup plan."

They kept on through the building's windowless, unlit innards. Deeba heard Curdle sniff its way.

"Something occurred to me," the Unbrellissimo said. "The bullets that the Smog fires: they're rain. An aggressive kind of rain, but rain all the same. The Smog's a cloud. And clouds have one natural enemy. The umbrella."

"Hang on," Deeba said. "Your umbrellas are broken."

There was an awkward silence.

"*Your um*brellas are sticks," Brokkenbroll said coldly. "My *un*brellas are *awake.* And still protectors. So I decided to train them, with a little finessing, to protect UnLondoners.

"I needed an army. It wouldn't be enough to rely on the discards that usually dribble through. So I've been recruiting. All the way from here.

"Then I heard something had happened. I listen to the gossip of clouds, which come and go between this sky and yours, and they said the Smog was cackling, that it had defeated its enemy. I wondered if something had happened to the Shwazzy. So I called a watcher to check. Hoped the information was wrong. That's what you saw, young lady."

"Zanna didn't get hit," said Deeba. "It was another girl."

"Ah . . ." said Brokkenbroll. "Blond? Tall? That explains the confusion. I was under the impression that the Shwazzy had been incapacitated. Which, sadly, has now turned out to be true. So it's just as well I've been preparing, after all."

There was a faint light in the hallway. Brokkenbroll stood by the outline of a door.

"But how?" said Deeba. "Umbrellas can't stop bullets."

"Please," hissed Mortar. "You're being rather brusque."

"Leave her alone, Mortar," Lectern muttered. "What our visitor is trying to say, Unbrellissimo, is that, uh . . ."

"She's absolutely right," Brokkenbroll said. "Neither *um*brellas nor *un*brellas can stop bullets. Not untreated, they can't. But as I say—the Smog's bullets are just rain, and my subjects keep the rain off. I knew there must be ways of reinforcing them."

"So they're like bulletproof vests?" said Deeba.

"Almost. The problem is that the Smog can change its chemicals, can fire missiles in many different compounds. The only way to make unbrellas effective against anything it might produce was to know everything about the Smog."

"So that's why we're here," Deeba said. "You got into Unstible's workshop and read his books, innit? He knew more'n anyone else, and you've been learning."

"Smart girl," murmured Lectern.

Brokkenbroll laughed.

"You flatter me," he said. "I couldn't make head or tail of those texts. Believe me, I've tried. No, I knew I'd need help from an expert."

He opened the door. The illuminations in the room beyond made them blink.

It was an enormous workshop. The ceiling soared. There were shelves crammed with books and dusty machines, and flasks and scrolls and pens and junk. There were piles of plastic, and bits of coal. By a huge fireplace was a freight elevator.

The chamber was filled with boiling kettles and glass and rubber tubes, boilers and conveyor belts. In the center was a bubbling brass vat.

There were no windows in the room. The light came from an enormous number of placid-looking insects the size of Deeba's fist, which sat on shelves and stools and crawled sluggishly up the walls. Their abdomens were lightbulbs, screwed into their thoraxes. Their slow motion made the shadows crawl.

The room was a hubbub. Thronging every surface were broken umbrellas. They trotted in spidery motion through turning cylinders, in front of sprays of liquid. They hauled up a ridge to the edge of the vat, and one by one jumped in.

They darted in the liquid like penguins underwater, and emerged again, shivering, leapt out and slotted themselves into an enormous rack. Rows and rows of unbrellas dripped and dried.

Mortar and Lectern gasped.

Standing by the ash-filled fireplace was a man in a filthy white coat. He looked pale in the glow of the shifting insect bulbs. He was short and fat, with bloodshot eyes and an enormous bald head.

He looked tired, but he smiled at Deeba and the Propheseers.

"No!" Mortar said at last. "Is that you?"

"Hello old friend," the strange little figure said.

"Ben?" said Mortar. "Benjamin Unstible?"

Hope Hiding with a Cauldron

After his delight, Mortar was angry.

"How long have you been here?" he demanded. "I can't believe you didn't tell me! We thought you were dead . . ."

"I know, I know," Unstible said. "I'm sorry. There were reasons."

He wheezed when he spoke. He shook Deeba's hand, and his flesh felt taut under her fingers. He looked terrible, though he moved energetically and spoke quickly.

"What reasons? What could possibly justify—"

"The Smog's still looking for me."

"Ah."

"I'll tell you all the details," Unstible said. "I promise. The short version is this. While I was in London, *I found the Armets.*"

"*What?*" said Mortar. "How? No one knows for sure that they even still exist."

"Huh? Oh, yes. Well, you know, they may be a secret society, but nothing can hide from someone determined. So I found them. There's a few of them left. Hiding. And they taught me their spells."

"Did they show you the Klinneract?" said Lectern reverentially.

"Unfortunately, ah, that is long gone. Magic weapons don't last. It did its job and now it's broke. But they did teach me about the Smog. I know everything. I know what it's made of, and more importantly, I know what can stop it. That's what I went for, and I found it.

"But the Smog must have realized what I was doing. Because I found out it was *following* me.

"If I wasn't studying it so close I might not have realized it had crept through, but I had some . . . feelers out. I had to hide. Go to ground. No one from here knew where I was, for sure. Or even if I was alive. But the Smog was looking for me. Once, it came very close to finding me. I was able to get away and slip back here, but I hadn't yet made preparations. I knew that as long as the Smog thought I was lost or gone it would leave me alone. So I *had* to stay hidden. I couldn't come out, because I hadn't got things ready."

"We made a plan together," the Unbrellissimo said.

"Exactly. Brokkenbroll's servants found me. When he asked me how to make his umbrellas into *shields,* I realized the concrete applications of what I'd learnt."

"It could stop the Smog," Brokkenbroll said.

"Exactly." Unstible waved at the strange machinery and the vat full of fervently swimming umbrellas. "It's a slightly more supernaturally interesting version of vulcanization. A cocktail of chemicals, technique, and magic that can fend off anything the Smog throws at us. Anything it can do."

"And we're almost ready," Brokkenbroll said, his voice tense with excitement. "I've been amassing troops. Unstible's been getting them ready. In a few days I'll start issuing treated umbrellas to everyone in UnLondon. It'll take awhile, but everyone'll get one. I'll keep pulling them in from London. Until everyone in the abcity's protected."

"But we can't all move those things like you do, Unbrellissimo," Lectern said.

"You don't have to. That's the beauty. *They obey my orders.* I'll tell them to protect whomever carries them. With Unstible's liquid and my soldiers, we can protect everyone in UnLondon. If the Smog tries to rain its bullets at us . . . just pull out your umbrella, and you're safe."

"That's . . . brilliant," said Mortar.

"It's a plan," said Lectern. "A real plan."

"So UnLondon don't need the Shwazzy after all?" Deeba said. "With your umbrellas or unbrellas or whatever they are? The Smog doesn't seem to know that. It's still in her lungs. What's it *doing* to her? What if she's really sick? If something happens to her, I don't care how scary the Smog is, I'll find it."

There were a few moments' silence.

"I think you might at that," said Brokkenbroll thoughtfully. "It says a lot about you that you came with your friend. You must have been very afraid. It says you're something to be reckoned with. I wonder what we can do . . ." He narrowed his eyes and seemed to be evaluating her. "Give me a second," he said, and beckoned Unstible over.

The two men muttered together. ". . . we could . . ." Deeba heard. Lectern shuffled a little closer to her, as if protectively. The two men seemed to be disagreeing. ". . . absolutely not . . ." she heard, and ". . . might work . . ." and ". . . worth a try . . ." and ". . . not unless we have to . . ." They bowed their heads together and muttered.

"Alright then," Unstible said suddenly, and shrugged.

"I've had an idea," Brokkenbroll said. "I think I might be able to get the Smog out of your friend."

"The trick," he said, "is to get the Smog so rattled it has to gather every bit of itself to fight. And it's not used to facing someone with the weapons to keep it at bay." He pointed to his unbrellas.

"Really?" Mortar said. "You honestly think you can scare the Smog? If you can do that . . . well." His expression left little doubt that if the Unbrellissimo could achieve that, he'd win Mortar's respect and loyalty.

"And how can you help the Shwazzy?" said Lectern.

"I'll attract its attention," Unbrellissimo said. "Somewhere away from here, some waste ground where no one can get hurt. Light a couple of old tires, go Smog-fishing."

"You're going to call it *deliberately?*" Mortar said.

"I can't believe this," said the book miserably. "For centuries I've known what was supposed to happen. Ins and outs. And with that whack on the back of the Shwazzy's head . . . that was all gone. Turns out I don't know *anything*. But for the record, it sounds to me like you're an impressive general. Maybe your plan will even work. Even without the Shwazzy, maybe UnLondon *does* have a chance."

"Propheseers, Propheseers, please," Brokkenbroll said. "We're not just talking about the abcity. We're also talking about a *young girl,* lying back on that bridge, struggling to breathe. Now, if I can make this work," he said to Deeba, "then you can rest. Your friend will be safe. The prophecies . . . well, they'll still be wrong, but that won't matter, because UnLondon'll have a new way to protect itself." He twirled an umbrella. "So there'll be no need for the Shwazzy to come running back, and no need for you to worry about her."

"What can I do?" Deeba said. "I want to help. She's my friend."

"It'll be dangerous. I really can't . . ." He stopped and thought. "Perhaps there is one thing."

"Tell me!"

"It'll mean you going home. I need time to prepare, and we have to get her as far away from the Smog as possible, as fast as possible. So it's something you can only do from London."

Deeba almost sobbed with laughter.

"I *want* to go home!" she said. "That's what we've been trying to do since we got here."

"Alright then," said the Unbrellissimo. "Let me tell you what to do."

30

Taking Leave

The bridge certainly hadn't been there when they came out of the factory. But Mortar and Lectern led them just one or two quick turns, and its familiar towers and cables rose before them, and they were back on its tarmac, heading for the office.

The loon was high overhead. It was a fatter oval than the previous night, was almost full.

The Propheseers were waiting, gathered around Zanna's immobile body. Curdle scampered and rolled towards them.

"Come here, you stupid carton," Deeba said, and stroked her friend's head gently, listening to Zanna's breath rattle. Then Deeba cried out with delight as she saw three familiar figures on the Pons Absconditus.

"Obaday! Conductor Jones! Skool!" she shouted, and ran to hug each of them in turn—even Skool, who leaned awkwardly and patted her back with enormous clumsy gloves.

"Deeba!" Obaday shouted.

"How are you, girl?" said Jones.

"You made it," she said. "How did you get here? Are you all alright?"

"It was a bit hairy there for a while," Jones said. "We laid up south of the river. Rosa had to do some extreme driving there . . ." Skool nodded and made a zigzag motion with his hand. "We got rid of another of the grossbottles, but a couple of airjackers boarded us. Used up all my current getting rid of them."

"Then Skool took over," Obaday said, and Skool struck a strongman pose.

Somewhere between Jones's laconic descriptions, Obaday's enthusiastic gabbling, and Skool's hand motions, Deeba learnt that the bus had landed, and there'd been a fight: "It wasn't much," according to Jones, and "It was terrible!" according to Obaday. "Stink-junkies . . . smombies . . . some other horrible-looking things . . ."

"We held them off as long as we could," Jones said. "When they got inside the bus, they snatched the captive—that toga'd swine—and left."

"When they saw the Shwazzy wasn't there," Deeba said.

"Poor thing," Obaday said, looking at Zanna. Skool stroked her head.

"She'll be okay," Deeba said quickly. "We know what we're going to do."

"I couldn't believe it, seeing her like that," Obaday said. "This wasn't supposed to happen."

"Tell me about it," the book said miserably, from Lectern's arms.

"If she isn't going to save UnLondon, then who is?" Obaday went on.

"Well," said Lectern. "There may be another plan. Something rather extraordinary. A plan involving someone you will *not* have been expecting to see again." She glanced at the book, and added quietly: "Just not a plan that's written." The book sighed.

"You remember what to do?" Brokkenbroll said. Deeba nodded.

The loon shone down. The Propheseers and a few binja were lined up to see Deeba off. She looked down at Zanna, slumped, eyes closed, in the wheelbarrow into which the Propheseers had gently placed her. It felt disrespectful, pushing her friend like that, but she had no choice.

"Soon," the Unbrellissimo said. "I'll get everything prepared. Six in the morning. Be ready, won't you?" Deeba nodded again, and looked at the rest of her companions.

She'd been so desperate to go home for so long, and she was still, was frantic to see her family, but she was suddenly sad to say good-bye to these UnLondoners. By the look of their faces, they felt the same.

*   *   *

"You're a tough one, Deeba Not-the-Shwazzy," Conductor Jones said. "You . . . you have yourself a great life, you hear?"

"I might come back," she said.

"I . . . doubt it," Jones said slowly. He lowered himself, bringing his face to her level. "Not that easy. Believe me. I had to try for years." He looked down for a moment. "It would be lovely if you did, believe me. You've impressed me. But . . ." He gave her a sad smile, shook his head, and gave her a sudden hug. "I'm afraid it's good-bye." Deeba could hardly hear him.

Skool squatted, patted Deeba clumsily, gave her a hug and a thumbs-up for good luck.

"It was an honor to take you both to the bus stop," Obaday said. "Don't forget me. And . . . remember me to the Shwazzy."

"Or not," warned Brokkenbroll. "You'll have to be very careful what you say."

"I know, I know," Deeba said.

"Alright then," said Obaday forlornly. "Well, *you* remember me then."

"You." It was the book. Its voice was sulky. "Fing. You've given me an idea."

Lectern held the book up. Obaday leaned in, and the pinheaded designer and the redundant book of prophecies had a whispered conversation.

"As long as I can remember, I've been waiting for her," the book said to Deeba. "The Shwazzy's not to blame for my inadequacies. I always imagined how I'd be there, in the Shwazzy's arms, giving her advice as she does what's needed for UnLondon. I've been imagining that since a long time before you or she were born.

"I can hardly believe that's not going to happen. I want to think of her carrying me around in some way. I'd like to ask you to give her something for me."

"This is a bad idea," Brokkenbroll said. "We have no idea what state the Shwazzy's going to be in when she wakes . . ."

"Well, if it's not *appropriate*," the book snapped, "then *you* keep the gift, Deeba Resham. Agreed? For goodness' sake, I want to make a gesture. For her. It's not as if there's much point sticking to my original use, is there?

"Open me," it said to Lectern. "Somewhere near the beginning. A page of descriptions—they're not inaccurate. No matter what else is." Lectern did, and then she, Mortar, and Deeba all let out horrified shouts as Obaday leaned over and tore the page neatly out.

"What are you doing?" Lectern shouted. "Are you mad . . . ?"

"Calm down," said the book. "I told him to. My main job was foretelling, and it turns out that I'd be more useful as a recipe book. At least that way you'd get a decent lunch out of me. So this way these two can get a real remembrance of us."

Obaday was working on the sheet with his quick fingers. He whipped scissors from his pocket and cut shapes from it. He plucked pins from his head, attached bits together, pulled a white-threaded needle from his scalp, and began to sew at incredible speed.

In less than two minutes he was done.

"Here," he said to Deeba. "Hold out your hand." He pulled onto it the single glove he had made her.

Deeba flexed her fingers. The ancient paper was so soft it did not crinkle, but folded like felt. The glove was covered in words, snips of sentences and the ends of paragraphs, in ancient-looking print that was hard to read.

"Something to keep us in mind," the book said.

"It's gorgeous," Deeba said. "I . . . She'll love it."

"If she sees it," Brokkenbroll said, looking uncomfortable. "Which is probably not appropriate."

Mortar and Lectern were staring at the glove as if they were about to have heart attacks.

"Oh, leave it, you two," the book said. "My pages. I can do what I want."

"Now don't worry," said Unstible. "We'll keep UnLondon safe."

"And help your friend," said the Unbrellissimo.

Curdle came rolling out of the shadows and leapt up into Deeba's arms. The little carton nuzzled up to her.

"Sorry Curdle," she whispered. "But I can't take you." The carton whined. "You wouldn't like it. You'd get thrown out, by mistake. End up in a dump. Or burnt."

Curdle forlornly shook its opening.

"No," said Deeba. "You have to stay." She looked around for the most responsible-seeming person on the bridge. "Lectern . . . thank you for everything. And . . . would you look after it?"

Lectern looked surprised.

"Of course," she said after a moment, and took the carton. Curdle made a sound like whimpering.

"Be good," Deeba said.

"Remember," said Brokkenbroll quietly, crouching by Deeba's side. "We don't know what state this'll leave the Shwazzy in. Treat her gently. Give her no shocks. Don't force her to think about things she's not ready to.

"Mortar?" he said, and tapped his wrist. "If you would?"

Mortar beckoned Deeba. As gently as she could, she wheeled Zanna towards the end of the bridge.

She turned and waved. Lectern, Obaday, Jones and Skool, and even one or two of the binja waved back. Curdle was trying to pull away from Lectern's hands and follow Deeba.

"The farther from one end to the other, the harder," Mortar said. "And to stretch from UnLondon to London is a very long way indeed, across the Odd. We're going to have to tap into a lot of energy."

In the distance, Deeba could see the UnLondon-I speed up. The colossal waterwheel turned faster and faster, churning the Smeath into a froth.

"This is going to take it out of me," Mortar said.

The end of the bridge was close. The strange UnLondon streets were only a few steps away now. "Hold on . . ." said Mortar. He had a nosebleed.

"It's hurting you!" Deeba said.

"Just . . . a bit . . . farther . . ." Mortar said, his teeth gritted.

The whine of the spinning waterwheel sounded dangerous now, and Deeba was about to insist that they stop, and there was something funny about the streets ahead; then Mortar *did* stop, and pointed violently and suddenly, and Deeba stumbled forward, shoving the wheelbarrow off the end of the bridge—

—and into her estate. Onto the walkway on the first floor, next to her front door.

In London.

The moon was shining down through clouds. Somewhere nearby a cat called out; then silence returned. The windows around Deeba were dark.

Jutting from the walkway behind her was the Pons Absconditus. It arched out over the yard of the estate. She couldn't see its other end. Mortar stood on it, raised his hand.

From somewhere, there was the noise of scattering bottles. Deeba turned for a moment, and when she looked back the bridge was gone.

She stood still for a long time.

Eventually she unlocked her front door. She pushed it open with her right hand, wearing the glove made from the book. She stepped over the threshold into her house.

"Mum, Dad," she said quietly. She half expected them to be up, waiting for her, agonizing. The sitting-room light was off, though. She could hear the gentle breathing from their bedroom, where they were sleeping.

As silently as she could, she wheeled Zanna through to her bedroom, and put her gently in the camp bed. Then she took the wheelbarrow back out, and deserted it on the walkway, where everyone would think it was someone else's. Maybe it would even seep back to UnLondon.

Back in the flat, a light had come on in her little brother's bedroom. Hass came out in his pajamas, rubbing his eyes. When he saw her, he stopped, and gawped at her stupidly for several seconds. Then he shivered, and blinked.

"Hello Deeba," he said sleepily. He went into the bathroom and peed with the door open. "Why are you dressed?" he said on his way back to his bedroom. "I had a dream about spaghetti." He turned his light off and got back into bed.

Deeba scratched her head and furrowed her brow. She sat up on her bed, stroked her unconscious friend's forehead, and watched the clock.

"You can stop worrying, everyone," she whispered, forlorn and confused. "I'm back."

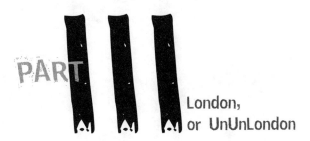

PART III

London,
or UnUnLondon

31

Clearing the Air

As the minutes went by and the sky stayed dark beyond her curtains, Deeba felt so anxious she could hardly breathe. She wanted to run to her parents' room and jump on their bed, wake them up and demand they be delighted and relieved that she was back. She wanted to examine the glove that Obaday had made, that she might have to give up in a little while. She wanted to read all the words on it carefully. But as the clock wound towards six in the morning, she knew she had a job to do, and she had to focus.

I'll work out all the other stuff later, she thought, her heart pounding. *Right now, I got to get ready.*

"Hang on, Zann," she whispered. "Brokkenbroll . . . do it right."

She crept through the dark house, quietly gathering the equipment she needed, for the mission the Unbrellissimo had given her.

The second hand of the clock circled, mercilessly slow. The minute hand crawled. Zanna wheezed on the camp bed, tossing from side to side.

"Not long, Zann," Deeba whispered.

Eventually it was five minutes to six. Four minutes to. Three. Deeba hesitated, then pulled on the glove Obaday had given her, for luck. In the half-light, she tried to read the words on it.

It was two minutes to six. One.

Deeba looked around, suddenly frantic. All the electrical points in the room were filled. She yanked a plug out of the socket, and the lights on her stereo dimmed. She plugged in her equipment.

The instant the minute hand touched twelve, dead-on six o'clock, Zanna began to shake.

"Come on, Zanna," Deeba whispered.

Her friend shook, and snapped her arms and legs violently.

Zanna moaned, and held her breath for terrifying long seconds.

Breathe, thought Deeba. *Breathe!*

Then Deeba let out a cry of alarm. Crawling with serpentine motion and speed through her window came a tentacle of Smog.

She flailed at the thing, but it moved too fast. It whipped soundlessly through the room, stinking like exhaust, unrolled, and clamped on Zanna's face.

"No!" shouted Deeba, and picked up her weapon. The Smog was *tugging* at her friend, and Zanna was *exhaling.*

I'll make it gather itself, Brokkenbroll had said.

Streams of filthy smoke jetted from Zanna's nostrils. She breathed out for a long time. The dirty spirals coiled over the bedclothes, coalesced into a dense clot, and hovered over the bed.

Deeba looked at the cloud, and she was sure it was looking at her.

Then, as filaments of smoke shot out towards Deeba's face, she switched on the fan she held.

"Choke my friend?" she said, and blasted the smoggler with air.

It recoiled, but Deeba pursued it. She shoved the fan right into it, and the Smog dissipated in panic. She could feel the faint pressure of smuts in the air.

Deeba chased grubby wisps around the room. They scurried like slugs into the corners, and she stretched the fan to the limits of its cord, harassing them. One by one they slunk away, soaking into the carpet, or squeezing through cracks.

The Smog tendril poking through the window, all the way from UnLondon, reared up at her, but she thrust the fan at it, and it hesitated, then snapped suddenly back out of the window the way it had come.

There was a long moment of stillness.

Did I . . . do it? Deeba thought.

Deeba turned off the fan. She sniffed suspiciously, but there was only a hint of the Smog's smell of petrol, coal, dirt, and sulfur. Its scum and muck was on her skin.

"Deeba?"

Zanna had opened her eyes.

"Zann!" Deeba said, and threw her arms around her friend.

"Deeba . . . ? What happened? Where am I?" Zanna began to cough. *You get it all up,* Deeba thought. *Get the last of it out.*

She hugged Zanna for a long time.

"What happened?" Zanna kept saying. She winced and touched the back of her head. "What's going on?"

Thank you, Unbrellissimo, Deeba thought. *Thank you, thank you. And . . . well done me, too.* For chasing the last of it away.

"It's okay, Zann," Deeba said. "You got hit by a stink-junkie and then the Smog got in you, but Brokkenbroll did something, and I just got rid of it, so . . ."

Deeba's voice dried up at the sight of Zanna's face.

"Deebs," Zanna croaked. "What are you *on* about?"

"The . . . the Smog," Deeba said. "On the bridge. With the Propheseers?"

Zanna shook her head.

"I don't understand," she said.

We don't know how it'll affect her, Brokkenbroll had said.

"What's the last thing you remember?" Deeba said.

"What do you mean?" said Zanna. "Yesterday? We . . . was it yesterday? I dreamt there was something outside my house, only . . . *What* is going on . . . ?"

She don't remember a thing, Deeba thought. *It's all gone.* She stared in astonishment.

"What is this bloody noise?" Deeba's mother opened the door in her dressing gown. When she saw the two girls, for a moment she stared at them blankly. Then she shook her head and blinked at them wrathfully. "It's *you* two," she said. "Banging around and shouting . . . It's early, girls! Deeba, what are you . . . ?"

She looked down in bewilderment as Deeba grabbed her in a big hug.

"Mum, Mum, Mum!" Deeba said.

"Yes, mad girl, it's me," Mrs. Resham said. "And despite this burst of endearing affection, you're still too loud."

Deeba looked up at her, too happy to care about her mother's reaction.

"Sorry, Mrs. Resham," said Zanna, and exploded with coughs again. "My *head*!"

Deeba's mother blinked again and changed her expression. "You don't sound well, dear," she said. "Maybe we should get you home soon."

Home, thought Deeba, and smiled.

"Maybe I should go," groaned Zanna, wheezing. "I feel *awful.*"

We did it, Deeba thought. Despite seeing her friend in pain, not knowing what had happened to Zanna's memories, the most important thing was that they were both *there.* Home. She felt overwhelmed.

"What are you grinning about?" her mother asked her.

We're home, Deeba thought.

32

Memento

As they took Zanna home, Deeba sent out mental thanks to everyone who had helped her in UnLondon: Obaday, Jones, Skool, the Slaterunners, Mortar and Lectern, and especially Brokkenbroll the Unbrellissimo.

Good luck, she thought. She knew that the UnLondoners still had a fight ahead of them. The Smog would not take kindly to their counterattack. But with Brokkenbroll and Unstible's plan, the UnLondoners might win.

It was their fight now. They had no Shwazzy, but they'd made their own plans, and she wished them luck.

Deeba's delight was overshadowed by bewilderment at her mother's strange lack of concern. But then she remembered what Mortar had said—the phlegm effect.

She went to the computer to look up the word *phlegm*. She found that yes, it did mean "snot," just as she had thought, but it also had an older meaning: "equanimity." And when she had looked *that* up, she learnt that it meant "calmness of temper."

So that was what Mortar had meant.

The phlegm effect was why when her mother and father stumbled sleepily in to breakfast, they cheerfully greeted Deeba as if she hadn't been missing for three days.

"Dad," she said. "You remember what time I got home yesterday?"

"Yesterday?" He looked thoughtful. "About six, wasn't it? No. I'm not sure." He shrugged.

"What was we talking about at supper, Mum?"

"At supper, darling? It was about . . . your schoolwork?" Her mother turned it into a question and forgot about it.

It wasn't as if time had stood still, and it wasn't as if they'd forgotten her, or as if she'd been replaced by a phantom. Instead, all the time she was in Un-London, they'd simply *not worried.* They'd all spent the time thinking that they'd seen her a few moments ago, or that she'd just popped into her room, or that they'd have a word with her in a second. They stayed calm—*phlegmatic*—because they didn't, and couldn't, realize that she'd really gone.

Deeba was pleased that her parents and brother and her friends and teachers hadn't been panicking. She would have hated for them to worry.

She had to admit, though, it made her a bit uncomfortable to realize that no one had been thinking about her and Zanna.

She was also uneasy when she thought of the moment of hesitation her family had shown on her return, the first time they saw her. Deeba tried not to think about it, even when her teachers and school friends did the same thing.

Zanna took a day off school, was laid up taking painkillers for her head and cough syrup for her lungs. In the playground, Deeba watched the sun and smiled into its fat, full little face. It was deeply strange not to see the empty hoop of the UnSun.

The sunlight was more vivid; she felt soaked in light.

"You're in a good mood," said Miss Edwards, looking at her oddly. "Haven't seen you this happy since . . ." she said, and then her voice petered out, because of course she could not quite remember when she had last seen Deeba, because of the phlegm effect.

Zanna's dad had gotten over the guilt of the accident, and that put Zanna in a good mood. Keisha and Kath were still a bit wary around Deeba, but something in the air between them had changed. They smiled at her cautiously during the lunch queue, and mentioned that Becks would be back in class soon. *If that one sight of the Smog scared you,* Deeba thought, *you wouldn't believe what I've been doing the last few days.*

She almost couldn't believe it herself. In the light of that bright little sun, all her memories of grossbottles and Slaterunners and bridges to and from anywhere and flying buses and her little carton Curdle seemed like daydreams.

When what had happened seemed impossible, she made sure no one was looking, and brought out the glove, and read it. *If Zanna remembers,* she thought, *I'll give it to her. Till then it's mine.*

Mostly it was single words or even just a few letters, but here and there were snippets of sentences. She soon knew them all by heart.

BRICK WIZARDRY AND THE PIGEONS
AT ALL, BUT ONLY TO REGRET IT
FICULT TO GET IN, AND NO EASI
ENTER BY BOOKSTEPS, ON STORYLADDERS
UNLIKE ANY OTHER

She read them again and again in the same order, reciting them quietly like a poem.

Zanna was soon back at school, and then Becks, and the slow patching-up of relations between the friends continued. Within a couple of weeks, things between them were all good again.

It's back like it was, Deeba told herself.

She said it to herself even though she knew that was not true.

Becks was still in her cast. Zanna suffered from headaches, and she wheezed a bit when she breathed too hard. She was physically slower than she had been, too. Only Deeba knew why.

Deeba could never talk to any of her friends about what had happened. If her conversation ever veered even close to anything even a little bit strange, Kath or Keisha or Becks would start to panic and get aggressive.

Once, when Deeba was alone with Zanna, she said gently: "Do you know what the word *Shwazzy* means?" In her pocket, Deeba felt the glove. *By rights it's yours*, she thought.

Zanna frowned with concentration. She opened her mouth and nothing came out, and a look of great alarm, even fear, crossed her face, and she began to cough violently. *She doesn't want to remember*, Deeba realized, patting her friend's back. *It's too scary.*

Of course it was frustrating, sometimes incredibly frustrating, not to be able to tell her best friends about the extraordinary, unbelievable things that had happened. To the *two* of them. But when she was with Zanna on the back of a bus and they were laughing or joking around, even though Deeba could hardly believe that all those events were gone from Zanna's head, she told herself it was worth it, and she tried not to think about the more unusual bus she and Zanna had recently taken.

Sometimes at night, Deeba would sit on her bed and look out onto the moonlit estate, and imagine UnLondon under the loonlight. She hoped everyone there was well and happy, and that the battle against the Smog was going according to plan.

It would be hard, but under the guidance of the Unbrellissimo, and Un-stible, and with the secret Armets' techniques, maybe UnLondon could win. Deeba read and reread the mysterious words on the paper glove that she believed was hers, by now, and wished the UnLondoners luck.

When she was there, she had wanted desperately to come home. Now, even though she was truly happy to be back, she was wistful that she could never say anything about the most amazing place she had ever been.

Deeba was certain that she would never see UnLondon again.

33

The Powerful Resurgence of the Everyday

Of course she was wrong.

34

Curiosity and Its Fruits

For a while, Deeba tried not to think about UnLondon, because it made her miss it. She soon realized, however, that she couldn't stop herself.

In the streets, she would eye passersby and wonder if they knew of the ab-city's existence. She was a member of an exclusive group.

Deeba wanted to know about the UnLondoners, and UnLondon, and the Smog, and the secret war. That war with the Smog, in particular, fascinated her. The idea that something like that had once gone on in her own city made all the impossibility she had seen feel closer to home.

There must be UnLondoners who've moved to London, as well as the other way round, she realized. *Maybe there's a secret group I can join, or something. Friends of UnLondon.*

After all, she knew now that there were real secret societies.

On the computer in her living room, Deeba went searching on the internet for information, while her mother and father watched television.

There were quite a few websites that said *UnLondon,* but she checked them all laboriously, and none of them were about the abcity. *There can't be* nothing, she thought, but there was.

All the references to *Unstible* were irrelevant spelling mistakes. All the listings for *Armets* were about the old helmets, from which the secret defenders had taken their name. Deeba tried countless different spellings of *Klinneract* and came up with nothing.

She tried to think of new strategies to research the hidden histories. She looked up how to toughen fabric. She looked up *weatherwitches,* and got loads of pages, but mostly ridiculous foolishness, and nothing at all helpful.

"Mum," she said. "What's it called when you study about the weather?"

"Meteorology, sweetheart," her mother said, and spelt it for her. "You doing homework?"

Deeba didn't answer. She typed *meteorology* into the search engine, and sighed as more than fourteen million hits came up. She combined meteorology with the words *smog, society,* and *London.* She still got lists of hundreds or thousands of websites.

She was amazed by the numbers of people studying the British weather. The Met office, meteorology departments in universities, departments of London's mayor's office, the Royal Meteorological Society. She clicked on them randomly, and skimmed articles about the London Smog of 1952.

And then suddenly, Deeba saw the web address of one of the sites she was reading: rmets.org.

The Royal Meteorological Society, it said at the top of the page, next to a logo that read *RMETS.*

Deeba stared, her eyes and mouth opening wide.

She'd found the society of so-called weatherwitches with whom Unstible said he'd studied. She'd found the Armets, and they weren't named after helmets at all.

It's got garbled over the years, she thought. *The name. People here saying* RMetS, *and UnLondoners mishearing, and thinking* Armets. *It's just a mistake.*

Deeba's delight at having worked this out was tempered by growing unease.

So . . . what was Unstible talking about, saying he'd studied magic with the Armets? There is no Armets. No weatherwitches. No magic. There's no secret society. It's all a misunderstanding.

So . . .

So Unstible must have been lying.

35

Conversation and Revelation

Maybe it's me getting it wrong, Deeba thought. *Maybe he was saying he worked with* RMetS *and I got the wrong idea.*

She dialed RMetS's number four times, always losing her nerve and disconnecting. The fifth time, she let it ring. When a man answered, Deeba was pleased to hear herself sound quite calm.

"Can I speak to Professor Lipster please?" She had written down a list of names from the website.

"What's it regarding?"

"I need some personal information about someone who worked . . . who I think worked at the society."

"I can't possibly—" he said in a bored voice.

"The name's Unstible," Deeba said, and to her surprise the man shut up.

"Hold on," he said, and there were a series of clicks.

"Hello?" a woman said. "This is Rebecca Lipster. I understand you wanted to know about Benjamin Unstible?"

"Yes," said Deeba. "I want to know what he was working on, please. It's quite important. I'm trying to find out as much as I can—"

"Look," Professor Lipster interrupted, very suspiciously. "I can't discuss this sort of thing. Who am I talking to?"

"I'm his daughter," Deeba said.

There was a silence. Deeba held her breath. She knew there was a big risk that Lipster would know she was lying. But Deeba had decided that if they'd even heard of Unstible, this was the best chance she had of persuading the meteorologists to hand over any notes he'd left. She got all her lies ready. *My dad says he forgot some of his papers. Can I come and pick them up . . . ?*

Then something completely unexpected happened.

"Oh, I'm so sorry," Professor Lipster said. "Of course I can understand you wanting to know. I'll tell you whatever I can . . . and I'm very sorry for your loss."

Deeba's eyes widened.

"You should be proud of your father, young lady," Lipster said. "He was working very hard. On the day he . . . of the accident . . . Ms. Rawley the Environment minister was coming on an official visit, and your father was very excited to be here. He was always saying what an excellent job she was doing, and he'd been wanting to meet her for weeks. He said he had some questions for her. And she said she was looking forward to meeting him, too.

"Then . . . well the visit had to be canceled of course, when we found him."

"What happened?" Deeba said.

Lipster hesitated.

"I'm sure you've been told . . . It was a heart attack, we think. At first we thought there might have been a chemical accident, there was such a strong smell of fumes in the room. But he wasn't doing anything like that. Just historical research."

"What sort of thing?" Deeba asked. Her mind was racing.

"The Smog of 1952, he said. What was in it, how much damage it did, that sort of thing. And what was done about it. What was it he was particularly interested in? Wait: I remember.

"It was the Klinneract."

"The *what?*" Deeba said.

"From 1956," Lipster said. "That was the law that really sorted out the problems of the smog." She repeated herself slowly. "The Clean Air Act."

"Oh," said Deeba slowly. "*Oh.*"

"What else would you like to know?" Lipster said.

"Actually," Deeba said, "that's more than I expected to find out." Lipster was saying something else when Deeba disconnected.

That night, to her father's surprise, Deeba went outside in a light shower of rain. She wanted to think in the fresh cold air.

"You splashing around?" her father said. "Don't go far. Stupid thing." He pointed at her umbrella, with its canopy of red fabric printed with lizards. "I don't think moisture in the air is reason enough—"

"Yeah yeah, Dad, to overturn society's taboo against spiked clubs, blah blah." She kissed him and went out.

She twirled her umbrella, watched it spin off the water in tiny droplets, remembered how Brokkenbroll's broken umbrellas had protected her.

Deeba went through what she'd found out.

Unstible had been about to meet Rawley the Environment secretary—who might know better than most about dangerous climate and how to fight it—and he had been stopped. By something that stank. Of chemicals. His colleagues at RMetS thought he was dead.

The Smog *had* found him. He *hadn't* managed to hide from it, as he'd told her.

Deeba thought about Elizabeth Rawley, the MP in charge of the environment. Maybe, Deeba thought, she could work out why the Smog had been so anxious to stop Unstible from meeting Rawley. Unstible had obviously thought she could help.

Deeba thought back to when she had last heard anything from Rawley on the news. *I can't remember exactly when,* she thought, *but I'm sure it wasn't long ago. Wasn't Dad saying something about her last night? He likes her, says she's the only one doing her job. Wasn't she in the paper? Yes, I'm sure she was . . . Anyway it doesn't matter. Why am I worrying about Rawley? I'll hear something about her soon, surely . . .*

"Oh my gosh," said Deeba suddenly. She froze her umbrella in midtwirl. She knew why it was hard for her to even think about when she'd last seen Elizabeth Rawley.

"I've got the phlegm effect," she said. "And that means . . . Rawley's been in UnLondon."

* * *

There was no Klinneract. Long ago, a few UnLondoners must have mis-heard what had stopped the Smog in London, and spread the inadvertently invented word, and eventually the whole abcity believed in a nonexistent magic weapon. That was how legends started. Then Deeba had been suckered into believing in it. By Unstible.

But if the people at RMetS were right, and Unstible had been killed by the Smog, then it wasn't Unstible in UnLondon.

So who was it Deeba had met?

And what was that imposter doing?

Something was happening in UnLondon. Something was happening *to* UnLondon. And none of the UnLondoners knew it.

36

Concern in Code

They'll be fine, Deeba told herself. She told herself that again and again.

UnLondon'll get through. The Propheseers'll work out what's going on. Whatever it is. Maybe I'm the one with the wrong idea. Maybe everything's fine. Anyway, the Propheseers'll see to it, one way or the other.

Whenever she thought that, though, Deeba could not help remembering all the confusion about the Shwazzy and the prophecies. She couldn't forget quite how wrong the end of the stick was that the Propheseers had got hold of there.

Still, she thought, *they'll have learnt their lesson. They'll be keeping more of an eye out.*

UnLondon would have to look after itself. She wasn't the Shwazzy. She was just someone. How could just someone be any help, whatever was going on?

It'll be fine, Deeba thought. *You saw how Brokkenbroll and Jones and the binja got on.*

But she was never a hundred percent convinced.

Besides . . . she found herself starting to think. She got ashamed of herself then. Because the thought that had been creeping out was *Besides, even if something terrible does happen, you don't need to know about it.*

* * *

"Zanna," Deeba said. "I need to ask you something.

"What if you knew something bad was going on somewhere, but the people there didn't know, and they thought something good was happening, but you knew it wasn't, and you didn't know for a hundred percent certain but you did know really, and you didn't know how to get a message to them, and you never hear from them so you wouldn't know if they were able to do anything if you *did* get a message to them . . ."

Deeba faltered and came to a stop. It had all seemed clearer in her head.

"Deebs," Zanna said. "I've got no idea what you're on about."

She walked away, glancing back at Deeba with confusion. And, Deeba realized, fear.

That was when she decided. Even though things were alright now for her and her friends, she couldn't ignore the fact that something might be very *not-alright* in UnLondon. She had to try to get word to the abcity. She could only imagine how hard that might be.

Deeba considered dropping messages in bottles down into the sewers. She wondered what she could write on an envelope that would ensure a letter's passage across the Odd. But whatever she tried, she'd never know whether the message had got through, and she had to be sure.

When she came to that conclusion, Deeba was surprised to realize that what she felt wasn't foreboding so much as excitement. Despite the possibility that something was badly wrong in UnLondon, she was excited by what she'd found out, and by what it meant for her: she had to get back.

So the question became how to *return* to UnLondon.

Deeba told herself repeatedly that she didn't want to go, even if she could. She didn't convince herself.

After several attempts, Deeba found her way back to the basement deep in the estate. But this time when she turned the big valve, London didn't ebb away. So she went looking for other ways into the abcity.

Deeba walked over several bridges, always trying to concentrate on somewhere else at the other end—somewhere in UnLondon. It didn't work.

She looked for hidden doors. She closed her eyes and wished hard. She clicked her heels together. She pushed at the back of her parents' wardrobe. Nothing worked.

What's going on over there? she thought.

In despair, Deeba wrote to the only other person she could think of in contact with UnLondon: Minister Elizabeth Rawley at the House of Commons.

She realized the letter would have to go through many secretaries and assistants, so she camouflaged her message.

Dear Minister Rawley,

You do not need to know my name. I know that you have gone somewhere quite like London but in other ways quite UNlike it. I think you know what I mean and you can see I know what I am talking about. I am writing to you because it is maybe more easy for you to go to that place than me, and I think that maybe that place is in trouble. You might know there is a plan for a fight against someone who SMOKES a lot—you know who I am talking about— and I think the man who is supposed to help is maybe not who he says he is and is actually an enemy working for that enemy. You know the man I mean, the one who is UNSTABLE. [*Deeba was particularly proud of this pun.*]

If you can go to that place or send other people I think maybe you should have a look at him and make sure he is doing what he says he is, or our friends are in trouble.

Thank you.

A Friend.

At least I'm doing something, Deeba thought, but she knew the minister would probably never get the letter. So she kept trying to think of other ways back to UnLondon.

At night she would sit up in bed, wearing and reading the glove that Obaday Fing had made from the book. "Brick wizardry," she read. "Pigeons. Difficult to get in. Enter by booksteps, on storyladders . . ."

And one night, reading those words as she had many times before, Deeba suddenly stopped, and slowly clenched her word-gloved fist. Because out of the blue, finally, she had had an idea. And though she immediately, carefully—almost dutifully—went through all the reasons she shouldn't act on her thought, Deeba could not stop worrying about her friends in UnLondon, and she knew she'd try whatever she could.

37

An Intrepid Start

When she came to school the next day, Deeba's bag was packed. It contained sandwiches and chocolate and crisps and drink, a penknife, a notepad and pens, a stopwatch, a blanket, plasters and bandages, a sewing kit, a wad of out-of-date foreign money she'd gathered from the backs of drawers all over her house, and other bits and pieces that she thought might just be useful. On top of them all, Deeba had put her umbrella.

That morning, she'd hugged each of her family members for a long time, to their amused surprise. "I'll see you later," she'd said to her brother Hass. "I might be away for a while. But there's something I have to do."

She reminded herself several times that her plan might not work. That all her preparations might come to nothing. Still, her heart was going very fast most of the day. She thought it was excitement; then she thought it was fear. Then she realized it was both.

That morning she didn't talk to anyone. Becks was watching her suspiciously, and Zanna looked confused. Deeba ignored them.

At lunchtime she went to the school library.

*   *   *

There were a few other pupils in the room, doing homework, reading, working at the computers. Mr. Purdey the librarian glanced up at her, then went back to his paperwork. Apart from a few whispers, the room was quiet.

Deeba walked past the desks and the other children, and in among the bookshelves. She went to the farthest end of the room and stared at the shelves in front of her. She pulled on the glove made of paper and words.

The multicolored spines of hardback novels stared back. They were slightly battered, and coated in clear plastic. Deeba looked up. The shelves rose a meter or so above her, to the ceiling.

"Right," whispered Deeba. She checked the contents of her bag one more time. "Enter by booksteps," she said, reading her hand. "And storyladders."

No one was watching. She stepped up carefully and put a foot onto the edge of a shelf. Deeba reached up and took hold of another. Slowly, carefully, she began to climb the bookshelves like a ladder. One foot above the other, one hand above the other.

The books didn't leave much space for her fingers or toes. She felt the bookshelves wobble, but they didn't collapse. Deeba concentrated on reading the titles just in front of her fingertips.

She knew she must be close to the ceiling. She didn't slow, and she didn't look up. She stared straight ahead at the books, and climbed.

A little way up the spines looked less battered. Their colors more vivid. Their titles less familiar. Deeba tried to remember if she had ever heard of *The Wasp in the Wig*, or *A Courageous Egg*.

It took a moment for her to realize that she was still climbing. The library floor . . .

Interlude

The Booksteps

. . . looked farther down than it should be.

In front of her was a book called *A London Guide for the Blazing Worlders*. Deeba kept climbing. She was definitely beyond where the ceiling had been. Still she didn't look anywhere but straight in front of her.

She clung to the edges of the shelves and climbed for a long time. A wind began to buffet her. Deeba tore her gaze from a book called *A Bowl for Shadows* and at last looked down. She gave a little scream of shock.

Far, far below her she saw the library. Children walked between the shelves like specks. The bookshelf she was ascending rose like a cliff edge, all the way down, and as far to either side as she could see.

Vertigo made Deeba nauseous. She had to force herself to keep going up.

* * *

She stopped to rest when her arms and legs were shaking. By this time, all she could see was an endless stretch of bookshelf. Behind her back was nothing but darkness.

Deeba tried to take a book off the shelf to take a look inside. She almost lost her grip. She heard herself shriek, and she clung to the storyladder while her heart slowed. She wondered if her friends below would hear a tiny tinny sound, and if she fell, whether she would keep tumbling until she landed back into the library.

Eventually she fished her umbrella out of her bag and climbed like a mountaineer, hooking a shelf high above with its curved handle, and hauling herself up.

Once there was a hard squawking and a noise from the void behind her. Something approached her on wings.

Without looking, Deeba grabbed a handful of books and flung them over her shoulder, rustling like rudimentary wings. There was a thud and an angry cawing. The avian noises receded. She did not hear the books land.

Though relieved, Deeba felt vaguely guilty about mistreating them.

She stopped being aware of time. She was only conscious of an endless succession of titles, and of wind growing stronger and louder, and of darkness around her. Deeba's fingers closed on leaves. She went through places where ivy had claimed the shelves and tangled roots into the books. She went through places where little animals scuttled out of her way.

I might be climbing the rest of my life, she thought, almost dreamily. *I wonder how far this bookcliff goes. I wonder if I should maybe start moving left. Or right. Or diagonally.*

It was growing slowly lighter. Deeba thought she heard a low noise of talking. With a sudden shock, she realized that there were no more shelves.

She had reached the top. She reached up and hauled herself . . .

PART **IV** Life during Wartime

38

Class-Marks All the Way Down

. . . over the top of the wall of books, and looked out over UnLondon.

Deeba clung exhausted. Below and all around her was the abcity. The loon shone down.

She was so tired and confused that for several moments she could not make much sense of what she saw. She hooked her umbrella carefully over bricks, and swung her leg over. Then she looked around.

Deeba swayed giddily. The wind pushed her hard.

She was straddling the rim of an enormous tower. It was a cylinder, at least a hundred feet in diameter, hollow and book-lined. Outside, bricks went down the height of countless floors past small clouds and flocking bats, to UnLondon's streets. Inside, it was ringed with the bookshelves she had climbed.

The vertical tunnel of books was dim, but lights floated at irregular intervals in the dark void below. It didn't seem to end. It wasn't a tower: it was the tip of a shaft of books that went deep into the earth.

At some point during her ascent, what had been a flat shelf-cliff must have curled around and joined up behind her back, so gradually she hadn't detected it. It had become a chimney poking from a vertical universe of bookshelves.

There was motion below her. There were people on the shelves.

They clung to the edges of the cases and moved across them in expert scuttles. They wore ropes and hooks and carried picks on which they sometimes hung. Dangling from straps they carried notebooks, pens, magnifying glasses, ink pads, and stamps.

The men and women took books from the shelves as they went, checked their details, leaning against their ropes, replaced them, pulled out little pads and made notes, sometimes carried the book with them to another place and reshelved it there.

"Hey!" Deeba heard. A woman was climbing towards her. Several men and women turned in their tethers and looked curiously.

"Can I help you?" the woman said. "I think there's been some mistake. How did you get past reception? These shelves aren't open-access."

"Sorry," said Deeba. "I don't know what you mean."

The woman moved like a spider just below her. She looked at Deeba over the top of her glasses.

"You're supposed to put in a request at the front desk, and one of us'll fetch whatever you're after," she said. "I'm going to have to ask you to go back." She pointed over at UnLondon.

"That's where I want to go," Deeba said, pulling off the glove and putting it in her bag. "But I came from inside."

"Wait . . . really?" the woman said excitedly. "You're a traveler? You came by storyladder? My goodness. It's been years since we've had an explorer. It's not an easy journey, after all. Still, you know what they say: 'All bookshelves lead to the Wordhoard Pit.' And here you are.

"I'm Margarita Staples." She bowed in her harness. "Extreme librarian. Bookaneer."

"Where did you come from?" Margarita said. "Lost Angeles? Baghdidn't?"

"I'm not from an abcity," Deeba said. "I climbed in from London."

"*London?*" The woman narrowed her eyes. "A young thing like you? You expect me to believe you climbed all that way? Straight up? Didn't have any trouble from wordcrows? None of the warrior booktribes of the Middle Shelves?"

"I dunno. Something had a go at me, but I got away. I climbed out of my library. And I came here."

"Oh my . . ." Margarita Staples stared at her. "You're telling the truth. Well. Well well.

"It's a good thing you didn't go left or right on your way here; you might have ended up almost anywhere. There are some terrible libraries, believe me, that you really don't want to emerge in. Not, I have to admit, that we're doing so well ourselves at the moment." She sighed.

"Why?" said Deeba. "What's happening?"

"We're in the middle of a war," Staples said. "Not just the library: the whole of UnLondon."

Due Diligence

From these heights, Deeba could see the UnLondon-I. The flickering of Wraithtown, the dark tiles of the Roofdom. She could see the glimmer of the river bisecting the city, the two enormous iron crocodile heads squatting on either side of it.

The night sky crawled with moving stars. A flying bus cut across the front of the loon.

"You see?" Margarita Staples pointed across UnLondon.

In the midst of the roofscape of mixed-up architecture, of huge tiger paws and apple cores and weirder things that served as houses alongside more conventional structures, was a darkness.

"Oh my gosh," Deeba said.

A clot of black enveloped a group of streets. It was hard to see, a shadow in the shadowy night.

As Deeba watched, tongues of substance unrolled from it and seemed to lick the buildings, leaving them smut-stained. It sent out cloud-tentacles like a dirty octopus.

Margarita pointed at another patch of roiling fumes, and another. UnLon-

don was dotted with clutches of malevolent smoke, where the abcity had fallen
to the Smog.

"My job was never boring," Staples said. "There's nuts-and-bolts stuff like
getting the tarpaulin over the shaft when it rains, and so on. Cataloging and
reshelving. The shelves are in a shocking state. And when you've got everything ever written or lost to keep track of, it's quite a job. And there's fetching
books.

"I used to really look forward to requests for books way down in the abyss.
We'd all rope up, follow our lines down for miles. The order falls apart a way
down but you learn to sniff out class-marks. Sometimes we'd be gone for weeks,
fetching volumes." She spoke with a faraway voice.

"There are risks. Hunters, animals, and accidents. Ropes that snap. Sometimes someone gets separated. Twenty years ago, I was in a group looking for a
book someone had requested. I remember, it was called *'Oh All Right Then':
Bartleby Returns*. We were led by Ptolemy Yes. He was the man taught me. Best
librarian there's ever been, some say.

"Anyway, after weeks of searching, we ran out of food and had to turn back.
No one likes it when we fail, so none of us were feeling great.

"We felt that much worse when we realized that we'd lost Ptolemy.

"Some people say he went off deliberately. That he couldn't bear not to
find the book. That he's out there still in the Wordhoard Abyss, living off shelf-
monkeys, looking. And that he'll be back one day, book in his hand."

Margarita shook herself.

"Sorry," she said. "I shouldn't go on. I'm just saying that I'm not scared of
a bit of danger. But I never thought I'd be working in a war zone. And it's going
to get worse. The Smog could attack anytime.

"We have to keep watch for attacks against the tower. That was never what
the job was supposed to be. We're hoping the winds this high'll put the smogglers off."

"What happened to the people who lived there?" Deeba said.

"In the Smog zones? Those that were inhabited, people had to get out.
Those that weren't fast enough . . . ?" Margarita shook her head. "No one can
go back now. You can't breathe there. They say there are things that creep out of
the Smog zones at night and set fires, or lie in wait and snatch people. Stink-
junkies . . . the dead returned . . . and smoglodytes—weird things, born out of
the chemicals."

"I dunno what's been going on," Deeba said. "But I know who's part of it. Benjamin Unstible."

"Oh yes," Staples said. "You're quite right."

"Really?" said Deeba. *They've worked out for themselves that they can't trust him*, she thought.

"Yes," Margarita Staples went on. "If it weren't for Dr. Unstible, we'd all be dead."

Ah, thought Deeba.

She was about to interrupt the bookaneer and explain why she thought she was wrong, but something stopped her. There was a fervor in Staples's voice.

"I haven't yet got my unbrella," she said. "The Unbrellissimo's distributing them as fast as he can, all of them vulcanized with Unstible's formula. I was saving up to pay. But Brokkenbroll won't even accept any money for them. Peter Nevereater . . ." She pointed across the bookpit at a colleague. "He's got one, and he was caught in a Smog attack.

"They're amazing! He told me. You don't even have to know how to defend yourself! They've been given their orders; they're all fully trained. Peter didn't even have to get under cover. The unbrella just danced in his hand and kept all the rain-bullets from touching him."

"I've seen it happen," said Deeba.

"It's an honor to help him," Margarita said. "Every day or two we get requests from Unstible, for more and more arcane volumes. Chemistry and sorcery. And chemico-sorcery. And sorcero-chemistry. Some pretty hard expeditions to find them, I can tell you. But worth it, for whatever he's learning.

"The Smog's been spreading badly. But if it weren't for the unbrellas it would've taken over the whole abcity by now. With Unstible's help, we're in with a chance."

It was obvious how much trust she put in Benjamin Unstible and his formula. Deeba thought quickly.

Her plan had been to announce to everyone who'd listen that Unstible wasn't what he seemed, but she realized that might not go down well. At best, Margarita would think she was mad. At worst, she might consider Deeba an enemy of UnLondon.

Deeba didn't want to end up in an UnLondon jail, or on the run. And besides, Margarita's certainty made her question her own conclusions. Wasn't it possible Deeba had got the wrong idea?

Maybe I should just go back, she thought, and shuddered to think of climbing all the way down again. She didn't even know if it would work. But more than that, uncertainty gnawed at her.

I can't say anything until I'm totally sure Unstible's lying, she thought. *I might be totally wrong. But if not . . . UnLondon is in real trouble.*

She cast her eyes over the abcity, wondering what to do. Nearby, the flickering outlines of Wraithtown caught her eye. She remembered something that Obaday Fing had told her about its inhabitants.

The roofs of Wraithtown weren't consistent. Their shapes shifted. From this distance they seemed to move like pale cold flames.

Deeba did not like the direction her own thoughts were going. She tried to work out some other way of finding out the information she needed. Unfortunately, she couldn't. She sighed. She had just thought herself into a dangerous expedition.

But I have to be totally certain, she thought. *So no one can think I'm mad.*

"Can you tell me how to get down?" she said. "Also . . . what do you know about Wraithtown, and the ghosts?"

40

Ghostwards

Two iron ladders stretched down the outside of the tower. They were rickety and rusted, but after her epic clamber up the cliff of books, they couldn't intimidate Deeba.

She waved thanks and good-bye to Margarita the bookaneer, and began to descend. Beside her was the other ladder, for readers coming up, to avoid the nightmare of bottlenecks.

After a minute or two, she heard the rattling of a typewriter. Beside the steps jutted a shelf of bricks, only slightly larger than the desk that sat on it. A suited man sat behind the desk, staring at Deeba.

"I don't have nothing to check out," she said.

"Wait . . . how did you get up here?" he said. "Did you sneak past?"

"No I didn't," Deeba said indignantly. She continued down. "Ask Margarita," she shouted up to him. "I come from inside."

"*Really?*" he said. "A visitor!" He leaned over the edge of his little work space and called down: "Welcome to UnLondon!"

Yes, it's really welcoming, Deeba thought sarcastically, thinking of the boroughs of bubbling Smog. *And now I have to go and beg a favor of a bunch of ghosts.*

But despite herself, Deeba could not pretend that she was not excited to have returned.

At last she touched down onto the pavements of the abcity. Streets meandered away in various directions, their bricks and mortar interrupted by moil technology and other oddities. Bits and pieces of feral rubbish moved skittishly from shadow to shadow.

"You don't scare me this time," Deeba said.

The sky was growing lighter, from the random direction in which the UnSun was going to rise. Deeba shouldered her bag and swung her umbrella. She looked up at the enormous pillar of the Wordhoard Pit, towering so high it looked as if it were falling.

Deeba got her bearings and set off in the direction of Wraithtown, considering what she had learnt about its inhabitants.

No one knew why certain of the dead came, as ghosts, to live in Wraithtown. The vast majority of those who died in UnLondon and in London went straight on to wherever it was they went. Of the few who did stick around, many stayed elsewhere, typically haunting the site of their death. A few others would roam.

The majority of the ghost population of the city and abcity, however, did settle in Wraithtown. Sometimes they stayed for years, before fading gradually and moving on, going wherever the dead go.

Wraithtown was an area of UnLondon but was also a suburb of the land of the dead, so far from the necropolis city center that it was hazily visible in the living world. Those dead who lived there must be those with some reason 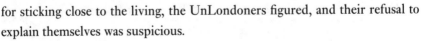 for sticking close to the living, the UnLondoners figured, and their refusal to explain themselves was suspicious.

It was very difficult to make sense of Wraithtown, as the dead were extremely uncommunicative. This led to thousands of rumors. Why else would the Wraithtown dead stay around, unless they were jealous of the bodies of the living?

Deeba was afraid. But it was in Wraithtown that she knew she could find out some vitally important information about Unstible. She tried to work out how she could get safely into its streets, learn what she needed to learn, and leave again without having her body stolen from her. She had a mile or two to decide.

"What am I going to do?" she said out loud.

As she walked quickly through the unlit alleys, Deeba had to admit she wasn't quite so sure as she had been that UnLondon didn't frighten her anymore. Margarita had warned her that the empty and emptish streets on the way to Wraithtown weren't safe. Deeba told herself that because it was almost dawn, and because she was impatient, it would make sense to set off straightaway. She wondered if she'd made a mistake.

She began to hum to herself, to keep her spirits up.

It can't be very far, she thought. She still hadn't worked out what she was going to do when she got to the Ghost Quarter. Deeba shivered in the damp, cold air.

From somewhere nearby came the smashing of glass.

She froze.

There was an awful scream, that might be a dog or a fox or possibly, just possibly even a person. Abruptly, it was cut off.

Deeba crept close to a nearby building, a moil house made of ancient record players. She listened.

There were no more cries. There was, though, another noise. A faint wet grinding. And something that was not quite padding, nor quite the noise of hooves. Something in-between.

Deeba crept forward. In those narrow streets and that close air, she could not tell where the sounds were coming from. They were moving.

Behind her, she saw a dark shape bobbing for a moment between roofs. Something was approaching, a street away, high over the pavement.

She edged slowly forward, and peeked around a corner.

Oh . . . she thought, her heart lurching. *Wrong turn.*

A few meters ahead, a huge animal loomed in the dark. It towered on legs like sinewy trees. From its muscular body jutted an enormous extended neck. It was poking its head into the remnants of a top-floor window.

Deeba heard the liquid-and-grinding noise again. The creature was chewing on the body of its prey.

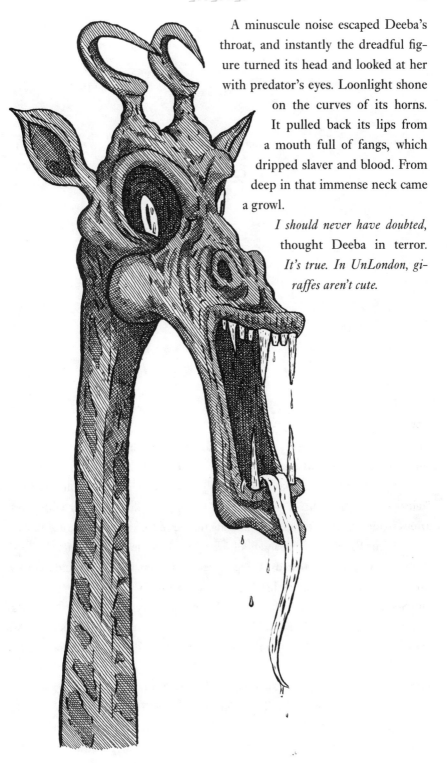

A minuscule noise escaped Deeba's throat, and instantly the dreadful figure turned its head and looked at her with predator's eyes. Loonlight shone on the curves of its horns. It pulled back its lips from a mouth full of fangs, which dripped slaver and blood. From deep in that immense neck came a growl.

I should never have doubted, thought Deeba in terror. *It's true. In UnLondon, giraffes aren't cute.*

41

Monsters of the Urban Savannah

Deeba ran.

From behind her came a snarl and a howl, and the drumming of those huge padded feet on the UnLondon pavement as the giraffe gave chase.

Deeba zigzagged, taking as many sharp turns as she could. She lurched left and right, breathing hard. She glimpsed the beast, galloping at her with enormous strides, flailing its head and hauling its chewed-on monkey like a gory flag.

With its banner waving, and emitting hyenalike shrieks through its clenched teeth, it was calling its friends, as Deeba realized when she tore around a corner to see another giraffe facing her. They were hunting as a pack.

She took off down an alley. Several more heads craned over nearby roofs, staring at her with ferocious yellow eyes. Deeba ran, and knew it was hopeless. The sound of giraffes came from all around. She turned and turned, looking for somewhere to go.

Behind her, she heard bestial noises of expectation.

The giraffes were close. They licked their teeth and horselike lips with tongues like cuts of meat.

There were six or seven coming at her. Deeba held her breath.

In their jostling to get to the front, two giraffes wedged next to each other in the tight alley, and were momentarily stuck. They bit at each other bad-temperedly.

Deeba turned and ran hard.

Bleeding from the wounds they had given each other, the enormous carnivores galloped after her again. Deeba accelerated. She turned to watch them approach.

Except that they weren't. Something changed in the air on her face, but Deeba was focusing on the giraffes.

One by one, a few meters in front of her, they stopped.

They shied, like racehorses who didn't want to jump a fence. They ducked their enormous necks, and trotted on the spot in frustration.

Deeba backed away.

"Why aren't you coming?" she whispered.

The giraffes circled and snarled, and leaned their necks towards Deeba, but they would not come any closer. They reared their massive bodies.

What are they scared of? she thought. It was only then that she realized where she was, and the answer was plain.

On all sides was the flickering of pale houses. From their windows, scores of phantom eyes watched her, their owners too dim or fading or moving too fast for Deeba to see clearly.

She was going to have to rethink her intention to wait outside Wraithtown and make a plan. Without realizing it, Deeba had just run into it. And the ghosts of UnLondon were watching.

Haunts and Houses

This had most definitely not been the plan. Deeba's delight at having escaped the giraffes changed instantly to a new anxiety.

And she couldn't run out, with the giraffes hovering, watching. She put up her umbrella, uselessly, and held it like a shield. Deeba began to turn on the spot.

"No one come close," she shouted. "I'm watching. First sign of anyone trying to possess me, I'll . . ."

I shouldn't really have started that sentence, she thought, because there was nothing she could finish it with.

Deeba walked cautiously farther into Wraithtown, turning as she went. It wasn't just the inhabitants of Wraithtown who were ghosts. It was also the buildings.

Each of the houses, halls, shops, factories, churches, and temples was a core of brick, wood, concrete, or whatever, surrounded by a wispy corona of earlier versions of itself. Every extension that had ever been built and knocked down, every smaller, squatter outline, every different design: all hung on to existence as specters. Their insubstantial, colorless forms shimmered in and out of sight. Every building was cocooned in its older, dead selves.

From all the ghost-windows, the ghosts of Wraithtown watched.

Deeba turned faster and faster as apparitions came onto the street to meet her.

In the light of the lowering loon, translucent figures emerged. They faded up out of nothing, men and women in costumes from throughout history. Some looked like Londoners, in antique wigs and old-fashioned coats. Some looked to Deeba more like UnLondoners, in their peculiar outfits. All were colorless, completely silent, and insubstantial. Deeba could see them through each other.

They wafted closer.

"You stay back!" Deeba said. "Don't come no closer! I know what you're trying to do! I just need one piece of information, and then I'm gone."

The Wraithtown ghosts circled her, and began to talk. She could see their mouths working, but there was not a sound. Deeba shook her head.

They grew agitated, and even looked as if they were shouting, but the only things she could hear were the sighs of the wind, and the far-off cries of dogs and foxes. One ghost sound-lessly stamped its foot in frustration. The loonlight glimmered through them.

"I need to see a list. I need to see *the list*," Deeba said. She mouthed the words slowly, as if she were talking to some-one who didn't speak good English. "One of you must be able to talk to me," she said. "Don't come any closer! I'll be gone in a second! I just need to see the list!"

Deeba stepped back from a nebulous figure dressed like Shakespeare, who had come close enough to touch.

"Stay away!" she shouted. "Don't any of you understand?"

"They all understand you," someone said. "You don't understand them."

She turned. Through the spectral layers of the crowd around her, leaning against a flickering ghost-house, she could just make out the boy Hemi.

"You!" she said.

He walked towards her, straight through the ghosts, one by one.

"Don't come too close," she said warningly. "Stay back! How long you been watching?"

" 'Don't come close'?" he said. "How rude *are* you? *You're* the one came here asking for *help.*" A nearby ghost looked down in surprise as Hemi stepped through his chest and stood before Deeba.

He wore a shabby old suit. His skin was as pale as she remembered, his eyes as shadowed, his voice as sarky. "Blimey, look who's back," he said.

"Just stay away," Deeba said. She backed up warily, raising her umbrella. "Why do you keep following me?"

Hemi made a rude noise.

"Follow you?" he barked. "Don't be soft."

"You were on the bus," Deeba said. "With that man." Hemi looked sheepish.

"Alright, yeah . . . I did sort of follow you on the bus. But just because your mate's . . . y'know, the *Shwazzy,*" he said. "I wanted to know about you, and anyway . . ." He stopped suddenly. "What do you mean, 'with that man'?" he demanded.

"And you followed us on the roofs. And you *stole* Zanna's travelcard!"

"Hold on! Alright, granted I was sort of behind you on the roofs, too, but how *dare* you call me a thief! I was looking *out* for you on the roofs, you dozy ingrate. Who do you think whistled up to the bridge when those junkies were coming? I *blatantly* never stole nothing! And what do you mean 'with that man'?"

"You tell me." Deeba's voice was guarded.

"I knew it! You're saying I was one of them grossbottlers." He put his hands on his hips and shook his head. "Outrageous. Blame the wisper, right? It was me who *stopped* that bloke!"

"Why . . . ?"

" 'Cause he was trying to hurt the Shwazzy! I mean . . . 'cause . . . y'know."

Deeba said nothing. She thought back to what had happened: the ghost-boy, or half-ghost-boy, emerging somehow from nowhere—sending the attacker neatly into Obaday's head. She'd never actually seen him touch Zanna on the roofs, either. "I . . . never realized," she said at last. Maybe Zanna had simply lost that card—it wasn't as if Deeba'd never done that. "Why didn't you *say* nothing?"

"Like *you* lot would've listened to the wisper." He raised an eyebrow. "You just said I was following you, and I don't even know where you came from! *You* came here! This lot called me as soon as they saw you," he said. "They know you're too deaf to hear them. Now put down your bleeding umbrella, tell us what you want, and bog off."

"Sorry," said Deeba. "But I know what you lot do. I don't want anyone taking my body. I just have to find something out—"

Hemi interrupted.

"You really do take the Michael don't you? Why'd any of us want your nasty body?"

Deeba was taken aback. In fact, many of the ghosts were shaking their fists at her angrily, mouthing what looked like swearwords.

"You barge in here," Hemi said, "spouting nonsense, and then you demand help?"

"I . . . I'm sorry," Deeba said. "I was told—"

"What next, you going to join in with the rest of them saying we're in league with the bleeding Smog?"

Deeba looked around the gathered ghosts. "You . . . don't want to possess people?"

"For Deadsey's sake, of *course* not!" said Hemi. "Look, you," he said to Deeba, jabbing his finger at her. "I'm not going to tell you *no one* from Wraithtown's ever nicked a body. Just like you can't tell me that no one from UnLondon's ever stolen clothes. But do you see me blaming you *all* for that? Do you?"

"So . . . why do you live next to living people if you don't want that?" Deeba eyed the ghosts.

"They don't *choose* to stick around!" Hemi said. "After we die, a few of us just wake up again. Sometimes for a few days, sometimes centuries. Isn't that right?"

A ghost by his side in an ancient dress nodded and rolled her eyes.

"And most of us end up here," Hemi said. "So what? At least we can talk to each other here. And then we get accused of everything! Next thing we know, there are gangs of UnLondoners snipping at us with exorscissors! D'you know how often some UnLondoner passes over and wakes up in Wraithtown? And then when they see what's going on, we have to hear all about how sorry they are, blah blah, they had the wrong idea about us, yak yak. Of course, by then it's too late."

There was a long silence. Of course, it might have been a hubbub of angry ghosts, but to Deeba, it was a long silence.

"Well . . . sorry," she said. "I was told wrong."

"Whatever." Hemi sniffed.

There was another silence. Deeba waited for Hemi to ask her what she was doing there. He didn't.

"Maybe . . . you could help me?" she said at last. Hemi eyed her.

"Me help you?"

"Please." She began to speak more urgently. "It's really important. I need to check something. Someone told me there was . . . Is there like an official list of all the dead?"

Hemi, and several ghosts, nodded.

"Yeah," he said nonchalantly. "In the records office. Wraithtown's a borough of Thanatopia—that's the city of the London and UnLondon dead. We can't move to the city center yet—don't know much about it—but we've got access to some of their offical files. The dead are way more organized than the living."

"Cool," said Deeba. "Listen . . . I really need to find out if someone's on that list."

Hemi struggled not to look interested, and failed.

"Why?"

"Because I was told he was dead. And that he died *before* I'd met him. But he's definitely not a ghost. So I want to know what's going on."

43

Flickering Streets

The giraffes bleated hungrily in the distance as Hemi led Deeba through the unstable streets of Wraithtown, past shops and offices clouded with their own remembered selves. Most of the spectral entourage dissipated. There were only a few flickers of ectoplasm as a curious dead or two flitted around Deeba.

"I cannot even believe," Deeba said again, "that you're taxing me for this."

"Um, excuse me!" Hemi said. "This ain't my business. And the way you've been talking about us, I think you're dead lucky I'm helping you at all."

" 'Help,' " Deeba muttered bitterly. "Half my cash . . ."

"Yeah." Hemi grinned. He fanned himself ostentatiously with the out-of-date currency he'd insisted Deeba pay him before he'd escort her. "Pleasure doing business."

"I am *out* of here the second we're done," Deeba muttered.

"Oh boo hoo," said Hemi. "No, please stay." They eyed each other.

"I know, I know," Hemi said occasionally to one or another wisp they passed. "It's alright, she's with me."

"We're not used to heartbeaters in Wraithtown," he told Deeba.

They passed phantasms of streetlights, in old styles, where illuminations had been and had gone. Little groups of ghosts gathered at street corners. They stood—or wafted, their legs disappearing—in costumes from throughout history.

"When you talk about them, you keep saying 'us,' " Deeba said. "But you're not like the rest." Hemi looked away. "Someone told me that you're half . . . How come I can hear you? Plus . . ." Deeba reached out and shoved him. "You're solid."

Hemi sighed.

"Mum was a Londoner like you," he said. "Born two hundred years ago, died a hundred and sixty-five years ago. Dad wasn't dead at all. He was an UnLondoner, came to Wraithtown out of curiosity.

"Mum tried to spook him. So she was all floaty sheets and *woooo!* and *wooaaah!* and so on. But he wasn't scared. The way they told it . . . he just fell for her, right then. And so one thing led to another."

"But *how*? If she wasn't even . . . solid . . ."

"Some ghosts can get physical. A bit. A few. She was one." There was a silence.

"Problem was," he said glumly, "his family didn't like it, and her friends thought she was sick. They managed to make everyone angry."

"You the only one?"

Hemi shrugged.

"I dunno," he said. "Never met any others."

"So you live here with your parents?"

"Mum went to Thanatopia when I was ten.

Dad said she tried to stay, but when that tide takes you . . . Dad disappeared a bit later." Hemi spoke briskly. "Some locals didn't like him living in Wraith-town. Maybe they scared him out. Or worse. Or maybe he did what he had to to be with Mum again."

"Sorry," Deeba muttered, shocked.

"Don't matter," he said, perhaps too brightly. "There are some great people here. Even if there are some dead who don't like me because I'm half-alive, that's not all of them. It's the living who *really* don't like me around, 'cause I'm half-ghost. I can look after myself. Full ghosts don't eat, but I do. Luckily my ghost half makes it easy to, ah, go shopping out there." He winked.

Before them was a building and its ghosts. It was a cement office, en-shrouded with the specters of a Victorian house, a tumbledown Georgian struc-ture, and a medieval-looking hovel. They shimmered around it and each other. Over its front door was a printed plastic sign, ghosted with an older hand-painted version, that read: WRAITHTOWN COUNCIL.

Hemi pulled the front doors open for Deeba, and the ghosts of all the ear-lier doors went with them. Deeba entered many layers of history.

44

Postmortem Bureaucracy

If it was confusing being in Wraithtown itself, surrounded by the ghosts of earlier forms, being in the building was overwhelming.

The corridor seemed to grow thicker and thinner as its ghosts eddied. The walls were lined with certificates and pictures, each surrounded by more in spectral form. Overlaying the lights were the ghosts of bare bulbs and of intricate chandeliers.

"I think I'm going to throw up," Deeba said.

"You're just ghostsick," said Hemi. "It'll settle down."

Behind a desk—and countless ghost-desks—on which was a computer, sheaves of paper, pens, and all their ghosts, sat a fat ghost in a tracksuit.

Can I help you? he mouthed, then looked up. He bolted to what would have been his feet, had his legs not terminated in wafts of nothing. He began to shout, silently.

Hemi shouted back.

"Don't you talk to me like that," he said. "Yes, she's living, and yes, I *am* 'that boy.' I don't care what you think, it's your job to give information. No she's not, she's a *Londoner,* you idiot." He rolled his eyes. "No, of course that's not a banishgun, that's an umbrella." Deeba was impressed with how fierce Hemi was.

"Now," he said. "Tell us what we need to know. Or I'll report you."

The fat ghost sat down sulkily. Deeba saw him eye Hemi and say something.

Hemi didn't react. What had the ghost said? She made the shapes with her own lips, to work it out.

She knew suddenly what he had called Hemi, and she stared at him with dislike. *Half-breed.*

"Alright, what do you need?" Hemi said.

"The record of all the deadists," Deeba said. "I need to check if someone's listed.

"The name is Benjamin Hue Unstible."

"What?" said Hemi. *What?* mouthed the ghost.

"What are you talking about?" Hemi said. "Unstible's not dead. He came out of hiding! He's doing his whole plan, he's sorting out UnLondon from the Smog, he's vulcanizing the unbrellas . . ."

"I know, I know," Deeba said. "I'm paying for this, aren't I? So just do me a favor and look. It's probably nothing."

"You are out of your mind," Hemi chuckled.

The ghost ostentatiously threw up his hands, and opened a filing cabinet by yanking its ghost-drawers, which drew the solid drawer at the center with them. He riffled through papers.

"Nope," said Hemi eventually, when the ghost shouted something. "No Unstibles in Wraithtown."

"Okay," said Deeba slowly. "Well . . . that's good." *Have I come all the way to UnLondon for nothing?* she thought. *The people in the RMetS must have made a mistake.*

"What about in Thanatopia itself?" she said. "Is there another file?"

"You heard her," said Hemi. "Double-check! Chop-chop!" The bureaucrat ghost looked sourly at him but, obviously deciding it was the easiest way of getting rid of them, rose and wafted to a back office, miming *wait* and mouthing something.

"He says new paperwork gets here from the Thanatopian office every couple of months," said Hemi.

"Couple of months?" said Deeba. "If I'm right, Unstible might have . . . moved to Thanatopia in the last few weeks."

Hemi sighed, then looked craftily around, and spoke quietly. "Well, it's your money. I suppose we could log into the database on the afternet if you really want. That'd be more recent. You know what red tape's like. This lot're still happier dealing in hard copy and its ghost. I bet they only use that thing for playing Minesweeper and bog all else." He nodded at the computer and its riffling halo of older computer ghosts. "Tell me if he's coming," he said, and grabbed the keyboard. Hemi found the officer's password on a ghostly piece of paper stuck to the side of the monitor.

"Does the afternet connect to . . . what was it they called it in UnLondon . . . the undernet?" Deeba said.

"Yeah. And both of them to your internet. But not many people can make the connections work. Ah, here we go."

Deeba saw the fat ghost closing drawers in the other room.

"Quick," she whispered.

"Alright," he said, "so if I just . . . click here, and feed in a few . . . there we go. We're in. Now." He looked at her sideways and shook his head as he typed. " 'Benjamin Hue Unstible,' " he said, and hit return.

The screen went blank, then whirred, then flashed up a single entry.

BENJAMIN HUE UNSTIBLE.

THANATOPIAN CITIZENSHIP GRANTED. *New immigrant.*

CAUSE OF IMMIGRATION: smoke inhalation/poisoning.

There was a very long silence.

"Oh. My. Gosh," said Hemi.

"I was *right*," Deeba said, and clenched her fists.

"Unstible died weeks ago," said Hemi. "Killed by . . . the Smog?"

"So . . . could it be his ghost, handing out unbrellas?" Deeba said. "It doesn't look anything like any of you lot . . ."

"No," said Hemi. "If he were a ghost he'd be listed as having moved to Wraithtown. Unstible's passed over completely. Whatever that thing is, whatever it looks like, whatever it's doing . . . it's not Benjamin Unstible."

45

Nasty Rain

Hey! the ghost mouthed, seeing them on the computer. It scattered the ghost-papers it held, and floated towards them shaking its fist.

"Print it!" said Deeba. Hemi stabbed at the buttons. "Quick!"

The chubby ghost reached for the paper as it emerged, but Hemi snatched it and gave it to Deeba. The ghost banged on the keyboard and the screen went blank. *What you doing?* he bellowed silently as Deeba and Hemi ran.

The paper was hard to read. The typeface was surrounded by whorls of ghost-print, a flickering of all the fonts once used on official forms. And the paper had obviously been recycled. Its previous forms—scribbled messages and newspaper pages—floated around it.

But through all the spectral interference, Unstible's name and the details of his "immigration to Thanatopia"—his death—could be made out.

"That proves it," said Hemi, pausing in the building's entrance. Deeba folded the printout carefully into her pack.

"I *told* you," she said.

"Alright, alright," said Hemi, shoving her towards the door as behind them a crowd of irate bureaucrat ghosts appeared.

*　*　*

When they emerged, the UnSun had dawned. Deeba stared at the strange, familiar shape.

"We got to tell Brokkenbroll," said Deeba urgently. "And the Propheseers."

"Whoa, whoa," said Hemi. He looked behind him nervously as they walked through Wraithtown. " 'We'? This is your thing. I'm sorry, but I did what you paid for. Good luck, I'm gone."

"Wait, what?" Deeba stopped and stared at him. "You *can't.* You're joking. *It isn't Unstible* who's doing things. Don't you see? Something's really wrong. I need to get to the Pons Absconditus. Can you help?"

"Its touchdown's nowhere near here," Hemi said. "You could get a bus but . . ." He seemed to sniff the air. "It's a Rogueday. I don't know how often they run on a Rogueday."

"Hold on," Deeba said. "Rogueday. You remember where I first met you?"

" 'Course," he said. "I was breakfast shopping." *Stealing,* Deeba thought. "In the market, just up the way."

"I've got a friend there who might help us."

"There's no *us,*" Hemi said. "I don't know *what's* going on, but I can*not* get involved."

"But . . . don't you care?" Deeba said. "It's UnLondon . . ." She stopped suddenly. She'd never seen him so agitated. She realized that it wasn't that he didn't care—it was that he was overwhelmed. And she remembered what had happened to him in the market.

She needed his help. Deeba almost despaired. One thing that stopped her was that though Hemi kept acting as if he was about to walk away, he didn't. She thought quickly. He obviously had to fend for himself.

"Look," she said, thinking carefully. She took out the rest of the money she'd brought. "This is all I have. It's yours, all of it, if you'll help me. I can't do this on my own." Her voice almost caught.

Hemi eyed the cash. He hesitated. He reached for it slowly.

"Nuh-uh," Deeba said, pulling her hand back. "Cash on delivery. Get me to the bridge—it's all yours. Or at least to the market—we'll work something out. Promise. Please."

"I'm not sure about this," Hemi muttered. "I'm *really* not sure about this."

They were at the edge of Wraithtown, peering across a stretch of concrete at the market, the traders and shoppers. A wall must have stood there years before, and they were huddled behind its ghost. Deeba squinted through misty spectral bricks, past the upside-down bathtub and concrete mixer and supermarket trolleys that were growing at the plaza's edges.

"It'll be fine," Deeba said.

"It will *not* be fine," Hemi said. "They hate me."

"Well, I guess now I'm here, you don't have to come *in*," Deeba said hesitantly.

"Whatever," Hemi said vaguely. "I might as well stick it a bit longer, earn the rest of the dosh."

"Okay," said Deeba without looking at him.

She held on to his hand and walked through the ghost of the wall. She felt a faint resistance, and then she was through.

"And I promise," Deeba added, "I won't let them chat any rubbish at you. And that includes Obaday."

Halfway to the market, Hemi stopped.

"Wait," he said. There was terrible urgency in his voice. He pointed up.

Light was leaving the sky. Racing across the pale circle of the UnSun came black cloud, like squirted ink. It was rushing up from the streets, spreading above the roofs, tugging itself through the air, approaching the market.

People had seen it. Some were standing their ground and looking up, scared but trying to be brave. Many were running. They scattered towards the surrounding houses.

"Quick, quick, quick," said Hemi. "We have to get under cover. It's the Smog."

"What about your unbrella?" he said as they ran.

"It's not an unbrella," Deeba said breathlessly, "it's an *um*brella . . ."

"Can it protect us? No? *What's the point of that?*"

Hemi looked around quickly, and ran to a manhole cover in the street.

"Help me!" he said, and he and Deeba began to pry it from the ground.

Hemi's hands moved fast. He tensed with effort, and for a moment she couldn't see what he did with his fingers.

"Got to get the lock," he muttered, then: "Yes!" Something clicked, and they hauled the cover from the street. "Get in, quickly."

He followed Deeba onto the ladder in the dank hole. Hemi hauled the covering back over them, wedged it with a stone, so they could peer through the crack.

Ankles in shoes scampered around them, as well as wheels and other odder limbs. The air was darkening.

There was a clattering. The metal lid began to ring like a cymbal. Pellets ricocheted.

Some way off, Deeba could just see a woman who had been issued an umbrella standing unafraid as the onslaught began. The umbrella leapt, pulling the woman's hand above her head, spun, blocking the Smog's attacks, sending its missiles flying.

Chunks of carbon were slamming into the pavement, centimeters from Deeba's face. The air was full of slugs of metal that hit hard enough to chip the pavement.

"It's too dangerous," said Hemi, and lowered the lid.

They clung in darkness. The noise was enormous. Below the hammering of the Smog's attack Deeba could hear shouts, and screams of pain. And underlying everything a noise that could be thunder, or could be an enormous growling voice.

"It's showing what it can do," Hemi whispered. "It's been attacking like this every few days. And it's had its addicts or its smombies start fires. It's declaring war."

The cacophony eventually eased, and stopped, and only the moans of injured could be heard. Slowly, Hemi pushed back the lid and they stepped out.

Throughout the market, injured people lay. A few were lying still, punctured and bleeding from where the Smog's missiles had hit them. The stalls were ripped and smoking.

All over the pavement and between the rows of tents the market was littered with remnants of the attack. Nuggets of metal and mineral from thumb- to fist-sized lay and smoldered. As Deeba watched, they slowly evaporated. They fizzed like dissolvable pills, and their matter boiled off in smoke that wafted away.

The sky was clear. The Smog had gone.

People emerged from dugouts and the cellars and the barricaded emptish buildings into which they had leapt. They examined the shredded awnings.

There were also the lucky few with unbrellas.

"This is going to work," said a woman. She twirled her broken unbrella, its spokes bent into an ugly claw, its upper surface boiling with smoke from the attacks it had deflected. "Did you see?"

Her companion was a man in an outfit of tied-together ribbons. "You're right," Deeba heard him say reverentially. He twirled his own unbrella. It was bent in its shaft. "Nothing could touch us. I wasn't even doing anything—were you? It's all Brokkenbroll. They're all obeying him."

Hemi knelt by a victim of the terrible mineral rain, a woman in a puffy dress interwoven with ivy. He looked up at Deeba and shook his head.

Some of the injured were being carried away, or tended to by various strange-looking doctors. There were a few others beyond help.

The market after the attack was a strange mixture of the exhilarated and the destroyed. Deeba and Hemi walked through the triumphant, the injured, and, here and there, the dead.

46

Old Friends

"Obaday!"

The needle-headed designer looked up in astonished delight.

"Deeba!"

Obaday was dressed in a natty suit of poems. He was sweeping up chunks of coal and iron into a big pile in front of his stall, which effervesced back into little threads of smog and drifted away even as he built it. He swept Deeba up in a hug. She laughed and hugged him back. "Deeba, what are you *doing* here?" He held her at arm's length and looked at her.

From the rear of Obaday's stall came an excited snuffling.

"Is that . . . ?" Deeba said, and Curdle came bouncing out from behind the curtain. The little milk carton rolled its cardboard body at them and leapt into Deeba's hands.

"Curdle!" she said. She tickled it and it squirmed. "What's it doing with you, Obaday?"

He looked sheepish.

"Well," he said. "After you left, the silly little thing was miserable. It was pining. Lectern was going to let it go back in the Backwall Maze, but I thought that maybe it would rather . . . live with someone who knew you and the Shwazzy . . . sort of thing."

"Oh right," she said and smiled. "You're keeping it for *its* sake. *You* don't care one way or the other."

"Alright, alright," he said. "Anyway. How on earth did you *get* here? Why did you come? It's a difficult time . . ."

His words petered out. He stared at Hemi.

Hemi stood tense and ready to run. If you didn't know, you wouldn't take him for part-ghost—but you'd know he wanted to be somewhere else. He looked at Obaday suspiciously.

"Obaday," Deeba said. "Think what you say."

"But Deeba," he hissed. "You don't know who that is. He's a—"

"I know exactly who that is. His name's Hemi, and he's a half-ghost. He's a pain in the arse, but he's also who got me here, and who helped me."

"But he'll try to—"

"Shut up, Obaday. No he won't. I mean it." Deeba spoke sternly. "He helped me. And we've got something really important to show you. Hemi's with me, and I don't want to hear anything about it."

Obaday thinned his lips.

"If you say so, Deeba," he said. "You are of the Shwazzy's party, after all. If you say so. Come and have a cup of tea. And . . ." There was a long pause. "And your guest, too."

They sat in the sumptuous fabric-lined back room, now shot through with hundreds of holes through which the UnSun shone. The stink of the Smog's missiles filled the air.

"You've chosen a pretty terrible time to come and visit us," Obaday said. "Did you see what happened?" Deeba nodded. "Well then. You see the war's hit . . . rather a complicated stage."

"That's what I'm here about," Deeba started to say, but Obaday continued.

"Thank God for the unbrellas, that's all I can say." He tapped the one at his belt. Its fabric was torn on one section of webbing. "That little split—that's what makes it an *un*brella—doesn't stop it protecting me. If it weren't for Unstible's formula—

and if it weren't for Brokkenbroll's orders, too—none of us could face the Smog. Shame so many of us still can't—there aren't enough unbrellas yet. I tell you, though, they have the Smog rattled."

"I think there's a reason the Smog's attacking more," Deeba said.

"Yes, Unstible was talking about it the other day. I read it on the walls. He explained that the Smog's getting worried. Because it can see we've got a new strategy."

"Yes," Deeba said. "But about that. About Unstible . . ."

"So really," Obaday continued, "it's actually a *good* sign that it's being more aggressive. It means we can be pleased with our progress. That's what Unstible said."

"Obaday, will you listen?" Deeba snapped. "I'm trying to tell you something. The reason the war's getting worse isn't 'cause the Smog's worried, but 'cause Unstible's *not on your side.*"

She showed him the piece of paper with its official Wraithtown stamp.

"What is this . . . ?" he said.

"Look. Unstible died. The Smog killed him. Whoever that is giving orders and making up potions, it's *not Unstible.*"

"This . . . this doesn't mean anything," Fing said uncertainly. "It might not be real."

"Obaday," Deeba said. "Don't be stupid. Look at it." The paper flared with ghostliness as she spoke: around its edges a leaf even became visible, a momentary haunting by the wood that had been made into the paper. "Why d'you think I'm here? I sort of realized something weird was going on. Now I got proof, I need to show that lot at the bridge."

"Well . . ." Obaday glanced at Hemi. "I'm sure your friend here wouldn't do anything deliberately, but you can't trust the Wraiths. Some people even say they're in league with the Smog."

Hemi jumped to his feet. "I knew it," he said. "I *told* you, Deeba."

"I'm not saying you, and I'm not saying I believe it," said Obaday. "If Deeba says you're alright, then . . . you're probably alright. But maybe, I don't know, someone in the office wants to undermine Unstible, or something."

"I saw it in the database," said Deeba. "On the computer."

"Well . . ." Obaday turned the paper over and examined it. "I'm sure there's an explanation. Maybe this is *another* Unstible. What do you think's going on, then? It doesn't make any sense. Unstible's *helping.* He's obviously on our side."

Before Deeba could answer, there was a shout. "Obaday Fing!" one of his assistants yelled through the Smog-tattered cloth. "Quickly. Something's coming."

"What?" he said, leaping to his feet and swinging his unbrella. "Is the Smog back?"

"No. It's a bus."

The Other Abnaut

The bus came in low over the roofs, swinging in its harness below a balloon.

The market traders stopped their reconstruction and gawped. No bus was scheduled to stop at the market.

There was more than one balloon-tethered bus in UnLondon, but the symbol on its front was unmistakable. It was the Scrollscrawl. Leaning out from the platform, Deeba could see the tiny waving figure of Conductor Jones. She waved back excitedly.

"Ahoy," he shouted as the bus came to a stop a few meters above. He dropped the basket on the rope. "Deeba, I can't believe you're back, girl! You actually came back! I didn't think it could be true . . . Come up! There's someone here wants to speak to you."

A little crowd had gathered.

"Hi Jones!" Deeba shouted. "Who is it?"

Another man appeared on the platform at Jones's side. He was thin and fidgety, carrying a briefcase.

"Ah, Miss Resham?" he said nervously. She could only just hear him. "I'm from Minister Rawley's office. The minister was very intrigued by your letter."

"*What?*" she said. "She got it? How . . . how did you get here? And *how did you know it was from me?*"

"Who is that?" Hemi whispered to her.

"Well now." The man smiled briefly. "We, ah, have our ways. Reconstruct a letter's journey, check video footage, that sort of thing. We were able to work out that you must have sent it. We tried to contact you at home, Miss Resham, but we realized you must've come here. We're very keen to, um, speak to you, please, as soon as possible."

"What did I tell you?" Deeba said to Obaday. He was staring foolishly at the bus, his mouth open. "D'you think they'd have sent him all the way from London if there weren't something going on?"

"I . . . but . . ." Obaday could only stammer. "There must be a mistake . . ."

"Nuh-uh," Deeba said. "I think things are kicking off. Watch yourself. I think things aren't what you reckon. Hold on, Jones!" she shouted up. "I'm coming. Do you want to come?" she said to Hemi. "You don't have to."

"I said I'd get you to the bridge," he said carelessly. "Might as well do that."

"And I'm bringing a friend." Hemi raised an eyebrow. Curdle refused to leave her grasp. "Two friends," Deeba said.

The basket spun, but Deeba had lost any fear she might have had of heights. She leaned over and waved good-bye to a still slack-faced Obaday Fing. Curdle bounced in her hands and looked down, too.

Hemi clung to the sides of the basket. His eyes were firmly shut.

"You're half-*ghost*," said Deeba. "How can you be scared?"

"Just because half my family are unquiet dead," he hissed, "why should I like this sort of thing?"

He didn't open his eyes until the conductor pulled him into the bus.

"Hello Jones," said Deeba, and hugged him. "You're not going to start insulting Hemi, are you?"

"Your friend's got ghost in him." Jones eyed Hemi judiciously. "Not my business. He's my passenger now, and that means he's under my protection. Although that *does* mean, young man, no more climbing the outside of the bus, no more dropping through floors, no more leaving clothes in dirty piles. Are we clear?"

Hemi didn't look at him, but his pale face darkened, just slightly.

"Dunno what you mean, Conductor," he muttered.

"How come you came here?" she said. "I thought you didn't like going off your route."

"There's always exceptions. When Mr. Murgatroyd here came and explained the situation, we didn't hesitate. He needed some help to find you, said they'd had a message from you, back in the old city, and could someone help him track you down. Well, the Propheseers knew I wasn't going to pass up the chance to see you again, was I? I knew if I were you I'd head back here, where you've got friends. But I didn't really believe you'd be here!"

"I *had* to come," Deeba said.

"Miss Resham." The nervous man stepped forward, interrupting. He looked quite gray. He carefully did not get close to the edge of the platform. "I'm Murgatroyd, of the Ministry of the Environment. I'm Rawley's man." He shook her hand. He did not even look at Hemi.

"What do you do?" Deeba said. "For Rawley."

"The lurch . . ." he said, then stuttered. "Th-that is to say, I, ah . . . I *lurch*. Minister Rawley's brainchild. It's, ah, a kind of experimental Odd-crossing technique. I 'lurched' here. I'm trying to perfect it."

"I can't believe you found me," Deeba said. Murgatroyd inclined his head modestly.

"We have certain methods," he said.

"What's this about, Deeba?" Jones said. He kept an eye on the sky, in case the Smog returned. The bus rose and set off over the city. Deeba watched the fabric of the market, and the ghost-slates of Wraithtown lapping like froth.

"This is what I'm telling you," she said, and reached for the paper. "I found something . . ."

"Wait," Murgatroyd said quickly. "I'm not sure what evidence you have, but we can't put this into the public domain just yet."

"But Jones isn't just anyone."

"I must insist."

"It's alright, Deeba," Jones said. "I just want to get you where you're going. I don't know what's going on and, right now, I don't need to. I'll find out if the time comes."

"But why?" said Deeba quietly to Murgatroyd. "D'you think I'm wrong?"

"On the contrary, Miss Resham," he said quietly. "On the contrary, Minister Rawley's sure you're right.

"But things have gone pretty far already. We need to work out what we're going to do. We have to put together a strategy. So to do that, we're going to meet someone who knows . . . the person you've expressed concern about . . .

better than anyone. Who'll be in the best position to really know what's going on, to take a look at your evidence, and to decide what to do about it. Someone who's going to be even angrier than you at having been misled."

"Mortar?" said Deeba.

"Better than that."

Rosa took the bus between shadowed patches of abcity.

"So . . . I told you not to worry about your family panicking, didn't I?" Jones said.

"Yeah," she said cautiously, remembering their reactions on her return. "I'm still not hanging around, though. The Prophs can take me back again."

"Got all the way here just to pass on this information?" He shook his head. "I take my hat off, girl. You'll have to tell me how you got over. And you're probably sensible. That phlegm effect does have its costs. Doesn't matter to one like me, no intention of going back, but you . . ." His voice petered out.

Jones pointed out over smoke-stained landscape like a smudged map. "Look at that smogmire," he said. He handed Deeba his telescope. Peering through it into those boroughs where Smog filled the streets, she could see dim shapes moving like malevolent fish below the smoky surface. "All kinds of things mutating into life in there," he said.

"Where are we going?" Hemi said.

"Yeah, where *are* we going?" said Deeba. "There's the Pons Absconditus." She pointed. She wondered how come it was there, when its ends were also in several other places.

There was a pause before Murgatroyd answered.

"We're going . . . nowhere in particular," he said. "To a little interstice between several areas. Hidden. Careless talk costs lives. We can't risk this getting back to the Smog. And until we know exactly what you know, we can't risk it getting back to . . . the subject of your discussions, either."

"We're close," Jones said. "Time we got out of sight." He rang the bell, and the bus descended.

It wove between buildings, hissing as it let out its gas and the balloon went flaccid, until its wheels touched down and it drove earthbound. They were in a deserted part of the abcity. There was no one on the streets, and no lights in any windows.

"Where is everyone?" Hemi said. "Is this emptish? A stopover?"

"No, these are empt*y*," Jones said. "The Smog took over only a few streets away. It's not safe."

"So why we here?" Deeba said, alarmed.

"People don't come here now—that's sort of the point," Jones said.

"We mustn't be observed," said Murgatroyd. "So long as we're quick, this is perfect."

"No one would dare come here," Hemi said to Deeba. He pointed down an alley they passed. At its end was a wall of Smog. Deep in its wavering filaments, predatory shadows moved.

48

Spilling Certain Beans

The bus puttered to a halt beside a church made of ancient, broken personal stereos and speakers.

"Can you wait?" Murgatroyd said to Rosa and Conductor Jones. "I and . . . our contact, may need a lift to the bridge to speak to the Propheseers. And Miss Resham, of course."

"I really think they should come," Deeba started to say, but Murgatroyd ignored her. He beckoned Deeba and Hemi, who followed him into the dark streets by the side of the moil church.

Deeba looked back again doubtfully at Jones.

"Go on," he said gently as she went. "We'll see you in a bit."

Murgatroyd led Deeba and Hemi past an ancient-looking pile of rubbish bags and trash into a concrete cul-de-sac. The UnSun drew sharp shadow-lines across the little lot, and put its farthest corners into darkness.

There was silence for several seconds. In that quiet, Deeba could just hear a faint tireless whispering.

What is that? she mouthed at Hemi.

"It's the sound of the Smog," he murmured. They were hearing it coil and unfold, a few streets away.

A voice emerged from the shadows.

"I'm here."

Deeba and Hemi jumped. Deeba dropped her bag.

"Mr. Murgatroyd," the unseen speaker said. "I got your message. You told me to come alone: I'm here. You told me not to tell a soul. You specifically told me not to tell my *partner*. I don't like deceit, Mr. Murgatroyd, but I've given you the benefit of the doubt. Now, prove to me that I should have done."

Mr. Brokkenbroll stalked into view.

"Deeba Resham." He nodded to Deeba and Hemi. "Young man."

"The Unbrellissimo," Hemi muttered. "Wow."

Curdle scampered behind Deeba's feet and cowered as Brokkenbroll approached, his trench coat sweeping. Behind him came a billow of fabric and the *skritch* of thin metal as his entourage of broken umbrellas fidgeted in the shadow.

Brokkenbroll folded his arms. "I'm glad to see you again. Is everything alright? Is your friend, the Shwazzy . . . did it not work?"

"No, no, she's fine," Deeba said. "It worked brilliantly. Thanks so much. That's not why I'm here."

Brokkenbroll raised an eyebrow.

"I'm glad she's well," he said. "But I'm mystified. And as you can understand—a little *busy*. The fight we find ourselves in has been difficult. So forgive me if I keep this brief."

"You see, Deeba?" Mr. Murgatroyd said. "You understand why we're here. It's the Unbrellissimo who's being used by this . . . imposter . . . worse than any of us. We don't yet know why. But he has the right to know what's going on. And, more than any of us, he might be able to do something about it."

"Mr. Brokkenbroll," Deeba said. She took the sheet of Wraithtown paper from her bag, and held it out to him. "You should see this."

He fiddled with it for some seconds, squinting past the fluttering specter-fonts. As he made out what it said, Deeba saw his face grow hard under the brim of his hat.

"I'm sorry," she said. "I don't know what he's doing, and I don't know why. I don't know who he is. But the man who says he's Unstible, isn't. He can't be, see? Plus I don't know what it is he's giving your unbrellas. I was thinking . . . maybe it's like poison, slow-acting, and they're going to get sick or something? I mean I know it works at the moment, but you don't know what it'll do in a few weeks."

Brokkenbroll said nothing. Deeba grew nervous.

"I mean, it might even be that whatever he wants to do isn't even bad," she gabbled. "But, it's just . . . it probably isn't great, because, I mean, why'd he lie? I don't see why he'd tell everyone he's Unstible when . . . he . . . isn't . . ."

Her voice petered out. Still Brokkenbroll was silent. He read and reread the paper.

"So . . ." said Hemi. He and Deeba shared a glance.

"So," Deeba said. "What should we do? Because, I mean I haven't been here long, but it don't look to me like it's going that well. And if you can think of something to do . . ."

"Why did you come?" Brokkenbroll said at last. "*Why* would you make that journey?"

There was a long silence.

"I was worried," Deeba said. Her voice grew quieter and quieter. "I found out something was weird, and I couldn't . . . I just . . . I wanted to make sure UnLondon was okay."

"You did the right thing," Brokkenbroll said eventually. "I don't like being made a fool of."

"You can see why I called this meeting," Murgatroyd said. "Why the minister insisted on getting to the bottom of this."

"I need to know everything," the Unbrellissimo said urgently, leaning suddenly down towards Deeba and making her jump. "I need to know what you know, how you worked it out, how you got hold of this." He waved the printout, leaving a brief trail of spirit-paper.

"If we're going to turn the tables I have to know exactly where we stand. We may not have much time."

Deeba told him everything. How she had been curious, and researched the Armets, and found the RMetS, and talked to them. How her suspicions had grown with news of Unstible's death. How she had tried to talk herself out of them, had not been able to, had eventually crossed over, and at last found proof in Wraithtown.

Brokkenbroll and Murgatroyd listened avidly.

"But how did you cross over?" Murgatroyd interrupted at one point. "There can't be more than a handful of people in London who know how."

"I read it somewhere," Deeba said. "It was sort of a lucky guess."

"But *how?*"

"I found a way in a library." She didn't explain further.

When Deeba finished, Brokkenbroll and Murgatroyd both stood silent for some time.

"That's everything?" Murgatroyd said.

"Yeah."

"It's not too late," Brokkenbroll said. "But whoever this man is, he's going to realize soon that we're onto him."

"The liquid does seem to work," Murgatroyd said.

"Oh, it works. It does what it's supposed to. But as she says, perhaps it does something else as well. Obviously he has some other plan. We have to decide how to proceed. Deeba, Hemi . . ." Brokkenbroll knelt before them. "Who knows about this?"

They looked at each other.

"No one," she said. "Only us here. Oh, and I said something to Obaday Fing. But . . ." Deeba made a *hmph* noise. "I don't think he believed me."

"Just them?" Brokkenbroll said. "No one else?"

Deeba shook her head. The Unbrellissimo smiled slowly.

"Good," he said.

He loomed suddenly and threw back his arms and spread out like a bat-wing shadow. For a second it looked as if he himself were a broken umbrella, his arms and legs crooked metal, his overcoat taut as a canopy, and then he swooped down on Deeba and grabbed her so fast he took her breath away. He bundled her into his grip and she could not scream or speak or even breathe, and everything went dark.

PART V

The Interrogation

Trussed

Deeba woke to voices.

"... was that? Not too much?"

"No, it was very good. 'We don't have time to waste!' I liked that." She heard laughter.

It was Brokkenbroll and Murgatroyd. Cautiously, Deeba opened her eyes a crack, but saw nothing. For a moment she thought it was night: then she realized that she was wearing a blindfold. She shook herself experimentally. She could not move.

"Deeba!" It was Hemi, speaking right behind her.

"Hemi," she whispered. "Where are you? I think I'm tied up."

"You are," he said. "You're tied to *me*."

Now she could feel his spine against hers, his slight wriggles. They were tied back-to-back, sitting on the cold pavement.

"Murgatroyd grabbed me," Hemi whispered. "While the unbrella man grabbed you. I can't believe what you got me into!"

Deeba's heart was racing. For a moment she thought she was afraid. Then she realized that she was, not surprisingly, but that more than that, she was *furious.*

"They tricked me," she hissed, struggling hard and ineffectually. "Brokken-broll's *in* on it. They must've been trying to find out what we know. I'm such an *idiot.* Oh man. What are they going to do? Have you heard anything?"

"No. Just that they'll find out quickly—I don't know what they'll find out—and Murgatroyd said he was on a schedule, and that people were counting on him. Hush a minute, I'm trying to . . ."

Something tugged at Deeba's face. She stifled a scream, then wrinkled her nose at a sudden smell of off milk.

"Curdle?" she said. Curdle clamped her blindfold in its opening and tugged, pulling it down and uncovering her eyes. "Good carton," she whispered. It shook enthusiastically and rolled onto her lap.

Brokkenbroll and Murgatroyd were talking, by the wall. They were lit by the dancing orange of a fire that Deeba could hear behind her. She thought she heard another sound, too. Very faintly, the padding of footsteps. They circled a little way away.

"Can you hear that?" she whispered. "Who's by the fire?"

"I can't see squat," muttered Hemi. "I'm blindfolded."

Curdle gnawed at the ropes fastened around them, but its cardboard flaps made no impact at all.

"We got to get out of here," Deeba said. "We got to warn the Propheseers. We got to warn everyone. Whatever that fake Unstible's doing, this lot are in on it."

"Hello," said a voice. Brokkenbroll and Murga-troyd had seen her, and were walking over. Cur-dle froze, lay hidden between Deeba and Hemi.

"How did you get your blindfold off?" Brokkenbroll continued. "You're awake. That's excellent. There are some things we need to ask you."

"Who have you told?"

"I already said," Deeba said. "No one."

"Maybe I should go back to the market," Murgatroyd said. "Have a word with that tailor."

"Not a bad thought," Brokkenbroll said.

"Leave him alone!" said Deeba. "I already told you, he didn't believe me."

"Well, we'll see, won't we?" Brokkenbroll said.  "You see, the thing is, in not very long at all, it won't make any difference. The unbrellas are still coming through every day, and those fools are lining up like baby birds to take them from me. Within a few weeks, everyone'll have one, and by then whatever you know or think you know and what-ever anyone believes or doesn't won't make an iota of difference. But I dislike being preempted. As do my associates. So we're keen to make sure that nothing complicates matters."

Deeba stared at Brokkenbroll furiously and resolved not to say a word to him. He raised an eyebrow.

"Well," he said. "That particular expression you're wearing is almost alarming. I'd be intimidated. If I weren't, you know, *incomparably more powerful than you.*"

He snarled the last words, suddenly lunging at her. Deeba could not help but jump, which enraged her even more.

"It's so foolish," Brokkenbroll said. "This whole thing was unnecessary. I did you so many favors!" He sounded seriously aggrieved.

"It was me who convinced my associate that it would be in our interests to let your friend, the bloody Shwazzy, go. *I* persuaded it to leave her. Went to some trouble to put on that little performance for you. Did you both a favor! At some effort, I might add. Made sure that little smoggler took all her memories with it, when it left, so there'd be no need for her—or you—to worry about Un-London anymore. We took her completely out of the picture. I really don't see the point in doing away with people if you don't have to.

"Besides, as I said to my partner—who believe me took some convincing, and who expended quite some effort on checking that everything was safe—everyone should have benefited. You got your friend back, uninterested in dangerous top-ics anymore. Your friend got to live. You get to feel good about having helped save her—so don't say I didn't give you anything. And *I* got to impress the idiots around me with my powers over the nasty smoke, so they put their trust in me. Which in turn benefits my partner. You were supposed to be out of the picture, and perfectly happy. You never, ever would have had to bother us, or we you.

"Now *why*, after I go to all that trouble to sort all that out for everyone, did you have to ignore it all and come back? You had *absolutely no need*."

There was a silence. Deeba stared at him pugnaciously until he sighed and looked away.

"He's sort of got a point," Hemi whispered. "Why did you come back?"

"Shut up," said Deeba. "Listen."

"We should get a move on," Murgatroyd said to Brokkenbroll. "I've got to get back, report to my superiors. Rawley was pretty worried by her letter, you can imagine. She wants reassuring that everything's in hand. Thanks for telling us who she was. I had to spin her some nonsense about tracking her movements from the post office." The two men laughed.

"How is it all up there?" Brokkenbroll said.

Murgatroyd shrugged modestly.

"It seems to be working well," he said. "Our LURCH program is proceeding excellently. It was hard building those trans-odd chimneys that send the fumes directly through to here, but worth the effort. My boss is getting lots of kudos for cutting down on pollution up our end." They both laughed. "Some people are beginning to wonder if all this might mean *Prime Minister* Rawley one day. She values her relationship with you and your partner immensely."

"Yes, I'm sure we'll do more work together."

"I know it's not so easy for it to make its way over . . ."

"Oh, it does when it has to."

"Absolutely. Now, I do have to report back that we've got the girl. She could have thrown a real spanner in things here."

"I'm sure we've sorted it all out, but just in case, we'll know everything she knows in a minute," Brokkenbroll said. "We'll know exactly who they've told. Did you hear that?" he said to Deeba, his voice chillingly gentle. "Lie all you want."

"I'm not lying!" Deeba shouted.

"It won't make any difference," he said. "We'll know the truth in . . ." He peered behind her. "In just a minute."

Murgatroyd was looking too, his face wrinkled with severe distaste.

"I'd rather not stay around for this," he said. "I'll go and wait by the elevator, so I can get straight back as soon as we've heard."

"Very well," Brokkenbroll said. "I'll take you back. It's been very handy, installing that elevator in the lab. Not easy, I know, and very appreciated. Meanwhile, we'll let things here . . . get on." He raised his voice and spoke to the something or someone behind Deeba. "Come along when you're done and tell us how it went. Good-bye, Miss Resham. I hope for your sake you impart whatever information you have swiftly."

"You pig," Deeba spat.

"Lanky dweeb!" shouted Hemi.

"You won't get away with this," Deeba said. The Unbrellissimo tipped back his hat and looked quizzical.

"Of course I will," he said. "Who's going to stop me? The *Shwazzy herself* couldn't. So much for the prophecies. If *she* couldn't, what on earth do you think *you're* going to do?"

Brokkenbroll reached into Deeba's bag and pulled out her umbrella. He looked at its unbroken shape with extreme distaste.

"How I do *hate* to see an umbrella in this unfinished state," he said, and roughly ripped a slit in its canopy.

He dropped it. It didn't fall flat, but tottered unstably on its handle. It swayed, snapped upright, looked eyelessly around. Brokkenbroll clicked his fingers, and the newborn umbrella leapt to attention.

"Come with me, you," he said. "Let's get you treated. But first . . ."

He gripped Deeba's shoulders, and spun her and Hemi on their backsides, scraping them on the ground. Now Deeba was pointed at the fire. She could see exactly what was waiting for them.

The flames poured out of a brazier, a big oil drum packed with coal and noxious rubbish, gushing black smoke. Beside it was a pile of trash with a shovel jutting from it.

Standing over the glowing drum, breathing in the stench and filthy fumes with an expression of hunger and delight on his ghastly face, was the thing pretending to be Benjamin Unstible.

50

Malevolent Breather

Deeba's eyes widened. She cried out.

"What?" called Hemi. "What, what, what?"

"It's him, it's the thing," she said. "Unstible. It's here."

Behind her, Deeba heard a beating like wings as the flock of unbrellas took off from the empty streets, the murmurs of Brokkenbroll and Murgatroyd receding rapidly with them.

Unstible's face looked terrible in the glow. He seemed plumper than she remembered, and his skin was oily and seeping and graying and unhealthy. His eyes were wide and bloodshot. He leaned over the fire and, still staring at Deeba, took another long, luxurious snort.

"*Aaaaaaaaah,*" he sighed. He seemed to fill out. Deeba saw his skin ripple, and strain.

"*Hello again,*" he said. His voice was different from when she had heard him before. He was relaxed, now, and it was a slow grating wheeze.

"*Now it's just you . . . and me.*"

*   *   *

"Unstible" moved slowly around the fire, breathing deeply, keeping his eyes on Deeba. He rummaged in her bag.

"Have to know what you've seen," he said. *"Have to know who you've told. And why you came."*

"Who are you?" Deeba whispered.

A slow and ghastly smile came over "Unstible's" face.

"You know," he said. He wagged his finger at her. *"You're not fooled by this silly puppet."* He prodded himself in the chest. *"You know, don't you, little girl?"*

Deeba did know.

"Why?" she said. "Why are you all doing this?"

"Everyone's happy. The minister gets what she wants. Unbrella man what he wants. And me . . . why am I doing this? Because of her LURCH . . . because I'm hungry," he crooned.

The Unstible-thing brought out the word-glove from her bag, and looked at it quizzically. Then it threw it on the fire, and sighed happily as smoke wafted up.

"Old . . ." it said. *"Powerful . . . And this? From the boy-thing's pocket."* It held up the Shwazzy's travelcard. Deeba stared at it in astonishment. "Unstible" dropped it on the fire too, and crooned happily, sniffing its smoke. *"More Propheseer power!"*

"You *did* steal it!" she said furiously, and tried to bang Hemi's head with her own.

"I wanted to see if she was really the Shwazzy," he said through his teeth, and butted her back. "I was just going to have a look and put it back. Could we *possibly* discuss this *later?*"

Like a tide coming in, little lapping wavelets of dirty smoke were edging into view around the corner. The smoggler a few streets away was stretching. Within it, Deeba could see creeping figures. As the Smog came, so did a few of the smaller intrepid smoglodytes.

No two were the same shape. There were things like crosses between rats and fungus, or bodiless things like two monkey arms attached together, or milli-pedish creatures the size of Deeba's forearm, each of its legs ending in tiny hands.

The smoglodytes were graveworm-pale and colorless. All had either enormous dark eyes, all pupil, to see in the filthy half-light of the Smog, or no eyes at all. And all had some adaption for breathing the poisonous stew, like enormous nostrils, or many pairs of them, to suck what little oxygen there was out of the clouds. Deeba saw one thing like a cat-sized snail, watching her with a bouquet of retractable eyes. Below them its face was an organic gas mask.

"You surprise me," Unstible said. *"Why would you come back? Thought we could forget about you . . . and the other one. Where's* she?*"*

For a moment Deeba didn't understand. Then her eyes widened.

"Nowhere," she said. "She don't remember nothing."

"Was more worried about her," Unstible said. *"Wasn't expecting* you *at all. But Brokk persuaded me it would work, and when I came to fetch what she breathed, it did seem to be the end of it. But now . . ."* He smiled at Deeba and widened his mad-looking eyes. *"Seems it wasn't. Perhaps she'll remember. If* you *got back, I certainly better go back and take care of her. Can't have the* Shwazzy *coming back here."*

"She's not!" Deeba shouted. "Leave her alone! You took all the memories out with your smoke! She don't know nothing!"

"Safety first, safety first. Make sure. Seeing you here, I think I'd better sort her out. Just as soon as we've taken care of you."

"No . . . !" Deeba gasped in horror.

"Oh yes. Not easy to stretch all the way . . . but I can. And do. A few favors for a few Londonsiders, here and there. Best to make the effort with your friend, as soon as it's less . . . busy here. Soon as I have a moment. I'll be sure. Anyway the practice'll be good for me. There'll be other, bigger reasons to go back to London, soon, I think. Best get good at the journey.

"But that'll be nothing for you to worry about. Soon, everything'll *be nothing for you to worry about."*

The smoglodytes crawled, flopped, and scuttled into Unstible's company, cooing and slobbering with interest as the Smog grew closer.

"Now," the man-shaped thing said, and unfolded the Wraithtown printout that proved that Unstible—the real Unstible—had died. He sniffed it, licked it like a connoisseur. He folded it and tore it in half and half again, smiled, and dropped the pieces into the fire.

The paper combusted with a flare of phosphorescence, and a swirl of released spirits. The heat pushed one little piece in an updraft, wafted it over the edge and onto the ground.

The thing in Unstible's shape exhaled, then breathed in hard, and a stream of smoke gushed up from the fire and into him through his mouth, and into each nostril. He breathed in the paper's smoke.

"*Aaaaah,*" he exhaled, smacking his lips appreciatively. "*Never eaten ghost-paper before. Unstible's death certificate. Clever to get it. Clever girl. It's gone now, though.*" He waved his empty hands. "*Nothing to show.*"

He tipped a spadeful of rubbish into the fire, and sucked at the resulting burp of stink. He poked around in the garbage, looking for something, sighed ostentatiously. The smoglodytes whickered.

"*No books,*" he said. He looked at Deeba. "*I love books.*"

"They'll stop you," Deeba said, trying to sound brave. "We'll stop you. You won't win. They'll get rid of you just like we did before, in London."

There was a pause. Unstible stared. Then he screamed with laughter. He opened his mouth so wide its sides split a little, and wisps of smoke exhaled with each guffaw, and curled up out of the corners of his eyes till he dabbed them with a handkerchief.

"*Got rid? Ha. 'Rid.' Yes. Of course, there was no arrangement then. Oh no. Just like there's none now. Of course.*

"*But . . . you're wrong, Deeba Resham.*" He stalked closer, his whisper crawling into her skull. "*They will not win, here. They have already lost. I will rule. And everything will burn, and burn, and burn, and smoke.*

"*I will print blueprints for smokeless chimneys, and build modern factories with filters to keep the air pure, and then I will* burn *them in old old furnaces and I will drink the smoke and grow strong. I will go to the galleries and burn the pictures and have them in me. Because I like art, you see.*"

His face was inches from Deeba's, and she almost choked on the reek of burnt plastic. The smoglodytes jabbered.

"*And books,*" he whispered. "*Lovely lovely books, all burning. Fires of paper and print. I will breathe in histories and stories, learn it all in the smoke. I learn and learn all the books you burn. But soon I'll choose what goes up. No more breathing leftovers then. I'll burn them all.*

"*My partner wants to run things, and make you burn things for me, so I grow.*

"*In my UnLondon you will print books over a furnace, so I can breathe them while the ink's still wet. You will fire the libraries. Light the shelves of the Wordhoard Pit, and fire will take them all, and the bookcliff below, and spread out and take all the libraries in all the worlds. And I will wait at the top and breathe the smoke of them all, and I will know everything.*"

"It won't fit in your lungs," Deeba said desperately.

"*Not* this *I*," he said, prodding his chest carelessly. "*The* other *I* . . ." He breathed the word out, lengthily, until he wheezed smoke.

"*And there's no reason to stop there.*" It spoke almost as if to itself, now. "*All the books in the London libraries too. No act to stop me this time. No weapon, no truce, no deals, nothing. Not when I'm finished here, not with the strength I'll have . . . But I'm getting ahead of myself.*" Unstible smiled in a ghastly way.

"*Now,*" he said. "*Time to make sure. Time to find out what you know.*"

"So you're a torturer too?" Deeba said, and felt Hemi shake. She tried to keep her voice from trembling. "Going to hurt us till we talk? I already told you everything."

"*Torture?*" the Smog-Unstible said. "*Silly. Silly girl. I don't have to make you tell the truth. I know everything in all the smoke I breathe into me.*" He looked at the brazier, and back at Deeba. "*So to find out what's in your head?*

"*All I have to do is burn you.*"

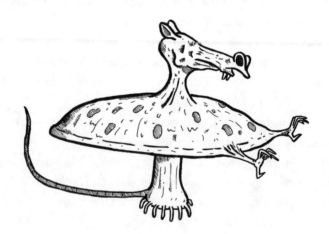

51

Out of the Fire

"Jones!" Deeba yelled. "Mortar! Obaday! Help!" The knots that held her were very tight. "Hemi, he's going to put us in the fire!" Hemi strained.

"Hush now," the man said. *"No one to hear."* He walked towards them, his arms outstretched. *"It won't take long,"* he whispered. *"It'll be over quickly. And then your memories live on as smoke in me."*

Deeba began to scream.

As the Unstible-thing leaned close, his eyes gaping wide, and Deeba's voice choked in her throat, Hemi moved. He strained against the ropes, and feeling the peculiar motion, Deeba realized what he was doing.

Not being pure-blood ghost, it was harder for Hemi than for his mother's side of the family, but with effort, he could pass through solid matter. That was what he was doing. The flesh of his arms was oozing through the sleeves of his jacket and the cords that held them.

The rope passed sluggishly through him. He was not transparent like his ghostly relatives, and the bonds disappeared completely within his skin, until they emerged reluctantly out the other side.

Unstible lunged. Hemi yanked off his blindfold and whacked Unstible in the face, grabbed his leg, and tugged. Unstible roared and fell, and the smoglodytes scattered in confusion. Hemi grunted and pulled himself free of his bonds—and of his clothes, which, not being ghost-clothes, had stayed where they were, like the clothes on the bus. Only his shoes and socks remained on him. Without him there, the ropes around Deeba went slack.

"Quick!" Hemi said.

So swollen it was hard for him to rise, Unstible bellowed and smoked. Hemi kicked him, dancing between smoglodytes as they snapped and grabbed for his nude pale legs. Curdle rolled aggressively among them, wheezing sourly as they snapped.

Deeba grabbed Hemi's clothes. She hesitated for one second, then picked up the tiny scrap of ghost-paper that had drifted out of the fire. It was unmarked, with only a very few ripped edges of spirits clinging to it.

Unstible grabbed Hemi's ankle. Hemi tugged his leg, and Unstible's fist closed through the skin and Hemi pulled himself free.

"Come on!" he shouted, and took Deeba's hand. Behind them, Deeba heard Unstible hauling himself up and growling, and kicking the smoglodytes, judging by the animal squeals. Deeba and Hemi ran.

They tore along the deserted streets of the empty quarter, through an alley where the streetlights coiled and lunged at them like enormous snakes.

"This way! This way!" Hemi said. Deeba called to Curdle, and the milk carton leapt into her hands.

Deeba could hear running, and she knew that Unstible and his smoglodytes were close. Hemi led her to a brick dead end.

"Hold on a second," he said. Deeba blinked as he shoved his head through the bricks, then brought it back.

"I thought so," he said. "Jones and the bus are just there." He held his hands cupped together in a step. The noise of their pursuers got closer. "Quick!"

Deeba struggled up and over with Hemi's help. She dropped the clothes and Curdle onto the pavement, dangled, and followed them. She could see the top of the bus nearby. A pair of shoes came sailing over towards her, trailing socks.

A hairy mass grew from the wall, then burst out. It was Hemi's head. He strained through the bricks as if shoving through jelly.

"Come on," he said, emerging with an audible slurp. "Give me my clothes! Go! Unstible's still coming."

"Jones!" Deeba called, realizing that to shout might tell Unstible where they were but too terrified to care. "Jones! Rosa! Quick! Go! Let's go!"

52

Skeptical Authorities

"I'm sorry, Deeba," said Jones. "I still just don't understand."

The bus was flying low and fast, heading half-hidden through the roofscape for the Pons Absconditus.

"Like I said," said Deeba. "Unstible's not Unstible, he's *Smog*. And the Unbrellissimo and the man from the MP's office are in on it."

"But why?" said Jones. "Why would Brokkenbroll be part of something like this? He's *helping*."

Hemi was pulling on his clothes, nodding vigorously at everything Deeba said.

"The Smog wants to burn everything," he said. "Murgatroyd's boss is putting smoke from London down *here*. Feeding it. And Brokkenbroll—"

"When you've all got unbrellas, Brokkenbroll runs things," Deeba said. "You have to obey him or he can just let the Smog kill you. They're partners. Brokkenbroll can't force you straight off, so he has to make you think he's on your side."

"Deeba . . ." Jones looked doubtful. "Why would he do that? I don't think he'd really do that, would he? Are you sure?"

"Unstible just tried to *burn* us!"

"Well I can't say anything about *him*," Jones said, "but Brokkenbroll—he seems to be fighting on the right side. Maybe he's been taken in by this imposter, too."

Deeba shook her head and stamped her foot in exasperation. She stared out of the back of the bus. There were birds, beasts, and clouds in the air, but nothing seemed to be following them.

"There's the bridge," she said. "Come on! I'll explain it all to the Propheseers, too."

Deeba, Hemi, and Jones descended by rope ladder, right into the office in the center of the Pons Absconditus. Deeba recognized many of the Propheseers' voices calling to her in astonished welcome.

"Deeba!" Lectern said delightedly, reaching up to pluck her from the ladder.

"We heard a rumor that you were back," said Mortar. "How wonderful. But . . . the Shwazzy's not here? No? Ah well, we thought there might have been . . . miscommunication." He tried to hide his disappointment. "And is this your friend? Hm. Well . . . hello. So . . . Jones and Murgatroyd found you? They've been looking—"

"Mortar!" she said. "Lectern! Where's the book? Everyone, listen. It's not Unstible. The man who says he's Unstible wants to burn everything. And Brokkenbroll's not on your side. The unbrellas . . . they're part of a plan, and he's got something up his sleeve . . ."

In her haste and anxiety, Deeba knew she wasn't making much sense. Hemi's garbled agreements and enthusiastic nodding weren't helping. She could see the Propheseers frowning in confusion. She stamped.

"I explained to Conductor Jones!" she said. "Hemi was there, he'll tell you."

"She's right," said Hemi. "It's a trick."

"The Unstible-thing wants to burn the libraries," Deeba said. "And build factories . . . and burn *me* . . ."

"You're saying the unbrellas don't work?" Lectern said, frowning.

"No, they *do*. But the Unbrellissimo's giving them out for a reason—"

"Let me clarify," Mortar said. "He's giving us a weapon against the Smog on behalf of the Smog?"

There was a long pause. Deeba and Hemi looked at each other.

"Well . . . yes . . ." Deeba said.

"I don't understand," Mortar said. "Unstible's dedicated his life to fighting for UnLondon, and now you're saying he's—"

"It's not Unstible," Deeba said.

"Who isn't Unstible?" Mortar said.

"Unstible."

In the silence that followed all the Propheseers stared at Deeba. She clenched her teeth in frustration.

"Where's the book?" she said. "Get it. I know it's not perfect, but it might have something written about this."

"The book, ah . . . might not be too much help," Lectern said. "It's not in the best mood recently . . ."

"Just get it!" Mortar inclined his head, and Lectern wrestled it out of a drawer.

"Why are you bothering me?" the book said morosely. "Is that . . . Deeba Resham? Why are you here?" Then it asked in sudden excitement, "Is the Shwazzy back?"

"No," said Deeba. "She don't know anything. She don't remember—"

"Well of *course,*" said the book, its voice sulky again.

"But listen!" Deeba said. "She's in *danger.* I been trying to tell you. Unstible's going *after* her, soon as it's sorted *me* out."

"Danger?" said the book. "Unstible? What are you talking about?"

"Just listen," Deeba said. "I want to know if you've got anything about a double cross . . ."

"What?" the book interrupted. "Are you making fun of me now?"

"No! I just—"

"Because we've already established I don't know anything."

"That's not true," Deeba said. "Not everything went how it was supposed to, but that doesn't mean there's nothing useful in you."

"I do beg your pardon," Lectern said. "It's been a bit snippy."

"Of *course* I'm snippy!" the book said. "I just found out I'm completely pointless! My prophecies are bags of nonsense!"

"This is UnLondon's seat of knowledge?" Hemi muttered. "Deadsey help us, what a farrago." Deeba almost stamped in frustration.

"We're wasting time!" she said. "Wait! Look!" She held up the little slip of ghost-paper. "This is the certificate from Wraithtown that says Unstible died." The Propheseers squinted at it.

"It's blank," one said.

"He burnt the rest," she said desperately, clenching her fists in frustration.

"Deeba," said Mortar in a kindly voice. "I've known Benjamin Hue Unstible for years. I'm sure you think you've found something, but it makes no sense. That's just a scrap of paper. The thing is, it's no surprise if you make a mistake. I mean, you're not the Shwazzy. You don't have any destiny here. Perhaps you got the wrong end of the stick."

Deeba gaped at him.

"Give me that." It was the book. Deeba looked at it in surprise. "The paper. We all know I don't know UnLondon like I thought I did, blah blah, but I do know paper."

Deeba held out her hands for the book. Lectern hesitated.

"Get on with it, it's fine," the book said testily. "Hand me over." Deeba took it, slipped the paper between its pages, and closed it. The book made a sound like chewing.

"Mmm . . ." it said. It sounded surprised. "Well . . . it's definitely genuine Wraithtown—"

"Wait!" A voice interrupted them. Everyone looked up.

Swooping down in a shadowy cloud of broken umbrellas, Mr. Brokkenbroll was dropping towards them out of the sky.

"Hold on!" he shouted as he careered for them. "There's been a terrible misunderstanding."

"Ah, Unbrellissimo," Mortar shouted up. "Perhaps you can clear things up."

"What?" Deeba said. "He's in on it! You have to stop him! How come he can get on the bridge?"

"Of course we showed him how," Mortar said. "He's an ally in the battle."

"Calm down, Deeba," said Lectern. "There's no need to worry."

"Actually, you know, I think we should hear her out," the book said, but the Propheseers weren't listening. Hemi edged towards Deeba.

"Unstible frightened the girl," Brokkenbroll said. He landed on the Pons in a swirl of steel and cloth, and walked briskly towards them. The umbrellas fluttered about him. "He's not used to dealing with children. He was trying to explain that she was in danger, and she misunderstood."

"That's not true!" Deeba said, backing away, clutching the book like a shield. Everyone on the bridge was staring at her.

"It's a lie," Hemi shouted.

"It's not her fault," Brokkenbroll said. "Unstible feels terrible about what happened. I had to come quickly to explain, because she's still in danger. The fact is, she *has* been tricked. By *him*." The Unbrellissimo pointed at Hemi.

There were expostulations all over the bridge.

"Oh *what?*" gasped Hemi. "Here we go." He backed away.

"I'm not sure about this," the book said, in Deeba's arms. "Something funny's going on."

"This is lies," Deeba said. "He's lying." But Deeba could see the Propheseers listening to the man they knew, blaming the ghost they had never trusted, for misleading her, the girl who was not the Shwazzy.

"Surely this can't be right . . ." said Jones, but he was drowned out.

"That ghost has been filling her head with nonsense, trying to drive a wedge between us, trying to stir up trouble, at a very delicate time in the war. The Smog's redoubled its attacks, and we really have to pull together. And he's misleading our honored guest in this disgraceful way, for his own nefarious purposes."

Brokkenbroll came threateningly on, his umbrellas bounding towards Deeba and Hemi on their points. The Propheseers looked accusingly at Hemi.

". . . disgraceful . . ." Deeba heard.

". . . comes causing trouble . . ."

". . . what's he planning?"

"I *told* you this was a bad idea," Hemi said, backing away.

"Are you crazy?" she wailed. "This is stupid! He's lying! He just knows you'll blame Hemi and not listen!"

"Give me back the book, Deeba, and come away from that boy," Lectern said.

"Deeba," said Brokkenbroll. "We can help you."

Deeba tried desperately to think of some way she could persuade them to listen, that Hemi wasn't the problem, that Brokkenbroll was lying. She looked into the Propheseers' faces and realized she could not.

"We'll sort out that little troublemaker," Mortar said.

* * *

Deeba turned, still clutching the book, and yelled at Hemi, "Run!"

"Where are you going?" shouted the book. "Stop! Let me go!"

But Deeba did not let it go. Pursued by frantic Propheseers, commanded unbrellas, and the trench-coated Mr. Brokkenbroll reaching out with long fingers like an unbrella's tines, Deeba and Curdle and Hemi the half-ghost ran.

53

A Hasty Leave-Taking

Deeba and her companions sped along the bridge that crossed from somewhere to somewhere else.

The Unbrellissimo and the Propheseers ran after them, shouting various things ranging from "Please wait!" to "Let's sort this out," to "Just you wait, ghost!"

"What are you doing?" the book screeched. "Put me down."

Deeba did not slow. She didn't have a plan: she just ran to get off the bridge as fast as she could, before Brokkenbroll reached her.

"Stop them!" she heard Mortar shout. "Before they get off!"

With a start, Deeba realized that the streets at the end of the bridge were unclear. They flickered between several configurations. She kept going.

"What's happening?" Hemi shouted.

"I dunno," said Deeba. "Just run!"

They were only a few feet from the end of the bridge, and the streets ahead were changing so fast they were a blur of architecture. The bridge was strobing between destinations.

"No!" shouted Mortar. "Stop it! There are too many!"

Deeba glanced over her shoulder. The general of the broken umbrellas was only a few paces behind, his unbrella hordes bearing down. He caught Deeba's eye. An unbrella lurched out and snagged her rear pocket, and with a little cry Deeba pulled free, ripping her trousers.

"Come on!" Deeba sped straight at the rush of images. "Together!" She tucked the book under her arm, grabbed Hemi's hand and held tight to Curdle. Hemi cried out, the book wailed, and they leapt off the end of the bridge—

PART **VI** Renegade Quester

54

Crossroads

—and tumbled onto tarmac in sudden silence.

Deeba rolled over frantically and threw up her hands. But nothing was coming. There was no bridge behind them.

They were lying in a wide road, in the late afternoon of UnLondon. They were quite alone.

"Oh now you've done it, now you've really done it," the book moaned.

"What happened?" Hemi shouted. "Where are we?"

"There were lots of Propheseers," the book sighed. "All trying to control the bridge. They each wanted to end it in a different part of UnLondon, where they thought it would be easier to catch you."

"The bridge got confused?" Deeba said.

"It was trying to go everywhere at once. It's only because you were all together that you ended up in the same place. It must have gone elsewhere instantly."

"Brokkenbroll . . ." said Hemi. "He was right behind us."

"By the time he got off the bridge it ended somewhere else," Deeba said. She stood up slowly and looked around her. "So where are we?"

They were at a crossroads. No landmarks were visible. They were surrounded by nondescript houses, without even any moil buildings or strangely shaped dwellings evident. If it weren't for the UnSun, it could be a scene from London.

"We could be anywhere," the book muttered.

"We've got to do something," said Deeba urgently. "I've got to get out of here."

"They think I did it," said Hemi. "The Prophs. They're going to be after me."

"They was just being stupid," said Deeba. "Brokkenbroll knew what to say to stop them listening for a moment. That's all he needed. *You* know, though, don't you?" she said to the book. "I could tell. You believe us."

There was a pause.

"I'm not sure," the book said. "I don't know what happened."

"It was that paper. You could tell, couldn't you? You know we're right."

"All I know is that paper's from Wraithtown," the book said. "That's all. I don't know anything about the rest of that stuff."

"Yeah, but," Deeba said, "I can tell. You believe me."

"I'm not saying that," the book said guardedly. "We need to get back to the Pons Absconditus and talk it over with Mortar."

"Maybe," said Deeba. "Maybe I shouldn't have run. I was panicking. It was the Propheseers got me home last time . . . But . . ." She looked around, stricken.

"But you can't go back now," Hemi said. "They think *we're* the ones who need stopping. Even if they don't know it . . . they're working with . . . that Unstible-thing. The one trying to get you." He and Deeba stared at each other.

"Book!" said Deeba desperately. "You *do* know, don't you? You *did* believe me."

"You had no right to take me," it replied. "This is booknapping!"

"Don't change the subject. Tell me straight. You know something funny's going on."

There was a pause.

"Some of what you say . . . would explain some things," the book said. "Maybe. At least . . . I think we need to do a bit more investigating. Something odd's going on. That's true. And Brokkenbroll's story doesn't make much sense. I don't see why you'd be attacking the rest of us, young man. Besides, I don't know how you could've got the wrong idea, Deeba, like Brokkenbroll said. You're not the type. Something funny's going on."

Deeba sighed with relief, and kissed its cover.

"Thank you," she said.

"Hey, I still don't think you should've run like that. Now we don't know where we are. And it just made you look guilty. We need to get back as fast as we can and talk to them."

"But you saw what was happening," Deeba said. "Mortar and that lot, they *love* Unstible. He used to be one of them. And with Brokkenbroll too, they're not going to believe us."

"So what do you propose we do?" the book said.

"I dunno," Deeba said in despair.

"Brokkenbroll's convincing everyone," Hemi said.

"Right," said Deeba. "So no one believes he's working with the Smog. Against UnLondon. And Hemi, you heard him, he's looking for me *and* he's going to go after Zanna! My friend! *Because I came back!* I have to get out of here, warn her. Maybe I can sneak back to the Pons. Book, you know how to direct the bridge, don't you . . . ?"

"*I* can't do it—" the book started to say, but Hemi interrupted.

"Wait. On the bridge you'll get caught straightaway, and like they said, they'll bring you to Brokkenbroll, and that means back to that . . . other thing. And they'll think they're *helping*."

"Alright then," she said. "I'll go back to the library and climb back down. There's got to be other ways in and out . . ."

"They'll be putting the word out right now," Hemi said. "They're looking for you. And *me.* Places like the Wordhoard Pit'll be guarded. And anyway, listen: how's it going to help being back in London?" Deeba stared at him. "No, seriously. Like you said, the Smog's coming after your friend—and you. If it comes at you there, how you going to fight it?"

"It got beat before . . ." Deeba said, but her words dried up. Whatever the circumstances of its apparent previous defeat—which the Unstible-thing had hinted might be more complicated than she thought—there was no "Klinner-act" in London with which she could fight it. The instrument of the Smog's banishment had been an act of Parliament, a weapon Deeba couldn't possibly wield. She'd be helpless.

Seeing her face, Hemi spoke quickly.

"Remember what it said? It still isn't easy for it to go up there. And it said it wants to . . . to sort you out first. It's going to be looking for you here."

"How's that supposed to make me feel better?" Deeba asked in a strangled voice.

"What I mean is, it isn't going to go after your friend. Not while you're here. Not till . . . But if you went back now, it'd follow and try to sort you both at once."

"But I *have* to go," Deeba whispered. "My family's waiting . . ."

In fact, the truth, she knew, was that because of the phlegm effect they were *not* waiting for her. And the truth was that was worse. It was that not-waiting that frightened her, made her so eager to get home.

That and the fact that a carnivorous intelligent cloud was only a few miles away, hunting her. But Hemi was right. Even if she *could* get back now, the Smog would still come for her—and for Zanna, too. And they'd have no defenses.

"If you go back," Hemi said, "it'll come for you."

Deeba could hardly breathe, thinking of it. She struggled to think the situation through. Panic welled up in her, but she fought it down. *Stop,* she thought. *You've got to be clever here. You've got to think hard.*

"Okay," she muttered. "It's all down to the Smog, and Brokkenbroll. I have to get out of here soon, but I can't while everyone's looking for me like I'm the trouble. And even if I *could,* it wouldn't be safe with the Smog after me, 'cause it's come for me and Zann. And I can't persuade the Propheseers to go against it: they think they already are. So . . ." There was a long silence. "We have to stop it ourselves."

"What are you talking about?" the book said. "Who's 'we'? What do you think you can do?"

"Leave her alone," said Hemi. "We're all in a mess here. She's smart, though." The area they were in was no longer deserted. Going about their business, a variety of figures had appeared. Many were carrying umbrellas. Deeba saw a robot made of glass, and a figure with a vegetable face, and men and women and other things in rags and elegant gowns, in tuxedos made of plastic and suits of armor made of china, and several in the strangely simple uniforms that London trades had copied.

Some of the UnLondoners were walking their way, and were looking at Deeba and Hemi with curiosity.

"Oh, I just want to get out of here and go home," Hemi moaned.

"Yeah but they're looking for you, too," Deeba said. "We're both being hunted."

"We have to be careful," Hemi said. "We don't know who's on what side. And now the Propheseers . . ."

"He's right," the book said. "They'll put out word. People will start looking for us."

"Shut up and listen," Deeba said. "*Something* has to stop the Smog, or I can't go, and I . . . we're the only ones that can." She waited, but neither Hemi nor, this time, the book raised any objections to her plural. "And there's nothing in London I could use against it. But there *must* be stuff here. That's why it didn't want Zanna here. So. Book, we know you got it wrong about the Shwazzy. That prophecy went wrong, right? But you still must have all the details of what it was she was *supposed* to do, right? To stop UnLondon's enemies, right?

"Okay then. The destiny didn't work with the Chosen One. So I'll do it instead."

55

Insulting Classification

"You'll what?" the book said after a flabbergasted silence.

"I'll do it," Deeba said. "Whatever it is that needs doing."

"Can we please talk about this privately?" said Hemi, ushering them into an alley.

"There's no choice," Deeba said to the book. "Why's it a bad idea? You might not be wrong about *what* needs doing. Just about *who*. I bet there's some choice stuff in you about what'll knock out the Smog."

"Well . . . Certainly there are references to a weapon that the Smog's afraid of, the implication that it might be for UnLondon what the Klinneract was for London . . ." The book sounded thoughtful.

"Not that there was a Klinneract," Deeba whispered.

"What?" whispered Hemi. "Don't tell it that; you can see how it hates being wrong."

"But you're forgetting two things," the book went on. "One, I have no idea what's right and what's not, anymore. Might be nothing in these stupid things—" Its pages riffled. "—is any use at all. And two, you're not the Shwazzy! You can't do this."

"How do you know?" Deeba said. "You don't know nothing about me. Except . . . wait a minute. You said I *was* mentioned, didn't you? You said there was something about me in there somewhere. So what does it say? What do you know?"

"It doesn't matter," the book said. "That's not important. Let's just—"

"Yes, it is important," Deeba interrupted. She yanked open the book's cover and started turning over pages.

It was the first time she'd seen what was inside. It was chaotic and confusing, different page to page, an extraordinary patchwork of columns, pictures, and writing, in all sizes and colors and countless scripts, including English. Deeba could hardly imagine how anyone would learn to make sense of it.

"Stop it!" the book said. "Get your hands off me!"

Deeba turned to the back and found a very long index. She scanned through all the entries, running her finger down the columns.

"You're tickling," the book said. "Stop." But Deeba kept reading.

The list of entries went straight from "Regal Garb" to "Restitution"—there was no "Resham." She flicked over some pages and looked for "Deeba," but the list went straight from "Decalcomania" to "Defcon Scale."

"There's nothing," she said.

"Good," the book said. "So close me and let's talk." But Deeba thought of one more thing.

She looked up "Shwazzy." There it was, with hundreds of pages listed. Underneath, slightly indented, was a long list of subheadings. Deeba skimmed the story of what Zanna had been supposed to do, chopped up out of sequence and laid out in alphabetically ordered episodes.

" 'Shwazzy . . . Bramble-Dogs Attack the,' " she murmured, reading entries out loud. " 'Enters the Bathysphere' . . . 'In the Court of Vegetables' . . . 'Laments and Tasks' . . ." Deeba stopped. Read and reread.

"What is it?" Hemi said, seeing her face.

" 'Sidekicks'?" Deeba said.

There it was, in the index. "Shwazzy, Sidekicks of the." Below that were sub-subheadings, each with a single page reference. "Clever One," she read. "Funny One."

"Look . . ." the book said. "It's just terminology. Sometimes these old prophecies are written in, you know, unfortunate ways . . ."

"Was it Kath who was supposed to be the clever one?" Deeba said. She thought about how she and Zanna had become friends. "So . . . I'm the funny one? I'm the *funny sidekick*?"

"But, but, but," the book said, flustered. "What about Digby? What about Ron and Robin? There's no shame in—"

Deeba dropped the book and walked away. It yelped as it hit the pavement.

"Deeba?" said Hemi eventually. "What d'you think we should do?"

She said nothing. She stood by the junction with the main road and watched the strange crowds of UnLondoners go by. After all the stress and fear of the Smog and the Propheseers and the running away, that little insult in the book's index was one thing too many for Deeba to bear. She shook her head.

"We can't just wait," Hemi said. "The Propheseers'll be looking for us. With Brokkenbroll. And if they catch us . . . You got me into this," he shouted at last. "Now what we going to *do*?"

She still refused to speak. Curdle whiffled and wound round and round her feet. Deeba didn't stroke it.

"Deeba." It was the book. Hemi carried it closer. "I want to apologize. I didn't write me. I've no idea who did. But we already know he or she was a moron." Deeba refused to smile. "They didn't know what they were on about. I'd probably be more use if I were a phone book. Even if my idiot authors didn't know it, *I* know you're not a sidekick—"

"No one is!" Deeba shouted. "That's no way to talk about anyone! To say they're just hangers-on to someone more *important*."

"I know," said the book. "You're right."

"Come on," Hemi said. "We're being hunted. Brokkenbroll might even persuade them to attack Wraithtown or something. We have to *do* something."

"Please," the book said.

Deeba watched them for a long moment.

"Alright then," she said at last. "I've told you what we have to do. I can't think of anything else. We can't go back to the bridge, book. UnLondon needs us, even if it don't know it. And Zanna does, and I do, and maybe London does, too. The Propheseers are working for the Smog now, even if *they* don't know it.

"The Smog'll expect us to hide. So it probably won't expect us to . . . to attack."

* * *

"Book," she said, raising her voice over the volume's objections. "Book, if you don't shut up I'll just leave you here. Answer some questions." Hemi stared at her with admiration.

Deeba began to flick through the book, referring to the index and checking various pages.

"How's this organized?" she said. "It's all over the place. There's no order."

"There is," the book said. "Just not a very obvious one. What is it you want to know?"

"Zanna the Shwazzy, in the end . . . she was meant to save UnLondon, right? How? What was she *supposed* to do? In what order? Because that obviously worried the Smog."

"Well . . ." the book said. "It was sort of a standard Chosen One deal. Seven tasks, and with each one she'd collect one of UnLondon's ancient treasures. Finally she'd get the most powerful weapon in all the abcity—as powerful as the Klinneract. The Smog's afraid of nothing but it. With it she was meant to face it and defeat it."

"I wouldn't get too excited about the Klinneract if I were you," Deeba said. "What was she supposed to collect?"

"The seven jewels of UnLondon," the book whispered. "What they call the Heptical Collection. A featherkey; a squidbeak clipper; a cup of bone tea; teethdice; an iron snail; the crown of the black-or-white king; and the most powerful weapon in the history of the abcity . . . the UnGun."

"The *UnGun*?" Hemi said. "Cor. I thought that was just a story."

"It's a story *too*," the book said grandly. "But it's also . . . the *Shwazzy's weapon*." There was a pause. "Well . . . I thought so, anyway," it added.

Deeba counted off the seven items.

"The Smog doesn't want us to get hold of them," she said. "So that's what we're going to do. Hemi . . . will you help?"

"Are you mad?" he said. "What *else* am I going to do? I've gone from being chased by the stall holders to being hunted by Brokkenbroll and the Prophebleedingseers. Can't run from *them* the rest of my life. This lunatic plan of yours is all we got. Besides," he added grudgingly. "Like I'm going to let you get the UnGun on your own."

"Thank you," she said. She smiled at him till he blushed.

"Well come on then," he snapped. "Let's get started."

"Curdle? You coming?" The carton jumped up and down. "Alright then," Deeba said. "*You* don't have any choice, I'm afraid, Book. You have to tell me what to do. And . . . one more thing." She swallowed.

"Look. No one's really said, but there's hints . . . if you stay too long in UnLondon, the phlegm effect gets stronger, doesn't it? When I came back, before, I saw the way people looked when they saw me. Book, be straight with me. If you stay too long, people can forget you. Right?" There was a silence. "Right?"

"Well . . ." said the book uncomfortably. "Theoretically . . ."

"How long?" Deeba said.

"You have to understand," the book said. "Most people who cross have no intention of going back, so it makes no odds. There are techniques to avoid it, they say, ways of making lists and mnemonics and so on, if you want to make sure to remember particular abnauts, but . . ."

"How long?" Deeba said. " 'Cause my mum and dad don't know any of those ways. So how long've I got?"

"Well . . . it's speculative. But there is a theoretical danger of acute abnaut-related memory deficit disorder affecting Londoners after about . . . nine days."

"Nine days?" said Deeba. "Is that all?"

"It might be possible to do the quest in that," the book said doubtfully. "It's not quite clear what happens after, but the Shwazzy must've been meant to go home afterwards. *Surely* . . . But then . . . she was . . ." *She was the* Shwazzy, Deeba thought as the book stopped itself. "Even so. It's . . . a little tight."

Deeba's heart was speeding up.

"Well then," she said. "We have to get started. What was the first one? Let's go and get the featherkey."

56

Incommunicado

"The featherkey's in a forest," the book said.

"A forest? In UnLondon?" said Deeba. "Where?"

"Where most things are in cities and abcities," the book said. "It's in a house."

"If you say so," Deeba said. "How do we get there?"

"I know where the house is," the book said. "But we don't even know where *we* are."

"Actually . . ." said Hemi. He was standing by the alley entrance. "Listen."

Deeba strained. She could make out a noise like a constant grinding, a sliding and slamming like very heavy machines.

"What is that?" she said.

"You know where we are?" Hemi said to the book. "It's Puzzleborough."

"Of course," the book said. "That would make sense."

"What?" Deeba said.

"It's like one of those games," Hemi said. "In crackers. A square with a picture in it chopped into nine or sixteen little squares, and one of them taken out, then they're all slid and mixed up, moving them one at a time into the empty space. And you have to try to make the picture again? In Puzzleborough, the houses are like that."

"A house was taken out, years ago," the book said. "And the rest of the buildings got moved around, and now there's a load of streets where none of the houses is in the place it should be.

"Every few minutes they all shift around. One of the ones next to the empty lot slides into it, and behind it another slots into the space it left, and it goes all through the borough. But there aren't nine or sixteen or twenty-five houses, there are hundreds. That means thousands of possible arrangements. You never know where any house is going to be. Everything's jumbled up.

"Maybe the only people in UnLondon as intrepid as the Wordhoard Pit librarians are the Puzzleborough postal workers. They're still trying to deliver the mail from decades ago. But the house numbers keep moving. Some of those posties have been tracking a particular house for years, now. Everyone's waiting for the day the houses land back in the right order."

"Anyway the *point is* . . ." Hemi interrupted with ostentatious yawning motions. "Point is we know where we are."

"So how do we get to this forest?" Deeba said.

"Well, if we were going direct," the book said, "we'd cut this way south, but that would take us through the Talklands of Mr. Speaker, and you never know with him, so instead we should go round—"

"Hold on," Deeba said, and clicked her fingers. "Mr. Speaker? I've heard of him. Doesn't he have working telephones?"

"I think so," said the book. "He's interested in everything to do with talking. But so what?"

"I can use it to buy some time. I can call home. Talk to my family," Deeba said. "To stop them forgetting."

Hemi looked at the book and then at her.

"It would be pretty risky," Hemi said.

"Why? Is this Mr. Speaker on the Smog's side?" she said.

"No," said the book. "But he's on no one's side."

"Don't tangle with Mr. Speaker," said Hemi.

"If we go through his yard it'll be quicker *and* I'll get to use his phone."

"It'll only be quicker if he doesn't . . . do something to you," said the book.

"You know," said Deeba, "for someone who doesn't want to be here and thinks we should go back to the bridge, you care a lot about this."

"I . . . I . . ." the book spluttered. Hemi tried to hide a smile.

"Come on, then," Deeba said. "We haven't got time to waste. You're not the ones who are going to get for*got* in a few days' time if you don't phone home. We're going to go straight through this Mr. Speaker's place, and I'm going to call my family on the way. You said yourself nine days wasn't very long. But if I communicate with them, the countdown starts again. And if we have any trouble, I'll just have to *amuse* him, won't I? After all, I'm the *funny sidekick*."

57

The Quiet Talklands

There were several maps of the abcity in the book, but Deeba couldn't make much sense of them. Their scale seemed to change from one section to the next, and the angles of their projections, and their orientations. Deeba simply followed the book's directions.

They hiked through the streets, avoiding crowds and the pedaled vehicles of UnLondon. They crept into empty and emptish buildings when suspicious balloons or helicopter-style things with blades like huge flat corkscrews flew overhead, in case they were Propheseer spy vehicles. Deeba eyed the unbrellas in the hands of many of the people they passed.

"No one knows who we are yet," Hemi said. "When the Propheseers get word out we'll be in more trouble."

When Deeba mentioned that she was hungry, Hemi disappeared and reappeared almost instantly with food from a street vendor.

"Figured we should stay out of sight," he said as they ate. "So that was half-ghost shopping."

As they walked, she told him about London—he didn't ask, but she wanted to talk about it. She told him about her family, and it made her miss them, but feel good too, even though it was a sad kind of good. She tried to learn more about his life in Wraithtown, and he grunted monosyllabic answers.

By late afternoon they reached the river, and crossed by the BatSee Bridge. Deeba was captivated by the sight of the utterly straight river Smeath running like a ruler through the abcity. She felt exposed on the bridge, under the big sky, but Deeba couldn't help stopping in the center for a moment and staring along the river, to where the two iron crocodile snouts formed Towering Bridge.

The enormous half-submerged heads stared at each other, blinking occasionally, each wearing a crown as tall as a tower, connected by a walkway at the top. As Deeba watched, the two huge mouths opened slowly, showing enormous riveted fangs, and closed again.

Hemi pulled Deeba on, past brown towers on the other side of the river. They were a little like London's Parliament if it had been made by giant termites.

"This is it," said the book as they stepped onto the north side of the river. "This is Mr. Speaker's Talklands."

"Why's it so quiet?" said Deeba.

The streets were not empty, but the few people they passed were walking quickly, and looking down. No one was speaking.

"Shhhh," the book said. It spoke in little bursts of whisper when no one was near. "Mr. Speaker. Laws. No unapproved talkage."

"No *way*."

"Shhh. Could get us arrested. He has . . . special servants. Could be anywhere. Shouldn't antagonize them. Keep shtum till we're at the phone."

"What then?" Deeba whispered. "How'm I supposed to keep shtum there?"

"Well, talk fast. It was your stupid idea."

It was eerie, walking in completely silent streets. Deeba found herself scuffing her feet just to make a sound.

"So where is the phone?" she whispered.

"No idea," said the book. "Let's get out of here."

"Shut up," Deeba hissed. "I'm making this call. So look in your index and find it."

It took them until almost the setting of the UnSun, but by a combination of trial, error, and deduction, under the book's complaining direction, they found their way into thickets of backstreets.

"He's built a maze around the telephone," the book said. "So people can't find it."

The streets emptied as they went on. They passed between terraces that loomed and leaned and became overhangs, until they walked in a tunnel between buildings.

The turns grew sharper, the streets shorter and more cramped. The alleys seemed to double back impossibly. Deeba and her companions passed dead ends, spirals, carefully confusing blind alleys.

"I think I've got a map," the book said. "Check around page three-sixty."

There was a plan of the maze, so extraordinarily complicated it looked like a human brain. Below it was printed: THE BLABYRINTH.

"I can't follow this," Deeba said, staring in the light of the streetlamps and the moving stars.

" 'Course you can," the book said. "You see the entrance? Put your finger on it. Now follow as I tell you. Don't press too hard on the page, you'll tickle. Are you ready?

"We've gone left, left, right, left, left, right, right, left, and right. Then left. Stop. Where your finger is is where we are."

"How can you remember that?" Hemi said.

"I'm a book," it said smugly. "We have good memories. Mark that place. *Gently.* Do you have a pencil? Now find a way from where we are to the center. When you've found one, move your finger along it."

It took Deeba and Hemi several minutes of false starts and retracing their trails, but eventually they traced a twisting route to the center of the maze. Deeba moved her finger slowly along it, and the book translated her fingertip journey, murmuring directions she and Hemi cautiously followed.

At last they turned into the cul-de-sac at the center of the Talklands maze. In front of them was a red phone box.

58

Touching Base

"Dad?"

"Deeba?"

The phone had accepted the coins in various currencies that Deeba had fed it. It wasn't a good line, and Deeba's voice and her father's were separated by long pauses, and heavily distorted, but they could hear each other.

Hemi, Curdle, and the book waited outside the phone box, looking into the rapidly encroaching night.

"Dad, can you hear me? I'm so glad to talk to you!"

"What are you up to, darling?" he said after another long pause. Even knowing about the phlegm effect, Deeba could not help being shocked by how calm he sounded. She had not been home for so long.

"I'm okay, Dad, I just wanted to say I'll see you soon. And to tell you I love you and . . . and don't forget about me."

As she spoke, Deeba was astonished to see through the glass a dense clot of wasps emerge from the phone outside the box and tear off into the night. They flew close together, extraordinarily fast, disappearing in an instant.

After a moment, they, or another group, zoomed back down out of the sky and into the phone again. They buzzed together, and through the receiver, Deeba heard her father's voice.

"Forget about you?" he laughed. "What are you talking about, mad girl?" She laughed back, a little hysterical with happiness.

"Get Mum, will you?" she said, and watched the insects zip off again to buzz her voice down the phone to her father. But only half of them came back, and when she heard her father's response, it was broken up and faint.

". . . can't . . . not . . . gone out . . ." he said.

"Say that again, Dad, I can't hear you." Deeba sent the wasps skywards. "Tell her I said hello! Tell her I called!" *Make her think about me,* Deeba thought. Hemi knocked on the phone box. Deeba didn't even look at him, just made an irritated motion.

Her father said something else in an even more fragmented voice, and Hemi knocked again. The book muttered her name.

"Will you shut up, you two?" she said with her hand over the receiver.

"Deeba," said the book. "Get out here now."

When Deeba turned, what she saw through the glass made her hang up in the middle of the static that was all she could hear. She stepped back outside to join her companions.

Dark figures were bearing down on them.

They moved furtively, and fast.

"What are they?" Deeba said. She saw a quickly scuttling thing moving like a crab, something dark red and simian, a stiff-legged man the size of her little brother. They and others came towards the travelers, with no sound.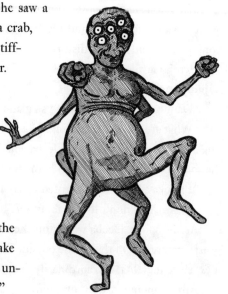

They approached with slow and threatening motions, in an amazing variety of shapes and colors and spikes and limbs. None of them had mouths.

"They're Mr. Speaker's court," the book whispered. "They're going to take us back to him. We've been done for un-authorized speaking in the Talklands."

"Maybe I can explain," Deeba said.

"Explain? You've done enough talking. Just keep your mouth shut from now on."

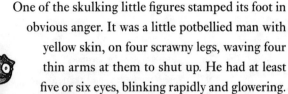

One of the skulking little figures stamped its foot in obvious anger. It was a little potbellied man with yellow skin, on four scrawny legs, waving four thin arms at them to shut up. He had at least five or six eyes, blinking rapidly and glowering. He made a *shhhh* motion, with his forefinger in front of where his mouth should be.

His companions grabbed Deeba and Hemi roughly by their arms. A big mouthless squirrel with wings and something like the cross of an armadillo and a centipede squabbled silently over the book, until the squirrel-thing bore it away.

"Careful!" Deeba heard the book say. "You'll scratch my cover!" She struggled but could not break free.

"Deeba," Hemi muttered. "D'you think you could have a plan that *doesn't* involve me being attacked?"

"Leave us alone," she shouted. Each word seemed to make her captors more angry. "I just wanted to talk to my mum and dad. I wasn't causing trouble. I have to go!"

But Deeba, Hemi, Curdle, and the book were swept away, out of the Blabyrinth and through the streets. For the first time since entering the borough Deeba heard noises. The night rang with extraordinary cries, single words spoken with an amazing, resounding voice.

"KETTLE!" she heard, and "MAGNANIMOUS! SEPTIC! GULLY!"

These and other words emanated from an enormous building shaped like a drum, towards which the silent figures dragged them.

59

Despotic Logorrhea

"So," the enormous voice said as Deeba and her companions were dragged inside. The sound of the words echoed everywhere. "Un-licensed speaking. That's a serious of-fense in the Talklands."

In the dead center of the huge hall, a man sat on a raised throne. At least, Deeba thought, *sort* of a man.

Under sumptuous robes, his limbs and body were twig-thin. His head was extended and misshapen, to accommodate his ab-solutely enormous mouth. It was al-most as big as the rest of his body. His huge jaw and teeth moved exaggerat-edly as he spoke with that astonish-ingly loud voice.

He wore a crown of inverted spikes,

each of which, Deeba realized, was a speaking trumpet that swung down in front of his mouth, to amplify him further.

"TERMINUS!" he said. "SPOOL! BRING THE CULPRITS CLOSER. GECKO!"

When he spoke, Deeba saw quick motion in front of Mr. Speaker's mouth.

"What was that?" Hemi whispered.

"QUIET!" Mr. Speaker shouted, and Deeba gasped to see something living slip from his mouth, scuttle like a millipede down his shirt, and disappear. "NO TALKING WITHOUT PERMISSION!"

With each word, another strange animal-thing seemed to coalesce and drop from behind his teeth. They were small, and each a completely different shape. They flew or crawled or slithered into the room, where, Deeba realized, hundreds of other creatures waited. Again, none had mouths.

"Sooooo," Mr. Speaker said slowly, watching her, a snail-thing popping out from between his lips. "YOU'RE JEALOUS OF MY UTTERLINGS?"

Five more animals emerged. One, when he said *jealous,* was a beautiful iridescent bat.

"SOLILOQUY!" Mr. Speaker said. His enormous lips stretched around sound that seemed to coagulate. The word thickened and tumbled out, taking on color and shape, rolling into his lap in a trembling ball.

It unfolded shyly and looked around. The word *soliloquy* was a long-necked sinuous quadruped. Mr. Speaker raised his eyebrow at it. The utterling scrambled off him, shook itself, reared on its hind legs, and grabbed hold of Hemi.

"Eeurgh . . ." Hemi said, then shut his mouth sharp as Mr. Speaker stared at him.

"UTTERLINGS," Mr. Speaker said. "MY WORDS MADE FLESH." More fleeting things left his mouth. "GUM!" he bellowed, and a slug-snake oozed out and around Deeba's ankles.

"Good thing they don't last forever," the book whispered. "Or he'd take over UnLondon."

"ARE YOU SPEAKING?" Utterlings tumbled from Mr. Speaker's maw. "I GAVE NO PERMISSION! QUIET! CARTOGRAPHY!"

The last word was a thing like a bowler hat with several spidery legs and a fox's tail. All through the hall, the utterlings trembled.

After a silence, Deeba raised her hand. Mr. Speaker sat back, obviously pleased that she had asked permission to speak. He nodded.

"Um . . . I'm sorry I didn't know the rules and that . . . but . . . we really need to get out and find something. It's really important. We're in a hurry."

"WHAT IS THE NATURE OF YOUR SEARCH?"

The utterlings *the* and *search* were tiny beakless birds. Deeba ignored them as they fluttered. Hemi nodded at her, and the book whispered, "Go on."

"Well," she said. "We're looking for something to fight the Smog. Please let us go. For UnLondon's sake."

"THE SMOG? WHAT DO I CARE ABOUT THE SMOG?" The two utterlings for the word *Smog* were similar little monkeys, but each had a different skin color and number of limbs. Deeba supposed it must be to do with Mr. Speaker's intonation.

"THE SMOG DOESN'T BOTHER ME, AND I WON'T BOTHER IT. WHAT DO I CARE IF IT RUNS UNLONDON? AWKWARD!" He spat out *awkward,* a two-headed chicken-bodied utterling. "YOU BROKE THE LAWS OF THE TALKLANDS. WHAT AM I GOING TO DO WITH YOU?"

Deeba thought quickly. The utterlings were strong. And even if she could break free, Mr. Speaker would just say more words and they would be overpowered.

"I could pay a fine," Deeba said. "I've got cash. (I know I said it was yours but I assume you're not going to kick up a fuss?)" She whispered the last sentence to Hemi out of the side of her mouth.

"Just get us out of here," he whispered back.

"NOW THAT," said Mr. Speaker, "IS AN INTERESTING IDEA."

"It's in my pocket," Deeba said. "I don't know how much, but—"

"NOT *MONEY.*" A humpbacked lizard undulated down Mr. Speaker's front. "YOU PAY ME IN DIFFERENT CURRENCY."

"What is it you want?"

"WORDS."

* * *

"What?" said Deeba.

"PAY IN WORDS. TELL ME NEW WORDS." Deeba winced to see Mr. Speaker's vast tongue lick his enormous lips. "GIVE ME GOOD PAYMENT, YOU CAN GO. PROMISE.

"AND NO INVENTING! A WORD'S NO GOOD IF YOU'RE THE ONLY ONE SAYING IT. I'LL KNOW IF YOU MAKE IT UP. SUCH!" *Such* was a football-sized mouthless beetle in blue.

"Well," Deeba said, thinking carefully. "I might be able to. 'Cause I'm not from here. So I know some words you might not've heard." She paused and thought about things she and her friends might say—or might once have said: she wasn't going to give up anything too good or new.

"I like your crown," she said. "It's a nice bit of bling."

Mr. Speaker gaped in absolute delight.

"BLING!" he said. A big silver-furred locust crawled out of his mouth. "I don't like the way you're talking to me, though. You're getting lairy."

"LAIRY!" Mr. Speaker crooned, emitting a baby-sized thing with one staring eye.

"Yeah. Don't diss me."

"DISS!" *Diss* was a six-legged brown bear cub. Mr. Speaker was almost crying with delight.

"So that's enough, brer," Deeba said. "Now you have to let us go."

"BRER!" Mr. Speaker said, and sighed as a big bumblebee with human hands flew drunkenly from his throat. "LOVELY! LOVELY!"

"There," said Deeba. "I'm sorry we spoke without permission. Now . . . would you let us go, please?"

"LET YOU GO?" said Mr. Speaker. "OH, I DON'T THINK SO. I HAVEN'T HEARD WORDS LIKE THAT IN MY LIFE. I CAN STILL TASTE THEM COMING OUT. LOOK AT THEM!"

It was true. The slang utterlings looked particularly healthy and energetic. Mr. Speaker stared at Deeba greedily.

"NO NO NO. NOT GIVING THAT UP. YOU'RE STAYING HERE. YOU GET TO TALK TO ME WITH THOSE LOVELY WORDS. TEACH ME ALL THE LANGUAGE YOU KNOW, FOREVER AND EVER."

60

Insurgent Verbiage

"No way!" Hemi said. "That's not on!"

"You promised!" the book said.

"I CAN DO WHATEVER I WANT," MR. Speaker said. "A PROMISE IS WORDS. I'M MR. SPEAKER! WORDS MEAN WHATEVER I WANT. WORDS DO WHAT I TELL THEM!"

His voice echoed in the enormous room, and the utterlings jumped up and down enthusiastically. Deeba looked around at the utterlings holding her, felt the strength of their grip. She thought quickly.

"I don't think that's true," she said.

Silence settled, and all the eyes in the room turned to Deeba.

"WHAT?" Mr. Speaker said.

"Well," said Deeba. "I don't think words do what *anyone* tells them all the time."

Hemi was looking at her with at least as much bewilderment on his face as Mr. Speaker had.

"What are you on about?" Hemi said.

"YES, WHAT *ARE* YOU ON ABOUT?"

Deeba paused to admire *about*, an utterling like a living spiderweb.

"Words don't always mean what we want them to," she said. "None of us. Not even you." The room was quiet. All the people and things in it were listening.

"Like . . . if someone shouts 'Hey you!' at someone in the street, but someone else turns around. The words misbehaved. They didn't call the person they were meant to. Or if you see someone at a party and they're wearing something mad, and you say 'That's some outfit!' and they think you're being rude, but you meant it really.

"Or like if someone says something's bad and people think they mean *bad* bad and they mean *good* bad. Or . . ." Deeba giggled, remembering one of the Blyton books her mother had given her, saying she had enjoyed it when she was Deeba's age. "Or like that old book with a girl's name that just sounds rude now."

The utterlings were twitching, and staring at her. Mr. Speaker was flinching. He looked sick.

"Or even," Deeba said, "like some words that mean something but they've got like a feeling of something else, so if you say them, you might be saying something you don't mean to. Like if I say someone's really *nice* then I might mean it, but it sounds a little bit like they're boring. You know?"

"Yeah," said Hemi. "*Yeah.*"

"The thing is," Deeba said, eyeing Mr. Speaker, "you could only make words do what you want if it was just you deciding what they mean. But it isn't. It's everyone else, too. Which means you might *want* to give them orders, but you aren't in total control. No one is."

"THIS IS OUTRAGEOUS NONSENSE!" Mr. Speaker spluttered, burping four confused creatures, but Deeba interrupted him.

"So, you might think all these words have to obey you. But they don't."

"NO MORE SPEAKING! UTTERLINGS, TAKE HER AWAY!"

The utterlings were staring at Deeba, absolutely still, their eyes enormous. None of them moved. Mr. Speaker's face went dark purple with rage.

"UTTERLINGS!" he shrieked.

"Even *your* words don't always do what you want," Deeba said. She wasn't looking at Mr. Speaker, though. She was looking at the utterlings, and she raised her eyebrows.

"TAKE HER *AWAY!*"

Some of the utterlings tightened their grips, but others were loosening them. Standing in a little group nearby, looking at Deeba uncertainly, were the silver locust, the many-legged bear, the bee, and the staring thing: the utterlings of London slang.

"I bet you could shut him up," Deeba said to them. "I bet you don't really have to do what he says."

Hesitantly, the four utterlings turned and looked at Mr. Speaker. They moved towards him.

For a moment it was only those four, but very quickly, others joined them. The four-legged four-armed little man who had captured Deeba was one of a crew bearing down on Mr. Speaker, who was so apoplectic with rage he wasn't even saying words—just screeching.

Other utterlings stood protectively before him, and the two groups began to struggle. But it didn't last long. The loyal utterlings were confused. The others, the rebellious words, started in a minority, but grew in numbers quickly. Deeba felt the hands gripping her let go one by one.

"STOP!" shouted Mr. Speaker, and spat out one last enormous utterling, a bewildered three-legged blob, but then the renegade words swarmed him. They clambered over Mr. Speaker's body, and he flailed his weak arms and legs, trying and failing to bat them away.

Something like a long saggy hat wrapped a tentacle around his mouth, and others held him down. Mr. Speaker squashed down in his throne, and struggled and *mmmmm*ed and tried to look fierce with only his eyes.

It was no good. His obedient utterlings had scattered. His words had revolted.

"What d'you reckon they'll do?" Hemi said.

"Dunno," Deeba said.

It was dawn. Awhile after the utterlings had subdued their speaker, they had ceremoniously ushered Deeba and her companions to sleeping quarters and given them supper, all with immense exaggerated bows. The travelers had slept, and woken refreshed, and Deeba was eager to get going.

They were escorted by a gaggle of the silently squabbling utterlings that were attempting to organize things. The utterlings showed them out with pomp and politeness.

"Might not last," the book muttered. "The smaller ones'll ebb and disappear before long. Mr. Speaker'll be trying to whisper new ones all the time, and he'll try to talk more loyal ones into existence. And there must be some who want to get back to obeying him, waiting for the right moment . . ."

"God, don't you ever stop moaning?" snapped Deeba. "Miserable git." She could see Mr. Speaker, still trapped and gagged in his chair. "Give them a chance."

The utterlings made *Where?* motions.

"Where *are* we going?" said Deeba, stroking Curdle.

"That way," Hemi said, pointing into the streets.

"We're looking for a forest," Deeba said. "We have to find something. Quickly. In fact . . ." She looked at the utterlings. They were small, but strong, and inquisitive. "In fact, do any of you want to come with us?"

"What?" said the book.

"Why not? The more the better."

The utterlings looked at her and at each other. After a few seconds, the majority, with ostentatious mimes of *Thanks* and *Regret for not being able to accompany you,* went back to the rest of their silently squabbling kind. But three came to stand with the travelers.

One was the silver-furred locust; one was the bear with a pair of legs too many; and one was the four-armed four-legged several-eyed little man. They looked at Deeba and Hemi shyly.

"That's brilliant!" said Deeba. "Cool. Let me see if I remember . . ." She pointed at the bear. "You're Diss," she said. It nodded and reared on its hind four legs. It had no mouth, but Deeba knew it was smiling.

"And you . . ." She pointed at the locust. "You're Bling." The arm-sized insect fluffed up its silver coat.

"I'm afraid I don't know what you are," she said to the many-limbed man. "You got spoke before I got here. What are you?" The man sketched shapes in the air.

Deeba shook her head. "What is it . . . ? Paraffin? Paintbrush? Purpose?"

The utterling shook its mouthless head.

"Redcurrant?" said Hemi. "Blackjack?" *No,* it mimed.

"Quiddity?" said the book. "Sesquipedalian? Oh this is ridiculous. We're never going to guess like this. Out of all the words in the whole language, how—"

"Cauldron," Deeba said, looking at the utterling with her head on one side.

It jumped up and down and nodded and threw up its four arms and spun in a jig.

Hemi stared at Deeba in openmouthed delight.

"How could you *possibly* tell?" the book said.

"I dunno." Deeba shrugged airily. "Doesn't it look like the word *cauldron* to you?"

They set off under the early light of the UnSun, leaving the utterlings to bicker and bargain with each other and chaotically start to make decisions. Deeba, Hemi, Curdle, and the book walked out of the Talklands to look for a forest in a house, accompanied by the words Cauldron, Diss, and Bling.

61

Hired Help

"So you know where the forest-in-a-house is?" Deeba said.

"I do," the book said. "It's written in me. And I've no reason to think *that's* wrong. But we're stopping off somewhere else first."

Deeba could not help being self-conscious at the head of such a peculiar group, but no one they passed paid them any particular attention. People were too busy keeping an eye on the skies for Smog attack, their umbrellas at the ready.

"Why?" Deeba said. "We should hurry."

"How much money do you have?" the book said.

Deeba sifted through the few out-of-date pounds, dollars, a little pack of marks and francs and pesetas from before Europe got the euro, and many dog-eared rupees. As she gathered it, Hemi hesitated, then pulled out the notes she'd given him and added them to her pile.

"You can *owe* me that," he said. "If it'll help to have a bit extra now. Pay me back later, alright?"

"Right, cheers," she said, carefully not looking at him. "That's what we've got. Why?"

"Perfect," the book said. "Because where we're going, we'll need some help. We're going to hire someone."

"When we get into the forest-in-a-house," it said, "we're looking for a bird. A particular bird. Its name's Parakeetus Claviger. We need something it has."

"The featherkey," said Deeba.

"Exactly. And it's going to be nigh-on impossible to get it. The chapter in me about the Shwazzy getting hold of the featherkey makes a point of telling lots of stories about how many people've failed because they can't find Claviger, or understand it, and so on."

"And hiring someone'll help?"

"Just wait," the book said. "It'll be indispensable."

It led them to an area of old wooden buildings, interspersed with the reconstituted junk of moil tech.

"So who is this bloke?" said Deeba.

"There's no shortage of hireable bravos in UnLondon," the book said. "And I was wondering who we should approach, when I remembered one in particular. He doesn't live far. His name's Yorick Cavea. He has all sorts of the usual qualities necessary for endeavors like this: once he fought off an entire horde of giraffes armed only with a corset-stay, believe it or not." The book let that sink in. "He also fancies himself a bit of an explorer, which combined with the money's why we'll probably be able to entice him. Let me do the talking. Here we are." They stood by a front door.

"Have we got time for this?" Deeba said to Hemi. "Do we need him?"

"Yeah, and are we going to have to go up against *giraffes*?" said Hemi.

"How's this Cavea going to help with Claviger?" Deeba said. Then the door opened, and she said, "Ah."

Yorick Cavea was a tall man. He wore a silk dressing gown and held a glass of whiskey or something. But on his human shoulders, Cavea's head was an old-fashioned bell-shaped birdcage. Inside it was a mirror, a cuttlefish bone, and a small pretty bird gripping a little swing.

The bird chirped.

"Ah, Yorick," the book said. "Nice to see you again too." Cavea shook Deeba's hand, Hemi's, and Cauldron's with its human arm. The bird whistled.

"Always straight to the point, eh, Yorick?" the book said. "Well, this young lady has an offer she'd like to make you. Deeba?"

Deeba fanned out a chunk of her money. The bird stared at it. "Tweet," it said, and Cavea's man-hands steepled together.

"Well of course," the book said. "I wouldn't expect you to be swayed merely by something so vulgar as money. But there's more at stake. You wouldn't expect me to go into detail here—one never knows who's listening. But suffice to say . . . it's going to be quite the expedition."

Cavea pondered. The bird twittered.

"Dangerous, certainly," the book said. "And suited to your unique capabilities."

Another whistle.

"Yes, of course we'll wait."

Yorick Cavea disappeared for a minute in his house, emerging in an old-fashioned khaki safari suit and swinging an unbrella.

"Wait," said Deeba. "You can't bring that."

The bird sang a few questioning notes.

"Sorry old chap, rules of this particular engagement," the book said. Cavea stood still for a moment. In the cage-head, the little bird sang on its swing. "It'd take too long to explain, but she's right, it's for the best."

Cavea threw the unbrella back in the house and closed the door, complaining in vociferous avian tones.

"Don't worry," the book said. "We'll keep watch for Smog. Half up front. That's only fair."

Deeba tucked a wad of the cash into Cavea's inside pocket. They followed the book's directions into the UnLondon afternoon, through different landscapes of the abcity, at last into a warren of narrow streets.

* * *

Deeba tried to make conversation with Cavea, but while it was obvious that the bird in the cage could understand her polite questions, she didn't understand any of its whistled answers. Mr. Cavea took the book under his arm. The bird plumped its plumage and warbled.

At some points the streets were crowded: at other times they were the only people they could see, and Cavea's lovely singsong was all they could hear, apart perhaps from the tiniest whisper of houses. Hemi and Deeba walked side by side.

"What you looking for?" said Deeba. Hemi was examining chalk- and scratch-marks on some of the houses they passed.

"Just seeing who's who and what's what round here," Hemi murmured.

"What you on about?"

"There are signs only a few of us know how to read," he said. "For stashes, caches, emptish houses, that sort of thing."

"Signs for who? Ghosts?"

"No, for . . ." He scratched his chin. "Alternative shoppers."

"Thieves?!"

"Right then," the book interrupted.

They were by an anonymous brick terrace. The houses were three stories high, in conventional red brick with black slate roofs. Shoppers milled where the road met others, and people leaned at several of the front doors, chatting to neighbors. If it weren't for the eccentric look of some of the inhabitants, it could almost have passed for a residential street in London. Almost.

"We're here," said the book.

"We never are," murmured Hemi.

One house was bursting with leaves. They pressed up against the glass of every window from the inside, blocking off any view within. They squeezed out from below the panes, and through the gaps at the top and bottom of the front door. A little plume of ivy poked from the chimney.

The caged bird on top of Mr. Cavea's body began singing fervently, the book interjecting.

"Come come," the book said. "I'm not denying it's dangerous. That's ridiculous. There were no false pretenses. Well then there's no problem—just walk away. Of course. But then there's no payment. And you won't be part of the expedition that gets deep into the forest." Mr. Cavea hesitated, the bird fluttering in agitation.

"No one's asking you to do anything much," the book said. "Honestly? All we want you to do is engage someone in conversation. Aha. That's right, you've got it."

The bird stared at the money, its head cocked on one side.

"You're not heading in, are you?" The speaker was an elderly man, sitting on the doorstep opposite. He was dressed in a skirt of animal tails. He scratched his beard and sipped a hot drink and shook his head wisely.

"I'd not," he said. "See them there?" He pointed at a rope stub emerging from behind the front door. "That was where the last lot of explorers set off. That's where they set up a base camp, they did, but never saw 'em again. Heard rumors though. Heard noises at night. It's a rum place, the forest, full of noises. No one knows its paths. I've lived here near on fifty years, and I've never been in nor never would. No, if I was you—"

Cavea squawked an interruption.

"I agree," muttered the book. Mr. Cavea's human body yanked open the front door. "He says he'd go in even if we weren't paying him anything. Just to get away from that bloke."

Deeba followed them. The utterlings and Hemi went with her. The old man opposite was left watching openmouthed as they hurried into the dark interior of the house, and into the forest.

62

Into the Trees

Deeba stepped into a realm of rustling hush, and warmth, and green light. The door closed behind her. She gaped.

"Oh my gosh," she said.

To either side were walls in bright wallpaper, and some way ahead she could just see stairs leading up on the left, and a corridor on the right. It was hard to make out the details of the inside of the house, because everywhere around them, filling it, were plants.

The carpet and the floorboards were rucked with lichen, moss, ferns, and undergrowth. Ivy clotted the walls. The corridor was full of trees. They were old, gnarled things that twisted around themselves to fit into the cramped space. Vines hung from them, and from the ceiling, and trembled as little animals and birds scampered up them.

Deeba could only just see through trees and bushes to where thick brambles and creepers plaited through the banisters. She could hear the call of birds, the whisper of leaves, wood knocking gently against wood, and somewhere, the gurgle of running water.

Light shone greenly through leaves from a bulb Deeba glimpsed hanging from the ceiling.

"We should get going," the book said. "It isn't that long till dusk."

What happens at dusk? Deeba thought. She didn't say anything. They were all too busy dragging themselves through the thickets.

The utterlings were making the most of their new freedom, roaming and foraging as the little group made their way. Diss snuffled enthusiastically and rooted around in the tangles and thickets and leaf mold, emerging from piles of old vegetation wearing temporary hats of compost. Bling leapt from tree to tree with ostentatious springs and backflips. If they strayed more than a few feet from their cautiously progressing companions, Cauldron would click his little fingers and beckon them back.

Having the forest wedged into the house seemed to have done something to the space. The walls' dimensions didn't work quite as they should. Deeba felt as if she couldn't see as far as she should be able to, and as if shadows sometimes fell in odd directions. It took them a long time to reach the base of the stairs, and Deeba didn't think it was just that the plants were so thick they impeded their progress—although they were.

She was quickly exhausted. She ducked under branches, climbed over others, held them gingerly in front of her and let Bling and Diss and the others pass, so the thorns wouldn't spring back and whack them. Sometimes, when they were confronted by a particularly

tangled thicket, Deeba saw Hemi roll up his sleeve or trouser leg, strain his half-ghostly muscles, and pull his flesh right through the blockage.

It was warm. The leaves were rubbery and thick. Deeba gripped a vine, and a tree frog crawled over her fingers, making her jump. Strictly speaking, she thought, this place was a cross between a forest and a jungle.

"This is a jorest," she said to Hemi.

"Yeah," he said. "No, it's a fungle." They grinned.

She hopped over a rotted stump jutting from the carpet and wiped sweat from her face. Mr. Cavea leaned against the stair's bottom rail, the bird in his cage-head staring at her. Through a gap in the forest canopy, Deeba saw the lightbulb, the air around it dusted with midges.

"Which way do we go?" said Hemi.

"My chapter about the featherkey isn't clear," the book said. "We could go right. That's probably the kitchen at the end of the hall. Or we could go up the stairs."

Mr. Cavea whistled.

"He's right," the book said. "We don't want to go the wrong way. There are predators in here. This isn't a safe place."

Cavea whistled.

"Are you sure?" the book said.

"What?" said Deeba.

"He says he'll find out where Claviger is. Cavea's the only one who can ask the locals. And he can get about quicker than us. And probably stay out of trouble easier."

"Can he?" said Deeba doubt-fully, eyeing him.

"We should camp," the book said. "It's late. We can't keep going all night."

He was right. Deeba needed to stop.

The caged bird sang.

"He has nocturnal cousins he can ask," the book said. "And he's too polite to say so, but he thinks he'll be safer if he *doesn't* spend the night with us. Isn't that so, Cavea?"

Deeba had never seen a little bird look sheepish before.

They decided it would be too risky to sleep in the open corridor, so they fought through tangles of stalks and leaves to a door nearby. They shoved it open past the resistance of months of plant life, and entered the living room.

Past a copse of twisted trees there was a sofa and several chairs in front of a television, burrowed through by voles and little digging beasts, and wound around with leaves. The TV was on, with the sound turned down. Through the ivy that crisscrossed its screen, it lit the clearing with the colors of a game show.

The travelers swept the little hollow free of stones and sticks, and made camp. They were just in time. Twilight came, and one by one, the lights in the house went out. The noises of the forest changed. A new chorus of night-things began.

"Are you really going to go looking now?" Deeba said. Mr. Cavea nodded his cage.

She watched him in the television's colors. Mr. Cavea reached up and opened the door to his birdcage-head. The bird twittered.

"He'll be back by morning," the book said. "He says to keep his money fresh."

"I have to admit he's earning it," Deeba said.

The bird hopped onto the threshold of the cage and gripped it with its little claws, then took off. The instant it flew out, Cavea's human body froze, swaying slightly on locked legs.

The bird fluttered away, through loops of vine and under the dark shadows of trees, through the doorway, out of sight. As it went, it sang.

When no one was looking, Deeba gave Mr. Cavea's leg an experimental prod. It was warm and fleshy—it felt like a leg. But it didn't move or respond. Cavea's vehicle just stood, the door to its cage open in its hand.

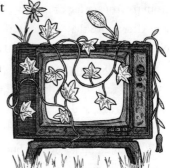

63

The Source of the River

Deeba woke several times to growls from nocturnal predators, but every time Hemi or whichever utterling was on watch duty would reassure her and go back to quietly chatting with the book or, in the mute utterlings' case, listening to its murmurs. When she woke to the weak first light from the room's bulb she realized that they had let her sleep through.

"Why didn't you get me up?" she said to Hemi crossly. He didn't answer, but looked away in embarrassment.

Cavea's body still stood as it had when the bird left. Deeba flicked a snail from its trouser leg as they breakfasted.

After more than an hour, the bird that was Cavea shot into the clearing. It circled them several times, adding its voice to the incessant backdrop of bird-song, then flew to the cage.

Its feet closed on the metal rim, and the human body jerked. The bird entered the cage, and Mr. Cavea stood up straight, stretched all his human limbs, and closed the cage door. The bird sung lengthily.

"Thought so," said the book. "Where else would you expect a high-flying bird like Claviger to go? Upstairs."

* * *

It was a long and difficult climb. Each step was thick with vegetation, and the travelers had to negotiate a brook that descended the length of the stairs.

They rested on the little mezzanine where the staircase changed direction. Mr. Cavea was at the front, carrying the book, his explorer's suit becoming more and more filthy. The bird sang at them to hurry, and Deeba and Hemi and the utterlings did their best to obey. The three utterlings helped each other, clambering silently over each other's bodies in a constant chain of themselves.

"I wish I could do that," Deeba said. Hemi raised an eyebrow at her. "Oh shut *up*," she roared. "Not with *you*." At the top of the stairs they stopped again. Through the thick leaf-cover they could see doorways on either side of the hall, and at its very end a window. Only a little daylight could struggle through the leaves that covered it and reach them.

Three times they had to move fast. A sinuous green creeper emerged quietly from under a nearby door and wrapped around Hemi's leg. It tightened and, shaking its leaves, hauled him towards the doorway, which opened onto darkness. He fell and gripped the roots around him. It was only his phantom heritage that saved him. Hemi strained, and Deeba saw the vine tighten on his trousers as the flesh beneath went semi-incorporeal. With a grunt of effort, Hemi dragged his half-ghost limb out of the thing's grip, leaving it with only a torn patch of his trousers in its trendril.

From the next door came a horrible slobbering roar, and a long, vicious-looking claw curled around the frame. Hemi and Deeba pulled the door closed on it as fast as they could, and heard a screeching and a bulky wet body slamming against it on the inside.

Little raccoony-skunky things watched them as they panted. Deeba stopped to examine fat berries in the thickets over her head, only to scream in disgust as the thumb-sized nuggets squirmed and she realized they were not fruit but leeches. "Run!" she shouted as the revolting sluglike things stretched their pliable bodies towards them.

"Quick!" said the book. They staggered as fast as they could along the first-floor hallway, Hemi and Deeba hurrying the utterlings along, just in time to avoid a shower of the bloodsucking things. Behind them was a patter of plops as the leeches landed.

"We've actually got quite lucky," the book said. Deeba and Hemi looked at it incredulously. "Given the number of things that live in this forest."

Mr. Cavea sang.

"It's not too much farther," the book translated. "The other birds told him. All of them know where the parakeets and whatnot live. He's had a look."

Cavea pointed. Through gaps between low-hanging foliage Deeba saw a door at the end of the corridor.

"So . . . is it going to give us this feather?" Deeba said. "Can we just ask it?"

"Doubt it," the book said.

"Why? Do you know it? Does it have a reputation?"

"It's just that's rarely how things work out with this sort of thing," the book said. "It's normally trickier than that. That's why they're *tasks*."

Cavea's bird trilled.

"We'd better have a back-up plan, then," the book translated. They stood silently for some moments.

"Bling, Diss," Hemi said thoughtfully. "How well can you climb?"

When they pushed the door, it opened onto a tiny room full of greenery. It was little more than a cubicle. To one side, brimming with water, tiny lilies, and water snakes, was a sink, its taps coiled with the roots of plants. The ceiling was surprisingly high, and was thick with branches above a dangling bulb. It rustled with life.

In front of them, rising like a deserted little temple from the undergrowth, below a dangling mass of creepers, was the toilet. Clear water gurgled over the rim of its ceramic bowl, wound its way along the floor, under the door, down the corridor and the stairs.

"We've found the source of the river," whispered the book.

Jutting from the wall of plant life, the square cistern was just visible. Among the hanging vines dangled its chain.

"Go on then Diss, Bling," Hemi whispered.

"Just in case," Deeba added. "Might not need you. But if you hear your names . . ." The utterlings nodded. They knew what to do.

They crept into the foliage on opposite sides of the tiny room and began to climb, Bling with its hooked claws, Diss with its six little paws. They stayed as hidden as possible under the leaves.

Deeba, Hemi, Cauldron, and Cavea stepped forward and stood in front of the forest toilet. Cavea hefted the book and sang, and hidden in the branches, scores of birds answered in harsher voices.

"He's calling the keyfeather-bearer," the book whispered. "Really giving it some flowery stuff. 'You most honored bird of paradise, of whom it is written in the book,' et cetera. The other birds are laughing."

Cavea seemed to be having some sort of argument. His human body cupped its hands to either side of the cage, like a man shouting, and the bird sang loud. Its unseen cousins answered.

"And they look so sweet . . ." said the book in a shocked tone.

The avian bickering went on, and Cavea grew more and more agitated, until all of a sudden, scores of birds dropped out of the leaf-cover and surrounded them, perching on ledges and branches.

They were parrots, cockatiels, macaws, and cockatoos, ruffling their feathers and calling raucously from nasty-looking beaks. They all spoke at once in ugly voices, and Deeba had to put her hands over her ears.

"They're telling Cavea to show proper respect in the Claviger's court," she could just hear the book say.

"Um, Cavea?" said Hemi, and pointed up.

A bird was perched on the rim of the toilet tank, watching them. It was a parrot, and it was huge. It cawed once, gratingly.

It was absolutely beautiful, a vivid patchwork of reds, blues, and yellows. As it shuffled on its feet and eyed the travelers, several of its smaller companions swept around it in a quick aerobatic dance.

"So where's the . . ." Deeba started to ask. As she spoke, several of the birds raised crests on their necks and heads. Vivid colors swung upwards into temporary tiaras, in the center of each of which was a large, bright feather shaped like a key.

The one adorning the big parrot was huge.

"Never mind," Deeba whispered.

64

Alpha Male

Claviger's head-feather smoothed down again, and was invisible in his plumage. Deeba stepped forward.

"Don't bother," the book said. "He doesn't speak any Human."

"Cavea, could you translate?" Deeba said. The caged bird nodded. "Parakeetus Claviger, I presume," Deeba said, and waited for Cavea to whistle. "Pleased to meet you. Sorry to crash round yours like this. I'm sure you know about the Smog, Mr. Claviger. I want to ask if you'll help us fight it."

The parrot cawed, and Mr. Cavea whistled.

"He says no," the book said.

"Who does?" said Deeba.

"Parakeetus Claviger."

"But . . . why did you wait for Cavea to say it? Do you understand Bird or not?"

"Yes. But Claviger has a strong parrot accent I can't make out."

Deeba rolled her eyes.

"And . . . he says no? Claviger?"

The parrot called again, and Cavea twittered.

"Yes, he says no. He says he knows what you're going to ask for, and we can't have it. He says we should be ashamed of ourselves, wanting to take his crest. The males all use them to show off, and when they're being aggressive. He says without it he won't be a hit with the ladies. He says, uh . . . that the chicks dig his threads. Don't look at me like that, Deeba, that's what he says."

Deeba had been feeling guilty about having to take Parakeetus Claviger's feather. Now she felt considerably less so.

"He says that? Aggressive? Well . . ." She paused. She saw climbing motions in the foliage on the water tank, and looked quickly away. "We don't want Mr. Claviger's head-gear. Is he stupid? What sort of idiots does he think we are?"

Cavea twittered.

"What?" said Hemi.

"What are you doing?" said the book.

"Why you getting angry?" said Hemi.

"Shut up," whispered Deeba. Then, more loudly, she said, "Maybe *we* aren't the idiots."

Cavea hesitated and translated.

All the birds were squawking angrily. Claviger jumped up and down in outrage, and screeched.

Deeba didn't wait for Cavea to translate. "Easy to say things like that from up there," she said. "Who wants your minging feathers anyway?"

"Oh, I get it," murmured Hemi.

Claviger must have understood from the tone of her voice. He screeched, and leapt down from the top of the tank to swing from the toilet chain, close to Deeba's face—and below the cistern.

"Up yours," Deeba said, and jerked her hand in a rude motion. Outraged,

Parakeetus Claviger ruffled his feathers into a fight-posture. The featherkey stood up on his head.

"Alright," Deeba said loudly. "I admit it. I'm sorry I had to *diss* you, but actually I do want your *bling.*"

The utterlings hidden in the leaves heard themselves spoken, and they burst out. They dropped on vines and flung themselves at Claviger's head.

The birds of Claviger's court filled the air, screaming in rage, raising their own featherkeys. Before Parakeetus Claviger could fly, Diss, the six-legged bear, grabbed him and clung on. With the sudden extra weight, the two bodies pulled the chain.

Even as they descended, Diss was pulling out the featherkey still raised on the bird's head. Parakeetus Claviger's cry turned into one of pain as the utterling yanked his plume.

Claviger was beating his big wings as the chain jerked at its full length, and the toilet started to flush. Diss lost its grip.

Hemi, Deeba, and Cauldron couldn't reach the tumbling bear through the barrage of enraged birds. As Deeba raised her hands to defend herself from beaks and claws, she saw Bling the locust reaching with its foreleg for Diss. The two utterlings clung to each other for a moment, but Diss couldn't hold on, and plummeted into the bubbling bowl, leaving the featherkey in Bling's grip.

Deeba's cry of triumph turned immediately into one of concern. She reached to plunge her hand after Diss, but the toilet was swirling madly, the water foaming, the level suddenly rising. The toilet overflowed violently, and the little brook that bubbled from it gushed and became a river.

"Where's Diss? Where's Diss?" Deeba shouted, but the little utterling was gone, lost in the clear water.

Parakeetus Claviger and several of his followers were dive-bombing Bling, and Deeba grabbed the terrified utterling and the featherkey.

She tried to fight her way through the increasing current. The water took her feet from under her and sent her sprawling.

"Come on!" shouted the book. Cavea's human hands swatted birds. "We can't help the utterling. We have to go!"

"Ow!" Deeba crawled out of the water. A fish with a vicious jutting jaw was attached to her leg, biting her even through her trousers. The explorers got out of the toilet, shielding themselves from parakeet attack and trying to stay out of the water.

They stumbled along the side of the new rising river, which tore down the corridor and to the stairs. Its waters bubbled with more than just its current.

"Don't fall in," yelled the book. "It's teeming with piranhas!"

They retraced their steps as fast as they could, hurrying under a new crop of leeches, leaping over predatory creepers. The birds followed them, scratching, through several layers of trees, but gradually began to leave them alone. Deeba heard harsh cawing. Cavea whistled.

"It's the beta males," the book said, jostling under Mr. Cavea's arm. "We've done them a favor. Now they get to fight to become the alpha, the main key-carrier."

"Less talking . . ." said Hemi. "More getting out."

It took them some time, even traveling as fast as they could, to get all the way down the stairs. No one said very much.

"I . . . I'm so sorry about Diss," Deeba said to Bling.

"It's not your fault, Deeba," the book said. She didn't answer.

They were descending beside what was a dangerous river, now, rather than the trickle it had been. Every so often a particularly voracious piranha would hurl itself from the water and at them. They dodged and climbed and slipped down muddy slopes, clinging to roots and stumps.

They paused at the bottom of the stairs to catch their breath. There were only a few meters—though they were those oddly behaved meters, Deeba remembered—to the front door.

"It's not far," Hemi said. "Let's get out of here."

"Can you hear something?" Deeba said. They listened. "There it is again."

Coming towards them, faint at first, but growing quickly louder, was a hacking, whacking sound. The leaves and trunks of the corridor were shaking with each stroke.

"What the . . . ?" Hemi said.

Cavea whistled.

"He says he'll go and look," the book said. But even as Cavea reached up to undo his cage door, the sound was suddenly right up close to them, and the curtain of leaves beside them was violently split open.

Standing before them was a man swinging a big blade. There was a hacked path behind him. He stared at the travelers, who were momentarily frozen.

His skin was wrinkled and mottled. His face was slack, his jaw hanging. He leaked dark smoke from the corners of his mouth and from his empty eye sockets.

The man had obviously been dead for some time. He raised his machete and stumbled towards them.

65

The Smoky Dead

Deeba stumbled. She heard Curdle squeak in her bag. Cauldron leapt at the attacker, but the dead man backhanded him away.

An awful stink of old meat and burning sulfur filled the air. Deeba tried to crawl away, but the man bore down on her with his fast shambling step and raised his blade.

Deeba screamed as it swung down.

But the blow stopped descending. The man looked up with smoke eyes. His weapon had caught on a vine. He struggled clumsily to free it.

"Come on, come on!" Hemi hauled Deeba up.

"What is it?" she shouted.

"A smombie," Hemi said.

The aggressive corpse lurched at Hemi, who ducked wildly.

The travelers backed onto the banks of a pool where the river's waters had collected. The horrible smelly attacker blocked their path and came at them. With each blow it devastated a huge swath of forest: it was terrifyingly strong.

Bling flew at it, scratching with hard insect claws. Where it tore skin, wisps of smoke rose. The dead man ignored the injuries and headbutted a tree trunk, stunning and dislodging the utterling on his face.

Mr. Cavea sang and stepped in front of him. He threw the book to Deeba, put up his hands, and dropped into an odd crouch, like an antique photograph of those old boxers wearing what looked like women's swimming costumes. He waggled his fists.

"He says, 'I must warn you, sir . . .' " the book translated, but got no further, as the dead man swung the machete and Cavea had to dance away.

"Don't try it!" Hemi shouted. "Smombies are strong!"

Mr. Cavea skipped nimbly over the roots, jabbing swiftly and punching. His blows didn't seem to do any real damage, but they were obviously annoyances. The smombie shambled, following Mr. Cavea at the water's edge.

He's turning him round! Deeba realized. *He's giving us a way out!* She gestured at Hemi and the utterlings, and they began to creep behind the smombie's back.

But while the man was dead, he wasn't stupid. He saw them moving and turned. Mr. Cavea punched and shoved him, tried and failed to knock him down. The man ignored him, and raised his machete again.

The bird in the cage whistled once.

"He says, 'Oh, dammit!' " the book said.

With that, Cavea grabbed the dead figure and twisted in a kind of judo throw, hauling the corpse over his shoulder. Their attacker arched towards the water and the avidly waiting fish. As he sailed over, the smombie gripped Cavea himself, and pulled him with him into the pool.

The two bodies vanished into the deep water.

"No!" Hemi and Deeba shouted.

The smombie's head and Mr. Cavea's birdcage both broke the surface. The water rippled as excited piranhas came to investigate. The smombie hauled clumsily at roots, to get out, but Mr. Cavea kept batting his hands away. The bird shook water from itself and trilled and hopped around its cage.

"He says go!" the book shouted. "Now! Before the Smog gives up on this body."

"We can't leave him," Deeba said.

"No way!" said Hemi.

Cavea chirruped at them furiously.

"Go. He says he won't be able to hold him much longer."

Deeba could see hundreds of fish nibbling at the men in the water. The piranhas around the smombie swam away, to join those attacking Yorick Cavea.

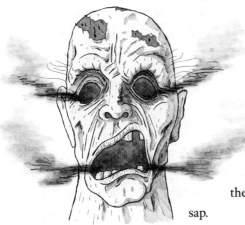

They don't like old meat, she realized.

"He says thanks for inviting him," said the book.

Hemi dragged Deeba. "We got to go," he said urgently. He pulled her through the passageway the smombie had cut, under the sliced ends of vines dripping sap.

Deeba looked back. Mr. Cavea was sinking. He gripped the smombie with one hand, and with the other, he threw open the door to his cage. As his body slipped into the piranha-infested water, the little bird flew out.

Immediately, the human body stiffened, its hand still tight around the smombie's neck. The two figures sank below the surface, the smombie still moving, the little bird circling above the pool.

There was a rumbling, bubbling noise.

The water of the pool was thick and foul with the juices of the fight and the dead body. It was unsettled like a stomach. Big bubbles rolled up in it.

There was a farting sound, and a mass of gas erupted out of the deeps. Bubbles of black smoke gathered, and sent out tendrils.

The bird-part of Cavea, still soaking, launched itself from a branch and circled the bolus of Smog.

"Move," whispered the book.

"No, everyone stay still," whispered Deeba.

The bird whirled around the Smog so fast it tore off strips of cloud-matter. After several such provocations, it raced off up the stairs. The Smog billowed in a dirty mass after it.

"He led it away," Hemi whispered.

"Good man," the book said.

"*Brave* man," Deeba said.

"Now can we *please* get out of here?" Hemi said.

They opened the front door, and stumbled out of the forest in the house, bedraggled, sticky with resin and plant juice, scratched, bruised, hungry, and exhausted, into the afternoon of UnLondon.

66

Skipping Historical Stages

People stared at them curiously. Sitting on his step opposite was the old man they had spoken to before entering.

"So in my opinion," he said, "you should avoid going in."

Deeba gave him a scorching look. "Let's get out of here," she said. "Hemi, can you find somewhere?" They stumbled off to a less crowded street, and Hemi read the signs until he found them an emptish house, where they washed as best as they could under the taps, went to the living room, and collapsed.

"What exactly was that . . . smombie?" Deeba said.

"They used to be really rare, but these days there are more of them," Hemi said. "Smog gets everywhere. Into cemeteries, and through the earth into the graves."

"How do you know so much about this?" said the book.

"Do you remember where I'm from?" Hemi snapped. "There's not much gets people in Wraithtown more riled than mistreating the dead. We've been complaining about this for ages. Not that anyone listened.

"Smog gets inside bodies and pulls them around like puppets. Some are nothing more than skeletons with clots of Smog around their joints. Some are like the one we saw in there."

"Aha," said Deeba. "And sometimes they might look even more as if they're still alive."

"Yeah . . . Of *course*," Hemi said, his eyes widening as he remembered the Unstible-thing.

"And how'd it find us?"

"The Smog must've sent them all over the place."

"It probably didn't expect to find you," the book said. "There'd have been more than one. But the forest is well known enough that it was worth staking out. Which means that there may well be others, waiting for us elsewhere."

Deeba held up the feather and turned it in her fingers. Its key-shape was made of intricate whorls and beautifully plaited threads of matter. Its reds and blues glinted like colored glass.

"So what now?" Hemi said.

"Well," the book said. "That was the first task. There are six more. The next thing we have to fetch is the squidbeak clipper. That'll mean going to the docks. After that we need the bone tea. After that . . ."

"We can't," Deeba said, twirling the feather.

"What?" said the book.

"What?" said Hemi.

"Look . . . what are we supposed to do with all these things once we've got them?"

"It depends," the book said. "The clippers are supposed to, well, to snip something open. The bone tea's there to send something to sleep. The snail . . . it's not exactly clear what the snail's for, but there are two distinct schools of thought—"

"What do you mean 'it's not clear'?"

"Don't take a tone with me! I told you, prophecies can be vague."

"Yeah, and wrong," muttered Hemi.

"A lot of these things," the book went on, "the idea is that as situations arise you'll . . . sort of know what to do. Some stuff is explained in detail, some isn't. Or it's . . . well . . . contradictory."

"This is *ridiculous*," Deeba said. "Trying to follow prophecies is obviously way too hard."

"But this was your idea," the book said. "And look, we got what we needed, didn't we?"

"Yeah, and it took us *two days*, and we lost *two people*!" Deeba yelled. There was silence.

"Diss is dead, and Cavea probably is," she said. "Do the maths. We still have *six more* things to get. At this rate that's going to cost us *twelve people*, and there are only six of us left, and that's if we count you, book, and Curdle! And, it's going to take *twelve days*. And I haven't *got* twelve days! You *know* that. I've got seven at the *most*."

"That started again, though," the book said tentatively. "After the phone call. And the number may not be accurate . . ."

"It's *too long*. And too risky. You saw what happened to Diss! We can't do it this way. Like you said, we don't even know what we're supposed to do with this stuff." She held up the featherkey. "Like, what do I do with this?"

"Well, you open a door, obviously," the book said.

"*What* door?"

"A *very important* door. A door without the opening of which the Smog cannot be stopped!"

"You don't know, do you?" Deeba said.

"No," said the book.

"No idea?"

"Not really." It sounded quite defeated. "I think it's the doorway to the room where the squid beak is, but . . . no. Not really."

Deeba stamped around the room in rage.

"We spent two days crashing around in a forest, and people *died*, and we aren't even sure what for! I'm supposed to use it to get something to get something else! Why don't I just get the last thing in the *first* place?"

"As I say, the occasions tend to present themselves, and then it's clear . . ." the book said.

"I'd shut up now, if I were you," Hemi muttered to it. The book took his advice.

"If Diss hadn't died getting us this," she said, staring at the key, "I'd tear the bloody useless thing up. I know it's not your fault," she said to the book. "It was my idea. And I know it would be nice for you if what's written in you turned out to be sort of true. But *we don't have time*. And it's too risky. So go through the tasks, and tell me what each one's supposed to do."

"Well, as I say, the squidbeak clipper's supposed to hold on to something in the tearoom—"

"Forget it," Deeba said. The book hesitated, then continued.

"The bone tea's refreshing—"

"No."

"But . . . we need it to give to the aleactor, to send him to sleep when we play ludo, so we can take the teeth-dice—"

"I said *no.*"

"The teeth-dice we need to chew up a—"

"No."

"The snail, I *think,* can prove to us that slow and steady wins out—"

"Are you joking? No."

"The black-or-white king's crown explains an outcome—"

"Whatever. Don't even know what that means."

"—and the UnGun's a weapon."

There was a pause.

"Is it? A weapon? For real?"

"For very real," Hemi said. "I didn't know it was in the prophecy, but everyone's heard of the UnGun."

"It's the most famous weapon in UnLondon's history," the book said.

Hemi nodded—surreptitiously, so the book wouldn't see that Deeba wanted independent verification of everything it was saying.

"Why?" she said. "What did it do?"

Hemi looked at the book, and Deeba was sure the book was looking back at him.

"I dunno," said Hemi. "Heroic stuff."

Deeba rolled her eyes. "What is it?"

"A gun," the book said, "only an un one. It says in me, 'The Smog's afraid of nothing but the UnGun.' That's what all this, all the seven tasks, leads up to. The fetching of the UnGun. It was put in a very safe place, where no one would mess with it, years ago."

"Smog's afraid of nothing but the UnGun, eh?"

"Yes," the book said, then added nervously, "Well to be honest it actually says 'nothing *and* the UnGun,' but we realized that must be a misprint."

"You're kidding me," Deeba snapped. "So you *did* know you there could be mistakes in you?"

"It was three letters," the book said forlornly. "We didn't think anything of it . . ."

"Alright. Whatever." Deeba thought. "A weapon. Alright. Right now we haven't got much to fight the Smog with. We need a weapon, and the Smog's obviously scared of this one.

"So that's what we're going to do," Deeba said. "We'll skip the rest of the stuff. Save us some time. We'll go straight to the last stage of the quest. Let's go get the UnGun. Then we can deal with the Smog, and I can go home."

Weapon of Choice

"This is ridiculous." Deeba could tell from the book's voice that if it could walk, it would be refusing to. It would be digging in its heels. Unluckily for it, it was tucked under her arm, and she was walking rapidly. "I said this is *ridiculous.*"

"I heard you," Deeba said.

"So? Are you going to stop?"

"Nope."

Hemi, Curdle, and the utterlings ran after the arguing duo. Deeba was turning decisively but randomly down side roads as shadows lengthened in the UnSun.

"Look," said the book frantically. "You can't pick and choose bits from a prophecy. That's not how they work."

"Let's be honest," Deeba said. "We all know you have no idea how prophecies work."

Hemi winced and sucked in his breath, shook his hand in an *ouch* motion.

"In fact," Deeba went on, "it looks a lot like prophecies *don't* work."

"The whole point is you *need* each of those things to get the next one, until we get to the UnGun," the book said.

"Even if we had *time* to try that, you don't know," Deeba said. "You're the one that keeps saying what's in you's wrong. You want to do it your way to make some of it work again. But if we know it's the UnGun we really need to deal with you-know-what, we're going straight to it, instead of messing around with in-between bits. Unless," she added with sudden interest, "there's any more telephones on the way?"

"N-no, there's not," the book said. "But in any case—"

"We are *not* walking through each of your chapters, book! So. *Give me directions*, or . . . or I'm just going to keep wandering in circles until the Smog finds us."

Deeba and the book sulked at each other.

"I vote you give her directions," Hemi said.

"Alright," the book said at last, as they turned yet another corner pointlessly. They passed a tumbledown piano, one of UnLondon's random pieces of street furniture. The book sounded beaten down and miserable. "I'll tell you what's written.

"It's going to be harder to get the UnGun than the key. Even if we had the crown of the black-or-white king. To get the UnGun we have to get past something truly terrifying, one of the most deeply feared creatures in UnLondon—"

"Get on with it," Deeba snapped.

"Alright. It's protected by the Black Window."

Hemi gasped. Deeba stopped.

"The Black Window?" Hemi said in a hushed voice. Then he said to her more normally, "Are you laughing?"

"Sorry," said Deeba. She tried to stop. "Black Window!" She sniggered again, making Curdle turn excited circles. The utterlings watched her, bewildered.

"I do not see what's so funny," the book said.

"It doesn't matter, it doesn't matter," Deeba said. "Tell me about this *Black Window*. What do we have to do?"

"This is no joke, Deeb," Hemi said. "The Black Window's nasty UnKin. Someone must've really wanted to protect the UnGun if they put it there."

"That's why we're supposed to work up to it," the book grumbled. "In stages . . ."

"Yeah yeah," Deeba said. "*Who* must've really wanted to?"

"Well," said Hemi hesitantly. "Whoever . . . wrote the prophecies, I suppose."

"That makes sense," said Deeba. "Sadists. Tell me what it is."

"The Black Window lives in Webminster Abbey," the book said.

"Oh you *didn't* say that," said Deeba, and laughed more.

"I wish you'd treat this information with the awe it deserves," said the book plaintively.

"Webminster, though!" Deeba said, but her laughter died at Hemi's face.

"It is serious," he said. "You wouldn't catch me going near there normally."

"The window doesn't just kill you," the book said. "It takes you right out of the world. No body left, no clothes, no trace. Swallows up whatever comes close. It's the perfect predator."

"I thought that was a shark," Deeba said.

"Alright, the shark's the perfect predator. The Black Window is the *pluperfect* predator."

Deeba still wanted to tease them, but there was a fear in Hemi's and the book's voices that made her uneasy.

"So how do I get to Webminster Abbey?" Deeba said.

Deeba's heart sank when she looked at the map. There were miles to go. Some of the areas they would have to cross were inhabited, some were empty—and now some were smogmires.

"It'll take *ages*," Deeba said. "Oh *no*. Can't we . . . I dunno, take a train or something?" Hemi stared at her as if she were mad. "There's going to be more and more people coming after us, every minute."

She was proved right much sooner than she had expected.

For an hour or so the rather dejected little group followed the route they had mapped, as briskly as their exhausted limbs would let them. They did nothing to attract attention to themselves, and apart from their clothes being a little more dirty than most people's, there wasn't much noticeable about them. In the streets of UnLondon, a group of a girl, a half-ghost, a talking book, a piece of rubbish, and two living words was unusual, but not very.

That was why, when Deeba first heard a motor approaching, she didn't think it was anything to do with her.

It got slowly louder and louder, until suddenly Deeba heard a voice call her name. She turned and looked up in dismay. Descending towards them, through a brief flock of scurrying laundry, was Rosa and Conductor Jones's bus, the Scrollscrawl Sigil clear on the front.

Murgatroyd was leaning from the platform, shouting, "Deeba Resham, stop! We need to talk!"

68

The Functionary's Tireless Hunt

Deeba and her companions ran.

"Wait, Deeba, wait!" It wasn't just Murgatroyd leaning out now. He had been joined by Conductor Jones, Obaday Fing, and even Skool, the brass helmet peering down.

"This way!"

"No, this way!"

Deeba and Hemi dithered at every turn, while the book barked directions. They were in an area of moil houses and streets littered with skips and obsolete machinery, with no arches or overhangs under which they could hide. The bus followed them through the intricate streets, while UnLondoners watched curiously from windows.

"Wait, Deeba!" The voices were insistent. "We want to help!"

Deeba turned in to an alley full of clotheslines and clothes gyrating as if they were in a dryer, though there was no wind. They ran through layers of cloth like curtains, until at the end of the streetlet they reached a blockage, a steep wall of broken clocks, slippery as scree.

"Listen," whispered Deeba. The noise of the bus had ebbed.

"They've gone," whispered Hemi.

"I think we lost them," Deeba said, and indicated the tight alley. "It's too narrow for the bus here."

Even as she said that, though, cords dropped out of the sky, from the bus hovering above the buildings. Conductor Jones rappelled down, landing in front of them.

"Deeba, Hemi, Book," he said, and held out his hands as they backed away. "Please wait. *Listen.* We're on your side."

"Leave us alone," Hemi said. "Leave her alone."

"Stay back," Deeba said. "You don't know it, but you're working for the Smog."

"These crazy allegations have to stop," said a voice. Climbing clumsily down a rope ladder was Murgatroyd. He stumbled to the ground and dusted himself off, stood by Jones, and pulled a strange-looking gun out of his suit. He aimed it at Deeba.

Following him down the ladder came Obaday Fing, in an outfit stitched of monochrome book jackets.

"Careful, now, Deeba," Fing said. "Don't move suddenly; there's no need to get hurt."

"You let him pull a *gun* on me?" Deeba said, aghast, staring at Jones and Obaday, who shifted uncomfortably.

"It's a tranquilizer," Murgatroyd said. "I don't want to use it, and I'm hoping you don't make me. It's purely in case you refuse to listen to reason. We're here to help."

"How'd you find me?" said Deeba. She refused to look at Murgatroyd, only addressing Fing and Jones.

"Jones came and asked my advice," Obaday Fing said. "Together we figured out how your mind works, Deeba. When the Propheseers told us about the tasks in the book, we thought we knew what you might try to do."

"And there's been sightings for days," Jones said, and winked. "You're noticeable, girl, been making an impact. I been sticking close to Murgatroyd. He made sure he was the first person who heard all the rumors that came through."

"Your friends've come along, to prove that you've no reason to be anxious," Murgatroyd said. "This is all for your own good. We just want to stop this misunderstanding."

"You going to try to blame everything on Hemi again?" Deeba said.

"We'll sort out the truth about this half-boy later," Murgatroyd said. "Please come with us. The Unbrellissimo's program to hand out umbrellas is continuing—nearly a third of UnLondon've been issued protection now, and just in time, because the Smog's attacks are increasing. We urgently want you on-side, Deeba. We want all this unpleasantness and misunderstanding to stop."

Cauldron and Bling looked one way and another, trying to work out if they could rush past their captors.

"Listen here," the book said with a pompous voice, "I think you should know that I believe Miss Resham may not be wrong—"

"Shut up, book," Murgatroyd interrupted. "We all know about *your* failures. Deeba, come with us. And you, boy. We'll deal with you too."

"Jones, Obaday," Deeba said. "Please, *listen*. The Smog's working with Brokkenbroll. They want to make everyone rely on umbrellas, 'cause that means on Brokk. Then they can rule UnLondon together. They're going to make everyone work in factories, burning stuff to make the Smog stronger."

"Really . . ." said Murgatroyd, and shook his head.

"And it's already getting stronger because Rawley, *his* boss in London—" Deeba pointed at Murgatroyd. "—she's been feeding smoke straight into UnLondon. We heard him saying so to the Unbrellissimo! Everyone in London, like my mum and dad, even, thinks Rawley's doing good things at my end, but she's not cleaning anything up; she's feeding the Smog over here!"

"That is enough!" Murgatroyd said. "I've had enough of your slurs."

"Ask him what, what the *lurch* is!" Deeba said. "It's something to do with all this. Are you going to believe him over me?" she begged. "This bloke holding a gun? You don't know him! After all we done together! Please . . . don't you believe me?"

Fing and Jones looked uncomfortable. Murgatroyd looked smug.

"The thing is, Deeba," Jones said sheepishly. He put his hand on Murgatroyd's shoulder. "He's explained things to us. On the bridge, in the air. About how you've been led astray." Fing nodded sadly. "And to be honest with you . . .

"Yes. Of *course* we believe you."

Jones sent a sizzling, crackling bolt of electricity through his hand. Murgatroyd's teeth rattled and sparked, and he made little burbling noises and danced like a ridiculous puppet. The current made his snubby gun burst.

"There," said Jones, and let go. The bureaucrat dropped to the ground, his shoulder smoking, his eyes wide, drooling and making noises like a baby. "That should keep him quiet for a good couple hours."

"Thank goodness for that," said Obaday Fing, and stepped over the smoldering man, his arms open. "He was really beginning to annoy me."

"Obaday!" said Deeba, and hurled herself into his hug. "And Jones!" she said, and grabbed him too, and he laughed and hugged her back.

"You knew?" she said.

"Not at first," said Fing. "But we've spent time with you. We know you. You're no fool, Deeba. You wouldn't misunderstand what Unstible said."

"And what this idiot was saying just didn't make sense. Like you say, it would be crazy for Wraithtown to join the Smog against UnLondon. I didn't want to admit that but . . . you were right. And I owe you an apology," he said to Hemi. He held out his hand.

For several seconds, Hemi just glowered. Then he smiled slowly, and shook his hand.

"Alright then," he said. "Glad you believe me now."

"Unfortunately, Mortar doesn't," said Jones heavily. "The man has too much history with Unstible. Can't bear there to be anything wrong. And Brokkenbroll's there every day, on the bridge, since they showed him how to get there. Whispering in Mortar's ear, and the old man won't question a word. Lectern doesn't like it, I don't think, but she's not rocking the boat. And what Mortar says, the rest of the Propheseers obey. Bunch of cowards, mostly. They don't think for themselves. So we had to keep very shtum."

"That's why we made sure we came with Murgatroyd," Obaday said. "We've been stuck to him like whelks. As soon as he heard a rumor about you, we told him we'd come too. They'd never have sent us along if they thought we were on your side. We couldn't say anything till we found you."

"So you going to help me, then?" Deeba said.

"If you'll have us," Jones said.

"But . . . you'll be going against the Propheseers."

"If they're too stupid to see what's what," said Obaday Fing, "that's their own fault. We're all packed and ready to go. Why d'you think I'm dressed like this? Book covers are tougher than their insides, and I needed something heavy-duty." Despite the swagger he tried to give his words, Deeba could tell he was afraid. She gave him another hug.

"Funny how it all turns out," he said. "I've never been a renegade before."

PART  VII

Arms and
the Girl

The Balance of Forces

"Good to have you back, Deeba!" Rosa shouted from the cab as Skool effortlessly hauled Deeba and her companions on.

Deeba hugged the ungainly driver, and Skool patted her clumsily on the back.

"Let me introduce everyone," Deeba said. "This is Bling and Cauldron." Cauldron stuck out three of his four hands, and shook the hands of Obaday, Jones, and Skool simultaneously. Bling reared up on its rear legs and gave a solemn locust bow.

"Where to, Deeba?" Rosa shouted.

"Webminster Abbey. Quick as you can."

"Really?" said Rosa.

"She knows what she's doing," Obaday Fing said.

"You're absolutely right, she does," said Jones. "So on we go."

"No, I don't," Deeba said. "I'm probably making mistakes. But we haven't got nothing to go against the Smog with, and we know it's scared of the UnGun, and we know that's at the abbey."

"Is it now?" said Jones.

"Webminster Abbey it is," Rosa said, and the bus began to chug through the sky.

"What's going to happen to him?" Hemi said, pointing at the immobile figure of Murgatroyd, hidden in a pile of rubbish. Deeba remembered how he had left her for the Unstible-thing to burn, and she'd imagined all sorts of bloodthirsty and fatal things to do while they had tied him up.

"I dunno," she said grudgingly. "We couldn't just do him in."

"See . . ." said Hemi. "Just not sure I agree . . ."

"I just couldn't."

"Well, he's not waking up for a while," Jones said. "And when he does, it'll take the same again for him to get out of those bonds. By the time he gets back to the Propheseers and Brokkenbroll, they'll know we've done a bunk."

Deeba stared out of the windows at the towers and spirals and steeples made of what looked like untold coiled wires. She had never flown over this neighborhood, and was frustrated that she couldn't look down at the abcityscape below, but she and Hemi stayed away from the platform, out of sight.

Obaday rummaged nosily through her luggage. He made rude noises about her sewing kit.

"What is the point of this dreadful equipment?" he muttered. He stitched up some of the rips in her and Hemi's trousers, and replaced her needles and thread with some from his own scalp.

"Can't we go faster?" Deeba said. "I'm worried about the phlegm effect."

"Not without drawing attention," Jones said. "They think we're looking for you. If they see us suddenly speeding up, they're going to think we've got a lead, or they're going to realize we're doing a runner. And either way they're going to come after us. Soon enough, they'll realize we're AWOL, and they're going to have to start choosing sides. But at the moment, there's enough stuff up here for no one to notice us. So long as we don't draw attention."

It was true. There were a few other buses, dangling below balloons or innumerable little spinning propellers. There were insects and birds, and high-flying rubbish like ragged dustbin bags crawling against the wind, and low clouds, and a flock of escaped washing hurtling around the sky with incomprehensible purpose. Deeba even glimpsed a grossbottle, but this one wasn't being ridden. It was wild—disgusting but not an enemy.

A little way off, Deeba saw a patch of the abcity, several streets by several streets, completely surrendered to Smog.

"I wish we *could* speed up," Jones said, seeing where she was looking. "We don't have much time. And I don't even just mean with you and your family. Look out there. I mean for UnLondon. The Smog's spreading."

"According to Brokkenbroll," Obaday said, "the Smog's gathering forces. Now—"

"Wait a sec," said Hemi. "Brokkenbroll's really on the Smog's side, even if Mortar doesn't know it. Why'd he tell the truth about what it's doing?"

"Because he *wants* people to be scared of it, so they'll trust him to protect them," Deeba said. "When they realize he's in on it, he'll already be in charge. That's what the umbrellas are for. He might even be *exaggerating* how bad it is."

"I don't think so," said Jones grimly. "Its attacks are coming more often, and smogglers are taking over more places."

"They travel underground, along the train tubes and the sewers," Obaday said.

"Smoglodytes and stink-junkies and smombies come with the Smog wherever it goes," Jones said. "People have tried to fight, but its forces are too strong. The umbrellas defend people, but they can't—or won't—disperse a decent-sized smoggler. Even electric fans sometimes don't. People just run, when the Smog moves in. UnLondon's filling with refugees."

"It's taking over in patches," Deeba said slowly. "Separating us into camps. Easier to control."

"You know, Brokkenbroll even said we'd have to give up certain areas," Jones said thoughtfully. "And Mortar went along with it. Telling us to make orderly retreats. Into designated 'safe' zones."

"Like they're herding us," said Hemi.

"There are a lot of rumors in UnLondon," Obaday Fing said. "There are mercenaries on the Smog's side. Like the man who attacked you and the Shwazzy in the bus."

"What happened to him?"

Obaday spat.

"A disgrace to the market. Barnabus Cudgel. He's worked alongside me for years. It turns out he was part of a group calling itself the Concern. They say there's business they want to do, factories and the like, that'll lead to more smoke and more emissions, so it makes sense to work *with* the Smog, would you believe? They want to do deals with it."

"They told you this?" said Deeba.

"They put out leaflets and graffiti and whatnot," Jones said. "Secret distribution. But it's not hard to find."

Skool gesticulated, drew large letters in the air.

"That's true. You see their sign on the walls," Obaday said. "More and more. 'E = A.' 'Effluence equals affluence.' " He smiled sardonically.

"And people have seen the Hex, they say," Jones said. "Fighting on the Smog's side."

"What's that?" Deeba said, seeing Jones, Hemi, and Obaday Fing exchange fearful glances.

"Nasty, nasty," Hemi muttered.

"A group of spellspeakers," said Jones. "Very powerful. If the Smog's got them on its side, life's going to be even harder for us."

"Don't we have any magicians?"

Jones and Fing looked at each other forlornly.

"I can make a sweet come out of your ear," Rosa yelled from the front.

"That's great," Deeba muttered.

"No, but I really can! Not just quick fingers, you know, I really pull it out of your ear!"

"Perhaps," Deeba said, "that'll come in handy."

The Gossamer Edifice

The bus continued its slow journey through the night. For the sake of appearances, like other hunting vehicles, they turned powerful searchlights down into the dim streets, and seemed to walk on light-beam legs.

Once a fat python of Smog rose curiously out of a lost quarter, nosing towards the bus. Rosa took them quickly up to where the wind was stronger, and the coil of cloud sank back.

Deeba held Curdle in her arms as she lay across the seats. The cardboard carton burrowed into her hug.

Tomorrow, she thought, *I'm going to get the UnGun. And then we'll have something that the Smog really doesn't want us to.* She drifted to sleep, thinking of the UnGun, and then, with sudden pangs, of her family.

She woke in the very early morning, as the bus's anchor snared in a tangle of aerials.

"Oh my gosh," Deeba said.

Deeba saw an area uncomfortably close to them that had become a smog-mire. That was not what made her catch her breath.

They were swaying before a huge building. It was like nothing she had ever seen.

It had no straight edges, was all long curving planes stretched like cloth or rubber. In several places it poked into steep cones, and pillars and jags like tree branches jutted from beneath its shimmering, moving surface. It looked like a load of giant tents, all stitched together at crazy random, as big as a stadium. Its entire surface was white, or gray-white, or yellow-white, and it rippled.

"Oh my gosh," whispered Deeba again. "It's a cobweb."

Tons of spider silk had been draped over an enormous irregular framework. It coated it completely, in layers, totally opaque. At its edges, strands of webbing jutted out at angles and anchored to the pavement and surrounding buildings like guyropes.

In one or two places, Deeba could see dark, immobile things smothered in the silk. It was wound around them in shrouds, suspending them in the building's substance.

"That'll be Webminster Abbey, then," said Hemi.

They all descended, and stood together, the bus above them, in front of Webminster Abbey: Skool, Obaday Fing, Rosa, Conductor Jones, Hemi, the utterlings Bling and Cauldron, Curdle the carton, Deeba, and the book.

The cobweb church loomed before them, its strands humming as the early-morning air passed through them. The UnSun was rising, but its weak light didn't make the abbey less threatening. It seemed to be smothered in shadow.

In several places, the silk curved inwards into tight funnels of darkness, jutting into the interior. Some were only a foot or two above the pavement, some up near the top of the steeple. They ranged from the size of a rabbit hole to that of a trapdoor.

"We're going to have to go in one of those, aren't we?" Hemi said.

"Book, do you know what's inside?" Deeba said.

"The Black Window. I'm afraid I've got nothing more than that."

"Alright," said Jones cautiously. "Any ideas?"

"Firstly we've got to see what's in there," said Deeba. "So we just look in, really quick, then get out again and make a plan."

They looked at each other uncomfortably.

*   *   *

The building was surrounded by a marquee of web, whorls of silk, and web archways. It was like twilight in the cobweb shade. Jones threw a stick into one of the cylindrical tunnels, and they all tensed.

The stick bounced and rolled out.

"Well, it's not sticky," said Deeba.

They crept up the silk slope towards the hole. It was like walking on a trampoline.

Skool had to stop. The diving boots were too heavy. They didn't rip the silk, but sank too deep to walk.

"You'll have to wait outside," whispered Deeba. Skool slumped, and backed out of the tunnel. Obaday Fing was clutching his box of scissors, thread, and mirrors as if for comfort.

"You should go with Skool, Obaday," she said.

"Are you sure?"

"Yeah. Make sure there's no trouble outside."

"Alright then," he whispered. "You be careful." He crept back.

Hemi, Jones, and Rosa were all smiling at Deeba. Even the utterlings seemed to be, in their mouthless way.

"That was kind," Hemi said.

"Shut up," said Deeba. "We needed someone outside."

"Oh, of course," said Jones.

Deeba grinned grudgingly, looked up—and froze. Something was plummeting out of the shade above them.

"Jones!" she shouted.

The thing came down at tremendous speed. It loomed out of shadow too fast to see clearly, dark, and big, and angled, with limbs splayed.

It dropped over Rosa, and rose again, and disappeared.

Rosa was gone.

"No!" shouted Jones, and jumped, but there was nothing above them. Their attacker had soared into the overhanging web, into the shadows and out of sight.

71

Men of the Cloth

They hollered and stared up into the webbed vault, ready for another attack. No motion was visible. They had no idea where the thing had gone. There was no trace of Rosa at all.

Back in the light of the UnSun, Jones stamped and shouted miserably, and kept saying Rosa's name.

"Years, we've been together," Jones said. "Years! She fought by my side in the Siege of the Battery Sea. Drove search-and-rescue to the coldmines for years. It was her came over from London with me . . ."

"I know, I know," said Deeba. They all stood in a circle, trying to work out what to do.

"Oh, dratted shame," said someone. "Are we too late?"

Deeba whirled around. Behind her were two tall, dry-looking priests. They wore big, silly popes' hats, and carried shepherds' crooks. They were incredibly ancient. One was stubbly, with very dark red, almost black, robes. His skin was the same color. The other was as pale as Hemi, and wore a long white beard and white—though dirty—cassock.

The men moved in tiny tottering zigzags, diagonally, forward and back.

"Who are you?" Deeba said.

"What's that?" said the pale man, cupping his ear. "Oh, who *are* we? I'm Bishop Alan Bastor."

"And I'm Bishop Ed Bon," said the other. "We know the secrets of this place, et cetera."

Their two voices were indistinguishable. They sounded extremely posh and elderly. Old English gents.

"May I say," said Bishop Bastor, "gather you lost a comrade. Awful business. Dreadfully sorry."

"Time was we met every arachno-fenestranaut, warned them with a few home truths," said Bon. "Didn't stop them all, of course, but at least they had due warning."

"Now we're older, there's always some we don't get to," said Bastor.

"Arackno—what?" said Hemi.

"Ah. Rack. No. Fenestra. Naut," said Bon. "Travelers like yourselves."

"You run this place?" said Deeba.

"Oh, no," sighed Bon. "Bless you."

He and Bastor looked sadly at each other. They were both coated in dust. Their eyes were as droopy and tired-looking as bloodhounds.

"We were military chaplains."

"Spiritual support for the troops."

"You were a team?" Deeba said. The two men looked shocked.

"Absolutely not," said Bastor. "Deadly enemies." He said this in the same vague, slightly tremulous tones with which he had said everything. Bon nodded judiciously.

"Quite right," he said. "Implacably opposed." The two men looked at each other mildly.

"What are you *doing* here?" said Deeba.

* * *

Bastor handed his staff absently to Bon, who took it without a word and waited while his companion scratched himself vigorously.

"Bastor and I were spiritual staff, for each side."

"Although that didn't stop me kicking a little bottom at times," sniffed Bastor with satisfaction. "A couple of knights rather regretted tangling with *this* His Eminence."

"Absolutely," said Bon. "I doubt your lot would've thought me very holy, either." They both chuckled in reminiscence.

"And?" said Deeba.

"We're on a bit of a *schedule* here," said Hemi.

"Sorry, sorry. Well, we both got taken."

"But his lot were shockingly lax on security."

"I didn't exactly get stopped at the fence myself, old chap."

"We bumped into each other here. We'd had a similar idea."

"Bishops, you know? Heard this was an important church."

"Turned out not to be quite what we'd had in mind," Bon said, waving at the silk. "Still—"

"—neither of us could very well let the place fall into enemy hands. But then we were both *hors de combat* as they say in Parisn't."

"So after a few stiff words—"

"Yes, I was awful, wasn't I?"

"—we came to an arrangement. You see, I'm watching to make sure he doesn't claim it."

"And I he. Until we find out who won the war."

"As soon as we find out my lot've won, you're for it then, I'm afraid."

"Keep telling yourself that," said Bastor placidly. "Soon enough you'll be in my power."

"Truth is, though . . . we've rather lost touch of the state of the campaign. Haven't had any communiqués for . . . how long would you say it was, Bon?"

"Oh, a few years now."

"I think they're talking about the Eight-by-Eight War," the book muttered to Deeba, apparently hoping that the two bishops were too deaf to hear it. "No one knows anything about it, except that it happened. *Centuries ago.*"

"Anyway," said Bon. "Once we realized what was in the church, and that people were trying their luck, we thought it only fair to act as warning. Gives us something to do."

"Or at least . . . try to do," said Bastor apologetically.

"We know as much about this place as anyone. We try to set the more *deluded* treasure seekers straight about what they're up against."

"Until we find out who's the victor."

"Someone'll come and tell us."

"Someone rather special's due."

"To whom we'll owe . . . well, I don't know what."

"Everything, I suppose."

"Good," said Jones. "You know about the Black Window. Then you have to help us."

"We have to get past it," said Hemi.

"Forget getting *past* it," Jones snapped. "We need to know how to *get* the bloody thing. It took Rosa."

"I'm sorry," said Bon gently. "Your friend is gone. Even if by any chance she isn't dead, we have no way of knowing which of them took her."

"What?" Hemi said. "It was the Black Window."

"Yes, but which one?" said Bastor.

The travelers stared at them, aghast.

"I think we've found another mistake in you," Deeba said to the book. "Defeat *the* Black Window to get the UnGun, you said. *Which bloody one?*"

72

The Truth about Windows

"Why do people come here?" said Hemi. "And what do you tell them?"

"To make their fortune," said Bon.

"To stay away," said Bastor.

"No doubt you'll be off now," said Bon.

"Hey, wait," Deeba said. "You don't understand—we *have* to get in there. We're trying to find something."

"Oh dear," sighed Bon. "You *are* an arachnofenestranaut."

"We're not going to encourage foolish greed by giving out information."

"What you on about?" said Hemi. "What sort of treasure seekers come here anyway? Not Deeba. She's here for UnLondon. We all are."

"The lad's right," said Jones. "I've had enough of this. That bloody thing took my friend. Now you'd better tell me what you know to help us." Skool tried to gently hold him back.

"Wait a minute," said Deeba. "Shut up a minute."

She scrunched up her brow in thought. "You've been waiting ages to find out what happened," she said to the bishops. "For someone special to explain.

Someone was due." She counted off on her fingers, mentally running through the things the book had told her that she, in Zanna's place, was supposed to pick up. When she reached the penultimate one, she looked at the bishops in their different-colored robes.

"It's me," she said. "I'm the one supposed to tell you. In return for help. I'm supposed to bring you the crown of the black-or-white king."

"You?" said Bishop Bastor.

"You've come with the crown of the king?" Bon said. "The crown that was surrendered?"

The two men looked absolutely kiboshed. They were talking so quickly Deeba couldn't interrupt them.

"We'll know, Edward."

"We will, Alan."

"After so long!"

"It's extraordinary . . ."

"Best of luck, Edward."

"You too, Alan, you too."

They shook hands vigorously.

"*Shwazzy* . . . Bishop Bon and I've been waiting for you for longer than I can even remember. Now that you're here . . . my goodness, our wait's complete. Happy, happy day."

"For one of us," said Bastor. There was a pause.

Neither of them looked anything but horrified.

"Listen to you two," the book said scornfully. "Have you actually read the prophecy? Jones, give them me, please, page four-twenty-one. Read the description!"

Bon peered at the text.

" 'And she shall be tall and with hair like the light of the sun and the UnSun, and—' "

"Well take that for a start," the book interrupted. "Look at her!"

There was a pause.

"Perhaps she dyes it," said Bon.

"I do not," said Deeba.

"She's not the Shwazzy!" said the book.

"Number one," Deeba said. "No, I'm not the Shwazzy. She couldn't come.

I'm her friend. And number two, no, I don't have the crown of the black-or-white king. We didn't have time to get it." The two men were staring in profound bewilderment.

"But number three . . . we still need to know everything about the Black Windows. Instead, in return I'm offering you . . ." She thought, and rummaged in her bag. "This feather in the shape of a key."

There was a long silence. The bishops' faces grew more and more confused. They reached out simultaneously and took Parakeetus Claviger's crest.

"Well . . . it is pretty," Bon said.

"But it's . . ."

"How can we put this?"

"Not what we were expecting."

"What do you mean the Shwazzy's *not coming*?" Bon said.

"Don't you know how long we've been waiting?" Bastor said. "How much we need to know . . . ?"

"Yeah but you *don't*," interrupted Deeba. "What's it going to matter? Imagine how it'll be. You'd have to go separate ways, for a start, which you don't want." The bishops looked quizzical.

"Alright," she snapped. "I *do* have the black-or-white king's crown. It's white."

Bon's face broke into a look of incredulity and delight. Bastor's broke into shock and misery. Almost as soon as he saw his companion's expression, though, Bon's smile faltered. Deeba ignored the surprised expressions her companions were giving her.

"Sorry, wrong way round," she said. "The crown's black."

Instantly the bishops' expressions were reversed. This time it was the beaming Bastor who began to frown at Bon's obvious horror.

"See?" said Deeba. "I got no idea who surrendered. We *haven't got* the black-or-white king's crown. But look at you two. *You don't want to know.*"

The two bishops stared at her, then at each other. For a long time.

"She may have—" said Bon.

"—a point," said Bastor.

"But Chosen One," said Bon. "Sorry, I mean, Unchosen One. Waiting to find out's been our whole purpose."

"We can't live without a purpose . . ."

"Okay," said Deeba thoughtfully. "I know what your purpose is."

"Do you?" Bon said eagerly.

"What?" said Hemi.

"Really?" said the book.

"If I tell you," Deeba continued, "you have to help. You have to tell us everything about the Black Windows."

"That seems perfectly reasonable," said Bastor.

"Alright," said Deeba. "You just got it back to front. I reckon your purpose is to make sure *no one ever* brings you the crown. Your purpose in life is to make sure you *don't* find out who won."

The wind whistled gently over the quivering web of the abbey. The UnSun warmed them.

"Again," said Bon. "She may—"

"—be onto something," said Bastor.

"I wonder if we've been barking up the wrong tree."

"I always had my doubts, old man." They were beginning to speak with more enthusiasm.

"Silly of us to have brought it up."

"Absolutely! No need at all! Perfectly clear!"

"Our holy task is to make absolutely damn sure we don't find out who won."

"Of course it is! Splendid! Do let's get on with it!" The two bishops beamed at each other, and at Deeba and her friends.

"We really can't thank you enough, young lady. You've been immensely helpful."

"Glad to hear it," said Deeba. "I'll even throw in the feather." She handed it over. "Now, *finally*—tell us what you know about the Black Windows. Maybe that way we can get past them."

"I'm not quite sure what it is you're after," Bon said. "But I suspect that it's not *past* you want but *through*."

73

An Unusual Social Ecology

Deeba crept, bouncing, on thick, candy-floss-filigreed darkness.

Hemi was beside her. Jones was ahead, struggling along the tunnel of web. She felt their vibrations. Jones lugged their trap.

They had spent hours making it. It had been complicated work.

"Do you think the straps'll hold?" Deeba whispered.

"Yes," Jones whispered back. "Like I did the last six times you asked me. Fing made them out of bits of the web itself, so we know they'll hold. I was more worried that his loops wouldn't tighten when we pull, but he said to me, 'Jones. I don't tell you how to guard a bus. Don't tell me how to tie off threads.'"

"The others better not get tired," whispered Hemi.

Deeba was very scared. Her breath came fast. She wished yet again that she'd been able to think of some other way of achieving their goal. She felt the cord playing out behind Jones from their bait, past her and Hemi, all the way to Skool's unseen hand. She gave it three quick tugs—*everything's alright.*

Outside, each standing by other funnels in the silk, the utterlings, Obaday, and even the bishops themselves were whacking the threads, sending vibrations inside in an attempt to distract the inhabitants while Deeba, Hemi, and Jones got inside.

Deeba heard faint sounds. A tiny rustling like air. Quiet rattling like twigs falling from a tree.

"What is that?" she muttered. Hemi bumped into her.

"Stop stopping," he grumbled.

"Hold on a second," Jones whispered. "There's a bit of light coming, and . . . *whoa!*"

The web bounced violently, and Deeba slipped down a sudden incline.

She couldn't help letting out a little scream. Jones grabbed Deeba in one hand, plucking her out of her slide, and Hemi in the other, pulling them close. He wedged them with him in a little hollow behind a cobweb-smothered ridge. The three of them were absolutely still, waiting to see if they had been noticed.

The cord stretching behind them was repeatedly tugging, Deeba realized. She pulled it three times, to reassure Skool.

Eventually, her heartbeat slowed down, and she looked into the interior of Webminster Abbey.

They were high up in an enormous space. It was dim, faintly illuminated by the light of the UnSun through the silk arcing above them.

The great room was dotted with supports, cobweb-swaddled minarets or trees, jutting at random in the irregular framework on which the web was stretched. In the very center was an ancient, ruined church, dwarfed in the chamber. Its steeple poked up into the cobweb ceiling, which smothered its weather vane.

"That must be where they started all this," whispered Jones.

Deeba could see black holes around the chamber: the ends of the tunnels that led outside.

"Alright then," said Jones. "Let's do this." He dangled their bait some way below them. Hemi took Jones's flashlight from his pocket and played the beam on it.

"We're ready?" said Deeba. She yanked the cord four times to say *stop touching the web.*

"Here, window window window," she whispered. Hemi waggled the light a little, and they settled down, very still, to wait.

A few seconds after their companions stopped vibrating the silk, something began to move.

Deeba saw motion. There were swaying beams of dim light, off in the distance of the darkness. She froze.

Out of the tunnels, back into the shadowy chamber, windows were coming.

There were tens, twenties, untold numbers of them. Crawling into view were heavy, painted wooden window frames, filled with thick, mottled old glass, through which Deeba glimpsed strange lights. From every frame splayed eight wooden arachnid limbs, four each side, clenching and un-clenching.

They dangled; they scut-tled with horrible bursts of spider speed or picked their way tarantula-slow over the floor. Deeba put her hand over her mouth so as not to make a horrified sound. She and Hemi clutched each other.

A Black Window descended out of the darkness, playing out silk. It twisted on the cord as it came, light from behind the glass rotating like the beam of a lighthouse, the same view, it looked like, shining from both sides. Deeba could see faint shapes beyond the panes of glass.

One or two of the windows trailed broken ropes from under slammed-shut panes. That must be where explorers had attempted to attach themselves, Deeba thought.

The Black Windows were not only clambering over every surface, raising their segmented legs high, through every loop and hole of webbing. They were clambering *in and out of each other.*

In some bizarre social interaction, windows pulled wide open, and in seemingly impossible motion, others would approach with furtive arachnid scurries and wriggle inside, the pane closing behind them. Others would open, and wooden forelegs would waver out from inside, and other windows would emerge and creep away.

All sorts of complicated maneuvers occurred. Windows that had just ingested others themselves climbed into yet others. A window opened and emitted three of its siblings, one of which then climbed into another, while the third spat out a fourth. Deeba saw one window emerge from another, then eat its own regurgitator. It was endless.

The web was dim. Noises were hushed. There was a soft clicking from countless wooden limbs.

Deeba saw glimpses through their glass. Through one window she saw a room full of tailors' mannequins; through another a pit of darkness; through another, frighteningly close to her, what looked like dark water full of weeds.

"What's that?" Hemi whispered; then his voice gave out.

A skeleton was floating among the kelp, beyond the glass.

There were other dead, Deeba saw. Bodies lying in empty rooms and corridors beyond some of the windows, rope tied around their waists. So this was what happened to the lost arachnofenestranauts.

If they managed to get out of the window they had entered, it might by then have entered another, which itself had entered another and exited a different one still. Even if they avoided the deadly realms that were beyond some of the panes, treasure hunters might roam helplessly through window after window, hunting for food and drink in a succession of alien rooms, never finding their way back to UnLondon.

"You didn't see what the one that took Rosa looked like, did you?" Jones whispered. Deeba and Hemi shook their heads. They had no way to tempt that particular window back. Rosa was lost.

74

Spider-Fishing

"Make sure you don't pull the wrong cord," whispered Deeba. There were two: one took the weight, the other tightened the loops.

Their trap dangled below them.

"No two are alike," the bishops had explained, and told them of the infinite rooms beyond the Black Windows' panes. They had glimpsed monsters and gas and mustard-colored limbos, as well as the more tantalizing vaults and stairways and arsenals, the glints of coins that attracted those foolish adventurers.

"We've got to get past them, and we've still got no idea where the UnGun is," Fing had said.

"Where do you think it would be?" Deeba had said. "It was put somewhere no one could get at."

Fing shook his head helplessly.

"It's *in* one of them," said Hemi. He and Deeba nodded at each other.

"Maybe . . . we can trick them," said Deeba eventually. "No two are alike, you said?"

"All different. We've seen a sword, a flame, a coal mine—"

"—the canopy of a tree . . . But all different."

"Because we're looking for one particular window, right?" Deeba said. "And we reckon we know what's in it. So, if all the windows are different, how d'you think they'd react if they saw one *exactly like them?*"

"They'd hate it," said Jones.

"They'd *love* it," said Hemi. "Maybe they'd, y'know . . . I mean, there are no baby windows, are there? Maybe they've been waiting."

"I agree with you," said Bon and Bastor simultaneously, Bon pointing at Hemi and Bastor at Jones. The bishops looked startled.

"It don't *matter,*" said Deeba. "If they're territorial and they attack, or if they're lonely and they want to, you know, whatever. Either way, if there's one just like them, they're going to come see."

With tools from the bus, Jones had pulled free a window from an empty building.

Following Bon and Bastor's description, they'd sawed and hammered, while the locals had ignored them as foolish treasure seekers. They made attachments to the frame, taking care not to crack the glass, and behind it nailed a flat piece of wood, on which Hemi drew exaggerated lines of perspective.

"Now the main thing," Deeba had said.

From his tool kit, Jones had taken a soldering iron with a grip like a pistol, stuck a length of pipe on its end, like a barrel, and attached it to the wood behind the glass.

The thing was inelegant. Its eight limbs swung stiffly on old hinges. It moved randomly when they jiggled it. Still, it was an eight-legged window with what looked like a gun behind it.

"It'll do," Deeba had said. "They won't have seen nothing like it before."

The bait swung below them, in the darkness of the web. A long time passed.

Every time a spider-window approached, Deeba gazed into its glass. There was one that contained nothing, one with a room full of lamps. When a third came close, Deeba squinted, and felt Jones's hand close around her mouth to stop her screaming.

Hammering on the inside of the glass as the Black Window rose was a gaunt, exhausted woman. She was thin, her hair was wild and dry, her eyes staring. She stared straight at Deeba and Hemi as the window passed.

*   *   *

The light was waning.

"It's evening," Deeba whispered. "Maybe this isn't working."

"Maybe it'll help," said Hemi. "It'll stand out more."

He shone his flashlight on it, and Jones swung their clumsy window from side to side. Its limbs waggled. Deeba saw several of the Black Windows stop moving, then, to her simultaneous triumph and horror, pick their way towards them.

"Here they come," whispered Hemi.

From the shadows in the rear of the hall, a window came fast.

"We've got something's attention," whispered Jones.

The Black Window ran with its unnerving many-legged motion, leaving the gloom. It leapt onto a thread between floor and ceiling, and raced towards them. It plunged on its silk right in front of their bait.

The window hung, its legs wide. Through its glass, Deeba could see a weak electric bulb, the gray of a little room, and attached to a wall opposite, a huge, antique revolver.

"That's it!" She grabbed Jones's hand. "It's the one with the UnGun in it! It's come to check out its double. Never seen another with a pistol in it."

The Black Window moved in agitation. Jones swung the bait gently, making its legs rattle. Other spider-windows watched and drummed their limbs.

"Is it angry, or flirting?" whispered Hemi.

"I dunno," said Deeba. "But it's interested. Get ready."

Deeba took hold of the rope that led out of the tunnel, and got ready to send Skool a message.

The bait twitched and jiggled. *Don't look too close,* Deeba thought. But the soldering-iron-and-pipe gun they'd rigged up seemed enough to fool the agitated Black Window. It drew back its limbs, paused, then pounced.

It gripped the dangling fake window.

"Now!" shouted Deeba, and Jones pulled hard on the second cord, as Oba-day Fing had shown him. The loops Fing had woven around the bait all tightened together. It was beautifully precise. The thick silk bonds clamped firmly, and pinned the Black Window's legs to the ridiculous marionette.

Instantly, everything went mad.

* * *

The captured window yanked its body, swinging at the end of the tether, trying to pull free. Jones staggered, was almost hauled off the little ledge.

All the other Black Windows began to run towards them.

"Quick!" yelled Deeba. "Help!"

Hemi pulled frantically at the rope, several quick tugs. "Anything more than four," they'd told Skool, "means *pull.*"

There were agonizing seconds of delay. Then the rope was hauled back hard, and the captured Black Window began to rise.

Deeba, Hemi, and Jones clambered as fast as they could up the slope of the tunnel. Their captive slid behind them, still shaking as it tried to escape, opening and slamming shut like a biting mouth.

Black Windows followed them into the funnel. Deeba felt the vibrations of feet closing behind, and thought in terror that she couldn't go any faster, until with one last heave, Skool yanked the tethered window the last few meters of the tunnel, sweeping Jones, Hemi, and Deeba with it.

They came spilling out of Webminster Abbey, to where Skool hauled, and Obaday, the utterlings, and the bishops waited anxiously. The Black Window they had snared skidded out, shaking furiously in its bonds, tied to the now distinctly unimpressive-looking fake. Curdle circled it, emitting aggressive puffs of air.

"We're okay!" said Deeba. "Don't let go of it!"

Giant wooden spiders' legs poked aggressively out of the hole, looking for prey, but the windows wouldn't come out of the abbey. None except the one that they had caught.

75

The Room Nowhere

"It's really not happy, is it?" said Obaday Fing.

It was early night, and the stars moved above them. Deeba and her companions examined their captive in the almost-full loon, and the faint glow from windows at the edges of the square. The cobweb curves of the huge abbey moved gently in the wind.

"I simply can't believe it," said Bishop Bon.

"I'm terribly impressed," said Bastor.

The window rattled and shook, still pinned to the bait. Skool kept the cord attached to its bonds taut.

"Let's get on with it," Jones said. "This bloody thing's strong."

They looked down through the glass.

In the room behind the window, the bulb dangled horizontally, and the wall the pistol was attached to looked like a floor below them. Next to it was a closed wooden door. It was only about six feet away.

"So that's the UnGun," said Hemi.

It was a very big, heavy revolver, like the ones Deeba had seen in cowboy films. She leaned close to the glass, and the window opened and slammed like teeth. They all jumped back.

"Right, so we get a rope with a hook, and we dangle it inside, and grab it," said Obaday.

Hemi wedged a hefty plank of wood in the window's opening, to its obvious fury. Its snared legs were twitching. Skool struggled to hold it.

"Come on!" said Jones.

"Here we are, here we are," said Obaday. But when he dangled a hook of bent piping on his spider-silk rope through the open window on the pavement, something strange happened. As soon as the rope passed through the window's opening, it immediately changed direction, and fell sideways.

Obaday stood with a rather stupid expression on his face. The rope dangled in an L-shape, down to the window, then inside at a right angle.

"It's 'cause down's a different direction there," Deeba said. "That's not a floor below us, it's a wall. We need something stiff."

They tried with the bishop's staffs, but they couldn't reach the UnGun.

"Whatever you're going to do," said Jones, watching Skool struggle, "may I ask you to speed up?" Deeba heard creaking from the wood keeping the Black Window open.

Everyone looked at each other.

"I knew it," Deeba said, and before she had time to reconsider, she sighed and stepped into the open window.

Deeba heard her friends' appalled shrieks as she slipped through.

She experienced a very peculiar fall, changing direction beyond the glass. She twisted, and rolled on the floor of the little room.

"Deeba!" she heard. "Get out of there!"

She looked out the window at her friends. They were looking down at her, from her angle seeming to jut straight out of a wall beyond the glass. Hemi was reaching urgently through the window.

"One second," she said.

Opposite her on the wall was the UnGun.

Deeba walked across the concrete floor, her friends urging her to hurry. She felt unnaturally sensitive, noticing the cracks beneath her feet and on the walls around her. She heard the lightbulb buzzing.

When she closed her hand around the wooden grip of the UnGun on the wall, she braced herself, expecting to be hardly able to pick it up. She lifted it.

It was lighter than she had expected. She hefted it in her hand, examined it.

It was
battered
and mot-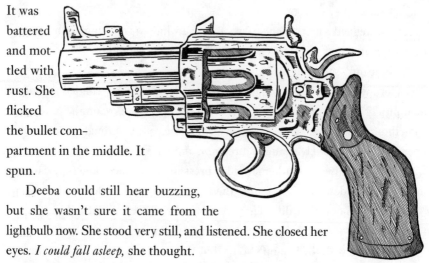
tled with
rust. She
flicked
the bullet com-
partment in the middle. It
spun.

Deeba could still hear buzzing,
but she wasn't sure it came from the
lightbulb now. She stood very still, and listened. She closed her eyes. *I could fall asleep,* she thought.

The noise was coming from behind the door. She put a hand on the wood. There were unclear sounds in the room, or corridor, or whatever was beyond it. *I could open it and go exploring,* she thought. *If this place has the UnGun in it . . . what else might be here? Maybe there's a garden. Or a bedroom. Or a phone . . . I could call home again!*

She put her hand slowly to the handle.

Something was bothering her. She paused and wondered what it might be. She couldn't think what was wrong.

"Deeba," she heard, for what she realized was the second time. "Turn around."

She did so, curiously, and there were her friends, staring down, sideways, through the window, beckoning.

The view beyond the window was shaking violently, and Deeba realized that the window must have nearly pulled itself free. With a cold rush, she woke back into herself. She had been in some kind of dream.

"Come on!" shouted Hemi. "Let go of the door!"

Even as he spoke, Deeba saw one of the Black Window's legs swing up into view, free of its bonds. It pulled the wedge of wood out from under its sash.

The window slammed shut.

* * *

Deeba saw the horror on her friends' faces, but she could no longer hear them. Everything seemed to move in slow motion. Deeba raised her arm, and hurled the UnGun as hard as she could.

The big pistol spun in the air, crossing the room, straight into the very center of one of the panes. The glass exploded into hundreds of pieces, and the window spasmed.

Deeba ran.

She watched Hemi, then Obaday, then Jones and the utterlings try to grab the pistol as it passed into UnLondon. It was traveling straight *up* to them, and at the end of its trajectory, it would pause and come back at her.

She was halfway to the broken window, and she saw another of its legs pull free.

The UnGun had reversed direction. She and it were racing towards each other. As she reached the jagged edge of glass, she saw one of the bishops' crooks reach out of nowhere, hook the pistol through the trigger guard, and yank it out of sight.

Deeba put her hands in front of her face, screamed, and dived through the broken window.

She felt her hair brush at fringes of glass still in the frame. She kept her eyes closed. As she passed through the window, gravity twitched around her again, and suddenly she was rising, not diving, and was grabbed by helpful hands.

"Deeba! Deeba! You're alright! You're back!" Her friends crowded around her, and she opened her eyes.

"What happened?" said Hemi. "You went all weird!"

"I dunno," she said. "I was sort of dreaming. It was something in that room, it . . . Where's the window?" she shouted.

"Gone," said Jones.

It was several feet away, where Skool had kicked it as she leapt free. The wounded spider-window was pulling itself away from the ruined bait. It limped back into the shadows around Webminster Abbey. Deeba let her heartbeat slow.

"I almost," Deeba said, "*almost* feel a bit sorry for it." She hugged each of her friends in turn, including, to their obvious delight, the bishops. Dangling on the end of Bon's staff was the pistol. He twirled it ostentatiously.

"We *got* it," Deeba said.

They crowded around the UnGun.

"It's amazing," said Hemi.

"It looks ancient," said Obaday.

"Someone actually managed to bring something back," said Bon.

"A successful 'naut. I never thought I'd see it," said Bastor.

"It's not loaded," said Jones. "Where are the bullets?"

Silence settled on them.

"Pardon?" said Deeba.

"I . . . it's . . ." Jones said, hesitant under her stare. He pointed at it. ". . . un-loaded . . . Bullets?"

"Ammo," said Deeba. "Right." And fainted.

76

Dwellers in the Smoke

Deeba listlessly played with the remains of her food.

After she had come to, her friends clucking frantically around her, they had agreed it was exhaustion and stress that had knocked her out. She seemed to have no ill effects.

The bishops had fetched food, chairs, and a table from an emptish house nearby, and they had sat down to eat in front of the abbey. It was the first hot meal Deeba had had for a long time, and though it was a bizarre, mixed-up picnic—eggs, potatoes, salad, curry, chocolate, fruit, olives, and spaghetti—it made her feel better, at least physically.

There was no improving her temper, however, nor that of her friends. The realization that after all they'd gone through to get the UnGun, they were missing a vital component, had put them all in terrible and argumentative moods.

"We have to go back," Jones repeated, glowering over the remains of supper.

"Are you crazy?" said Obaday. "We don't even know where the bullets are."

"They must be in same room as the UnGun," Jones said. "Stands to reason."

"That makes perfect sense," said Bishop Bon, just as Bishop Bastor said, "We can't assume any such thing." They stared at each other.

"Deeba is not going back in there," said Hemi.

"No one's asking her to," said Jones. "I'll go."

"It's too risky," said Obaday.

"The bloody gun's pointless without them!" said Jones.

"How are we supposed to get the window back?" said Hemi.

"It's an insect, not a philosopher!" Jones shouted. "We'll just trap it the same way again."

And on and on, around the argument went, repeating itself in loops. Deeba sat in surly silence, as she had since the beginning, playing aimlessly with the UnGun. *Spiders aren't insects,* she thought, but she didn't say anything. She didn't imagine the correction would go down well just then.

She rubbed the UnGun's smooth handle, opened the revolving cylinder as Jones had shown her, and stared for what felt like the thousandth time into the six empty chambers. Yet again, Deeba tried to remember if she had seen any bullets—or anything else at all—in the room behind the Black Window.

Yet again, she had to admit that her memory of that time was hazy, and that she couldn't be sure. But she didn't think she'd seen anything.

The loon shone onto the midnight meal and the billowing silk. In its gray light, Deeba saw a little caravan of ants crossing the table, passing morsels of food back along the line, rummaging among the remnants.

Her friends kept arguing. Deeba ignored them.

She tried to work out how the pistol was loaded. Deeba picked up a big grape pip and idly dropped it into one of the slots. She jumped when she saw that an ant was on her fingers.

It trotted off, following the trail of juice clockwise around the rim of the cylinder, crawled busily into one of the holes.

"Get out of there," Deeba muttered, and shook the UnGun. From her pocket she took a scrap of paper, twisted it, and poked it gently after the ant.

The paper wedged in the chamber, just as the ant crawled out from under it, and straight in to the next hole along. Deeba swore.

She tried to entice the insect out with a pinch of sugar from the table, sprinkling it on the edge of the cylinder. Then with a sudden suspicion, she licked her finger. The grains were not sugar but salt.

Deeba swore again, and laughed without any humor. Things were just not going her way.

Her friends continued their bad-tempered exchange. Deeba picked up one of the broken bricks from when they had made their bait window, which lay discarded and redundant. She carved her initials in the brick with her fork, sending little chips of it onto the table around her, and into the UnGun.

The arguments were exasperating her. She sighed, wound a hair around her finger and plucked it out to fiddle with it, huffily scrunched it into a little matted wad, and dropped it into the mechanism. With a sniff of impatience she closed the cylinder, the ant still inside it, and spun it, watched it whir, then slapped it still.

"There's no point to this," she announced. They were all quiet. "We're not getting anywhere."

"We should do something quick," said Jones.

"What are we going to do?" said Deeba. She turned the UnGun over and over in her hand. "We're knackered. You're right—this stupid thing's useless without bullets. But the rest of you're right too—we can't go back now."

"Propheseers and Unbrellissimo are going to track us down soon," said Hemi.

"I know, but what can we do?" said Deeba, meaning *I'm too knackered.* "Maybe tomorrow we'll have to take the bus back to the Talklands and I'll call my mum and dad again, and buy us a bit of time with the phlegm effect, and we'll come back then, or something."

She fiddled with the UnGun's cylinder, to empty it of the rubbish inside.

It wouldn't budge.

She frowned, and tried again, without success.

"Jones," she said. "Could you open this please?"

"What did you do?" he said grumpily, struggling with it. "It's jammed."

"I didn't do anything!" Deeba said, then hesitated. "I was seeing how it worked."

Jones pulled and twisted at it, but it stayed firmly shut. He eyed her.

"What did you put in this?" he said. Everyone looked at Deeba.

"Nothing. Just . . . stuff," said Deeba. "I was seeing how it worked. Give me that." She grabbed it back, and tried again and failed again to open it herself.

"Well, that solves that," snapped Hemi. "There's no point trying to get bullets when the UnGun's broken."

"I can fix it!" said Deeba desperately. "Just give me a minute."

"Deeba," said Obaday Fing gently, and laid his hand on the pistol's barrel. "Stop."

She stared at him, and her grip faltered. At that moment, there was a scream.

Something rushed overhead, with a noise like a flock of heavy wings. Several voices cried out maniacally together from the sky. In almost the same instant, Deeba heard the words "Boss," "Message," "In," "From," "Go," and "You," shouted in different, but similar voices.

"What's that?" she said as crazy laughter and the sound of rushing diminished above her. There was a creaking, the noise of heavy thumping.

"What *is* that?" Jones said.

"Can that have been—" Bishop Bon said.

"—the Hex?" said Bastor. They stared at each other.

"Passing something on?" said Bon.

" 'Message from Boss . . .' " said Bastor.

" 'In you go.' Who are they talking to?" said Bon.

There was another scream.

Lights came on in houses, and sleepy people of all shapes peered out.

Panicked UnLondoners came running into view. They wore pajamas or nighties, or T-shirts and boxer shorts, or nothing at all. They ran, children, adults, and the elderly; animals and people and the halfway things of the abcity.

"What's happening?" shouted Bishop Bon.

From behind a corner at the edge of the square, from the darkness beyond the trembling edges of Webminster Abbey, an enormous shape came lumbering out of the night.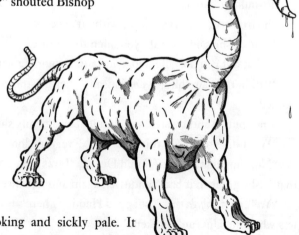

It was clammy-looking and sickly pale. It padded like a clumsy cat. Its body was a pudgy hairless lion's, but its head was that of an enormous, blindly groping earth-worm. It nosed into the bricks and concrete and tar, turning them by some chemical exudations into mulch.

Behind it were other grub-white figures, herding terrified locals before them. They seemed to drag darkness behind them. Deeba realized that they were walking in a bank of spreading, dirty smoke.

"Smoglodytes!" she said.

These were very different from the ones that had paid court to the Unstible-thing when it threatened her. Those had been small and tentative, living in the shallows of the poison. These, now, were mutants from the deeps of the Smog, and they were huge.

Behind the lionworm was a presence like a noseless man's face on stumpy caterpillar legs; something flying on one bat's wing and one vulture's; a gorilla with enormous whiteless eyes in its chest; and others, an impossible variety of impos-sible shapes. All were color-less. All had either large eyes or no eyes, and bulky filter-noses or huge nostrils or none.

The smoglodytes gnawed and clawed or suckered or whatever at buildings, and even, Deeba saw in horror, at a few UnLondoners too slow to get out of their way, who, with horrified wails, were pulled into the rolling Smog and dis-appeared.

"They're claiming the neighborhood!" Hemi said. Locals fled desperately past them, carrying what few possessions they had grabbed. Several gripped umbrellas, opening them in terror, and holding them like shields.

"Everyone move!" shouted Jones. Deeba grabbed one old man's bags, helped him to the edge of the square. Skool picked up a fallen escapee under each arm, and hauled them out of the road. Deeba and her friends struggled to help the UnLondoners away.

"We have to get out of here!" Hemi shouted. The smoglodytes and the thick Smog they breathed came ominously fast. The outer fringes of the Smog had reached the web, which shook strangely. From a couple of the dark funnels wooden jointed legs twitched.

They're going to come out, thought Deeba. *When the Smog gets inside, they won't be able to breathe.* Any moment, as well as predatory monstrosities and choking fumes, the streets would be full of panicking spider-windows. There was no way the locals would get away.

There was no way *she* would get away.

"Deeba!" Hemi shouted. A smoglodytic tentacled goat-thing was bearing down on her faster than she could run. With a despairing cry, she raised her hands.

77

Fruit

Deeba had forgotten she was carrying the UnGun. She didn't realize she was pointing it at the smoglodytes, or that she pulled the trigger.

There was an almighty *BANG!* and an explosion of smoke.

Deeba went flying backwards, sailing over the table, still holding the pistol, her hand stinging and her ears ringing, as something shot from the barrel of the UnGun with a little stab of flame.

Instantly, there was rumbling. The buildings shook.

A plant roared up from below the pavement, splintering the concrete and sending it flying.

Others leapt out of nothing beside it and beyond it, in a thicket and then a copse and suddenly in rows, clambering the sides of buildings and bollards and corkscrewing around lamps.

Deeba stared, her mouth open. In less than a second, the street ran with roots and stems moving so fast they looked like molten wax, setting in exaggerated gnarls. Trees hauled themselves vigorously out of nothing, shook off dust and debris, and were suddenly tall and thick and very there, filling the street and square. Fruit hung from them.

The UnLondoners who moments before had been running for their lives stood still, staring in shock. Deeba got to her feet and stared at the UnGun. She stumbled towards the vines.

"Deeba!" said Jones. "Careful!"

"It's alright," she said. "Look."

The vines had twisted themselves into position and grown in an instant around the smoglodytes.

Wrapped around with coils of stems so thickly they were almost mummified, the smoglodytes were immobilized. There must have been more than a hundred of them, frozen in the positions they had taken when Deeba fired.

She saw the squid-goat thing. It eyed her as she approached. She was sure it was straining against its bonds, but it could do no more than make the grapes hanging from its chin tremble.

Behind it, where the smoglodytes were closer to each other, the vines had grown together, connecting overhead from creature to trapped creature. They grew into fantastic shapes, stretching over the monsters. Their leaves and fruit shook as the smoglodytes struggled, but that was all.

Deeba boldly entered the new green-lined walkways.

"Deeba!" shouted Obaday, but she walked for a little distance between trapped smoglodytes, which watched her from beneath leaves. She plucked a bunch of grapes hanging from the horn of a thing staring at her with rage.

"It looks as if it's been an arbor for years," said the book in wonder, from under Obaday's arm. "Whole new meaning to the word *grapeshot* . . ."

Eddying around them, the Smog seemed confused and panicked. It thrust out smoke stalks like snails' eyes, swept down out of the air, and examined the vines that trapped its inhabitants. It coiled into a column and raced around the gathered UnLondoners, stopping in front of Deeba.

Deeba could tell it was hesitating. Slowly and ostentatiously, she raised the UnGun and aimed at it.

The Smog coalesced, poured out of sight down into a backstreet, and was gone.

"Oh, my, lord," whispered Hemi. Skool pointed at Deeba, at the Smog, at her again.

"You *scared it off*!" said Obaday Fing.

Deeba looked at the UnGun. There was still smoke rising from its barrel. Deeba sniffed it. It smelt of grapes.

Tentatively, UnLondoners explored the new groves.

"I'd stay out of them," Jones called. "You don't know how long until the vines disappear."

"They look pretty solid to me," Deeba said. "And if they do disappear, I'll bet the smoglodytes won't hang around. Not without the Smog."

Curious people in nightclothes were approaching. "Is that . . . ?" they said, and, "Are you . . . ?" Deeba ignored them.

"It still won't open?" she said as Jones fiddled with the UnGun. He shook his head and handed it back to her.

"Are you sure you can't remember what went in?" he said. "In what order? Remember, it turns counterclockwise."

"Not really," Deeba said. "I think it's my hair in the next one. Unless it's the salt . . . I thought it was sugar, you see . . . There was some other stuff, too . . ."

Jones smiled and shook his head.

"Well, if we'd known," he said, "we might have tried to plan it. But I don't know if we could've done, or if it'd make much difference. We know the Smog *is* scared of that thing, and no wonder . . ."

"You should use it," Deeba said suddenly, and held it out to him. He flung himself to the floor.

"Don't point it like that!" he shouted. "Is the safety catch on?"

Deeba held it awkwardly, twisting the little lever he indicated. Jones rose.

"You know how to use it," she said. "My hand still hurts. I don't know what to do with it. You take it."

"I do not know how to use it. I'm a close-quarters fighter. I'll twang a bow if I have to, but that's all. I'm no gunslinger. Each time you fire it—if you have to fire it again—it'll hurt less. This is *your* UnGun, Deeba. There's no way I'm taking it from you."

"Listen to you!" She stamped her foot. "You're acting like I'm the Shwazzy. I'm not. It's just a gun, and you should use it."

"The thing is . . ." Hemi said hesitantly. Deeba saw that he and the others were standing behind her.

"Skool," Deeba said. "You know how to fight." She held the UnGun to him, handle-first. Skool raised a glove and wagged a finger *no*.

"The thing is," Hemi said, "we all sort of think you'll do best with it."

Deeba looked helplessly at the pistol. From the growing crowd of onlookers, she heard a few whispered phrases.

". . . scared off the Smog . . ." she heard, and ". . . Shwazzy . . ."

"No," she said immediately, and turned to them. She tucked the UnGun into her belt. "I'm *not* the Shwazzy. I'm completely unchosen."

"There's no way this'll stay quiet," the book said.

"I know," said Deeba. "We have to go *now*, even though it's the middle of the night." In fact, she didn't feel nearly as tired as she had.

"You're right," said Jones. "We need to start traveling covertly. We couldn't take the bus now . . . even if any of us could drive it . . ." He looked up, stricken, at the vehicle bobbing overhead.

They kept their voices down as curious locals came closer.

"Where to now?" Hemi said.

"We've got the UnGun . . . time to move on the Smog," said Deeba.

There was sudden quiet. The travelers looked at each other.

"Just . . . like that?" said Hemi.

"Just like that," Deeba said. "That smoggler's going to find its way to the rest of itself. It won't be more than a day or two before the whole Smog knows. And it's going to figure out that we're coming for it. And that might make it move.

"Do you remember what it was saying, Hemi? When it had us? It's been trying to gather strength. That's what it's been waiting for, but I don't think it's going to wait anymore. And neither are we."

She looked at her companions.

"Look," she said. "I *have* to go. It wants me dead. It's hunting me. You . . ." She hesitated. "You don't have to come . . ." Her voice petered out.

Jones looked calm; Obaday scared; Hemi excited and scared. It was harder to tell how Skool, Cauldron, and Bling felt, but all of them, she was suddenly sure, were determined. Even Curdle circled like a dog that'd seen a cat.

"I think I speak for all of us," said Hemi, "when I say do shut up with that."

Deeba smiled with relief and delight. She was proud of them, and of herself.

"Anyway you still owe me money," Hemi added.

"Alright then," she said. "Let's go. Back to Unstible's factory. Hands up, Smog."

"Bishops," Deeba said. "Can we ask a favor?"

"Of course, dear girl," said Bon.

"Anything," said Bastor.

"We need to make sure we're not followed. And also . . . When people hear about this, they're going to ask questions. Businesspeople with plans—the Concern. And . . . the Propheseers. And I'd really appreciate it if you didn't tell them nothing."

Deeba was anxious. The Propheseers were the most powerful body of magicians and scholars in the abcity, with reputations built on generations of study and protection. But neither of the bishops acted even slightly surprised.

"Absolutely," said Bon, making a little locking motion by his lips with the featherkey.

"Don't look so shocked, my dear," said Bastor.

"Anyone who can outsmart the Black Windows is damn clever. But anyone who fights off the Smog is . . . well . . ."

"A friend of ours."

"No questions asked."

Deeba nodded, weak with gratitude.

"There's one more thing," she said. "Maybe this is the first time the Smog's not got a neighborhood it wanted. People are going to be excited. Tell them to enjoy the grapes." She grinned. "But if the Smog comes back . . . people *shouldn't use their unbrellas*. They should find other ways.

"I know they won't want to give them up, 'cause they work and all that. Really though, it'll be safer. They can't trust those things, or their boss. People round here know you two. It'll be hard to persuade them, but the more you do, the better. I promise."

There was a long pause.

"Funnily enough—" said Bon.

"—we believe you," said Bastor.

"We'll see what we can do."

78

Night Eyes

Deeba and her companions traveled through strange quarters in the orange illumination of streetlights and the glow of the fat loon.

They took backstreets, climbing over walls, and through holes in fences, and empty houses. They stayed out of sight, avoiding the few night-walking UnLondoners. To Deeba's frustration, they had to pause periodically, to let Skool catch up, heavy boots swinging with impressive quiet, but that was made up for by the times Skool pushed away some ridiculously heavy thing blocking their path. Once Jones led Deeba through what she thought for a moment were tree trunks, then realized were enormous skinny legs that supported houses, jostling each other gently.

"Come on!" whispered Jones. "Before any of them sit down."

When the first loop of the UnSun appeared over the horizon like a sea serpent's hump, Deeba had to admit even she needed to stop, and they found a building full of nothing but door lintels, and slept.

When they emerged that evening, the loon was a perfect circle.

"Look at it," said Hemi.

"Let's not go," said Obaday.

"Are you mad?" said Deeba. "Come on!"

"We've no choice, Fing," said Jones. "We'll just be careful. Shouldn't really travel when the loon's full," he explained to Deeba.

"Why not?"

"Things come out."

They passed a moil building made entirely of vinyl records. There was a glass tank the size of a house, full of earth tunneled by rodents. At the top of a steep rise they looked over the abcity, which was speckled with glimmering colors. Deeba could see for miles, to the lights of the November Tree and the Un-London-I, the high towers of Manifest Station.

Here and there, miles apart, the night was broken with the lights of houses on fire.

"The Smog," said Jones.

"You reckon the Smog's setting all of them?" Deeba said. "Some are them aren't even near smogmires."

"Could be the Concern," said Jones. "Smog's allies."

"It's growing itself," Deeba said. "Setting fires to suck up smoke. It's trying to get stronger, 'cause it knows it's time for war."

Even where the conflagrations were extinguished, the remains poured off black smoke for a long time.

"They have to put them out," Deeb said, "but then they feed the Smog."

Something flitted above them. They tensed, but the sky was clear. The sound came again.

"What is that?" said the book. Jones drew his copper club.

"I don't see any Smog," Hemi whispered. "But something's after us."

They ran down a narrow avenue of house-things. It was an empty zone of Un-London, and their footsteps rang hollowly in unlit streets. The strange noises kept coming.

They bolted down a side street, hurrying Skool along between them, twisting as fast as they could into narrow, convoluted roads. Flitting, hunting presences gusted overhead. They beeped and whirred faintly behind them, but suddenly seemed to circle confusingly, and sound ahead.

Deeba turned a corner, and stopped in astonishment. Above her in the night sky, a flock of winking green lights approached. They eddied and swirled like fish.

"Back! Back!" she said to her companions, but more of the lights turned the corner behind them.

As they neared her, Deeba could see what they were. CCTV cameras, racing through the air like little planes. They surrounded the travelers, every dark lens turned towards them. Deeba heard the faint mechanical wheeze of them adjusting.

The travelers turned down a tiny alley. The cameras stared mercilessly at the little group of explorers. Especially at Deeba.

Deeba and her friends ran hard, but it was too late. The cameras had locked onto them, and couldn't be shaken off.

"Who are they?" Deeba shouted as they ran.

"Might be Propheseers," said Jones. He swore. They had reached an empty space between warehouses, with only one way in or out, and too open to hide in. He stared up at the sky for airships or gyrocopters.

"I don't reckon so," said Hemi.

There was a rumbling. The ground shook. Everyone cried out, and stumbled.

In the corner of the empty yard, the concrete vibrated and cracked, then exploded up, sending huge chunks and shards flying. Something massive and pointed burst from beneath it, whining.

It was a spinning corkscrew drill, the size of a steeple. Behind it was a big cylindrical craft, sliding out of the tunnel it had carved.

It flashed with blue lights. It rose out of the earth with a familiar *nee-naw-nee-naw* sound, and emblazoned on its side Deeba saw the symbol of the Metropolitan Police.

The burrowing thing cut off the way out. A hatch banged open. Two men stuck their heads out, wearing the distinctive domed helmets of the London police.

"Deeba Resham," one shouted. "You're under arrest."

Constructive Munitions

Another, familiar face appeared beside those of the two men in uniform.

"That's her!" screamed Murgatroyd. "That's the little witch! Get her, Officers! Grab her! Tie me up, will you?" he shrieked at her.

"Mr. Murgatroyd," the taller policeman said sternly. "Do you mind, sir? You're not helping."

"We *should* have killed him, see?" Hemi spat.

Portals swung open the length of the vessel. Deeba and her friends moved closer together as police emerged in riot gear.

"Miss Resham," the officer in the hatch called. "I'm Chief Inspector Sound; this is Inspector Churl. We're with the Special Constabulary for Un-London Monitoring. We'd like to ask you some questions."

"What for?" said Deeba.

"You're nicked is what for," growled Churl. "For terrorism."

"*What?*" said Deeba. The CCTV cameras swarmed back to the police vehicle.

"Alright, alright," Sound said. "I'll deal with this, Inspector."

"You're coming with us, girl," Churl sneered.

"Hear that?" screamed Murgatroyd. "You're never getting out of jail! It's special rendition for you!"

"Will you two stop it?" muttered Sound. "Listen, Miss Resham, I'm sorry about all this. Let's just get it sorted out—"

"I'm *not* a terrorist!" shouted Deeba. "Listen—they're helping the Smog. *He* is. They're going to let it take the whole of UnLondon, and he's in on it, and his boss, Rawley the Environment minister, and you're going to help them!"

"You seem to have mistaken me for someone who gives a monkey's," Churl said. The three men climbed out of the vehicle. "Were you terri*fied*, Murgatroyd?" Murgatroyd nodded eagerly. "There you go, girl: you're a terror*ist*. You make me twitchy, and under Article Forty-one of the 2000 Terrorism Bill, that's all I need. Time for some reasonable force, I think." He cracked his knuckles.

"And her friends!" Murgatroyd shouted.

"Inspector, Mr. Murgatroyd, *enough*," Sound said. "We've no jurisdiction over locals, and so long as they stay out of our way I'm not bothered."

"*Except*," shouted Churl, "unless I'm very mistaken, *that* is Joseph Jones, originally of Tooting, now of no-fixed-abode. You're a Londoner, sonny-jim, and that means you're mine. *Bring 'em!*"

The rows of police began to march towards the travelers, truncheons raised.

"How do they *know* you?" Deeba hissed. "The phlegm effect . . . ?"

"There are ways round it," said Jones, backing away. "This lot never forgave the conductors; they weren't going to let themselves forget us, either."

"Miss Resham," Sound urged as the police bore down, faces invisible behind their masks, "listen to me. I know you've got certain concerns—there are certain parties you think you may have irritated—and I want to assure you *we can protect you*." He stared at her. "D'you understand? Let me help you."

Deeba's eyes widened. *Protection . . . ?* she thought with a sudden stab of emotion.

"There are too many," Jones said grimly. "We can't get out."

"*What about your family?*" Sound said to Deeba over the slow approach of the police. "Don't you want to get back to them, eh?" He watched shock and hope come and go on her face. "You know," he said gently, "I've got a daughter about your age. I can't imagine how I'd feel if she were down here." He held out his hand.

Deeba stared. His words reminded her painfully that her family were *not* worrying about her, and that was suddenly unbearable. She looked at Sound, beckoning her.

"Oh, them," said Churl. "Those three other enemies of the state resident at your address. Cause any trouble, I'm going to enjoy ensuring their arrest and detention."

"Leave them *alone*," Deeba screamed at him. "You *can't*—"

"In*spec*tor, hush *up*," hissed Sound. "Miss Resham, come quietly now, let me sort all this out, and you have my word—I'll make sure we lose that paperwork about your mum and dad. And don't you look at me like that!" he added curtly to Churl, staring at him until his assistant looked down sulkily. "None of us wants this, Miss Resham. *You* never wanted all this! I know there's just been a big misunderstanding, and I can sort it. Let me take care of it. And meanwhile you'll be safe, in our custody, and you can see your mum and dad. We'll make sure you're *all* protected . . . and your friend, too. Understand?"

"Protection . . ." Deeba said at last. Sound clicked his fingers, and the police paused in their approach.

"Guaranteed," he said.

"Deeba . . ." she heard Hemi say, but she ignored him.

I could go home, she thought. *I could see Mum and Dad, and they'll* remember *me.*

"Please," Sound said to her. "I can't stand seeing a nice young lady like you in this mess. The longer this goes on now, the harder it's going to be to keep your parents out of this . . ." He glanced at Churl, rolled his eyes, and shook his head in a minute apology to Deeba. "Come on now."

"This is taking too long," Murgatroyd said. "Just *get* them—"

"*Quiet,*" Sound interrupted him. "This is a police operation, and I am in charge." He held out his hand again. "Miss Resham, let me take you home."

Home, Deeba thought, with a feeling so sweet and painful she almost made a sound.

What if . . . , she realized she was thinking, *. . . what if I do?*

What if I go with him?

If I don't *go back, they'll take Mum and Dad away,* she thought desperately, glancing at Churl's unpleasant features. *And Hass! I can't let them do that . . . And even if I* could *get away from them now, I might not* ever *get out . . . and Mum and Dad'll be in prison and they won't even know* why, *and they'll* forget *me.*

The thought was too appalling. She stared at Sound, and tried not to look at her companions.

How can I beat the Smog? she thought. *Even with Jones and Hemi and every-*

one? It's way too strong. But with the whole government and the police protecting me . . . I could be safe.

"Deeba, don't," said Hemi in a horrified voice.

She couldn't look at him. There was a silence. The police waited.

"I'm sorry, Hemi . . ." she said at last, her voice tiny. "It's my family . . . It's a way back . . . And look at us. Look at *me*. I'm *not the Shwazzy*. We've got *no chance* against the Smog . . . But they can protect me. And Zanna."

"Don't you see what they're doing?" said Jones.

"Remember what the Smog said," said Hemi urgently. "It's still coming!"

"But they can keep me safe," she whispered.

"Come on, Miss Resham," said Sound gently. "Let's get you home."

It's my only chance, Deeba thought. *Hemi, Jones, don't hate me, it's my only chance . . .*

She took a tiny step towards the waiting police, and caught sight of Jones's face. She winced at his expression. *I can't just walk away and let them take him,* she thought. *But . . . but if I don't go home now I'll never make it.*

Deeba looked away from the smug cruelty on Churl's face and up at Sound. He kept his hand out for her, his face creased in concern. *Come on,* he mouthed gently, and Deeba came.

And then, for one fraction of a second, she saw Sound flick his eyes sideways, and glance at Murgatroyd, as Murgatroyd glanced at him. Just for a tiny instant, but the expression was unmistakable.

Sound and Murgatroyd had shared a moment of triumph.

Deeba stopped dead.

"What is it, Miss Resham?" Sound said, in the same gentle voice, but Deeba ignored him and looked at her friends in horror.

Sound's fleeting look had brought home to Deeba something she already knew.

They're allies, for God's sake, she thought. It was Rawley giving Sound his orders, and Rawley was in cahoots with the Smog. The Smog that had tried to burn Deeba alive.

They're on its side, Deeba thought. All *of them! It's a trick! Sound's the one making promises? The one I was going to let take my* friends? *Take* me? *Stupid! They're all* working together.

Why would they protect *me?*

She raised the UnGun in both hands, looked Sound in the eye, and fired.

*   *   *

A roaring *BANG* echoed. Deeba had tried to plant her feet more firmly this time, but she still couldn't stop herself being flung onto her back.

Fire stabbed from the UnGun.

From the ground around the police rose bricks. They soared upwards, layer after layer, incredibly fast, brick, mortar, brick and mortar in rows, walls lurching out of nowhere.

They zoomed up in front of the stunned officers, a low wall, then a tall wall, then a high building, tiles bursting into place with a noise like popcorn. Deeba glimpsed Sound's appalled look as he was enclosed.

In less than a second, the yard was filled with a tall, solid house containing the police officers and Murgatroyd. Their vehicle was a little way off, empty.

There were the outlines of windows in the building's walls, but there was no glass in them. They looked as if they had been bricked up decades previously. A door was concreted over.

Deeba and her companions stared. The bricks and slates were cracked and old. A fire escape curled from the roof, its black iron banisters ornate and old-fashioned.

Everyone looked at Deeba. Even Curdle turned its spout towards her. Deeba carefully turned the UnGun's safety catch back on.

"I think," she said slowly, "I must've got a bit of brick into the UnGun, after all."

She looked at her companions. "Sorry about that," she said quietly. She wasn't talking about ammunition.

"It's alright," Jones said, and smiled.

"They'd have got any of us like that," Hemi said.

"We'll get you back safe. *Really* safe. And," Jones said, "we'll get you back in time."

Deeba listened at the new house, but could hear no noise. She kept her face from her friends, so they wouldn't see how she was feeling, at having thrown away the opportunity to get back. Even knowing it had been a trap, she was still absolutely bereft.

"Maybe all the rooms have blocked doors," she managed to say. "But they'll get out eventually. And you heard what they said about getting my mum and dad . . ."

"Hold on a sec," said Jones. He trotted to the side of the burrowing vehicle.

"They wouldn't have helped you," Hemi whispered. He put his hand on her shoulder. "They would have *given* you to the Smog, when they were done questioning you. And your family, too."

"I know," Deeba managed to say. "I do know. It's just . . . first chance I'd seen to get back . . . hard to say no . . ."

"It's Rosa really knows her way around machines," Jones said, fussing at the panels below the contraption's huge spiral nose. He got one open, and made an *aha* noise at the mess of wires and tubes that sprang out. "But in my experience," he continued, "this sort of thing generally doesn't go down well with engines at all."

Jones gripped a fistful of wires, gritted his teeth, and sent a huge surge of current into the metal innards. There was a series of flashes and a resounding *bang,* and smoke began to gush from the hatch, and the machinery's seams. For good measure, Jones tugged out a handful of the charred, half-melting wires. He blinked and staggered a little.

"Now," he said. "I'm not saying that's unfixable, but it'll take 'em awhile, I'd think, even after they get out of their new abode. A little breathing space for your loved ones, Deeba. So let's *use* it, to get you back to them, sharpish."

They took the fire escape over the roofs.

As she went, Deeba glanced at the burrowing machine and wondered how often the secret squad came through to UnLondon. The vehicle had to dig not only through the crust of the earth, but through the Odd, through the membrane between the city and the abcity. *If I just climbed back behind it,* Deeba wondered, *into its tunnel . . . could I walk all the way home?*

But even if it would work—which she doubted—Hemi was right. It was still a trap. The Smog would still come after her, and there was no one to keep her, her friend Zanna, or her family safe but her. She had a job to do. And UnLondon needed her.

Deeba and her comrades descended nearby in a tangle of loud, late-night/early-morning streets full of shoppers and partygoers. Deeba realized she had missed crowds.

Even in such a boisterous area, filled with the tunes from several different music machines, and UnLondoners dancing in even more astounding costumes and colors than normal, Deeba could feel an edge of anxiety that had not been there when she first visited the abcity. Many people carried unbrellas. People watched each other suspiciously.

"UnSun'll be up soon," Jones said. "We should find some cover."

"Look," said Hemi. "Can you feel it? People know something's up. See people all tense? Rumors are out. Word's probably spreading about what you did up by Webminster Abbey, Deeba—people probably don't know who to trust anymore. But they know something's up. They know there's a battle coming. Maybe some of them even reckon they're going to have to pick sides."

Rendezvous

While the UnSun was up, they sheltered in emptish houses. When they emerged, they stuck to backstreets and moved as fast as they could, at Deeba's urgent insistence. Signs of trouble were everywhere. The abcity was growing more tense.

There were few people in the streets, even allowing for the fact that they went by night. Once, scouting ahead, Jones flapped his hand frantically and the travelers hid in the deeps of an alley till a group of binja trooped past the entrance, their weapons out, following a Propheseer Deeba vaguely remembered from the Pons.

"They're sending out squads," Jones whispered.

In some areas the streets were patrolled by nervous-looking locals swinging makeshift weapons and wearing cobbled-together armor. Most UnLondoners knew a fight was coming, but didn't yet know what the sides were, let alone which one they were on.

"Don't forget the Concern, and those they pay," the book said. "There are plenty who'll line up with the Smog, when it comes to it."

Order was breaking down: once, in the distance, the travelers saw the looming heads of giraffes in the loonlight, far from their usual hunting grounds. Once they thought they saw the distinctive helmets of London police, and hid until the officers, if there were any, went by.

"Was it them?" said Deeba. "The same ones? Did they get out?" But no one had seen them clearly: everyone was on edge. "Let's just get going."

Hemi led them to a moil house, with eccentric walls of variegated trash.

"How do you know this is safe?" Obaday said.

"Better avoid the obvious emptish houses now," Hemi said. "We don't want just anyone walking in on us. But that?" He indicated a set of scratches by the front step. To Deeba they looked random. "It's a sign from a local . . . guild. Safe house. There'll be a bit of food; it won't be watched."

"What guild?" said Obaday.

"Guild of extreme shoppers," said Deeba, and Hemi laughed. He strained against the door, oozed out of his clothes and through the entrance itself, opened it from within, and held out his hand for his outfit, to get dressed again before he'd let them in.

 Inside, Deeba leaned her head against the dark glass of an oven door, part of the moil wall. She rested her hands on broken toasters embedded in see-through mortar.

"This is a *thieves' hideout!*" the book gasped. Obaday looked up, startled. He nodded in horrified realization, opened his mouth to say something—then met Hemi's eye. The half-ghost raised an eyebrow.

"Oh . . ." said Obaday to the book eventually. "Hush up."

The house on Unshrink Street was opposite an official newswall, showing headlines like *ALL GOING WELL! BE READY TO RETREAT FROM ATTACKED AREAS!* and instructions such as *REPORT ANY UNUSUAL ACTIVITY OR YOUNG VISITING LONDONERS TO THE PROPHESEERS! THIS IS FOR YOUR OWN SAFETY!*

Like several they had seen, this one was scrawled over with counter-graffiti, from more than one group. $E = A$, someone had sprayed. It had been crossed out vigorously, and next to it written *PROPHS R SUCKY SELLOUTS!* Deeba read. On one patch was written *CHOSEN ONE ROOLZ!*

"Look at that," sighed Deeba, peeking out at it from under a curtain. The sky was not quite light, and airborne buses were trawling with searchlights. "Zanna's still getting all the credit."

* * *

Deeba woke to mutterings, and sat up in sudden shock in a newly crowded room. The travelers were no longer alone.

They'd been joined by a small group of locals, as varied and bizarre as most collections of UnLondoners, talking quietly to Hemi and the others, while Skool kept an eye on the door. They greeted Deeba with great, though hushed, excitement.

"It's wonderful to meet you," said a large woman wearing a dress made of insects' wings "May I see the UnGun? Of course if it's inconvenient . . ."

"You helped my sister up by the abbey," said a man shorter than Deeba but more muscular than Jones. "I wanted to say thank you."

"I don't know what's going on with the Propheseers," said a third person, who was tall and wore thick glasses and whose sex Deeba couldn't tell. " 'Course, people like us've never seen eye-to-eye with them *entirely*, but I always understood them before. But now their instructions make no sense."

"Who are these people?" Deeba hissed to her companions. "Why are they here?"

"Rumors travel faster than we do," Hemi said.

"How?" said Deeba. "I don't want nothing traveling faster than us."

"There was already rumors," Hemi said. "People must've been worried for a while. Now there's something they can do about it. The first people here are going to be those . . . extreme shoppers, or people who know them, but I bet you word's spreading."

"We have to get rid of them," Deeba muttered.

"Why?" Jones said. Deeba stared at him.

"What? What are you . . . ? If they can find us, the Propheseers will, too! We have to travel *fast,* and *quiet.*"

"People know you're on the move," Jones said. "A few—at first just people with connections, like this lot—might find you. There'll be more. There might be a few you can't trust, but not all."

"Don't panic, Deeb," Hemi said. He held her shoulders and looked at her steadily. "Don't you get it?" he said. "You knew the war was coming. This lot are your allies. More than that.

"They're your troops."

A slow calm spread through Deeba. She looked again at the newcomers. They might well be outlaws. Several of them would have attracted long glances in

London, and at least two would have brought the streets to a standstill and paranormal investigators to the scene.

Here they were just locals, and they were there to join *her*. None, she realized, carried an umbrella.

She smiled cautiously at Hemi, and he smiled back at her.

"Alright everyone," she said. The room went silent. In a moment of panic, her words dried in her throat. *They're waiting!* she thought.

The anxiety only lasted a second. She coughed and smiled.

"Thanks for coming. Thanks for joining. Let me tell you what's going on."

Deeba's rather convoluted explanation was helpfully intercepted and steered by Obaday and the book, and interrupted by expostulations of rage and disgust from the newcomers. Jones drew a crude map on the floor. There were at least two obvious routes to Unstible's factory, and they were taking neither of them.

"Rendezvous is *here*," said Jones. He didn't say which way they were ultimately going.

"And listen," said Deeba. "From now on, wherever you go, or come with us or not . . . tell people. Not to trust umbrellas. Find other ways to fight. And if the Smog comes for an area, *do* fight. Don't just give up like the Propheseers say."

When they left the house, Deeba saw that the altering graffiti had itself been altered. In front of CHOSEN ONE ROOLZ! someone had added UN-.

"Look at that," she said, delighted. "It's accurate now."

Hemi was blushing.

That night there were more fires, and Propheseer vessels above, and sounds of skirmishes. There was deeper darkness against the black sky: Smog on malevolent missions. The travelers stopped and started, hiding and scurrying, many times.

Twice, those disembodied car headlights swept mindlessly around the travelers as they went. NOT YET GOT UNBRELLA?? the official graffiti said. TOMORROW—BROKKENBROLL & UNSTIBLE TO HAND OUT LAST BATCH!!! DEFEND YOURSELF AGAINST THE SMOG!

Deeba heard the far-off grunting of smoglodytes, and the brutal pattering of coal nuggets and metal bullets.

"Big attacks tonight," she said. "They're going to terrify everyone, so the last people'll get umbrellas."

"Why doesn't he send unbrellas after you?" Hemi whispered. "He could fill the streets with them."

"He can't," said Deeba. "If people saw them going off all over the place, and didn't know why, they'd get suspicious. Brokk blatantly needs everyone to trust them. Right till the last moment."

When the morning came the skies didn't lighten as much as they should.

"What's that?" Hemi sniffed. The air was acrid, with a smell that wasn't quite burning.

"It's exhaust," said Deeba. "Like car fumes. I bet you it's from London. Murgatroyd must've got out of that house, back to his boss . . . They've turned up those chimneys. To bulk up the Smog. They know something's going to kick off."

"Today they hand out the last unbrellas," Hemi said.

"And the Smog'll make its final attack," said Deeba. "With only unbrellas to protect them people'll do whatever Brokkenbroll says. Which means what the Smog says."

"If we don't get in the way," said Hemi.

"So," said Deeba. "Let's make sure we get in the way."

They had to stop when it was light, but of course they couldn't sleep. They listened to the panicked UnLondoners beyond the safe-house walls.

"Bling, Cauldron." Jones beckoned. "Would you go on ahead, and pass on a note? Get things ready?"

Deeba watched them go. She squinted—there was something strange about the two utterlings, she thought, something shifting in their look, something not quite all there. She shook her head. It must be nerves. She was mad with impatience. She checked and rechecked what was in her bag, pointlessly. She whispered to her parents, and imagined their responses, until Jones came and told her it was time.

The top of the UnSun had only just sunk below the horizon when Jones motioned the travelers down, behind a clutch of dustbins. He pointed into the sky.

Way above them, a man was visible in a rowing boat, dangling from a balloon. He held a rod, on the end of which was metal cord thirty or forty feet long, and a burning tire.

"The crazy fool's fishing!" hissed Obaday.

"Smog!" They could just hear the man's voice. "Smog! Come and get it! I have a proposition!"

"What's he trying to do?" whispered Hemi.

"A deal," said the book.

"I'd like to discuss options with you," the man shouted. "I'm with the Concern, but I'm . . . not entirely happy with the way things are going."

From a smogmire a few streets away, a pillar of cloud rose. It hungrily engulfed the wisps of smoke pouring off the tire, followed the trail along the sky. A fat blob of Smog engulfed the burning rubber.

"Good, you enjoy that," the man said. He was peering over the edge of his boat, and his voice was trembling. "And, and I'd like you to consider the following options. I'm willing to set up, and run on *your* terms, at least two rubbish-fired plants, on the understanding that you and I are partners . . ."

Two stalks of smoke rose out of the mass, to the level of the boat, and eyed the fisherman. Deeba could almost hear his *gulp* from there.

"Oh no," she breathed.

"There's nothing we can do," said Jones grimly. "Stay still. We can't let it see us."

"So . . ." the man said. "What do you say?"

The Smog yanked the tire, the fishing rod, and the man out of the boat. He wailed as he fell. The Smog swallowed him. Deeba didn't hear him land. Perhaps the Smog bore him with it, in a grip of airborne dirt, as it disappeared back into its stronghold.

"We're doomed," whispered Deeba to Hemi as they trudged along. "We can't fight that."

"You don't mean that," he whispered back. "You *don't*."

Deeba said nothing. *We might as well just give in,* she thought. She looked at the UnGun and almost laughed. *What good is this?*

Slowly, Deeba became aware of a noise. A whispered hubbub.

Jones led them through a district of warehouses and moil buildings, and the bizarre one-offs of UnLondon—buildings like bottles, and radiators, by fences like upturned nails.

They made one last turn, and there was the river. Deeba gasped.

It wasn't the sight of its dark water under the lights and crawling stars that took her breath. It wasn't the extraordinary, bizarre collection of boats that jostled at the edge of the dock. It wasn't the outlandish silhouettes of the bridges and waterside buildings, which looked cut out and pasted on the sky. It wasn't even the sight of Bling and Cauldron, standing with obvious pride on either side of a grizzled harborman, waiting.

It was everyone else.

There must have been more than a hundred people on the dock, standing in little groups. All of them were looking at Deeba.

"Told you word would spread," Hemi said.

There were men and women in uniforms and rags. There were people who weren't quite human, and a few who weren't human at all. She saw a man and a woman in the bus-conductor uniform that Jones wore. There was someone wearing the clothes of the extreme librarians. There were animals, and even a couple of other utterlings.

"Joe Jones," said the man by Bling. He was older than Jones, and big, with long gray hair. He shook Jones's hand.

"Bartok Flumen," said Jones.

"I got your note," said Flumen. He unfolded the piece of paper. Deeba read what Jones had written.

Bartok! it said. *Boats please! Many. Joe Jones.* That was all.

"Boats," said Flumen, and indicated the collected vessels by the river-wall. He raised an eyebrow at the gathering around them. "You didn't tell me you were bringing so many friends," he said.

"We didn't know," said Deeba.

PART **VIII** Fight Night

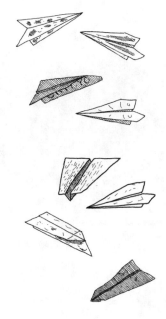

81

A Special Boat Service

Deeba smiled at the UnLondoners waiting. They carried bows and arrows, clubs, a few strange-looking guns. Standing on a roof overlooking them, Deeba saw a little group, one of whom was effortlessly standing on her hands.

"Slaterunners," Deeba said, delighted. She waved at them. "Isn't that a bit high for you?" she said. They grinned.

"Took a bit of getting used to," one said.

"A lot of our friends were against it," said another. "Said no good would come of leaving the Roofdom. But when we heard the rumors . . . well, we had to come."

"You finally did it, then? Came on *real* roofs?"

"It's *scary* up here! But, special times, ain't it? You're Deeba. Inessa Bad-ladder thought it must be you she kept hearing about. Well, at first she thought it was the Shwazzy, but then she changed her mind when she heard more. She says hello. We'd like to come . . . fight by you."

Deeba had to turn away. She felt a bit choked up by the sight of the little army.

Standing some way from the main body of volunteers, there was a wispy gang of Wraithtown ghosts. They looked ill at ease.

"Oh my gosh," she said. "Hemi, it's the man from the council! Maybe he *did* see what was on the screen."

"And he's brought others," said Hemi.

He walked over purposefully and began to talk to the chubby ghost, and the others. The bureaucrat smiled uncomfortably. Deeba saw their faint, spectral mouths moving inaudibly. She saw Hemi pointing people out, speaking in a voice that wove in and out of audibility for her. He stood and spoke with authority.

"Don't see what they're doing," someone muttered. "They couldn't do anything even if they wanted to."

Deeba stared unpleasantly at the woman who'd spoken. She walked ostentatiously to the gathered ghosts, standing by Hemi. He introduced her, and though she could not hear every word he said, she watched his mouth and, at the relevant moments, reached forward and shook as if she could feel the spectral hands they held out.

"There are others on the way," he said.

"I just wanted to say thank you very much for coming," she said. "I'm really glad you're here."

"There's more smoke," she said. "More fires. The Smog's trying to spread. And there's fumes coming out of chimneys. That's probably the Concern, lighting furnaces to help it."

"We need a diversion or two," said Jones. "No point us all trying for the break-in—"

"Jones!"

They froze. Approaching them from behind the crowd was a Propheseer, bodyguard binja walking in front of her.

Jones leapt and reached for his weapon, but the Propheseer threw up her hands and said, "Wait, wait!"

It was Lectern. She looked at the book, in Hemi's arms.

There was silence for several seconds. The Slaterunners, librarians, and others watched tensely. Lectern looked immensely uncomfortable. The martial-artist dustbins watched from below their just-open lids.

"Book," said Lectern in sheepish greeting.

"Come to fight?" the book said.

"Actually," Lectern said, "I came to apologize. And to join you."

"Some of us've been getting suspicious for a while now," Lectern said. "Brokkenbroll's *suggestions* have got more and more like orders, and they don't make any sense. And Unstible wouldn't let any of us help with his studies. He wouldn't even let us see his notes. That's our job! But then a couple of days ago," she said, "Brokkenbroll tells us that we might have to consider *abandoning the Wordhoard Pit*. That it's too costly to keep it safe. That we should let the Smog take it.

"Or, he says, another option's to build a few fires ourselves, or start up an old factory or something, and maybe *come to an arrangement* with the Smog! Says he's got contacts considering something like that! Well . . ." She looked at them.

"So you started remembering what I said," said Deeba. Lectern nodded. She couldn't meet Deeba's eye. "Is it just you?"

"I know there're others who don't like what's going on," said Lectern. "Some of them might be on their way. But I didn't know which of them to risk talking to. So when I heard the talk about what was going on, I just . . . walked off the Pons. Put my ears to the ground, listened out for where you might be."

"So word's spreading a bit too much," muttered Deeba. "We better be quick. Do the others know?"

"They must know I'm gone by now, but I made sure they didn't follow us."

"And the others are loyal to Brokkenbroll?" Jones said.

"Some. A lot of them . . . sort of pretend, to themselves, that they believe him."

"The binja?"

"These are the only ones I know you can trust."

"What about Mortar?"

She looked sadly at them.

"He's worst of all," said Lectern quietly. "He's been friends with Unstible so long, he won't hear a word of criticism. And the funny thing is, he gets *more* aggressive and *stupidly* pro-Unstible the more Unstible looks dodgy. Goes on and on about how brilliantly everything's going and how Unstible's going to fix everything and the Smog'll be routed soon. It's like he knows something bad's going on, and he has to prove to himself he doesn't.

"He's just being weak, really," she said. "You can't help feeling a bit sorry for him."

"Yeah," said Deeba grimly. She thought of Diss, and Rosa, and the locals by the abbey, and others across UnLondon. "Yeah you can."

Some of the vessels in the harbor were so old-fashioned they looked like they should be in museums; others were hung with streamers and ropes so they were like shaggy, floating, multicolored animals. Deeba saw one that didn't have just a figurehead at the front, but an entire hull made up of wooden animals, women, skeletons, men, and geometric curls.

But these weren't suitable for a secret mission.

Shapes jostled in the water. They were strange and ungainly, with slanted glass sections towards the front and back, and vertically along the sides. It took a moment for Deeba to realize she was looking at the metal-and-glass shells of cars, pulled off, turned over, and made watertight.

"What is that?" she said, pointing at the nearest.

"It's called a ɹɐɔ," Jones said.

The four grooves where the wheels had been were now the housings for oars. It didn't look like the most stable vessel, but it was low and nondescript from afar.

"Which is ours?" Deeba said.

"Traveling in style," Jones said, and indicated one that must have once been the body of a Rolls-Royce or a Jaguar or a Bentley or something.

"So this is a—" Deeba tried to remember how Jones had said it. ". . . a rack? No, that's not right . . ."

"It's a ɹɐɔ," Jones said.

"A . . . rack? I can't say it."

"Easiest way is to bend over and say 'car.' "

"Stay low in the water," Jones told the gathered army. "And don't go too fast. We need everyone to look like rubbish. There's no point avoiding the bridges if they catch us on the water.

"You've all been told where you should go. We want you to storm into the front, and—if you make it—we'll see you inside. There'll be defenses. No doubt about it. Probably a lot of them. So be prepared to fight hard."

People waited. After an awkward silence, Jones nudged Deeba, inclined his head.

Deeba hesitated.

"I wasn't supposed to be here," she said. "At first I just wanted to go home, but I couldn't, because you-know-what would've come after me. And back where I come from I couldn't have done nothing about it. So I *had* to stay and fight, even though that was crazy.

"That thing wants UnLondon—and who knows what else? It's poison with a mind—you do *not* want to be here if it runs things. Unfortunately, some people have been taken in.

"But you haven't. *We* haven't. You're fighting for UnLondon. And you know something? Me too. I want to get home, and I have to stop that thing coming after me, so I'm going after it . . . but that's not the only reason. I'm here for UnLondon, too." She realized it was true. "You lot—us lot—we're Un-London's last chance.

"We don't ask for much," she said at last. "Only to live in our abcity. Un Lun Dun!"

It wasn't much of a speech. But somehow spoken in a night so apocalyptic, beside the lapping river, under a sky crossed with the lights of flying machines and stars and Smog-feeding fires, it inspired.

"Un Lun Dun!" The crowd knew they couldn't risk shouting it, but they whispered enthusiastically, and it was almost a chant.

Deeba didn't realize for several seconds that she had said *our* abcity, and meant it.

"Does this thing have a name?" Deeba said as she settled onto a bench set between what had once been car doors, now upside down and sealed shut.

"It ought to," said Hemi. "Bad luck otherwise."

Her companions paused and considered, and all started making suggestions at once.

"Feather-I-Say?"

"Silver Belle Flower?"

"QV-66?"

"No," said Deeba. "This is the *Diss & Rosa*."

82

The Tangle

As Jones and Skool tugged on the oars, Deeba saw that the sky was darker, more stained with Smog than ever. Deeba was sure that those shreds would be mostly gathered over Unstible's factory, where they were heading.

One by one the ɹɐɔs began to cross the river, with faint splashes. Lectern and three binja huddled with Deeba and her companions in the *Diss & Rosa*. A widening wedge of vessels followed. The ghosts walked and drifted like thread over the river's surface, appearing and disappearing.

What had been the car's windshield and windows were below water level, and Deeba watched the brown swirl. She thought she could hear the noises of fighting in the wind.

"Sounds like trouble," Hemi said.

From the shore they had left, Deeba heard the song of a bird.

She looked back sharply. Jones stopped rowing, and looked through his telescope. He swore excitedly.

Running around the corner of a warehouse was a familiar figure, in an old-fashioned khaki jerkin, trousers, and big boots. In place of a head, he had a bird-cage, within which a little bird sang.

"Mr. Cavea!" said Deeba, and jumped up, swaying the ɹɐɔ dangerously. She waved her hands excitedly over her head, and Yorick Cavea waved back, desperately, without breaking stride. "But we saw him get et!"

"That was just his vehicle," the book said. "He must've got a new one."

"What's he singing? What's he singing?"

Cavea had reached the ɹɐɔs that had not yet cast off, and was shoving them towards the river hurriedly.

"He's saying . . . 'Quick,' " the book said. "He says: 'They're coming.' "

No one on the shore seemed to understand Cavea. One or two even shoved him back.

"Too late," said Hemi. Lectern let out a cry.

Masked figures were emerging into the docks, following in Cavea's footsteps, stepping in time. The nightlights reflected in their goggles. Pipes clanked and rattled from their helmets and the sacks over their heads. Deeba heard the hissing of gas sluiced through tubes.

"Stink-junkies," she said. "Hundreds."

The UnLondoners still at the river's edge stared a moment in horror at the oncoming army, then tried to race onto the water.

"Too slow, too slow," said Jones. "They won't make it!"

They could not all launch onto the Smeath before the Smog's slaves reached them. The front line of stink-junkies was already raising hoses, preparing to spray their enemies with flame or poison. Deeba's army was way outnumbered.

Flumen and a few others stepped forward, swinging spanners and planks. The Slaterunners somersaulted to the edges of the roofs, blowpipes at the ready. But these brave efforts could only slow the remorseless march by a few seconds.

"They're doomed!" said Jones, stricken.

"No they're not," said Deeba. Her voice was suddenly hard. *Everyone who's not a stink-junkie!* she shouted as loud as she could. *"Get down right now!* Jones, catch me."

Every Slaterunner, librarian, marketeer, utterling, nomad, adventurer, and birdcage-headed explorer hit the pavement, leaving Deeba a clear line of sight to the horde of stink-junkies. She raised and fired the UnGun.

The recoil slammed her backwards, but this time Jones was there behind her, braced and ready. In the split second of the roar, Deeba was trying to remember what was in the cylinder.

Ant? she thought. *Salt?*

Light flared from the barrel, and the stink-junkies froze. For one, two, three seconds they were all immobile, and the rebels looked up from where they crouched. Then the Smog's army began to shake, and their masks to bulge.

"What in . . . ?" Obaday said.

The stink-junkies' helmets shifted. The sacks that covered their faces blew up like lumpy balloons. They split, and from the rips burst out yards and yards of hair.

Oh . . . that's *what it was,* thought Deeba.

Stink-junkies tugged ineffectually at their heads, but their hair kept growing, shooting out of their scalps like waterfalls. Sideburns and stubble erupted from the seams of their masks, and the edges of the eyeglasses. Sudden fat dreadlocks pushed the pipes out of the headpieces, and clogged them so only trickles of Smog escaped.

The attackers reeled under the weight of the sudden shaggy swamp. It oozed out of their heads and mingled in a matted slick. In seconds they were just shambling mounds in a streetful of hair. The odd arm, leg, or split-open helmet poked from the tangle, but nothing could get out of it.

Deeba's allies got slowly to their feet and stared in astonishment.

With a little swagger, Deeba blew the smoke away from the end of her UnGun. She wrinkled her nose at the reek of scorched hair.

"He says that was amazing," the book said, translating Yorick Cavea's twitters.

Cavea opened his head-cage, and the bird flew over the river and joined Deeba on the *Diss & Rosa.*

"It's so good you're here!" Deeba said. "How'd you find us? Where did you get . . ." She pointed vaguely at the human body on the shore. Cavea whistled.

"He says over the last few days, everyone's been talking about the Shwazzy and what she's doing. Then he says other people tell them off and say she's not the Shwazzy at all, but that she's doing something anyway. He's been looking for us. He intercepted the stink-junkies, and realized they were coming for us."

"Yorick, mate," said Jones as he rowed. "Keep it down a bit."

The bird whistled more quietly.

"The Smog's attacking on several fronts," the book translated, "and the Unbrellissimo's flying from place to place, ordering his umbrellas into action defending people."

"Yeah," said Deeba. "Defending them so long as they retreat, I bet. While the Smog takes what it wants."

"Well yes, but apparently some people are saying they don't want to go, and they're trying to use the unbrellas to fight back. So Brokkenbroll's having to order them into action against the people who carry them. Telling everyone it's for their own good, and they have to pull together."

It was, Deeba realized, a very confused war. She looked back at the giant hairball still twitching on the docks. Cavea whistled.

"He says he has to go. He doesn't want to leave his body unguarded tonight. He says good luck, good luck, good luck." The little bird circled, and Deeba blew it a kiss. Then it scudded over the surface of the river back to its body and its cage.

The higgledy-piggledy procession of upside-down cars proceeded along a river full of obstacles. Hemi steered them past the hulks of sunken ships, and half-submerged old guns, and oddities, and amphibious trees with roots in the sludge on the bottom, leaves emerging from the black water and rustling on the vessels that passed them.

83

Wracked

One by one the rɐɔs pulled away onto the shore, and each crew set off into the streets. It was less than a mile to the factory.

Soon only the *Diss & Rosa* was left in the water. In the river-walls, Deeba saw the ends of tunnels, above and below the tide line. They were fringed with slime, and rippled as lizardly things slipped out of the abcity's underside.

The ghosts around them faded from view, until they were only glimpsed as an occasional half-visible pair of eyes. Deeba felt very exposed in the river.

"Here we go," muttered Jones, looking over his shoulder, and veering the *Diss & Rosa* slowly towards a darkness Deeba realized was a gate sluicing into the river. It led into a narrow channel that cut into the back of the abcity, behind rows of buildings in brick, moil, and magic.

"Where are we going?" Deeba whispered.

"Into the canals," said Hemi.

The concrete walls were so close rowing was difficult.

The houses backed straight onto the water. Sometimes they connected and made a tunnel, their big windows high over the canal. Levers and brackets jutted from the walls, and old chains swung. Wooden doors rose out of the water ahead.

"It's blocked," said Deeba.

"It's a lock," said Jones.

He climbed from the *Diss&Rosa* and operated a mechanism on the bank, opening the gateway slightly so water poured through. The ɹɐɔ went forward to another gate. Jones closed the first and opened the other. This time the water level rose.

"Like steps," Jones said, "up into the backstreets."

The locks continued, to a quiet, narrow stretch of water. *We must be way above the river now*, thought Deeba.

"Everyone hush," Jones whispered, pointing to the windows of the houses that backed onto them.

"I think they've got other things to worry about," Deeba said. From the streets beyond the buildings, they could hear shouting, and running.

Through the *Diss&Rosa*'s windshield, Deeba saw fingers of weed rise from the murk and stroke the underside of the metal. Deeba put her face close to the glass to watch them, then sat hurriedly back.

"It moved," she said.

The stuff floated around them. It drifted by in little islands. As Deeba watched it, one *quivered*, and reached out a tendril to grab a passing piece of rubbish. It hauled it in—it was a mouldy fish carcass—and the slimy clot of weed quivered more.

"That's shudderwrack," said Lectern. "Keep your hands out of the water."

"That's it," said Jones, and drew in the oars. "Too narrow. I'll have to pull from the shore . . ." He stopped. The houses came right up to the water. There was no towpath.

Skool held up a glove.

"Skool . . . ?" said Obaday Fing.

Skool took hold of the rope attached to the *Diss&Rosa*'s front. Then, with a wave, Skool tapped the glass and brass of the diving helmet ostentatiously, and stepped off the bow into the water. There was a splash so quick it sounded like *shloop*, and Skool was gone.

The rope descended into a widening ring of ripples. Clumps of shudderwrack drifted over to examine the disturbance, and Obaday batted them away. "Skool!" he said.

There was a knocking at the inverted windshield. Looming out of muddy darkness, a glove rapped at the glass.

"There!" said Deeba.

The water was too dirty to see much, but Deeba could just make out Skool's arm, and a hulking shadow that must be the brass bowl of the helmet. Skool put thumb and forefinger together in an *everything's okay* motion.

Obaday and Deeba returned the signal. Skool's hand disappeared, and a few moments later the rope angled out in front, and the ıɐɔ began to move. For a long time, there was no sound except the gurgle of its progress.

Weed ducked under, investigating the intruder, but Skool was unintimidated. Several times, clots of shredded shudderwrack bobbed to the surface.

"There." Jones pointed over the roofs. Around a curve in the canal, a brick chimney rose, sooty plumes gushing from it. There was a big clock halfway up one side.

"Unstible's factory," Deeba said. She remembered the first time she had come. It felt like a whole other life.

"We're coming in at the back," said Lectern nervously. "There should be a loading stage."

"Time to be on guard," said Jones. "This is Unstible's stronghold. He and Brokkenbroll are going to have allies here."

The bank opened into a yard at the rear of the factory, deserted but for clumps of crabgrass. Deeba looked up at the red brick, the unlit and boarded-up windows. In one corner a door hung ajar. From this angle, she could be looking at a view of London.

As the boat drifted closer, something moved by the doorway. A broken umbrella jerked up. With its effortful open-and-close strokes, it flitted into the air and away.

"It saw us," said Deeba. "We have to move."

She knocked on the windshield. Skool's faceplate appeared below. Obaday beckoned.

"What's that?" said Lectern.

Something dark was circling Skool in the water, in little spasms, fingering the leather suit with filaments.

"Just a bit of shudderwrack," said Obaday.

"There's another," said Deeba.

Suddenly there were several, and Skool was waving as vigorously as the water would allow, to disperse them. The utterlings jumped up and down in agitation, Cauldron pointing all his arms.

Something moved behind Skool's back. Ropelike limbs snaked out of the black and coiled around Skool's legs, arms, chest, and faceplate. There was no sound at all.

"No!" said Obaday, his hands flat on the glass. A huge mass of weed loomed from the mud and enveloped the diver, folding in on itself again and again, pulling Skool out of sight into the dark.

"The shudderwrack," said Deeba. "It's got him!"

Everyone scrambled onto the concrete shore. They leaned out over the water as far as they dared, hissing Skool's name.

"I'm going in," said Obaday frantically, searching his bag for a weapon, finding nothing but a heavy hand-mirror.

"No!" said Deeba. "That won't help."

They were sticking planks and ropes into the water, but for several seconds nothing happened. Then the surface began to bubble. The canal shook and fountained, and a gloved, weed-smothered fist punched out of the water.

"There!" said Obaday.

The fight below the surface was brutal. Thick shudderwrack emerged in temporary claws and mouths, and went swiping back under. Skool's heavy boot came kicking up at an amazing angle, through a chunk of waterweed.

With huge strength, Skool began to stagger from the deeps, weighed down and bent by weed. But pieces of shudderwrack trembled across the water, alerted by the commotion. They coagulated together, leapt up, and dragged Skool down. Deeba could hear the slimy noise of shudderwrack gnawing.

Deeba took the UnGun from her belt.

"Stand back," she said. Everyone obeyed.

"Quick," said Obaday.

"Don't you . . . need that?" Lectern said, but everyone ignored her.

Only one of Skool's hands was in the air now, and as Deeba stepped to the edge and aimed into the water, whips of weed spiraled out, and pulled it under.

Deeba fired.

*   *   *

There was a roaring boom, a spit of flame. She staggered, but this time Deeba didn't fall.

The air was filled with the smell of cordite, and also, Deeba realized, of the sea. *What's that about?*

Then she saw what was happening in the canal. The water was boiling, frothing, and then was choppy, suddenly covered in waves and white foam that jostled the boats and spattered against the concrete walls.

The UnGun had fired the salt crystal. The fresh—though dirty—water of the canal for meters around had been instantly transformed into brine.

The water seemed confused. It was attempting to mimic the sea. Deeba was sure she heard a gull somewhere overhead. Waves were surging as if the canal were tidal, and slapping against the *Diss & Rosa*.

Meters to either side, Deeba could see where the new patch of ocean met the regular waters. The edges of the join were perfectly sharp.

Clots of shudderwrack drifted to the surface. Their trembling didn't look like the healthy, unpleasant motion from which they took their name. One by one they stopped moving.

"What's happening?" said Deeba.

"That's what happens when the freshwater variety of shudderwrack suddenly finds itself in . . . the sea," Lectern said. She eyed the UnGun in awe. *Whatever it is, it always uses its bullet well,* Deeba thought. *No wonder it's such a legend.*

There was one sudden big wave, and the water broke over the concrete wall, and deposited Skool at their feet, flecked with dying weed, and highly bewildered.

Across the Yard

There were noises from the factory.

"They must've heard the UnGun," said Deeba.

"Quick," said Jones. "Let's get in before they get here."

But before they were even halfway across the yard, the door flew open. With a waft of fumes, death, and rotting clothes, smombies began to stagger out of the building.

With Lectern and three binja, the rebels were a decent-sized little gang. But there were twice as many smombies.

Angry-looking corpses swayed and lurched in their direction. The wisps of smoke that curled from their mouths and ears and eyes made them look as if they were smoldering.

The binja stepped forward, twirling their nunchucks and their staffs. They somersaulted into action.

Within seconds they were spinning kicks and twirling blows into the smombies' bodies. But despite the binja's skills, the animated dead were tough with the Smog controlling them. They hacked and smashed and kept coming.

Jones joined the melee, but his current was ineffective. Skool swung enormous punches, but so slow even the sluggish smombies could evade them. Deeba leveled the UnGun, but she couldn't get a shot clear of her friends.

Then, as the smombies seemed to be getting the upper hand, Hemi put his hands to his mouth, and shouted.

At least, it looked like he did. Deeba couldn't hear a sound.

But in the air around him, faint shapes began to appear. *The ghosts!* Deeba had forgotten about them. They emerged out of invisibility. There were definitely more of them than there had been when they set out.

Some were in ancient costumes, some in fashions only a couple of years old. All looked stern and aggressive. They put up their hands like boxers and swept through the air towards the smombies.

"But they can't touch nothing!" Deeba said.

"I told you we don't take over bodies?" Hemi said. "There's exceptions. If someone else has done it first, it's only fair to take the bodies back."

One by one, the ghosts stretched out their arms like divers and hurled themselves into the smombies. As the dead men and women were entered, they staggered to a stop and began to twitch. Here and there, ghost-hands emerged from the smombies' chests or backs, and flew back in, pummeling. The smombies rocked on their feet.

"They're fighting the Smog!" said Deeba. "To take back control!" She widened her eyes at the thought of the battle going on inside those poor, misused bodies, the Smog pouring through innards, chased by the ghosts' ectoplasm, spectral juices and chemical fumes vying.

"Quick!" Jones ushered them towards the door.

A ghost flew out of a smombie and lay, dazed-looking and semitransparent, on the ground. But elsewhere, Smog was being expelled from smombies' ears, and the dead bodies were shaking.

"Yes!" said Hemi. He grabbed at the Smog emerging from the nearest smombie, and flexed his hand into an ectoplasmic ghostly state. His spectral hand grabbed the smoke, and he whipped it out of the body and flung it away, dissipating it as it went.

The last Smog-controlled smombies began to hurl stones and lengths of iron past the binja, at the infiltrators.

"Stay down," said Jones, crawling rapidly for the entrance. Scooching down, Deeba heard a horrible splintering. She turned.

Skool was slow, and could not crouch. A smombie had thrown a particularly heavy jag of iron, and it had landed right in the middle of Skool's faceplate.

Deeba stared in horror at the asterisk of cracks spreading out in the glass.

"Skool!" shouted Obaday. "Go! Get back to the canal!"

There was no time. Skool reeled and leaned back against the wall, and the glass exploded.

Water burst out of the hole, as if from a broken main.

As the pressure dropped, the diving suit began to crumple and slide down the wall, wrinkling, its head drooping. It looked horribly like a body collapsing.

With wet slapping noises, fish began to gush out of the broken helmet. There were silver ones the size of Deeba's arm, tiny multicolored ones, an eel, an urchin, a seahorse, a little octopus. They poured onto the lap of the suit and the concrete, and began to flop and gasp.

"Skool!" said Obaday. He crawled over and tried to pick up the fish. They were slippery and flapping frantically.

"Where Deeba shot, it's still the sea!" he said. "Quick!" He scooped up handfuls of the fish that had worked together to be Skool, and threw them over the heads of the binja, ghosts, and smombies. One by one they landed in the brine. Deeba and the others fumbled to help him.

They worked as quickly as they could, but there were too many to save them all. Slowly, one by one, some fish stopped moving, by the wrinkled-up, emptied-out diving suit.

"Skool never did anyone any harm," said Obaday, staring stricken at a cod that hadn't made it. "They spent years refitting the suit, trudged all the way out of the sea to come and live with us, and this is what happens!"

"At least half of Skool made it, Obaday," Jones said urgently. "I know you want to give the others a decent send-off, but we have to go now." There were still smombies controlled by Smog, and they were regrouping. Obaday bit his lip, and nodded.

"We can't let the smombies get back in," said Lectern. "Or anyone else." The ghosts were confused, shouting soundlessly, emerging from smombie mouths. Hemi watched.

He opened his mouth and yelled orders that Deeba couldn't hear, gesturing commands with sudden authority. The ghosts listened, rallied, obeyed, and re-doubled their attacks.

"Binja," hissed Lectern. "Keep them out! Guard the door!"

"There's only three. They need help," said Hemi. He hesitated several seconds, and caught Deeba's eye. "I . . . I'd better stay too. I can tell my lot what to do."

"Hemi, no!" said Deeba.

"Look at them!" he said. The ghosts swept in little sorties into the smombie flesh, harassed the Smog inside, rushed out again in guerrilla raids. "They can win, but they need re-inforcements and they need my help. And *you need to go.*

"I'll be right here. I'll see you afterwards." He smiled at her as if he was sure there would be an afterwards.

Deeba was about to argue. Then she slumped, realizing there was no time, and that he was right, so instead she hugged him.

"Now go," he said urgently, hugging her back hard. "All of you. You saw the umbrella: it's going to tell Brokkenbroll we're here, so go *now.*" He motioned to the door.

"See you soon," Deeba said. "*Soon.*"

With one last look at him, Deeba turned, and leaving a little ocean, guards, a chaotic battle, and the bodies of half of one of their friends behind, she entered the darkness of Unstible's factory.

85

Six of One

Unlit brick passageways stretched in both directions.

"How do we know which way?" she said.

"Sniff," said the book. The burnt-chemical smell of the Smog was in the air. "Follow that."

They inhaled experimentally.

"I think it's stronger . . . this way," said Lectern hesitantly.

"Move fast," said the book. "If you can smell it, it's around us, and that means it knows you're here. Hopefully right now it's too diffuse to be much of a mind, but as it gets thicker, it's going to think better, too."

"So by the time we find it, it'll be ready for us?" Deeba said. "Wicked."

She hefted her pistol, and moved.

"Be careful with the UnGun," Jones said.

"But I'm getting better and better with it," she said.

"That's not what I mean," said Jones. He held out his hand and she passed him the weapon. He fiddled with its mechanisms, shook his head, and returned it. "I mean it still won't open, we can't reload, and you've only got two bullets left. We know the Smog's scared of it, and you can see why. You're going to have to use it. Husband your resources."

They stood together a moment at a junction, the utterlings blinking, Curdle scuffing the floor, Lectern following them reluctantly.

"Jones, Obaday," whispered Deeba when they moved on. "Is it my imagination, or are Bling and Cauldron . . . disappearing."

"It's not your imagination," said Obaday. They stared surreptitiously. The silver locust and the eight-limbed little man were both definitely slightly see-through.

"Utterlings don't last forever," Jones said. "These two've already hung around much longer than most. Maybe getting independent of Mr. Speaker's the reason, somehow. But we can't expect them to be here much longer."

"But . . . I hate that," whispered Deeba. "They're part of the team. There must be something we can do about it."

"I'm not bananas about it myself," said Jones.

The smell grew stronger and stronger.

"The workshop was on a top floor," Deeba said when they reached some stairs. "And . . ." She sniffed. "There's more smoke up there."

"There's definitely *something* up there," said Lectern nervously. Noises of cackling, and gobbling, and animated talking were audible in the stairwell.

The infiltrators ascended, to a closed door. It was from behind that that the sounds were coming. The Smog-stench was thick.

Deeba listened. There were several voices emanating from behind the wood, and they were talking over each other, interrupting and finishing each other's sentences, in aggressive, boisterous chat.

"I bet you there are six of them," whispered Jones.

"Oh no," said the book. "It's true, the Smog *is* working with them. That's the Hex."

". . . long are we going to be waiting?" roared one of the voices.

"Hush—"

"—up, Aye-Aye."

"Soon, Brolly man says."

"He *says*, Ivv."

"King Smogra's roaring around, to put the wind up 'em, make everyone practice with brollies—"

"—and tomorrow he'll move them all around."

"So what are we, Vee?"

"Don't you ever pay attention? We're helping with removals, Vee-Aye."

"Brolly and Smogula haven't decided yet, Broll says."

"They dunno how long they can get away—"

"—get away yourself, AyeAyeAye!"

"Shut up! Get away persuading the UnLondoners that Unbrell and Smogenstein are enemies."

"They *are* enemies! Hasn't Brollwah clocked that yet? He's nothing with his poxy shields. Smogzilla don't need him."

"And he thinks it was all his idea! Silly hombre!"

"Its Smokeliness has other plans."

"Not that the Brollington Prime realizes it. He did well to get the Propheseers on his side, though."

"Yes. I seen them here."

"Pay attention! They think Unstibulus is one of them, Ivv!"

"Don't know he's . . . puppet."

The voices snickered.

"My, they're going to be unhappy . . ."

"The Concern?"

"Propheseers! *And* the Concern."

"How'd it get so strong so fast? I remember when the Smogtopus was just a wee little puff of stink. Now it's all over the place in bits and bigger than ever . . ."

"Been feeding, ain't it?"

"Suckling on chimney teats. They been sending down gunk-smoke from that other place."

"The weird version of UnLondon? Lodno, ain't it?"

"Something like that, Vee-Aye. Anyway, they been feeding Smogli. On the quiet."

"Where *is* unbrella man anyway?"

"Things are going wrong, ain't they? Trouble all over."

"Hence no one here for supper?"

"Yes, what is all this for?"

"What, the spread? Broll meant it for a meeting with the Concern, tonight. Plans over repast."

"Not happening."

"No, things a smidge too chaotic for them to get here."

"People are up and arguing early! He's off like a bat-squid here and there, trying to stop trouble. There's *fighting*! People not doing as told and clearing off when Smogus comes on!"

"Shouldn't we be out, scary as bugbears, then? To frit them?"

"No need to frantic. Smogosaurus ain't concerned. Preparing still."

"I don't think it's caring if Unbrell's having a bad night."

"Don't care at all."

There was unpleasant tittering.

"They're just *nasty*," whispered Deeba. "How are we going to get past? Can we face them?"

"Absolutely not," hissed Lectern. "They're the *Hex*. Most powerful magickers in UnLondon. Each of them was strong originally. Two were Propheseers, a long time ago. But since they joined into one . . . No we can't face them."

There was a pause.

"So what do we do?" said Deeba.

"You know a funny thing?" whispered Obaday, his ear to the door. The utterlings mimicked him: locust, little man, and him, the three of them pressed up close.

"Maybe I could try to lure them out here one by one," said Jones.

"There are six, right?" said Obaday.

"That's crazy, Jones," said Deeba. "They'd never buy it. We have to try to find another way round."

"Well," said Obaday, "I've been listening carefully, and I can only count five voices in there."

One by one, Deeba and her companions stopped speaking, and turned to Obaday.

Whistling jauntily and doing up his fly, a man sauntered around the corner towards them. He was very tall and fleshy, and he squinted behind dark glasses. He wore a long pointed hat.

When he saw them, he froze. They froze too.

"*She's here!*" the man bellowed. "*She's here!*"

There was a commotion within. The door was pulled open, sending Obaday sprawling and the companions tumbling inside.

* * *

They were in a hall, in the center of which was a big table covered in food. Meats and cheese and fruit were piled in pyramids.

In one corner stairs led up. Deeba saw layers of smoke drifting from them, thankfully too dispersed to pay attention. The room was full of junk: suits of armor, old globes, game pieces, oily engines, and all manner of other moil.

The man from the corridor ran in behind them and slammed the door. Deeba and her companions faced the Hex.

There were three men and three women, all freakishly similar to each other. They wore identical jackets and trousers and conical hats. Each hat had different letters neatly stitched into it. The man who'd followed them in had *i*. The others had *iv, ii, v, vi,* and *iii.*

"Quick!" shouted the book. "Before they cast a spell!"

"Get her!" shouted the man wearing *i*. "It's the girl."

"You heard Aye," said a woman who wore *iv*.

Jones reached for his club. Before he had a chance to move, the Hex pointed at Deeba with a simultaneous motion. They all spoke a word at the same instant.

"Alive!"

"Come!"

"Girl!"

"That!"

"And!"

"Get!"

A crackle of light burst from each of their forefingers, flew together, and became one. It zipped through the air, whining.

Obaday appeared in front of Deeba. He still held his little mirror, and he swung it like a racket. He intercepted the humming light and belted it out of the air, as if returning a serve. It slammed with a *phutt!* into the table.

"How'd you move so fast?" gaped Jones.

The couturier looked rather amazed himself.

"But . . . I don't think it was going to hit her," said Lectern.

"They were aiming at that armor," said the book. "That was an ordersquito."

The companions looked at the armor, then at each other. Then at Obaday's mirror, and finally at the end of the table, where the little spell had been deflected.

On the table, one of the huge piles of fruit rumbled, spilled, tumbled into a new configuration, and stood up.

86

The Unintended Attacker

The fruit-thing rose, and unfolded.

It was taller than Jones. Deeba saw pears and peaches, apples and grapefruit all moving together like muscles. It stretched out arms at the end of which were bunches of bananas splayed into open hands. Its head was a watermelon, with bulging kiwi-fruit eyes.

The thing looked ridiculous.

"We're being menaced by *fruit*?" said Obaday sarcastically. "Oh *scary*."

"Wait!" said the book, and "No!" said Jones, but Obaday had picked up a knife from the table and swung it casually at the thing.

The fruit-figure caught Obaday's wrist with one of its bunch-of-banana hands, and it began to squeeze. Obaday stared at it in astonishment, and then cried out in pain. The melon-head was mouthlessly snarling.

"Not what we had in mind," said one of the Hex.

"We were thinking of a tin-man sort of thing," said another.

"But a fructbot will do," finished a third.

There was a crack from Obaday's wrist, and he screamed.

The fruit-monster swung cherries and strawberries and black currants sausaged into a tail, ending in a pineapple like a spiked club. It sent Obaday sailing through the air to land with a horrible thud.

The fruit-devil raised its banana claws, and ran at Deeba.

The Hex laughed and watched their inadvertent creation on the rampage.

Deeba leapt away from it. Jones grabbed it and tried to electrocute it, but the charge seemed only to annoy the fruit. It flicked him away. The little half-transparent utterlings could only scamper out of its path and occasionally slap it, completely without effect. Lectern cowered.

The towering fruity menace slammed its bananas and its pineapple into the wood of the table, sending food flying. Each blow bruised and smashed the fruit that made it, but the fragrant stuff still held together. Deeba dodged its sweet-smelling blows.

It stamped, and snarled, its fruit-face terrifying and malevolent, crouching like a murderer.

"Deeba!" Jones shouted. "Get out of here! Finish the job! I'll hold it off!"

She grabbed Curdle and tensed. But she hesitated.

One of the Hex was watching her. Before she got three paces, she realized, they'd cast another spell, and this time it would hit her full-on. Obaday was unconscious, the utterlings and Lectern were useless, and Conductor Jones was being pounded by the fruit. It smacked him with blow after terrible blow.

"Right," she said, and pulled the UnGun from her belt.

"No, Deeba!" said Jones. "You need the ammo!" He ducked, but got hit anyway by a pineapple smash. "You'll only have one bullet left," he groaned.

"You've seen what the bullets do," said Deeba. "Whatever they have to. One's all I'll need."

She pulled the trigger.

There was a reverberating UnGun roar.

The report stung Deeba's hands, but she kept her stance, lowered the UnGun a little, to aim at the astonished Hex.

From the tiny spaces between the fruit of the attacker's body rushed rapacious black specks. A tide of hungry ants.

The fructbot turned and spun on its heel, raised its hands, and beat itself with its tail. But though it must have mashed thousands of the insects, millions remained, racing over it and its crevices and chomping with their little scissor-jaws. Deeba could actually hear a whisper of munching.

"It's not enough to hit it," she said to Jones. "You have to actually take bits away."

The fruit figure was shrinking fast, its struggles weaker and weaker.

A trail of ants was crossing the floor in a line, disappearing into a crack in the floor, each bearing a nugget of fruit-flesh.

"To be honest," Deeba said, "I was sort of hoping it might be one giant one."

"Stop staring at that thing and look at the Hex!" the book shouted. Deeba spun.

The Hex stood grim and angry, their hands clenched in a complicated six-way clasp. Jones tried to vault the remains of the table to get to them, but he was way too battered. They glanced at him and spoke simultaneously.

"Where!"

"Now!"

"Are!"

"Stay!"

"You!"

"Right!"

Jones froze. His eyes shifted from side to side, but he couldn't move.

The Hex stared at Deeba.

"Forget taking her for questioning," spat the one called *ivv*. They shouted words again.

"Time!"

"It's!"

"Heart!"

"Your!"

"Beating!"

"Stopped!"

In the split second they spoke, Deeba rearranged the words in her mind, and a dreadful fear gripped her. She wanted to pull the trigger, but—absurdly, even at that moment when everything was about to end—she remembered that she would need one bullet at least to face the Smog and she hesitated.

She could almost sense the Hex's words flying across the air between them and her. *Oh no,* she thought. Her chest constricted, and she went numb.

Words of Persuasion

But even as a chill began to creep through Deeba's limbs, the utterlings leapt in front of her.

Bling and Cauldron were getting fainter and fainter. She could see right through them. But it didn't seem to affect their energy. They were jumping up and down frantically, waving their limbs.

Deeba couldn't quite make anything out, but she had a strong sense that something was decelerating. A point of focus. A particular vibration in the air. The utterlings leapt on the spot and gesticulated. No one but the utterlings moved.

"I can't help noticing," Deeba said eventually, "my heart's still beating. What exactly's going on?"

The utterlings signed quickly at the strange patch of air. The Hex stared at them in rage and shouted again.

"Banished!"

"Words!"

"You!"

"Renegade!"

"Are!"

"Spoken!"

The utterlings redoubled their motions, and another invisible-but-detectable oddity racing towards them slowed, and stalled.

Renegade spoken words, you are banished, thought Deeba.

"Oh my," said the book. "I think I know what's happening. The Hex are spellspeakers—"

"But the utterlings are making their words disobey," said Deeba.

"They're words, and they rebelled themselves," the book said. "They know what to say to persuade other words to follow suit."

"Somebody bleeding well gag the Hex!" the book shouted. The six magicians were opening their mouths to try a third time, but Deeba swung the UnGun at them and they froze.

Jones shoved cloth torn from their own clothes into each of the Hex's mouths. He picked up lengths of chain from the cluttered room and connected all six of them. He sat wearily on the stairs holding one end of the metal.

"If I hear a word out of any of you," he said, "I'm conducting the juice, and you won't like that. So *shhhhh*."

The Hex looked wide-eyed, and nodded to show how carefully they would obey.

Deeba circled the utterlings, which were talking silently and animatedly with their hands, pausing sometimes, presumably as the Hex's words answered them.

"So," Deeba said. "Somewhere in there—" She pointed at the air in front of them. "—are the words to banish them and kill me?"

"Yes," said the book. "But the utterlings are doing a good job of persuading them to do their own thing."

"What if they decide to do what they were supposed to, later on?"

"I don't think they're very interested in that," the book said. Bling had begun walking around the room, pointing things out to the rebellious words. "See? It's showing them around. They want to be tourists. They only just got born."

"If they do what they were supposed to, then they're finished," Deeba said. "I suppose the last thing they want to do now is what they were told. Then they'd be done."

The last of the ants was carrying off the last shreds of the fruit. There was nothing left but pips, stones, and stalks, lying on the floor very vaguely in the shape of a man.

"Isn't there something we can do for the utterlings?" Deeba said quietly to the book. "They're nearly gone."

"I don't think so. They've already lasted longer than most of their kind."

"But . . . we can't just let them disappear!"

"I don't want them to, either," the book said. "But it's not under our control." Deeba watched the dwindling figures.

"Can't I just speak them again? Cauldron. Bling."

"It doesn't work that way. You didn't speak them in the first place."

"Well, Mr. Speaker's certainly not going to speak them again," said Deeba. "Even if he could . . ." She stopped suddenly. "But they're not his things anyway, anymore. They rebelled. Why can't they speak themselves?"

"Don't be silly," the book said. "They haven't got any mouths."

"There are people who can't make sounds but they still talk," Deeba said. "They use their hands. Or they *write things down*. Why can't the utterlings do that? They *are* doing it, look. They could talk themselves back."

Cauldron and Bling were gesturing energetically to the Hex's invisible words.

"Tell them to say themselves," Deeba said. "That could work. Couldn't it?"

"It . . . might," the book said hesitantly.

"Of course it will," said Deeba. "Promise me you'll tell them to try, as soon as they're done talking to the spell-words. Promise?"

"What do you mean?" said the book. "Why can't you tell them?"

"Because I have to go," Deeba said. "Time's running out." She sat next to Jones.

Obaday was moaning and clutching his broken wrist, while Lectern tended him. The utterlings were escorting the newly independent words around the world that most words never had the time to notice.

"Come on then," said Jones. Deeba could hear the exhaustion in his voice. "The Smog's somewhere upstairs. Time to track it down."

"Jones," she said. She sighed. "Look at yourself."

"Come on now," he groaned.

"Seriously. That fruit-thing knocked you around. You can't even walk. And anyway . . ." She lowered her voice. "Do you really trust Obaday to keep watch over the Hex?" Jones laughed morosely. "*You* have to watch them, be ready to shock them if they get uppity. They can't come after me."

"Deeba, you can't go on your own."

"Do you think I want you not to come?" For a moment she could hardly speak. "I don't even want to go myself. But I got no choice. Look at you, man!" She prodded him gently, and he had to fight to stifle a moan. "You're a liability. Besides," she added. "I won't be on my own. I'll have Lectern." They watched the Propheseer.

She was dabbing at Obaday. Curdle butted gently against her, and Lectern gave a little squeak and twitched her hands and dropped her scrap of cloth. It fluttered down and snagged on Obaday's pins-and-needles hair. Lectern frowned and tried, and failed, to pluck it off.

"A milk carton, a bad-tempered book, and her?" said Jones.

Deeba and Jones began to giggle, a little hysterically. But there wasn't much time, and even as she laughed, Deeba knew she had to go.

The Baleful View

Deeba crept up the stairs, the UnGun raised. Lectern came hesitantly behind her, carrying the book. Curdle jumped energetically from step to step.

"Come on," the book whispered to Lectern. "Keep up, keep up."

After several twisting flights, they reached the top. At the end of the hallway was a door, from above and below which Smog oozed.

"We better be fast," Lectern said. "This Smog's going to sense us any minute."

The corridor shimmered in the vivid colors of night. One whole wall of the passageway was windowed.

"Look at that," breathed Lectern.

They stared out onto UnLondon at war.

There was the streetlamp glow, rising where the inhabited boroughs were, and between them the coiling dark of smogmires. But that night, UnLondon was also flickering in the illumination of many fires. There were the flashes of combustion, and the glowing beams of flashlights from the streets, from the dark cut of the river, where they danced with their reflections, and coming down from the sky, from aircraft and other flying things, racing in all directions.

"It's kicked off," said Deeba. "It really has."

She could hear the sounds of battle.

"Look," she said.

Below the rising and falling roofscape of the floors below them, they could see the factory forecourt. It was full of a huge fight. Behind the walls and thrown-up barricades, and on roofs to either side, battalions of smombies threw missiles. Stink-junkies pumped smoke and fire.

The attackers, just beyond the entrance, were the UnLondoner troops that had gathered with Deeba by the river.

They fired weapons and swung grappling hooks over the walls. Many wielded big fans, and swung them like axes at the Smog as it approached, blowing its smaller clots away. The dirty smoke scattered, gathered again at the edges of the yard, and re-formed for counterattacks.

"Un Lun Dun!" Deeba heard the rebels shout. "Un Lun Dun!"

"There are more of us than there were by the river," Deeba said. "People are joining."

"But most UnLondoners still think Unstible's on their side, don't they?" Lectern said.

"Maybe not, not round here. As soon as they see he's using smombies and that, they'll know he's with the Smog. In fact . . ."

"In fact word of that'll spread," the book finished. "And Unstible must know it. So it's decided, whatever it's going to do . . . tonight's its last chance."

"But *that wasn't their plan.*" Deeba frowned. "The whole thing I heard them talk about . . . it was all about how people would think Unstible and Brokkenbroll *were* on their side, and that's why they'd do what they were told. Why's he giving it away?"

"Maybe they're desperate," the book said uncertainly.

"Look," said Lectern. She pointed.

Among the vessels, birds, bats, grossbottles, and smogglers racing through the sky was a cluster of shadows. It was flying in a strange way. It was a dense mass surrounded by outriders. It careered towards them as chaotic and lurching as a crowd of moths, coming at tremendous speed.

"What is that?" whispered Lectern.

Specks flew up from the city as the mass approached, and joined it, and others dropped away from it and torpedoed into the streets. Deeba saw one of them fold its wings and fall like a crooked, hook-ended missile.

"Uh-oh," she said, and stepped back from the window. "It's the unbrellas."

* * *

In the umbrella flock's dark center, something dangled like an ugly fruit.

"Brokkenbroll," Deeba breathed.

The Unbrellissimo was holding on to one of the umbrella's handles, hanging below it as it opened and closed. He swung and reached with his other hand, grabbed another of the umbrellas. Again and again, he moved like someone on monkey bars, hand-to-hand, as if clambering his way through the sky. The umbrellas carried him each in turn.

The swarm swept into the factory's yard. They spread out among the fight. Then to Deeba's surprise they each flipped around, hovering in front of every woman or man, offering their handles.

"Friends!" Brokkenbroll shouted over the noise of the battle, dangling like a lunatic Mary Poppins. "It seems, uh, the Smog's forces must have managed to get into Unstible's factory. I'll make sure he's unharmed. It's heroic of you to rush to his defense like this. I'll check on him. In the meantime, I notice that none of you have unbrellas. The Smog's attacking all over! Please, take them! They'll protect you!"

Some of the rebels looked at each other in confusion. A few reached hesitantly and took the umbrellas flapping in the air before them. But even as Deeba began to hammer on the window and shake her head, she saw people smacking the umbrellas out of their comrades' hands.

"Are you mad?" Deeba heard one say.

"We know what you're about," shouted another. "Enough of your lies! Un Lun Dun!" He hurled a half-brick, and Brokkenbroll had to sway out of the missile's path.

The Unbrellissimo's face lost its expression of anxious concern. A look of rage replaced it. He bared his teeth and growled.

"That *girl*!" he shouted. He swept his free arm, and his umbrellas attacked. They reared and clubbed at the UnLondoner troops, joining the smombies and stink-junkies.

The Unbrellissimo rose to overlook the scene, and very suddenly, he was at the level of the window, looking straight at Deeba.

"Uh-oh," she said, and moved back from the glass. It was too late.

Brokkenbroll opened his mouth, and pointed at her.

His unbrellas hauled him, hand over hand, straight for her. His coat flapped. He loomed.

Like bugs on a windshield, unbrellas hurled them-selves at the windows, cracking and bursting the panes.

"Come on!" said Deeba. Lectern couldn't take her eyes off the oncoming Unbrellissimo. She would have dropped the book on the ground if Deeba hadn't caught it.

"I said come *on!*" said Deeba. She grabbed the book under one arm, tucked the UnGun in her trousers, and pulled Lectern along. Deeba dragged her down the passageway towards the Smoggy door. Curdle scampered after them.

Eddies of Smog tangled around Deeba's feet. They were thick enough to feel like cotton wool. She stumbled.

It didn't make any difference. There was no way she could have crossed the distance before Brokkenbroll arrived.

The Vengeful Man

With a dreadful crash, the Unbrellissimo kicked through a window ahead of Deeba and Lectern. He landed in a crouch, his coat billowing about him. The air around him was thick with umbrellas, and the incessant *click-click* as they flew.

Brokkenbroll stood, and glowered.

"Congratulations, Deeba Resham," he whispered. "You've managed to turn yourself into rather a pain. And now I learn you've poisoned I-don't-know-how-many UnLondoners against me."

Deeba, Lectern, and Curdle backed down the hall. Brokkenbroll made a hand motion, and umbrellas swept by them and opened, blocking their retreat. Only Curdle was small enough to squeeze through. Deeba heard it bounce off down the hall.

"I have worked, and worked, and worked at this," Brokkenbroll said. "Didn't I help? Didn't I persuade my associate to leave your friend alone? There was *no reason* for you to come back. *Everyone was happy.*"

"Everyone except all the UnLondoners," said Deeba.

"They'd have been fine! Holding out against an enemy! Under my careful guidance! Everyone happy!"

"You was lying just to take control!"

Brokkenbroll made *yak-yak-yak-you-talk-too-much* with his hands.

"I tried to treat you right," he said. "But you threw it back in my face. You are so ungrateful." He raised an unbrella high.

"Brokkenbroll, listen," said Deeba desperately. "The Smog's *your* enemy too."

He paused.

"What nonsense are you on about?" he said.

"Think about it!" Deeba felt the canopies of the unbrellas, some torn, some with metal poking through, pressed against her back. She pointed at the window. "Why's it showing its troops? That tells everyone Unstible's not on their side! They'll know not to trust him, and that means not to trust *you*. The Smog's sabotaging your plans!"

Brokkenbroll stared at her. For a second, Deeba saw his doubt in his eyes.

"You . . . *bad girl!*" he said. "I don't know how all this mess started, or what's been spreading such malicious thought in the abcity. But blaming my partner . . . you really are a disgrace."

He raised his unbrella again. Deeba reached for her UnGun.

It wasn't there.

Deeba panicked so hard she dropped the book. "Ow!" it said as it landed.

Deeba patted her waistband frantically, rummaged in her pockets.

Lectern was holding the UnGun. She must have taken it from Deeba's waistband. She was aiming it at Brokkenbroll.

He hesitated, staring at it.

"That's right," said Deeba. "We've got you covered. Don't move. Well done, Lectern. Now give me it."

The Propheseer looked at her with wide, dazed eyes, then down at the big pistol. Her mouth opened and closed. Brokkenbroll looked at her.

"Do you want to live?" he said. "You know you haven't got a chance. Give me that now and I won't kill you."

"Shut up!" said Deeba. "You don't scare us!"

Lectern stepped forward.

"Yes, he does," she said. She turned the UnGun around and offered it, handle-first, to the Unbrellissimo.

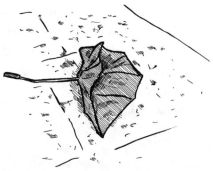

"*Are you crazy?*" screamed Deeba, and leapt forward to try to grab it. She was too late. Brokkenbroll had it in his hand.

"There's only one bullet left," Lectern said. She was speaking very quickly. "I heard her talking about it. They know the Smog's scared of it, but she's only got one last shot. Her friends are downstairs. They beat the Hex with some utterlings. She doesn't know exactly what she wants to do. She's following the smell of the Smog . . ."

Her voice petered out. Deeba stared at her, speechless with outrage.

"Sorry Deeba," said Lectern. She stood next to Brokkenbroll, and nodded her head in his direction. "But look at him. We haven't got a hope. I don't want to die."

Deeba lurched forward to grab her; but Brokkenbroll made a tiny motion, and unbrella handles grabbed Deeba from behind, held her still.

"Excellent choice, Propheseer," he said. "I'm sure we'll find something for you to do in the new government. One shot left, you say? Do be quiet, Miss Resham."

An unbrella clamped into her mouth. Brokkenbroll examined the UnGun curiously while Deeba struggled in the unbrellas' grasp.

"I don't have to listen to your unpleasant, troublemaking lies," Brokkenbroll said. "I will have a little word with my partner, however. I'll clarify exactly what has gone wrong, and what we can do about it. Nothing is unfixable."

He ran his fingers through his hair, looking decidedly wild for a moment. "But first—I'm not going to let you get in my way again.

"It might surprise you to hear that I can be extremely insecure. Particularly when someone seems intent on undermining my plans. Out of *pure malice*." He shook his head and looked wounded. "Well, since we had our last little altercation, I've kept something with me. To remind me that no matter how much trouble you've managed to make yourself, I still win."

He beckoned. From behind Deeba's back, one of the broken umbrellas came dancing forward. It was red, with a design of crawling lizards. Its canopy was torn, and flapped along the rip.

"Ass *ngine*," Deeba said through her gag.

"It is indeed yours," Brokkenbroll said. "Or, it was. One split, and it was mine. Do you want to see how *very* mine?"

He made a little motion. He turned and walked towards the door.

What had once been Deeba's umbrella leapt up, put its handle around her neck, and began to squeeze.

Deeba couldn't breathe.

Stitch

"Sir?" she heard Lectern say anxiously. "Do you have to? Couldn't you . . . send her home or something?"

"Don't be ridiculous. Now, I have to have words with my colleague."

But as Deeba ached and fought to get air into her lungs, the Smog wisps around her thickened. It regarded her, with globs of smoke like eyes on stalks. She heard a scraping voice.

"Brokkenbroll," it said. *"Stop. The girl . . . is intriguing. I want to breathe her. And I want her breathing while I do."*

"Ah," said Brokkenbroll, uncomfortably. "Good." He was looking at the fumes about him. "Have you been listening, then?"

Deeba's ears were starting to sing.

"The girl," said the voice.

Brokkenbroll snapped his fingers, and the unbrella released her neck. Deeba wheezed and gasped. The unbrella leapt down and hooked her ankles together instead. Another unbrella did the same to her wrists.

"Fine, there, it's done," Brokkenbroll said. "Now, I need to talk to you about what's going on."

He glanced irritably at Deeba. She was immobilized, unbrellas shackling her ankles and wrists.

"Bring the weapon," the voice said. *"I want to see what's so special about it. I don't like having something so . . . threatening floating around. I'll breathe it later. Then I'll learn it. All the prophecies are . . . unclear."*

"What do you mean you'll breathe it?" It was another voice coming from behind the door. A tremulous old man's. Deeba recognized it. "Who are you talking to, Unstible?" It was Mortar.

"Hush," the Unstible-Smog said. *"Quiet. Brokkenbroll . . . come."*

Brokkenbroll entered the laboratory, and with a last miserable look at Deeba, Lectern followed him. The Smog in the air around Deeba withdrew like a film of a fire run backwards, sucking back through the doorway, leaving the air cold, thin, and clean.

"Unstible," Deeba heard Brokkenbroll say. "Things aren't going according to the plan we made. What's happening? That awful girl was making all sorts of accusations—"

"Lectern . . . ?" Mortar said. "You've come to join us? And is that you, book? So . . . are we winning? Against the Smog?"

"Oh Mortar," Deeba heard Lectern say sadly. "Smell the air."

Deeba struggled.

The unbrellas' grip was unrelenting. She could shift her arms a little one way and the other, but she could not pull them, or her ankles, apart, or free.

There was a snuffling at her feet.

"Curdle," she whispered. The little milk carton crept through the immobile unbrellas and rolled into her lap, wheezing air in and out happily. "Oh, Curdle."

Deeba struggled again, but the unbrellas were too strong. Deeba sighed. She bit her lip.

"Put the UnGun down," the grating voice said.

"There's only one bullet left, apparently," she heard Brokkenbroll say.

"Where did you get that?" Mortar said, in a heartbreakingly feeble voice. "Might we be able to use it?"

"Brokkenbroll, UnLondoners are getting uppity. Things are going wrong. Hence change of plan. Need some more help. We're not ready yet. Take the elevator—find Murgatroyd. Or Rawley. Take the woman and go."

"You think?" said the Unbrellissimo. "I doubt Murgatroyd or his boss'll be willing to part with any more police, or come down themselves. They were doing us a favor in the first place."

"*Worth a try.*" The Unstible-thing's voice was loud and angry, and Brokkenbroll was silent. "*Put the UnGun down, put the book down, and go.*"

"Very well," Brokkenbroll said. "Of course. It's a good idea . . . I'll . . . go and ask . . ."

"*And leave an unbrella to help me.*"

There was a pause.

"I will not," said Brokkenbroll nervously. "I think you forget we're partners. The unbrellas are *my* servants."

Deeba heard the clank of metal, a gate slid into place. There was a receding mechanical grind.

"*Oh well,*" the voice muttered. "*Never thought I'd get rid of him.*"

"Oh my lord . . ." muttered Mortar. "What have I done?"

"*Sleep.*" There was a whoosh like wind, and Mortar's voice petered out to nothing.

I need to get these things off me, Deeba thought, and wriggled her wrists again. Curdle grabbed the unbrella with its cardboard spout. Deeba heard the book.

"Brokkenbroll'll realize you're double-crossing him," it said. "Probably does already."

"*Silly unbrella man,*" Unstible-Smog said. "*It's too late for him now.*"

"When he realizes and joins us, you know —"

"*Book.*" The voice was heavy. "*I am very busy. Last experiments. Chemistry. Working on this a long time. Breathed a lot of books. Very helpful, those librarians. Provided me a lot of fuel. Now I need to focus. I would rather not deal with you or 'Broll or the stupid old Propheseer. But make me pay attention to you and I will. In fact,*" it said with sudden greed, "*not got any chemistry chapters in you . . . ?*"

"No," said the book hurriedly. "Nothing but geography. And half of that's wrong. Shtum, me."

There was the sound of tearing, and a quick cry.

Deeba strained again, but it was hopeless. She slumped and closed her eyes.

It's no good, she thought. *I've come so far, I got so near what we had to do, and it's going to finish like this. I can't get out. Brokkenbroll controls the broken umbrellas completely.*

"Wait," she said aloud. Her eyes snapped open. *The broken ones . . .*

She examined her old umbrella. Its shaft and folded-up canopy lay flat beneath her, its crook around her legs. She examined the long gash in the canopy, which tore straight through several of the lizards.

Deeba frowned. There was an idea swimming somewhere in her head, and she strained to catch it.

"Curdle," she whispered. "I need you to fetch something. In my bag. See? The pouch! Fetch!"

The little carton followed her frantic nods eagerly. One by one, it began to drag things out of the bag.

"No," she said, "not the socks. Not the notebook. Not the . . . not my keys, no. The little black thing. No. No. No. *Yes!*"

With her hands gripped together, it wasn't easy to open her sewing kit, but eventually Deeba did so, and drew out a needle and thread. It was even harder to bend down to the unbrella holding her feet, with the other one around her wrists, but slowly and carefully Deeba managed it. She used one of the needles that Obaday had given her, and she would have sworn it seemed to help her, dipping and stitching with simple metal enthusiasm. Curdle hopped excitedly around her.

With crude, ugly loops of thread, all she could manage with her two hands working together, Deeba began to repair her umbrella. She listened to the murmurs of the Unstible-thing behind the door, trying to work out what it was doing. And as she did so, she clumsily sewed up the split that had ruined her umbrella's canopy.

The instant Deeba had put the last stitch into the unbrella, and closed the tear, it quivered. It trembled, and something changed.

The red-and-lizard thing shook itself like an animal waking up. Deeba held her breath. It moved fitfully, then slowly unhooked from her ankles and turned on its handle, opening and stretching its fabric in what could have been a yawn.

It turned, and the eyes of the biggest lizard faced Deeba.

"Yes," whispered Deeba. *"I did it!"* She bit her lip to stop herself shouting in delight. She watched what had once been her umbrella hopping around the corridor, bending to examine things around it.

"Hey," she whispered, and it turned to her. "Do you remember me? From a long time ago."

It paused for several seconds, then nodded its tip uncertainly up and down.

"Do you remember a minute ago you were gripping me?"

It nodded. Vehemently.

"But you don't want to hold my legs?" She gesticulated at her ankles. The unbrella bent to look at them. It raised its canopy a tiny bit and lowered it again. An umbrella-shrug. Then it shook it *no.*

"You had to. You were ordered. And now you don't have to obey."

It nodded and jumped and spun, and cartwheeled, and bounced from wall to wall and ceiling to floor. It opened and closed and flew in little jerks.

It's free! It doesn't have to do what Brokkenbroll says! Deeba thought.

It's not an unbrella at all, anymore. It's something else. When it was an umbrella, it was completely for one thing. When it was broken, it didn't do that anymore, so it was something else, and that's when it was Brokkenbroll's. His slave.

But if it's fixed . . . *It's not* un*broken—then it would be an* um*brella, just a dumb tool again. But now it's not* broken *either, so it's not his anymore.*

It's something new. It's not an um*brella, and it's not an* un*brella. It's . . .*

"What are you?" muttered Deeba. "A *rebrella?*" *Whatever it is,* she thought, *it's its own thing, now.*

"You like being free," she said. The rebrella nodded enthusiastically. "In re-turn . . . would you help me?"

The floor was littered with glass, and splintered wood from the window frames. There were little metal rods, too, a few inches long, that had secured the windows closed.

Curdle and the rebrella picked up random broken bits and brought them each to Deeba.

"No, not the glass," she said. "The rod. Yeah, that's it."

The unbrella that held her wrists was bent in the middle of its shaft. It took a lot of effort, but with the help of the rebrella—and the enthusiastic unhelpful participation of Curdle—Deeba held it firmly. The rebrella forced it open, and Deeba held a rod flush with the unbrella's shaft. Between them they managed to unbend it and wrap sticking-tape around and around her captor and the metal rod, binding them together, bracing the unbrella straight.

And suddenly, fixed like that, it wasn't an unbrella at all. It sprang away from Deeba's hands and did a dance of delight, like the first rebrella had.

*   *   *

With her hands and legs free, Deeba was able to get hold of the remaining umbrellas in turn. They didn't fight—their orders had been to hold still.

Two were so broken Deeba couldn't fix them. The others she patched up quickly. None of them looked good, but very soon Deeba was surrounded by four delighted rebrellas, jumping with the pleasure of no longer being Brokkenbroll's to control. They were like animals playing.

Her mind raced. She was painfully conscious of how time was passing, that her friends were waiting, and that she had only one last chance to stop the Smog.

"Will you help me?" she said. She had to say it a few times before the rebrellas lined up, seemingly eager. The exception was the red-and-lizard rebrella, which was quicker. *Perhaps because it was mine for ages*, she thought, *it understands me.*

"Here's what I need you to do," she said. "When I say 'Attack!' do this." She made exaggerated hitting motions.

She knew the Unstible-thing was very strong, but the rebrellas had been *umbrellas*, all treated with the chemical goo that rendered them invulnerable to the Smog's attacks. There was poetic justice, she thought—the props the Smog had made to help it take over the city with Brokkenbroll would now be turned against it.

There was a blue rebrella she had sewed up, a yellow one the shaft of which she had straightened, and a black one that had been the easiest to fix: it had just been inverted, and she had snapped it back the right way around.

"There's no way we'll be able to sneak in. There's one chance. I need you to help me," she said to the red rebrella.

For a moment, she remembered playing with it in the yards of her estate, twirling it like a sword. She wondered what those memories were like for it—for it, two whole lives ago. Perhaps they were like dreams.

"While these three are attacking," she said, "I need you to fetch something."

When she had done explaining, Deeba hesitated. Whatever happened in the next few minutes, she knew things were coming to an end.

Reactions

Deeba yanked open the door, and the rebrellas swirled inside.

As she entered, everything went slow. Deeba took everything in, in an instant.

The illumination in the workshop shifted. The room was full of the crawling and sluggishly flying lightbulb insects. A huge fire burnt in the fireplace. The big vat was still there on its swiveling stand. It was full of a vividly glowing, bubbling green liquid. Blue gas jets hissed below it.

Around the room, the benches and stands were the same amazing mess of chemicals in beakers, bubbling test tubes, and coils of glass that she remembered.

On a table in the corner, Deeba saw the UnGun and the book. Mortar sat back on a chair, snoring. His head was encased in a fug of smoke. The cage-door entrance to the elevator was closed, and the lift itself was not there.

The rebrellas went charging and twirling, opening and closing, swinging like swords. They moved more swiftly and impressively even than the unbrellas did. *Everyone prefers fighting by choice,* Deeba thought.

They bore down on the figure in the center of the room.

The Unstible-thing.

For an instant, it was frozen, examining a beaker full of the glowing gunk from the vat. Deeba stared at it in horror.

Unstible was grossly swollen, its skin stretched and puffy, pale and blotched and sick-looking. Its lab coat was tight on its body. It stared at Deeba with bloodshot eyes.

"Deeba!" shouted the book.

As the rebrellas spun aggressively towards it, Unstible opened its mouth and laughed.

It moved. Despite its new bulk, it was unnaturally fast. It cartwheeled out of the path of the oncoming rebrellas, seemed to bounce. It sprang on one hand, keeping hold of the glowing container in the other, twisting its wrist as its body turned so the glass didn't empty.

It laughed again, with a noise like a sack of dead animals being dragged across coal and broken glass. Unstible flung the beaker at the closest rebrella.

The glass shattered on the toughened canopy, and Deeba opened her mouth to shout in triumph at how easily it repelled his missile. Then her throat constricted.

The glowing liquid burst over the black rebrella, and where it touched the treated fabric, it *combusted.*

The rebrella went up in oily flames, with a ferocious outpouring of smoke. It burnt in instants, with a squeal of red-hot metal.

Unstible inhaled mightily, and sucked the fumes that gushed from the burning rebrella into its nostrils. They left behind a heat-coiled, twisted umbrella skeleton, and ash.

Deeba was aghast. For seconds, the rebrellas were motionless. Unstible moved again, like a ballet dancer, grabbing another glass full of the stuff.

"Move!" shouted Deeba, and the rebrellas spun off in different directions. But Unstible hurled the flask it held straight and hard, and it exploded across the stitched-up framework of the blue rebrella.

The liquid spilt across it, and spread fire. "No!" screamed Deeba, as it fell. In seconds it was gone, leaving its ruined metal bones behind. Unstible snorted the smoke in, and its skin stretched even tighter.

"*Boring,*" it grunted. "*Not very interesting minds. But a useful test. I thought I'd solved it. Thought it would work.*" It shook a test tube of the glowing stuff. "*Then 'Broll found a sliver of spine . . . wouldn't leave me a test subject.*" It looked at Deeba and grinned. Its teeth were the color of mud. "*Thank you for bringing me guinea pigs.*"

The other rebrella launched bravely at him. It hit his shins with two enormous *thwacks,* which sounded loud enough to crack wood. Unstible fell.

Deeba's heart lurched with hope, but the sick-looking figure bounced straight up again, like an inflatable. It was laughing.

With monkey swiftness, it grabbed the rebrella, and plunged it into a bucket of the liquid below the vat's spigot. Flames and fumes gushed up, and Unstible leaned over and breathed them in.

It turned and grinned. Its face was soot black, its hair singed off. In its smoking hand it held the remnants of the rebrella, a sorry tangle of ruined metal. With a *clank,* a piece fell off. Deeba recognized the rod with which she had made the yellow unbrella a *re*brella, only minutes previously.

"*You think,*" Unstible said, "*I let things wander around that I can't stop? That I can't breathe?*"

Deeba kept her eyes on the horrible figure, but out of the corner of her eye she watched Curdle and the rebrella she couldn't stop thinking of as hers, the red-and-lizard one, creeping quietly towards the UnGun and the book.

The motion seemed to catch Unstible's attention. Deeba held her breath. But the rebrella froze, and Curdle leapt away from it and rolled, wheezing aggressively, towards Unstible, drawing its attention.

"Curdle, stay back!" said Deeba. As Unstible reached for the carton, she picked up a chair and threw it with all her strength.

Unstible caught it, by one leg, with one hand. It threw it in the fire, and sniffed as it began to burn. Curdle bounded away and hid behind Deeba's feet.

" *'Broll's right. You are annoying. Distracting my attention. I had intended to breathe you later, for pudding, but congratulations—you're an hors d'oeuvre, instead.*"

Unstible stalked towards her, its newly pudgy hands out. Deeba backed towards the wall.

Her rebrella scuttled the last few meters to the table, leapt up, and hooked the UnGun.

"What . . . ?" said Unstible, turning, and snarling when it saw what was happening. It leapt with that unnatural grace, like a fat tiger, nails crooked into claws. The rebrella levered itself desperately like a catapult, and sent the UnGun soaring over Unstible's head.

The UnGun spun. It rose. Unstible seemed to change direction in the middle of its leap. It snatched at the pistol, its fingers millimeters from it, but the weapon arced just, just over its hand, and began to descend, and Deeba came forward, reached up as the UnGun came down.

And then it was in her hands, and Deeba aimed.

Auto-da-Fé Dreams

Even as Deeba raised the UnGun, Unstible was moving. The enormous figure jumped straight at a wall, and *bounced* behind the vat like a rubber ball. Deeba tried to keep her weapon trained on it, but it was so quick, and the room so cluttered, she couldn't. She kept her back to the wall.

Unstible's hand emerged from behind an upturned table, and reached for the controls at the bottom of the vat. It was too far. It poked its fat head around the edge of the table, and Deeba's finger tightened.

One bullet left, she thought. *Only one. Be sure.*

Unstible saw her aiming, and leapt back behind its barricade. Deeba kept her weapon up.

Come on, she thought. *Try for it.* But Unstible stayed put.

"Careful Deeba!" the book called.

"What's going on?" she said. "What's that liquid?" She wished she could talk to it without Unstible hearing, but there was no way.

"That's what it's been working on all this time," the book shouted. "All the books Unstible's had people fetching from the Wordhoard Pit. All research. It's been looking for something to make a magico-chemical *reaction.*"

"But why? The unbrellas have to *work* to make people believe this whole story him and Brokkenbroll are spreading, the whole baddy-goody thing. If they don't work, no one'll obey the Unbrellissimo."

"I think there's been a change of plans," the book said.

"Why don't you just ask me?" Unstible growled, and laughed.

"Don't talk to it," the book said. "Just be ready to shoot!"

"Unbrellas do work," Unstible said. Deeba could hear it moving. *"Protect against bullets. Against missiles. Against coal-rain. Without unbrellas, all the Un-Londoners stay hidden, whenever I come. Hide in holes. Hide in cellars. They stay out of sight. No good."*

"What?" whispered Deeba.

"I want to breathe. To suck in smoke and know. The lovely burn of books, and houses, and pictures, and people. *Silly UnLondoners. Silly Deeba. It's not like ending. Everything burns, and floats in smoke, into me. I keep it safe. Make it me. I am everything.*

"Everything is so fragile. So I set my fires, to breathe it in, and save it forever in my clouds. But the UnLondoners hide. Too scared. Then put out my fires."

Deeba stared at the convoluted rebrella remains.

"It wants people to think they'll be okay," she said. "So they'll come out."

"When 'Broll heard what Unstible was looking for, over your side," it said, *"he came to me, with his plan . . . But he wanted to rule, by lies. And feed me a little at a time, without UnLondoners knowing what they did for me.*

"He wanted me to be a secret pet.

"But I want to grow, and grow, and know. I wasn't strong enough for a long time. But I've been feeding. I want to know and know and grow. Lovely books. Burn and learn, burn and learn. Lovely people, lovely minds." The horrible crooning hunger in the voice made Deeba sick. *"But you all kept hiding. And Brokkenbroll gave me an idea. So I show them, boo hoo, how much they beat me with their magic unbrellas . . ."*

"Oh my God," said Deeba. "They'll all come out . . . It's going to attack . . . to rain . . . and they'll all come out, because they think unbrellas protect them . . ." *And it'll rain its new chemical . . . and everyone will burn.*

"That's what it's been researching," the book said. "A compound that reacts to Unstible's formula. It's not working with the Unbrellissimo at all, it's *double-crossing* him, using him. Brokkenbroll thinks the unbrellas are shields he controls . . . but they're matches, ready to light."

"They come out to show they're not afraid," said Unstible, its voice singsong and horrifying. *"And rain comes down and they'll go up, in light and smoke, and I will gather everyone. And fire will spread, and all UnLondoners and all their houses and their lovely books and all their lovely minds will float in smoke and come and be in me. And I'll know everything. And be everyone. No one will end. I will be all of you.*

"Is that so bad?"

Deeba saw visions of the abcity, and all its inhabitants, in flames. The Smog would be colossal, a supergenius, of millions of minds and millions of books, all mixed in its poison, ruling over a kingdom of ash. She went absolutely cold.

"I'll be so strong, then," it whispered. *"Strong enough to travel long ways, all of me, and burn, and learn, in a thousand places, in abcities . . . and cities."*

It was insatiable, Deeba realized. If it succeeded, tonight, it would become a poisonous, fire-starting smoke god, burning and learning everything it could reach.

"I'll learn everything I can get to. Understand?" It began to laugh.

Deeba couldn't breathe. This wasn't just about her or Zanna or her family or even the whole of UnLondon. The Smog knew the way to London, too.

One bullet, she thought, and thought of what she'd fired already, and wondered what the UnGun would do with what was left. *Do . . . not . . . miss . . .*

There was the churn of a motor, and the approach of clanking.

"Well, that was a total bust," she heard someone shout.

Brokkenbroll's voice came from the elevator shaft.

"Like I thought, the minister won't give us any more people. She was a bit concerned when I told them what's going on, too." The lift descended into view. Brokkenbroll opened the gate and stepped out, with Lectern behind him, and unbrellas on all sides.

"In fact," he said, "she asked me to keep an eye out for Murgatroyd. Can't find him. She said I should—"

He stopped. He stared at the chaos of the laboratory, at Unstible, hiding from Deeba, at Deeba herself. For a moment, no one moved.

"Turn up the gas!" screamed Unstible.

"Brokkenbroll!" shouted Deeba. "No! It's a trick!"

But as Lectern dropped cowering to the floor, Brokkenbroll grabbed the gas valve and twisted it. The flames below the vat roared, and the glowing liquid bubbled more vigorously.

Deeba swung her UnGun towards Brokkenbroll, then faltered as Unstible leapt into view and ran towards her with bouncing strides.

One bullet, one bullet, Deeba thought.

She ducked sideways, aiming down the barrel of the UnGun, until both Unstible and Brokkenbroll were in her line of sight. The vat of glowing chemical was beginning to steam and spit.

Brokkenbroll's unbrellas rose like ravens and came for her. Brokkenbroll raised his hand. Unstible was close, snarling, drooling smoke.

Deeba braced and pulled the trigger.

93

Shed Skin

An almighty explosion rang in Deeba's ears. The UnGun recoiled.

From every corner of the air came paper airplanes. Some were tiny; some were made from huge sheets. They were all different colors. Some were made from pages torn from books, some were written on in pen, some were blank.

There were simple folded darts and intricate models with recurved wings. The air was filled with thousands. They dive-bombed Brokkenbroll and Unstible as if they were carried in a hurricane.

They swept past the targets, brushing the two men with the edges of their wings, scoring lines. Brokkenbroll cried out.

Her aim was good. But Brokkenbroll was clicking his fingers, and a phalanx of his unbrellas opened and made a shield. With a drumming like rain, the paper missiles bounced from the reinforced fabric.

In the center of that shield, Deeba saw the red, lizard-covered rebrella.

No! she thought in despair. *With him so close, he's controlling it again.*

There were no unbrellas protecting Unstible. The paper edges scraped it hundreds of times. Had it been a man, the stinging onslaught might have hurt it. But it was not. It stood in the middle of the blizzard of darts and laughed. Behind it, the vat bubbled vio-lently, and thick steam poured off it. Unstible sucked, and the green swirls eddied into its mouth and nose. Unstible's body grew fatter. Its skin stretched.

"Come on!" Deeba shouted, and shook the UnGun. "Paper *planes?*" she shouted. "*Paper* cuts? Drop a ton of books on them or something!" But the on-slaught of folded planes was ebbing.

Unstible's skin was marked with little wounds, which didn't bleed, but oozed wisps of smoke. Brokkenbroll peered out from behind his unbrellas.

He looked at Deeba, holding her useless empty weapon. She desperately tried to snap open its cylinder to reload, but it wouldn't budge. The Unbrellis-simo looked at Unstible, still sucking in the stream of green fumes.

Brokkenbroll didn't look triumphant: he looked bewildered, and afraid.

"What are you . . . ?" he said to the Unstible-thing, and his words dried.

He snapped his fingers. The unbrellas folded their canopies and made towards Deeba.

The rebrella did not. Deeba saw it fold up under Brokkenbroll's nose, and understood. It had infiltrated his shield, to get close to him. When it did not obey him, Deeba saw a look of total horror cross Brokken-broll's face.

He did not have time to do anything. The rebrella whacked him resound-ingly in the head. He keeled over backwards.

Instantly, in time with his fall, the unbrellas stopped mov-ing towards Deeba, and eddied in confusion.

The rebrella smacked Brokkenbroll several times more, until he was definitely unconscious.

Deeba could not take her eyes from Unstible's horrifying transformation. It inhaled like an industrial pump, and swelled into a revolting parody of a human. The smoke pouring from the vat sluiced into its body. The vat itself was beginning to shake, and creak.

Unstible staggered towards Deeba, but it was too grossly inflated now to walk. Instinctively Deeba raised the UnGun, but it was empty, and she could only lower it again. Unstible smiled.

"It's," it spat out through an inrush of reeking steam, "time."

It smiled wider, and wider. It opened its mouth and stretched back its lips, and still kept smiling. Its mouth began to gape, and the skin at the corners stretched, and Unstible's jaw dropped and its head lolled back, and that mouth opened so wide suddenly its head hinged all the way open, turned inside out, and a huge, dense cloud poured out.

The Smog inside Unstible was so thick it completely blocked out light. It was dark and tinged with the green of the steam. It gushed out of Unstible as if from an exhaust pipe.

Unstible's skin collapsed. There was not a fleck of blood. It fell in on itself, as the fumes, the only things that had filled it for a long time, left.

The skin lay in a man-shaped rag on the floor. The Smog expanded luxuriously into the room. It seemed impossible that so much smoke had fit in Unstible, no matter how stretched. The Smog was everywhere, and Deeba couldn't breathe, or see.

She felt the grit of airborne soot and rubbish sting her, and she tried to keep her eyes and mouth shut. The chemical stench was inescapable. She spat. She fell to her knees.

The room began to shake. For a second Deeba thought it was her imagination, but she could dimly hear the roaring of the huge cauldron as the magic compound boiled into gas, and joined the Smog's substance.

There was a bursting roar, and Deeba felt the Smog rush from her, and the air clear.

Wind tugged at her hair. She opened her eyes, and was staring up into the crawling stars, and the loon, and a dark, soaring cloud.

Deeba looked around in confusion. Dust was settling everywhere, coating the aimless unbrellas, the ruined furniture, and the room's other coughing inhabitants. She saw Unstible's skin where it had fallen.

The vat was burst. The liquid had reached some critical heat and exploded. It had blown off the roof. Deeba looked up again and let out a cry of terror. Rising directly above the room, the Smog flew.

It was growing as it rose, spreading out into its full dimensions. It indulged itself, played, gave itself momentary smoky wings, or claws, or teeth. In the loonlight, Deeba could see thick green spread through it as it mingled the chemical with the rest of its substance. All the fumes in the room were sucked up in its wake, merging with it.

The factory's great chimney was trembling. It began to collapse at the top, falling in on itself and roaring as it tumbled down, sending bricks and brick dust into the fireplace a few feet from her.

Deeba put her head in her hands. But as she cowered, she heard ricochets.

Her rebrella was open by the fireplace. It was darting from side to side and up and down faster than she could see, using its reinforced fabric to shield her—and coincidentally Lectern, Mortar, and even Brokkenbroll—from the falling bricks. She watched its beautiful life-saving performance in amazement.

After several seconds, the top of the chimney had collapsed inwards and clogged the shaft. The remaining stub swayed and held.

One by one, the walls of the room fell away. The rubble of the laboratory was open to the air. The rebrella clicked closed, and spun into Deeba's hand.

"Thank you," she whispered.

"Deeba . . ." It was Mortar. The soporific little smoggler that had covered his face was gone, sucked into the growing cloud above them. He staggered to his feet, raising a plume of dust, and shuffled towards her, blinking.

"I don't know what's happened," he said, "but I do know I've been a terrible, terrible fool. Please forgive me. I simply . . . couldn't believe my own old friend Unstible was . . ." His voice failed him.

Deeba eyed him. She knew she should be extremely angry with him, and she would be soon, but not just then.

"He wasn't," she said. "Your friend didn't do nothing. It was the Smog." She decided not to show him Unstible's skin. He looked on the verge of collapse already.

"But . . . can you ever . . ."

"Yeah, yeah," she said hurriedly. "I'll forgive you later. Right now there's *no time.*" She pointed up. Mortar stared in horror at the growing mass of greening cloud.

"What's it doing?"

Deeba spoke urgently.

"It's getting ready to make every unbrella in UnLondon a firebomb—all them unbrellas it and Brokkenbroll told everyone to carry. For protection."

With your help, she thought, but didn't say. It was obvious from Mortar's face that he knew it.

"What can we do?" he said mournfully. "What can *I* do?"

"First, we need to . . . *stop her getting away,*" Deeba said suddenly and, without even thinking, hurled the rebrella at Lectern, who was creeping towards the elevator. It tangled into the Propheseer's legs, pulled her down. Lectern wailed.

"She went over to Brokkenbroll," Deeba said. "Deliberately."

"*Lectern!*" Mortar said.

"Yeah, it's terrible, but we don't have time to be horrified yet," Deeba said. She thought quickly. She looked up at the Smog, and out over the ruined walls across UnLondon.

All over the city, dark plumes were rising from the smogmires.

Everywhere were flashes of fires and battles, and the noises of struggle, as the great war for UnLondon raged. But something new was happening.

The Smog was oozing out of the streets it had taken over, tugging out of the sewers and the houses, floating up into a choking lid. It sat in the air in fat globs acres wide, dangling filaments of smoke like feelers, sucking the last of itself from chimneys.

All the Smog of UnLondon rose. Nightbirds, highfish, and flying vessels lurched, shocked, to evade it.

From every battleground, the Smog seeped out of the reanimated flesh of the smombies. They collapsed, or were suddenly controlled by surprised ghosts who'd been struggling to push the sentient smoke out of them. The Smog gushed out of the tanks and pipes on the stink-junkies. They fell to the floor and wheezed in withdrawal as the pollutants that had addicted them floated away.

All the clots of Smog billowed through the air and rolled into each other, like blobs of mercury. They joined into fatter clouds. They slowly approached the densest patch of all, over Deeba's head. After weeks in Unstible's skin, it was luxuriating in the open sky.

Deeba heard cheers from across UnLondon.

"They think it's over," said Deeba. "They think they won. But it's drawing together, so it can mix that chemical in. It boiled it so it could breathe it—now it's going to mix it into every bit of Smog there is. Then it'll spread again . . . and rain. While everyone celebrates. They'll see it coming, but they'll just put up their unbrellas."

"And then . . ." said the book.

"The unbrellas," Deeba said. "And the people carrying them. They'll all burn."

94

The Dreadful Sky

"Can you get to the bridge?" she said. "Mortar! Can you?"

With a visible effort, Mortar looked away from the growing mass of Smog.

"Yes," he said. "I may be tired, and an idiot, but I wouldn't be a Propheseer if I couldn't get to the Pons Absconditus."

"Right," said Deeba. She thought fast. "You have to go *everywhere*. Hundreds and thousands of people are out and about tonight. You have to go *everywhere*, and tell them the Smog's coming back, and that their unbrellas won't help them: they'll kill them.

"Maybe gather up more Propheseers. Move as fast as you can. Tell people to get underground, whatever. And throw their unbrellas away!"

"But what then?" said the book. "The Smog'll be everywhere . . ."

"First thing's to stop it *killing* everyone," she snapped. "Then we'll work out what's next."

"What are you going to do?" Mortar asked.

"I need to get my friends," Deeba said. "Jones and Obaday and the others . . . I have to make sure they're okay."

"I'll wait for you."

"*No.* You have to go *now.* There's no time. Spread the word. I'll . . . try to sort things out here."

Mortar looked for a moment as if he was about to argue, then changed his mind.

"I'll get the bridge," he said. He shook his head to clear it, and concentrated.

"She'd better go with you," said Deeba. "Don't want her escaping to London." She stretched out her hand, and her rebrella yanked Lectern towards her. Lectern squeaked.

"How did you do that with an unbrella?" said Mortar.

"It's not," Deeba said. "It's a *rebrella* . . . that's another thing! Everyone can *fix* their unbrellas. That frees them from Brokkenbroll."

"So if they fix them, they can use them against the Smog . . . ?"

"No, they'll still explode in the rain. Forget it. You have to get everyone inside, fast. We'll fix the unbrellas afterwards. Brokkenbroll's not the problem now."

Above them, the Smog was condensing. Its smogglers were congealing into it one after the other. The green tinge was spreading throughout its substance.

"Get the bridge here," said Deeba.

Mortar gripped Lectern's shoulder. Lectern was so slumped and defeated, Deeba didn't think she would run.

He should take Brokkenbroll, Deeba thought. But the Unbrellissimo was still out cold, and no one had the strength to drag him. She watched the Smog.

A cold awareness settled in her stomach. The Smog was seconds away from merging completely, mixing its new chemical, and spreading out again for attack. Even with the help of several other Propheseers, there was no way Mortar could warn more than a handful of UnLondoners.

It's not going to work, Deeba thought. *We have nothing.*

When she looked back at Mortar, the bridge was there, jutting from the edge of the building. She glimpsed the desks on its surface, saw its girders recede with perspective.

There was a bass growling from the sky. The last trail of smoke disappeared like sucked spaghetti into the thick green-tinted Smog, which rumbled.

"Go!" shouted Deeba. Mortar went onto the bridge, dragging Lectern. He looked at Deeba. A tentacle of Smog swooped down towards the roof, moaning like a monster. "*Go!*" she shouted.

Mortar waved once. Deeba ducked to avoid the swirl. When she looked back the bridge was gone.

The
Smog
churned its mur–
derous chemical
within itself. It made shapes with its
clouds, sank towards Deeba.

With Mortar gone, Deeba felt a strange calm. Perhaps it was certainty—the certainty of defeat. She knew she had no time to retreat to where Jones and the others were waiting, and she knew there would be no point even if she could. She tried not to think about all the people in two worlds the Smog had at its mercy.

She had stayed in the remains of the room because she couldn't bear to run from her enemy. Not after everything that had happened. *It's crazy*, thought Deeba. *I have nothing.* But still, she realized, that was why she'd stayed.

Brokkenbroll lay untrustworthy and unconscious. Deeba was alone.

The Smog descended.

Deeba made a brief move towards the remains of the corridor, then stopped. She wouldn't get farther than ten feet. There was no point. She looked up.

The Smog made itself a green cloud face. It loomed over her, and sent out a cathedral-sized smoke tongue to lick its smoke lips. It bashed air currents together in its miles-wide mouth, and with a voice made out of thunder, it said to her:

"APPETIZER."

Deeba closed her eyes as the Smog came down. All she could think, again and again, was: *I have nothing.*

95

Nothing

Nothing.
  Nothing.
  Nothing.
  And the UnGun.

Deeba opened her eyes.

Nothing and the UnGun!

96

Six-Shooter

The enormous Smog-mouth plummeted towards her. Deeba raised the empty UnGun.

It's no mistake! she thought. *In the book! It's not "Nothing but the UnGun" the Smog's scared of, it is supposed to be "Nothing and the UnGun."*

She held the weapon in her right hand, the rebrella with her left. The Smog was right above her. She could feel the wind it pushed as it dropped. All of the Smog was congealed into a dark, rushing shape. It concentrated itself so densely it looked almost solid.

It growled as it came.

Nothing's the opposite of something. If I fire something, anything, from the UnGun, it shoots it out, and exaggerates it. So if I shoot nothing . . .

Deeba fired.

There was an enormous implosive rush. This time, the UnGun didn't recoil. It didn't push her back. It pulled her *forward,* and she staggered to stay standing.

With a roar, the UnGun *sucked*. It sluiced with impossible strength into its barrel.

A huge chunk of the Smog's cloud-matter was drawn from the sky. In the instant that Deeba pulled the trigger, a tightly twisting vortex sprang from the Smog and funneled into the UnGun.

The Smog broke off from its dive and curved away. The face it had made boiled and re-formed. It looked confused.

It was noticeably smaller than it had been a moment before.

The Smog turned like a vast rearing horse, and snarled. It stared at Deeba, and the cloud swept down again, changing shape as it came.

Deeba hefted the UnGun. It was heavier than it had been. *Five chambers left*, she thought. She fired again.

The sucking sound roared across the heavens again, even louder than before, like water rushing into a cosmic drain. Another great whirlpool of Smog coiled superfast out of the cloud, slurping out whole banks of its stuff, which gushed out of the air in a dense stream, into the UnGun.

The weapon clicked in Deeba's hand, the cylinder twisted, and another empty chamber slid into place in front of the hammer. Deeba fired again, and suctioned in another swath.

With three bullet slots full, the Smog was at least half-gone. At last it understood what it was facing. It gathered itself, and in a rolling mass like a storm front, the dark, green-tinged cloud fled across the sky.

Deeba planted her feet and aimed carefully. She fired twice in quick succession. Huge clots of Smog yanked backwards like stretching dough, gushed into the pistol.

One nothing left, Deeba thought.

There was only a small, dense patch of Smog left in the air, but it was large enough to send down a murderous rain if it got away. It flitted frantically in a zigzag over UnLondon, curling around towers and behind high roofs. It was already miles away.

Steady, thought Deeba. She watched it sink towards unlit streets, to hide below roof-level. Deeba shifted her aim, pointing not at it, but at where it was heading.

As its front entered her line of sight, she fired.

One last gust swept into the UnGun. The big lump of Smog strained against the currents, but stretched and twisted, and spiraled, and was pulled in. For seconds, the night sky over UnLondon was full of a horizontal tornado, a corkscrew of poisoned smoke gushing into the UnGun. It hauled backwards over the abcity, the wind rushing through its eddying particles with a noise exactly like screaming.

Until with a long, loud gurgle the last of the Smog disappeared down the barrel, and the sky was clean.

97

Regroupment

For a long time, Deeba just stood in the rubble of the factory, swaying. She dangled the UnGun at the end of her arm, cautiously. Deeba thought she could feel the weapon twitching slightly.

She staggered to an unbroken stool and sat at the remains of a table.

"That," said the book slowly, "was great."

Deeba had forgotten it was there. She bent and picked it up, wiped the dust off its cover.

"Are you alright?" she said.

"Okay," the book said. "It tore out a couple of my pages and burnt them, to scare me. Worked, too. Are you alright?"

Deeba laughed tiredly.

"I think I am," she said.

Trailing dust, Curdle emerged from a pile of rubbish. It shuffled to Deeba's feet. She picked it up, too, and stroked it clean.

"And you," she said, and beckoned to the rebrella. It jumped onto her lap. They listened to the noises of celebration across UnLondon.

* * *

There was a cough and a shuffle nearby. Brokkenbroll was staring at her, from the ground. He looked as terrified of her as he had of the Smog.

"It . . . you . . . it . . ." he whispered.

"How long have you been awake?" Deeba said.

Sending up dust, Brokkenbroll fumbled for his unbrellas. All but one were buried under bricks, or lost.

"You stay away from me!" he whined. He scrabbled backwards, his single unbrella in his hand. He stumbled to his feet. "The Smog . . . !" he said. "It . . . you . . ." His mouth worked a few more seconds; then he ran across the remains of the room, leapt the rubble of the wall and out into the air.

Without any others to carry him, the unbrella lurched down a long way. It opened and closed frantically, struggling to stay airborne. Brokkenbroll clung to it, swaying, with his right hand. His clothes were ragged and flapping and left a trail of powdered brick.

As he flew slowly away, Deeba heard him wail.

She got to her feet.

"Quick," she said, and staggered. "We should . . . I should . . ." She wasn't sure what to say next.

"Leave it," said the book. "He saw you with the Smog, at the end. He's too afraid to do anything but run. We can deal with him later."

Deeba sank back onto the stool.

"If we even need to deal with him," she said. She patted the rebrella. "We know how to free his soldiers. Without them, he's got nothing.

"And not," she added, looking at the UnGun, "in the good way."

"Deeba . . . ?" Through the remnants of the door, staring at the wreckage, came Conductor Jones, leaning wearily on makeshift crutches.

Behind him came Bling and Cauldron, holding Hemi's hands. And behind them, bleeding, holding his wrist gingerly, but wearing a bewildered smile, was Obaday Fing.

Deeba called their names happily. She stumbled over and hugged those who weren't too bruised to take it.

"What," said Hemi, looking at the devastation admiringly, "did you *do?*"

"The utterlings persuaded those words to go exploring," said Jones. "And we heard all sorts of banging and whatnot. The Hex are all tied up. We shouldn't have left you alone." He hobbled slowly forward. "We tried to get up here as quick as we could."

"Look at the utterlings!" Deeba said. "They're back."

Bling and Cauldron weren't quite fully solid, but they were more substantial than when she had last seen them.

"You were right," said Jones. "It worked. Took them awhile to work out how to say themselves by signing, but they're getting it. Bling does it by rubbing his legs together."

"The smombies all emptied," said Hemi. "The smoke went up. Zoomed about the sky. But . . ." He looked about. "You know all about that, don't you?"

Deeba waved the UnGun vaguely.

"What?" said Jones. "Did you manage to reload?"

"Sort of," said Deeba. "It's a prison. It's full of the Smog."

They yelled and backed away, then paused as they realized there was no sign of trouble.

"What *happened* here?" said Jones.

Deeba paused a long time, then laughed.

"I'll explain," she said. "But basically . . . Nothing. *Nothing* happened."

The sky was beginning to grow light.

"There's lots of stuff to do," Deeba said. "We have to find Brokkenbroll. He got away. And we have to tell everyone in UnLondon what to do with the umbrellas." She twirled her rebrella, and it did a little midair pirouette of its own.

"There's all sorts to do. Let's find the Propheseers. I've got an apology to pick up."

"So we've got to get to the Pons, *now?*" said Jones, trying not to look horrified.

"Don't worry," said Deeba. "No more trekking. Give it a minute. The bridge'll come to us."

"What about Skool?" said Obaday. "And the binja, and—"

"We'll make some stops," said Deeba. "Trust me. Mortar's going to do exactly what I say."

She knew it would be awhile, and it was. It took a bit of time, in the confusion at the end of the war, while the Propheseers tried to work out what had happened, and how the abcity had won, and whether they could trust the victory. But after the UnSun had come up and shone gently on UnLondon, the end of the Propheseers' bridge poked into the ruins of Unstible's workshop, and Mortar beckoned them all on.

PART **IX** The Home Front

Fit for Heroes

"We're putting the word out," Mortar said. "All over UnLondon, unbrellas are being converted to rebrellas. Mostly they bounce off immediately into the Backwall Maze or somewhere and join bands of rubbish. But a few of them seem to want to stick around with us."

"Whatever," said Deeba. "The main point is Brokkenbroll can't control them. Does anyone know where he is yet?"

"No. But we're not worried. I'm sure he'll try to break a few rebrellas and reclaim them, and unbrellas are going to keep finding their way here, but everyone knows to fix them when found. What can he do? He's a bandit and we all know it. A nuisance, at worst, these days."

"Still," said Deeba. "I'll be happier when you find him."

"Binja are looking."

"Among others," said the book, tucked under Hemi's arm.

It was only one full day after that extraordinary battle, but UnLondon was adjusting to the news and ways of postwar life impressively quickly. All over the abcity, stories of heroism and betrayal and incompetence and luck were emerging. There were plenty of champions Deeba had never heard of, who'd done amazing things, in parts of UnLondon she'd never been.

"What'll happen to Lectern?" Deeba said.

"Oh, she's confessed," said Mortar. "She'll do some time. But she's by no means the worst of them."

"No," said Deeba. "She was just a coward. Although seeing as what she almost did to me . . ."

"Absolutely," muttered Hemi. He had become a go-between of sorts, a proto-ambassador between Wraithtown and the Pons, and he was wearing a suit of ghost-clothes. Around the cotton was a corona of older forms of dress.

"Quite," said Mortar. "There were quite a few people who worked hand in glove with the Smog. We don't know who they all are."

"The Concern. They could be trouble in the future."

There was a lot to do. Mortar was energized, now that he had finally stopped apologizing to Deeba.

"Is the UnLondon-I ready?" Deeba said. "I have to get back over."

"They're finishing it up now," Mortar said. "Don't worry, it'll be ready by tonight. And that still gives you a few hours in hand—you'll be fine."

The great waterwheel, like so much in the abcity, had been damaged in the fighting, its mechanisms clogged and banged about by rampaging stink-junkies. Nothing too serious before the Smog had dispersed, but enough that they had not been able to use it the previous day, to generate the current to poke the Pons Absconditus through the Odd into London.

A little part of Deeba had almost felt relief. Despite her eagerness to return, she'd been so battered after the showdown that a day of enforced rest and recuperation while the Propheseers worked to fix it had felt like a blessing. Now it was definitely time for her to go.

They strolled on the Pons Absconditus as Propheseers had its ends dip into various parts of UnLondon, gadding busily around the abcity. Elsewhere on the bridge were Deeba's companions, their wounds bandaged and tended by doctors and apothecaries, whose herbs, poultices, and spells had done amazing things.

"I like your clothes," Deeba said to Hemi.

"Oh yeah," he said, embarrassed. "I haven't often worn ghost togs. Too busy trying *not* to have that side of me noticed. Extreme shopping." He grinned.

"But the good thing is with these things I don't end up in the nude if I go through something—they come with me."

"It's all going well," Deeba said, looking around. "Be good to see what happens."

"The first thing," said the book, "is that I'm making this lot change their name. Now that we know things don't go as written at all."

"Tell me something I don't know," said Deeba. "You're talking to the Unchosen One."

"Yeah, but where's the skill in being a hero if you were always destined to do it?" said Hemi. He hesitated, and said, "You impress me a lot more."

"Destiny's bunk," said the book. "That's why this lot aren't the Propheseers anymore."

"From here on in," said Mortar, "we're the Order of Suggesters."

"And what *about* all those prophecies?" said Deeba. She poked the book gently. "In you."

"Oh . . . who knows? Who *cares* what's in me, frankly," it said loftily. "Maybe in a few years we'll open me up and read out what was supposed to happen and we can all have a good laugh. What Zanna was supposed to be doing. Whether you're even *mentioned*. Yes, maybe I'll end up a comedy. A joke book. There are worse things."

"You never know," Deeba said. "One or two of them might be true."

"Well," said the book. "Coincidence is an amazing thing."

"After all," Deeba said. "The only thing in your pages you thought definitely *was* wrong turned out to be right. Nothing *and* the UnGun?" There was a moment's silence.

"That," said the book with cautious pleasure, "is true."

Curdle and the rebrella bounded towards Deeba, as she approached them.

"Have you decided what to do with the UnGun, yet?" said Deeba.

"Well, we're ready for the first step at least," Mortar said. "If you'd do the honors?"

In the middle of the bridge was a huge mold, a cube five or more feet on each side, into which mixers were pouring liquid concrete. Jones, Obaday, and the others were gathered around it.

"Ready?" said Hemi.

Skool stood beside him. They'd rescued the little colony before the patch of seawater in the canal had ebbed away. The fish were still mourning the loss of several of their companions, but they'd come to say good-bye to Deeba. They were poured into a new suit. This one was smaller, and more up-to-date: a little wetsuit, complete with ungainly flippers. This time the mask was clear, and Deeba smiled at the seahorse and clown fish staring at her from the brine inside.

"I'm not making a big thing of this," Deeba said. "No speech." She chucked the UnGun, the Smog's prison, into the cement.

It splashed thickly and disappeared. They watched brief, thick ripples.

"When it's set, what then?" she said. "Got to make sure no one can open it."

"Opinion's divided," Mortar said. "Some people want to put it back among the Black Windows. It must have been one of our predecessors did that, yonks ago, so there's history. Some want to bury it. Some want to tip it in the river. Or the sea. We haven't decided yet."

"We might put it to a vote," said Jones.

"We'll see," said Deeba.

"Well," said Mortar, "*you* might not.

"You're talking as if you'll be back again, Deeba," he said gently. "But it isn't easy to cross between the worlds. Every time you breach the Odd, the membrane between two whole *universes* is strained. Think what that means.

"You have," he said, "to make a choice. You know we want you here. You . . . well, you saved UnLondon. We owe you our abcity and our lives. You're a Suggester, whether you join us officially or not. It would be an *honor* if you'd stay.

"But your family. Your life. All of these things . . . we understand. We'll miss you if you go, Deeba. But you have to choose."

There was a long silence.

"I can't stay," Deeba said at last. "I can't let my family forget me. Forget I even *exist*. Can you imagine? I'm going back. You know I have to."

She looked at each of them in turn.

"You know that," she said. Hemi looked away.

They all looked sad. Obaday sniffed. Jones dabbed surreptitiously at his eyes.

"The stuff that happened here," Deeba said, "I'll never forget. What we did. I'll never forget *you*. Any of you." She paused, looked at each of them in turn.

"And part of the reason I won't forget you," she said, "is 'cause I'll be back all the time."

* * *

Mortar and the Propheseers—the Suggesters—looked up, startled.

"Come *on*," she said, smiling. "What you even *talking* about, Mortar? It's *easy* to get from London to here. I got here by *turning a tap*, then by *climbing shelves*. Jones is here, Rosa got here, all the conductors got here. The police came in a digging machine. For God's sake, Unstible and Murgatroyd put an elevator in. People are *always* going between, and you don't see either universe collapsing, do you?

"You just think it's hard to go between the two 'cause you've always thought it must be. You're just saying that 'cause you sort of think you should."

Deeba's friends stared at her, and at each other. "She has a point," Mortar said eventually.

"You've spent all your time wanting to go!" said Jones.

" 'Cause I *couldn't get back*," she said. "Now that I *can*, I'll go back and forth all the time. You seriously think I'm not coming to see you again? Not coming to see this place?"

"But such methods," Mortar said, "they aren't reliable. They may not always work; the rules aren't always clear—"

"Well then, I'll try others. Till one of them does. Look, I'm not even making plans. I'm just saying there's no *way* I'm not coming back. There's things I want to do here."

"I've been thinking," Jones said. "I'm going to take a trip back to Webminster Abbey. I'm going to find Rosa, and get her out. And I'd be delighted if you'd join me."

"Of course," said Deeba. "*Yes*. Speaking of which, there's someone called Ptolemy Yes I was told about who went missing, and I want to find him. And I'd like to go back to the Wordhoard Pit, climb down, see what the libraries are like in other places."

"There's people in Wraithtown I'd like you to meet," said Hemi, still not meeting her eye. "And also, I wondered if maybe you want to go to Manifest Station? We could get a train. See another abcity together . . ."

There was a pause, and Deeba smiled at him.

"Absolutely," Deeba said. "*Yeah*. And loads of other things. I'm *blatantly* coming back. And you can come visit me." She smiled at Hemi again.

He, and then the others, began cautiously smiling back.

"You called it *our* abcity," Jones said. "Before the fight. And it is. It's your home too."

"And anyway," Deeba said, "Curdle and the rebrella are coming with me, and they might get homesick."

"You can't let feral rubbish cross into London," Mortar said anxiously. "It belongs in another world." Deeba looked at him and raised an eyebrow, and his voice dried up. "I suppose one or two can't hurt," he mumbled.

"So listen," Deeba said. "I'm not saying good-bye to any of you. I'll say 'See you soon.' And I mean *really* soon. Let me explain.

"I told you one reason the Smog grew so strong: 'cause it was getting help. There's one thing we haven't dealt with. Mortar, you said the police burrower was gone?"

"Yes. We checked where you said it had been. The officers must have got out and fixed it, gone home yesterday."

"Right. They threatened my family. It might have been only to scare me— there's nothing in it for them to actually do anything now. But I don't like it. And I don't like who they ally with. For the sake of me, and my mate Zanna, and my family, and London and UnLondon, it needs sorting. So I wanted to make a suggestion. An arrangement. It's going to involve clearing some rubble in Unstible's old place, but I think it's worth it."

Deeba looked at them all. Jones cracked his knuckles and raised an eyebrow. Hemi pursed his lips thoughtfully. Deeba smiled.

When evening fell, with a huge grinding, the UnLondon-I spun once more. With focus and effort, Mortar and the Suggesters directed the bridge.

Deeba hugged every one of her friends good-bye.

"Oh," she said to Hemi. She fumbled in her pocket.

"Tell me you ain't reaching for that money," he said. She grinned.

"It's no good to *me*," she said, and held it out. "You might as well . . ." He took her hand gently, and closed her fingers back over it.

"This way you still owe me," he muttered. "So this way you *got* to come back, to pay up."

Deeba swallowed and nodded and hugged him again. She held her breath, and turned and ran to the edge of the bridge. There was a strain, an effort, a whining in the air, and Deeba felt a membrane split, somewhere in reality. The bridge dipped across the Odd. She ran towards the walkway by her front door, which she could see beyond the girders.

I dunno what might happen, she thought, giddy, head spinning. *I could go back. I could live there, in a moil house with walls made out of wallets and windows made out of glasses. Or in a house like a goldfish bowl. I could catch a train from Manifest Station.*

But right now . . .

She stepped off the bridge, and breathed deeply in the London night. She looked all around her. Curdle exhaled at her feet. Deeba smiled.

"Hush," she told it. "And you." She held up the rebrella. "Remember. Over on this side, when other people're around, you stay still."

She turned. The bridge still soared out across the estate. Standing near its edge, waving at her, were her friends. Joe Jones; Skool; Hemi the half-ghost, biting his lip; Bling and Cauldron, their bodies quite solid; and Obaday Fing, carrying the book.

Deeba blinked through tears and smiled. She raised her hand. The Un-Londoners waved back. She and they looked across at each other, from city to abcity.

A cat yowled somewhere. Deeba glanced in its direction.

When she looked back, the Pons Absconditus was gone. Deeba stood alone on the concrete walkway, in the dark. In London.

Deeba gave a long, shaky sigh. She picked up Curdle, put it in her bag. She whispered to the rebrella: "Remember!"

Then she turned and unlocked her front door.

Memory

Deeba walked slowly through the living room. She was trembling. She heard voices from the kitchen.

She paused a moment, and looked at a photo on the mantel.

It was of her whole family. Deeba stared at it in horror. There was her mother, her father, her brother, smiling out . . . and there was she, but it was as if the film was underexposed in that corner of the picture. Or as if she stood in shadow. Or in fact, as if it was just hard to *notice* her there, smiling, her arms around her parents.

The picture was of four people, but it looked as if it was of three.

Her family were at the table eating supper. Deeba almost sobbed to see only three places set.

She walked in, looked at her parents and Hass, and brimmed with tears of relief, and nervousness. She wanted nothing more than to just run across the room to them, but she held back in fear, seeing their faces.

All three of them were staring at her blankly.

Her father had a fork halfway to his mouth. Food was dripping slowly off the metal tines. Her mother held a glass. Their faces were almost like voids. They looked slack, completely uncomprehending. Deeba saw a struggle deep inside each of them.

I was gone too long! she thought desperately. *The phlegm effect's gone permanent!*

"Mum?" she whispered. "Dad? Hass?" They stared.

It's only been eight days! she thought. *Since I spoke to Dad, in the Talklands! But . . .* A coldness hit her stomach. *But it's been more than nine since I* left. *Maybe it doesn't do it, to phone. The time counts from when you're gone. It's too late . . .*

"Mum? Dad? Hass?"

The Reshams quivered, and very slowly winced and blinked, and stared at Deeba, and something seemed to shudder and run through the room. One by one her family shivered as if at a chill, and they stretched their faces as if yawning, or shrugging something off.

"Can't you sit down like a civilized person?" Mr. Resham said. It took several seconds before Deeba was sure he was speaking to her.

"What are you wearing?" Mrs. Resham said. "You funny girl."

Deeba let out a little sob of relief and grabbed them both, and hugged them harder than she ever had before.

"Mad girl!" her father said. "You're spilling my rice!" He laughed.

Deeba hugged Hass, too. He looked at her suspiciously.

"What?" he said. "I drew a picture."

It took Deeba a few moments to convince her mum and dad that though, yes, she was crying, she was very happy.

"I'm just going over to Zanna's for a minute," Deeba said as the Reshams picked at the last of their dinner. Deeba did so too, her father having wordlessly got her a plate and cutlery, a faint quizzical look on his face when she sat down.

"You . . ." her mother said. "You think I can't see through this shameless attempt to get out of clearing up dishes?"

"Oh, please. Just for a second. I need to . . . give her something for school."

Deeba grew more and more nervous the whole short distance to Zanna's. She had to clench and unclench her hand to stop it shaking before she rang the doorbell.

It was Zanna herself who opened the door. Deeba stared at her, dumb, her mouth open. It felt like years since she had seen that familiar blond-fringed face.

For an instant, a cloud of confusion passed over Zanna's expression. Then she smiled and stood up straighter, looking fresher and better than anytime since she had returned from her own, unremembered, trip to the abcity.

"Hey Deebs," she said. There was no trace of debilitating breathlessness left in her voice—her lungs sounded completely clear. "Man," she said, "you look *happy*. So . . . you been doing anything interesting? What? What's so funny? Why you laughing?"

Much later, when Deeba crept out of bed and looked at the photograph of her family again, while everyone else was asleep and she was basking in having her house around her, the light in the picture had altered. Deeba's image was properly visible, and there were four Reshams again.

It was beyond extraordinary that she had only a few hours previously been in UnLondon, a place so far away from her bedroom that conventional measures of distance were meaningless. She thought, carefully and precisely, of all her friends in turn: Obaday, Jones, the book, the utterlings, Hemi the half-ghost.

She missed it already, she realized. *It'll always be me got rid of the Smog,* she thought. She felt the lack of UnLondon like a loss.

But at the same time, she couldn't remember being so happy as she was then, at that moment, luxuriating under her duvet, in her room, with her family close, and her image back and visible on the photos in the living room. She felt as if she glowed with contentment.

Deeba whispered to Curdle, which was making a nest under her bed. Before she turned out her light, Deeba checked her diary. She had an appointment coming up.

EPILOGUE

In the heart of Westminster, in the sumptuous, wood-paneled office of Elizabeth Rawley, secretary of state for Environment, it was an unexceptional morning. The minister worked through the pile of papers on her desk, checking reports, making notes and suggestions, preparing press releases.

There was a personal note from the prime minister. He was extremely pleased with the success of LURCH, the London–UnLondon Rerouting Carbon Hazards plan. Carcinogens and toxic pollution were down across the southeast, the ratings from environmentalists were up, and the government had established an invaluable relationship with a very powerful ally.

The prime minister was already raising the possibility of deploying their contact in various trouble spots. "A chemical weapon that can strategize like a general," he'd said. "Hidden among oil fires! Think of it, Elizabeth!"

She did think of it. She was very proud of her initiative. She didn't want to count her chickens, but she was hearing whispers of promotion. She eyed a door on her far wall.

Rawley only hoped the PM didn't find out that communications had dried up since just after Murgatroyd had made his way back in a half-crippled police burrower, cursing.

* * *

Her intercom buzzed.

"Minister," her secretary said. "There's someone to see you."

"There's nothing scheduled . . ."

"She came in the public entrance, Minister. She won't give her name, but she's insisting on seeing you."

"For heaven's sake don't be ridiculous."

"She says she can tell you what's going on in . . . in the other city. *She said you'd know what she means." Her secretary sounded nonplussed. "But only if you saw her now. I'm sorry, Minister, she wouldn't be more specific. She insisted I tell you. She said something about chimneys, and a war, and—"*

"That's enough." Rawley spoke quickly. "Send her in." She pressed another button. "Murgatroyd, for God's sake get in here. We've finally got contact."

Murgatroyd entered from his adjoining office, accompanied by secret service men with pistols out and ready: standard procedure when dealing with the abcities.

After a moment, the main doors opened, and a short, dark, round-faced girl with an extremely determined expression entered. She was carrying a red umbrella.

Elizabeth Rawley stared at her. The girl eyed her back.

Murgatroyed emitted a strangled sound. "You!" he screamed. He pointed with crooked fingers. The girl held up a hand and looked at her watch.

"Was hoping we'd catch you," she said. "Ten seconds." After a moment, she said, "Five."

It was that many seconds to nine o'clock.

An alarm bell sounded. The noise of machinery began to approach. In the corner of the room, a red light came on.

The elevator hadn't worked for days. The noise of gears came closer.

There was a bing *as the lift crossed through the membrane between worlds, and arrived. The door opened. "Hey, you lot!" the girl called happily. "You cleared the elevator shaft! I knew you could."*

Elizabeth Rawley stared.

Stepping out of the elevator came a big man in an antiquated London Transport uniform. He wore a conductor's ticket machine and carried a copper rod. Beside him was a man wearing printed paper, with needles and pins for hair.

There was a boy with them, a pale boy in flickering clothes. And leaping out from behind them . . . Was that a dustbin? *With arms and legs? And stern eyes glinting from under its lid?*

Rawley took it all in.

Murgatroyd drew his gun and aimed it at the girl. There was a shot, and the ping of a ricochet. The girl held her umbrella before her.

The agents raised their pistols. The conductor leapt out with a flurry of fists and feet, and the sound of crackling and bursts of sparks. Bodyguards tumbled to the floor unconscious. The dustbin somersaulted and, with a frenetic succession of windmill kicks, laid out a line of men and women.

The girl spun her umbrella so fast it looked as if it were the umbrella pulling her. She smacked weapons effortlessly out of several agents' hands.

Elizabeth Rawley stared in shock. In less than three seconds, most of her staff were incapacitated.

"I'll kill you!" Murgatroyd spat, and fired again.

The girl spun, and blocked with the umbrella, then swung like a truncheon. It caught Murgatroyd under his chin, and sent him soaring. He sailed backwards, over Rawley's desk, crashed into the wall behind her, and slid to the floor, groaning.

The dustbin handsprung over Rawley's desk and stood with one foot on Murgatroyd. The conductor stood poised, ready to strike. The boy and the pin-headed man ran to the door, checked it, and wedged it closed.

The girl stepped closer and stared into the minister's eyes. She jumped up and landed on the desk. She twirled the umbrella, stretched like a fencer with it pointed directly at Rawley's throat.

"Minister," said the girl. "We need to talk."

Glossary

Bin / Dustbin: Trash can / garbage can.

Bog off: Go away.

Bollard: A little post to divert traffic on a road; a traffic cone.

Class-mark: The numbers on the side of a library book.

Climbing frame: A jungle gym.

Comprehensive: A school for children aged 11 to 16 or 18.

Do a bunk: Run away.

Estate: Several big apartment blocks—a housing project.

Git: Unpleasant person.

Knackered: Exhausted.

Lairy: Cheeky and aggressive.

Manky: Disgusting.

Minging: Dirty/smelly/unpleasant.

Mobile: Short for "mobile phone"—a cell phone.

Nutter: Somebody acting crazy.

Quite: When Americans say something is "quite good/bad/etc.," you mean it is "very" good/bad/etc. When Brits say it, we sometimes mean it in just the same way—but then sometimes we mean something is only "fairly," or "moderately," or "kind-of-but-not-extremely" good/bad/etc. It can be confusing.

Rubbish: Trash / garbage.

Rum: Strange.

Sarky: Sarcastic.

Scrum: A confused situation involving lots of people.

Shtum: Silent.

Soft ("Don't be soft"): Foolish.

Take the Michael: Mock, make fun of.

Tarmac: What they make airport runways out of, but we use it to describe normal roads, too.

Tower block: Big apartment block.

Yonks: A long time.

ABOUT THE AUTHOR

CHINA MIÉVILLE is a two-time winner of both the Arthur C. Clarke Award and the British Fantasy Award, as well as the Locus Award and several other honors. He is the author of *King Rat, Perdido Street Station, The Scar, Iron Council,* and the anthology *Looking for Jake.* He lives and works in London.

ABOUT THE TYPE

This book was set in Ehrhardt, a typeface based on the original design of Nicholas Kis, a seventeenth-century Hungarian type designer. Ehrhardt was first released in 1937 by the Monotype Corporation of London.